Pro

by JJ Perri

For Tracey, who first inspired me; Mum, Wendy and Maria, who encouraged me by pestering me for the next chapters; Georgia, who painstakingly proof read, and Nick and Leo, who only saw my back for months and never complained.

Part 1

Chapter 1

I gasped as I moved forward into the room. The door to the stairs was wide open, and the glass coffee table had been smashed, but the most shocking thing was the fireplace. The makeshift altar seemed to have been purposely destroyed. If there had been a fight in here, things may have been knocked over, or even broken, but it looked like someone had deliberately swept everything off the mantelpiece. On the left hand side of the hearth, candlesticks and candles were strewn about on the carpet and the large gold crucifix lay on its side in the middle of the room, perhaps having bounced off the wall. A couple of the framed religious pictures which had covered the wall behind the altar remained hanging askew; the rest were on the floor on the right side of the fireplace.

The statue of the Virgin Mary was missing. I remembered her specifically because she had stood in the middle of the display, pale and almost luminous, and it was when I saw her that I realised the significance of the Catholic religion in this house. Scanning the room, I expected to see her lying on the floor somewhere or maybe on one of the chairs. She seemed to have disappeared, but why demolish the rest of the shrine and save her?

There was no sign of Dan, but as I crossed the room, preparing to check the upstairs, I saw what looked like a heap of clothes piled up next to the sofa, blocking the door.

Sticking out of the clothes was a bare foot.

'Dan!' I shouted, kneeling down to touch his shoulder. He was huddled up in a ball, on his knees, but slumped forward with his arms around his head, as if he was protecting himself.

'Dan,' I ventured, more quietly this time as I shook him gently. There was no response. I touched the skin at the back of his neck, feeling for warmth or a pulse. I couldn't feel either, but he wasn't cold.

As I took my hand away from his neck I saw the blood. On the far side of his head, half hidden by the sofa, there was blood, blood that was now covering my hand, soaking the neck of his T shirt and dripping down onto the carpet where a large stain was growing.

'Ring an ambulance!' I screamed at Tyler, who was standing in the middle of the room like a statue, staring, his eyes and mouth open and frozen. I remembered my feelings of shock when we'd found Dan in the street, and how they had rendered me helpless.

Pulling out my phone I rang 999, spoke with a strange calmness I didn't feel, and gave the necessary information. Taking off my jacket, I lay it over Dan and talked to him, stroking his back softly and telling him we were there and that the ambulance was on its way.

'Can you open the front door and wait for them?' I asked Tyler, my voice once again sounding relaxed and controlled, like someone else's voice completely, belying the terror I was feeling. How long had Dan been like this? hunched up here?

The light was still on. The light was on at ten o'clock last night, but why now, when sunlight was streaming through the gaps in the curtains? Had Dan been here like this all night?

'Please don't let us be too late,' I chanted silently as we waited for the ambulance.

I touched Dan's hair and thought back to the day it all began.

Chapter 2

It was raining on the day I first knew for certain.

Huge blobs burst on the windscreen, then slid down, joining streams of themselves, desperate to be together, desperate to belong.

I leant my head back on the headrest and watched, as one after another exploded, then slowly reformed and made their way back to the fold, regrouping and flowing down as one united river. It was strangely hypnotic, like seeing nature evolve in miniature, trickles becoming streams, then rivers, before gushing into the mouth of the scuttle.

I was vaguely aware that Mum was talking to me, but I heard the words as if from a distance, eventually snapping to attention when she bellowed, 'Have you listened to a word I've just said? Do you have everything? Have you brought the money for the science revision books? You haven't, have you? I can't believe this! What is the point…'

'I have it. I have everything.' I was calm. She meant well. She always meant well.

In the top left-hand corner of the glass, a lone drop wobbled, surface tension straining as it clung to the slippery surface. I wondered why it wavered there, seemingly unable to decide whether to join its peers rolling down to the right or the ones running down the edge of the windscreen to the left. For a while it appeared to be veering left, then right, but then it stopped for what seemed like an eternity, just standing alone there, unsure and isolated like a lone tear.

'I said, when is the first exam? I don't know why I waste my breath. I should just let you fail and that would maybe teach you a lesson. If you fail all your mocks now, maybe you'll realise how important it is to prepare…'

I didn't hear the rest. The raindrop began to wind its way warily down, slowing down at intervals, then making a sudden dash, before slowing again. Reaching the base of the windscreen, it spread sideways and simply disappeared, as if it never existed.

Shutting, not slamming the car door (that would earn me another lecture later) I waved and smiled before turning to trudge across the car park towards another long school day. I tried not to walk too fast – no point prolonging the agony, or too slow – same reason – no point getting a lates detention, but as I turned the corner I could see Amelia Clarke's huge Towie hair tumbling in curls down her back. Seriously, who gets up early enough to spend that much time looking good for school? She was surrounded by her coven, and there seemed to be plans afoot. Periodically, one of them would turn around, scan the area, then report back to the group, presumably to confirm that their victim was, or wasn't, in sight, depending on the 'prank'. I should have walked more slowly. Perhaps then I could have avoided them.

It was too late to retrace my steps and vanish among the students now beginning to surge toward the door; one of them was sure to spot me. So I walked on, slumped, attempting to disappear among the crowd. There was laughing and out of the side of my eye I saw a couple of them turn, although I couldn't see in which direction they were looking.

Suddenly someone shouted. 'Look where you're going, geek!' I recognised the nasal voice. Amelia's Henchwitch, Jilly. 'Oh no. Look what you've done.'

I stopped and turned with the rest of the students filing towards the entrance and saw a tall, dark haired girl stoop to retrieve her bag from the floor. But before she could reach it, Jilly kicked it away, the books and pencil case inside spilling out as it spun around, finally coming to a stop when it hit the bench in its path.

'Next time, watch who you're barging into!' spat Jilly maliciously. Amelia leaned against the wall, watching approvingly.

No-one moved at first. I was frozen to the spot. I knew what I should do, what any civilised, decent person would do. We all knew. But still nobody moved.

The tall girl eventually stooped again to pick up her pencil case, cheeks burning and heart probably pounding half way out of her chest. Then something weird happened. A boy stepped from behind me and began to sweep the books together one by one, until he had them all in his hands. He recovered the bag from under the bench, carefully replaced the books and then took the bag over to her, holding it open while she replaced the pencil case.

All this happened in about a minute, but I seemed to see it in slow motion. The boy was Dan Sweeney: Sports Captain and resident school heart-throb; tall, dark and film star handsome. A spiteful voice inside my head said, 'It must be so easy to do the right thing when you're the most popular boy in school'. I should have stopped it then but it continued, 'We could all be knights in shining armour if we looked like you and everybody loved us.'

'What must it be like to have such an easy life?' I thought.

I glanced over at Amelia and Jilly. They looked strangely alone, the rest of the clique having made themselves scarce. Jilly was staring at the floor and biting her lip, and even Amelia had the grace to blush. I didn't believe for a minute that this was as a result of any amount of remorse or shame, she was just mortified to have been exposed, especially by Dan, probably the only boy in the school she considered good looking enough for her. Allowing myself a secret smile, I started to make my way into school.

I may have imagined it, but at the very moment I turned, I thought I saw Dan looking at me. He had given the bag back to the girl but was walking next to her protectively. Both their heads bobbed along above the rest and I could have sworn, just for a second, that our eyes met.

For the whole day, I replayed that second in my mind. In some versions, there would be a look of recognition on Dan's face which made me feel that he could see deep into my soul, that he could see the real me. In others, ashamed of my own ridiculous notion that someone like Dan could be the slightest bit interested in someone like me, I saw it for what it obviously was; he was looking at someone or something behind me, or in-front of me, and the expression I thought I saw was of my own creation.

Still, every time I saw his face from then on, whether in my imagination, or across the dinner hall; every time I saw the back of his head at the front of my geography class, or his profile as the school bus pulled away, I knew for certain. I was falling in love with Dan Sweeney.

Chapter 3

It was easy being in love with Dan Sweeney, a bit like being in love with a famous singer or an actor. Everybody else is also in love with them, you all know it's completely unrequited and there's absolutely no chance anything will ever happen so you just enjoy it while it lasts. You can dream about them and not worry that it will be embarrassing next time you speak because you don't speak. They will never see you or hear you because you are nobody, and they are everything. I enjoyed being able to feel something, something that was real, but secret. I felt safe feeling this way about Dan because no-one would ever know, no-one would ever guess because we lived in different worlds, albeit ones that slightly overlapped, in geography, and English, and sometimes in the lunch queue.

The feelings ebbed and flowed. It was a busy time, what with mock GCSEs and practising for my piano exams. There wasn't always enough time for unrequited love, and sometimes I found I had gone a whole day without even thinking about Dan.

I was generally able to avoid the witches too. If I arrived before eight-thirty, I found that I could cross to the opposite side of the yard and sit happily on the steps waiting for my friends to arrive. Amelia, Jilly and the rest usually appeared between eight-thirty and eight forty-five, stationed themselves around 'their bench', flicked their hair and laughed at passing uncools.

The witches' 'bench' was indicative of their status in school. They were the popular girls, no matter how callous and malignant they were. All good looking, with rich parents who were able to kit them out in designer pieces to add to their uniforms. Shoes, bags and even skirts could be utilised to show how stylish and fashionable they were (something everyone wanted to be). Their wealthy backgrounds meant it was easy for them to be wearing and carrying the labels that others craved, and many of the other girls hung around them simply hoping that some of their popularity would rub off.

Appropriating a bench was a sign that you were in the top tier of the school hierarchy. I remembered being in year seven and witnessing a particularly vicious annihilation of some poor underlings by the then football team. 'Looks like somebody doesn't know whose bench this is?' sneered a big scary year eleven (although they all looked like men to me) and bounced a football hard on the head of one of the younger boys, before throwing it to his team mate.

'Looks like we'll have to teach them whose bench this is,' his friend smirked, and bounced the ball even harder on one of the other boys' heads.

They then circled the bench and threw the ball hard at each of the boys in turn, laughing like hyenas as their victims cowered, struggling to avoid the blows, until all but one of them had escaped, dodging the whacks of hooting year elevens, to safety. They took the last boy by the legs and arms and launched him onto the grass, sobbing, before sitting down and congratulating themselves on a job well done.

I never forgot their cruelty that day, and I heard a few weeks later that the last boy had left school, never to be heard of again.

Lower down the ladder, less popular, but still popular, groups would congregate on the amphitheatre steps in front of the main doors.

Our steps were off to the right of the school, and very much a third-rate location, not suggestive of the lowest rank, as we were year eleven, and obviously the year you were in did influence your status, but placing us definitely in the mid to lower echelons of year eleven society at least.

Below us, younger and even less powerful groups stood and sat on the grass, against the wall and in the case of the students unfortunate enough to belong to the social underclass of school, somewhere in the middle of the tarmac yard space. As a rule, as they moved up the years, they would hopefully relocate to more sought-after positions in the yard.

'It's all in your head!' my friend Olivia laughed one morning. 'They do it to everybody. You're just over-sensitive.'

'She's right you know,' Tyler echoed. 'No-one's safe from their evil powers.' He made a grotesque face, twisted his hands into claws and cackled. 'To them, everyone's a potential victim.'

Tyler was my oldest friend. We'd been born on the same day, attended the same nursery, the same primary school and now the same high school. Our parents became friends and we would all socialise together. It wasn't like we had lots in common; in fact, it was the opposite. But we had a connection. Sometimes we'd finish each other's sentences, and when we played games at family parties, people marvelled at how in tune we were. I'd adopt a certain expression and he'd know exactly what I was thinking, or he'd say one word and I'd know the correct answer instinctively. The others jokily accused us of cheating, but they knew we were just so close we knew each other inside out. We knew everything about each other. Well, almost everything, that is.

The bell rang and we started towards school. Tyler put his hand on my arm as Olivia ran on ahead to join some girls from her form. 'You ok?' he looked worried.

'I'm fine. It's fine.' I forced a smile.

'It's true you know. It's nothing personal. They pick on everybody.'

I suddenly felt an irrational sense of frustration, maybe even anger. 'They don't pick on you.' I said quietly, and I walked away.

By lunchtime, I felt almost happy again. We'd had a science assessment marked and I'd been given a grade nine. It was probably the first grade nine I'd seen, on one of my papers, or anybody else's. I tried to be cool about it, but I couldn't help the odd half smile that bubbled to the surface. Obviously, there was the requisite swapping of results and although I was beaming with pride on the inside, it was embarrassing to say the word 'nine'. I wasn't quite sure why. It seemed like showing off, and even though they'd asked me, I could feel slight waves of…what? Envy? Resentment? radiating from a few people.

Walking down to the dinner hall, I anticipated telling Tyler, Olivia and the others. I knew they'd be happy for me, even if some of my class weren't. Amelia being one of them.

She hadn't asked me what I got. Why would she lower herself to even care, let alone ask? But I could sense her bristling from across the room when the news reached her. Amelia was in most of my classes, although I had the feeling she struggled to stay in set one, that it wasn't easy for her. She gave the impression she was coasting, but there was something about her body language, something about the way she concentrated when she thought no-one was looking and glanced furtively around during assessments that gave me the impression that she cared a great deal, a great deal more that she'd ever stoop to admit.

Half way down the stairs I heard a stifled laugh behind me, followed by a chorus of muffled giggling, some muttering, and another burst of louder cackling. I strained my ears to find out what was so funny but I couldn't quite make out the words. It didn't matter really. I knew what they were laughing at. Perhaps the grade nine was a catalyst, because I'd actually felt pretty confident for a while that they were losing interest in me. It appeared not. My blazer was too tight and pulled across my stomach, making it ride up at the back. They were laughing at that. At the way my legs rubbed together as I walked. At the way I had to fasten my blazer because the buttons of my shirt strained apart and showed glimpses of flab instead of a six pack like the perfect people on Instagram. It wasn't like I was huge, I just wasn't perfect, and that was enough for them.

Reddening with humiliation, I sped up, passed a group of year sevens pushing and shoving each other in jest, and eventually reached our table. In the canteen, the same grading system applied, and our table was in a cramped corner of the room, far away from the top tier of tables next to the windows and near the door to the yard. To my relief, Olivia and Faye were already there, smiling and welcoming. I sat down gratefully.

'You ok?' Olivia asked. Had she noticed my discomfort or was it just an everyday 'You ok?' I avoided her eyes.

'Yeah'

She didn't push it. Just the usual, 'You ok?' then.

Tyler and George came next, punching each other playfully, flushed from PE and laughing at something that had happened there. Tyler jumped over the bench and flopped down. It was how he always moved, like a gazelle or a kangaroo, everything quick and full of energy. When he was still he was like a coiled spring or an unexploded bomb, ready to leap up and bounce off when least expected.

'I can't believe you did that!' George's eyes were wide with amusement and admiration. 'He was so shocked!'

'I can't believe it either,' Tyler was shaking his head in disbelief, his blond curls falling into his eyes. 'I don't think I've ever put one past him in four years. I can't beat him one on one with one hand and one leg tied behind his back.'

'What? What happened?' both Olivia and Faye were desperate to know.

'What did you do?' screeched Olivia as Tyler and George smirked conspiratorially. 'Come on. You can't leave us hanging like that. What happened?' She whacked Tyler's arm in mock anger.

'We were about seven goals down and Tyler was starting to mess about, like he does when he's losing,' George raised his eyebrows and nodded towards Tyler. 'Anyway, it was yet another kick off and I think Dan was getting bored at this point because he'd hardly even touched the ball. It hadn't been in their half more than a couple of times, let alone near the net!'

My ears pricked up at the sound of his name. Were they talking about the same Dan, or just any Dan? The conversation had just become hugely more interesting.

'He was just daydreaming. You know, kind of in another world, wandering up and down the goal line, not really paying attention to the game.' Tyler continued the story.

'He didn't have to, we were that crap.'

'I just saw the opportunity and took it. I never in a million years thought it would go in! I was as gobsmacked as anyone else when it did. Except maybe Dan!'

They both laughed as if he'd said something hilarious.

'What did you do?' bellowed Faye. 'For God's sake get to the point!'

'He scored from the kick off!' George's eyes were wide. 'Just walloped it as hard as he could and it went in. It was a cracking shot though. Even if Dan had been on it I don't think he could have stopped it.'

'Give over. He's an amazing keeper. He'd have had it definitely if he was focused on the game. It just took him a couple of seconds to snap back and by then it was too late. No-one would have expected it. I thought it would be somewhere off down the banking and Hughesy'd kill me because it was the end of the lesson and I'd made us all late in. I thought I'd be tidying up the gym by now!'

'His face though. His mouth just dropped open. It was priceless.' George shook his head and grinned.

'He's a good bloke though, Dan,' Tyler was thoughtful. 'I can imagine some of his cronies throwing a fit at that. Some of them would have lost the plot. I might not be so pretty now if it had been a couple of them. He took it really well. Yeah, he was surprised and it took him a while to even realise what had happened, but he actually thought it was funny. He just shook his head and laughed, and he even patted me on the back on the way back into the changing rooms. I like him. He's not like some of the team.'

'I know what you mean,' Olivia said. 'He's different. Obviously, he's gorgeous.' She elbowed Faye in the ribs and they both giggled girlishly. 'But it's not just that. He's kind of respectful, even though I've barely spoken to him apart from 'excuse me' or 'thank you' when he's held the door open for me. I can't put my finger on it. He's just…different.'

I felt a tightening in my chest. It couldn't be jealousy, because there was nothing to be jealous of, was there? It was jealousy though, or envy at least. Jealousy implies a sort of hostility towards your rival, and I didn't feel that, did I? I didn't think so. I just envied Olivia and Faye the fact that although Dan might be way out of their league, they were at least playing the same game. Not like me.

Chapter 4

The next few hours seemed to pass in slow motion that day, but afterwards I found it hard to remember certain sections properly, as if I'd been in a kind of daze.

When the paramedics arrived, they pulled me firmly away and started to tend to Dan. Tyler and I were ushered back to the other side of the room and were unable to see what was happening, but when it became clear that he was alive, I broke down crying with relief, deep sobs wracking my body.

One of the paramedics dragged the sofa away from Dan to give them more space to work in and when the light shone on the carpet there was more blood. Lots of blood. As I lunged forward to go to him, Tyler grabbed my arm, but I wrenched it away, losing my balance and falling to my knees. I knelt there, prostrate, holding my head in my hands and chanting, 'please God, please God…'

I'd never been religious, but at that moment, I believed, and I prayed to the God that just might be there to have mercy and help us. Opening my eyes, I found myself leaning over the shattered coffee table, looking directly into the eyes of the Virgin Mary herself. Her face was intact, but the rest of her was smashed into tiny pieces, mingling with those of the table top. Whoever did this had to have lifted her as high as he could and hurled her through the table with extreme force.

I dreaded to think what had happened the night before, but something told me Dan had cracked. I picked up the face from among the fragments and slipped it gently into my pocket. To protect her from further harm? I don't think I knew even then.

Tyler told me to go to the hospital with Dan in the ambulance. He seemed to have regained control of his faculties now and promised to let everybody know what was happening. 'Shall I tell your mum?' he asked tentatively.

I shrugged. What difference did it make?

Dan's face, exposed now he was lying flat on the bed in the ambulance, was hardly recognisable. His eyes were swollen shut and one side of his face was twice the size of the other, even half concealed by the blood that I could now see covering his neck, and sticky against the matte black surface of the T shirt he was wearing. There were marks on his neck as if he'd been strangled; I couldn't see the rest of his body.

'Will he be ok?' I whispered to the paramedic sitting with him.

There was a pause. 'He's stable now, but we can't tell what's going on inside. Somebody's certainly used him as a punch-bag. The doctors will tell you more after he's been scanned.' He turned and looked at me. 'It's a good job you found him when you did. It looks like he might have been there for a while.'

I should have knocked on the door last night. I could have stopped it, or maybe heard Dan call for help. I could have rung the police, or kicked the door in. He was being beaten viciously while we were eating chicken in Nando's. Maybe he tried to crawl to the door for help before he passed out? Maybe he was already lying there when I simply walked past the house and took the bus home.

Chapter 5

On the way home, I remembered I hadn't even told Tyler about my grade nine. Still, the day was spoiled anyway. I wasn't sure whether the witches had been the ones to darken my mood, or the way I'd felt when my friends had made it clear they fancied Dan. Somehow, that had changed movie star Dan into boy next door Dan. Dan who would, sooner or later, go out with someone I knew. I'd have to see them arm in arm, kissing and giggling over some private joke. It might be Amelia Clarke, which would be awful. But even worse, it might be Faye, or Olivia. I'd never looked at them as attractive girls before, they were just my friends, but now I began to see them as Dan might. Faye, blonde and willowy, a little too tall (I knew she was self-conscious about it and had developed a slight stoop as a result) and not what you'd call pretty, but interesting looking, like some of the top models. Then Olivia, dark hair and skin, shorter and stockier (athletic I suppose) and naturally good looking. She never wore make-up, but she didn't have to. Her eyes were fringed with the longest lashes I'd ever seen, and her skin was the colour most girls buy in a tube.

I could feel the familiar churning of anxiety in my stomach. The more I tried to block the thought out of my mind, the more I could see that if Dan actually met either of them, and realised how interesting and fun to be with they were, he'd probably fall for one or the other. It was ridiculous. He'd never even met them, but I was picturing their engagement party by the time I arrived home. Dan, looking stunning in a suit, and his fiancé, whose face kept changing from Olivia's to Faye's, like Sleeping Beauty's dress in the Disney film.

Mum wasn't home, so I went upstairs to play on my PS4, the only thing that blocked everything else out. When I needed to escape, I'd immerse myself in a game and miraculously an hour of complete oblivion would follow: worries, anxiety, any sign of reality annihilated along with the evil characters I'd defeat as the game progressed.

When Mum shouted that dinner was ready, my heart sank. Dinner was always stressful, as she pretended not to watch what I ate and desperately tried not to comment.

'I got a grade nine for my science assessment.' I blurted out; maybe the fact that I was clever could cancel out the fact that I was eating too much.

'What does that mean?' asked Dad. 'I can never understand these new-fangled systems. Why can't they just leave them as they are? I don't think they want us to know really. Is that good?'

'Yeah, it's really good Dad. It's like an A star, star, even better than an A star.'

'Brilliant, really well done.' He smiled at me. 'You get your brains from me.' Then he laughed. I smiled back. He didn't often have much to do with school, that was Mum's job, but I knew he was genuinely proud and it felt good.

'Yes, well done love,' Mum echoed.

I leaned over to help myself to seconds of the cottage pie in the centre of the table, willing her to ask me something about the exam, or what had happened that day at school, but she couldn't help herself. 'Do you need any more?' she asked quietly. 'Didn't you have quite a big first helping?'

Blushing, I took just a small spoonful from the dish. It was always the same. I took a smaller helping at first than I really wanted, because she was watching to see how much I took, then I was still hungry, but having a second helping would always elicit the same look or comment about 'not needing any more'.

I knew why she did it, because she was overweight as a teenager and couldn't bear the thought of me going through the same thing as she did. Unfortunately, her gestapo tactics simply meant I ate more rubbish: crisps, chocolate and anything I could get my hands on really, especially if I was stressed.

She must have thought I had the slowest metabolism in history, eating so little and still putting weight on. Although, did she know I was eating between meals? Or did she think we had a stowaway who made short work of the unhealthy treats in the house. She'd tried a system whereby sweets and crisps were completely banned for a while, but Dad soon put a stop to that, arguing that being responsible for half the household income surely gave him the right to influence what it was spent on.

I hated myself of course. It was pathetic. Why did I do it? I couldn't tell you. I read an article about self-harm once, and it struck a chord with me. Self-harmers felt a huge sense of relief when they cut themselves, like they were releasing all their tension and anxiety; maybe the physical pain replaced the emotional pain.

Not that I was comparing my over-eating to self-harm, but looking back, I suppose it felt a little like that. I would focus on food and eating to blot out whichever sense of confusion or hopelessness I was feeling. It was a huge temporary high. A relief to be eating after thinking about it for so long.

Afterwards though came the regret and the shame. I felt bloated, uncomfortable, and stupid. Why would somebody do that to themselves? How could someone have so little self-control?

I felt my over-eating was like an addiction. How else could you explain doing something that you knew would make you feel worse in the long run and being unable to stop yourself?

It was unfair, I thought sometimes, that being addicted to food was treated like a joke, but other addicts were pitied and offered support by strangers. There were even charities set up to fund therapy and rehabilitation if you were addicted to drugs or alcohol, or gambling, or any number of other things people abused themselves with.

When your addiction was food though, people just thought you were stupid, or weak, or just plain greedy. I wallowed in my self-pity while I revised for my geography exam. At least if you were fat there was nothing else better to go out and do. No-one was interested in you when you were fat so you might as well revise. At least I might end up fat and rich.

Chapter 6

The next day was a Friday, and under normal circumstances it would have been my favourite day of the week. Double science, maths and geography (I did have one period of English, but you can't have everything). Unfortunately, I was still brooding over the conversation with Olivia and Faye the day before. I knew it was pointless and I should have forced it out of my mind immediately, but I couldn't seem to escape the pictures of one or the other of them happily married to Dan, with two kids (a boy and a girl) and a dog.

To make it even worse, my trousers felt even tighter than usual, and I knew I'd have to do something about it soon or I wouldn't be able to fasten them at all. I needed to diet, which always made me feel better, albeit temporarily, and I decided that my diet would start on Monday, as diets always do. In the mean-time, I'd just keep my head down and try to make myself as invisible as possible.

The yard was pretty deserted when I arrived at school, and I made my way to our steps without incident, settling myself down to do a few more minutes of cramming for geography before everyone arrived. No sign of Amelia, Jilly or the rest of them. So far, so good.

When I looked up from my book ten minutes later, I was surprised none of my friends had arrived yet. Amelia and Jilly were in residence, hair and make-up as perfectly done as ever (I could see that from fifty meters away), but no sign of Tyler, Olivia and Faye or George. Studying Amelia from a distance, I wondered how long it took her in the morning to get ready for school. The hair alone must have taken half an hour, unless she had it in rollers all night perhaps, and surely she wouldn't put up with that sort of discomfort every night? Perhaps if she were going to a party, but every night? And the make-up. It looked like a work of art to me. I had to admit, it was impressive (if she was aiming to be a make-up artist she certainly had a head start) but it just screamed trying too hard. I wondered what she looked like underneath. It must be terrible having to wear a mask every day to conceal who you really were.

The irony hit me just as Tyler and George rounded the corner with a football.

They were playing keepie-uppies, alternating kicks while the ball bounced once in between them. As they moved past the witches, three steps forward and two steps back in order to keep the game going, Amelia turned to watch, leaning on the edge of the bench, sitting on her hands with her body thrown forward. The rest of the coven followed suit, watching the entertainment, making appropriate whooping and oohing noises when either of the boys managed to keep up a particularly unlikely ball. Eventually, Tyler had to lunge frantically to the side to reach a seemingly impossible ball which then veered out of range of George's feet on to the grass verge. He leapt forward, catching the ball in his hands and sliding to a stop just before hitting the leg of the bench.

The witches erupted, applauding and whistling in appreciation while Tyler and George lay on the floor at their feet, in fits of laughter.

The knot of anxiety which had been forming overnight in my stomach tightened, and a lump appeared in my throat. I didn't know which was worse, the sense of betrayal, or the realisation that things were changing. When I was younger, it didn't matter that Tyler and I were different: that he was good at sport and I wasn't; that he was funny and I just laughed at the right time; that he was popular and had lots of friends and I was just one of them. He liked me, and that was enough for me. Now though, I could see that it did matter. How long would it be until he was sick of carrying me, until the burden of looking after me became too much and he cut me loose.

How long would it be before my mask slipped and he could see the real me underneath? What would he think when he realised I wasn't even the person he had known for so long, however needy and disappointing that person might be?

Chapter 7

Slumped in my chair in the English classroom, I was so grateful that I sat at the back in the corner. If it was possible to be invisible, this was the best place. I had avoided Tyler and George so far, and assumed Olivia and Faye had arrived after I slipped through the school doors early on the pretext of having to visit the library (somewhere I'd barely been by choice in four and a half years). Unable to concentrate in science, I'd come straight to the English classroom at the start of break and was attempting, unsuccessfully, to immerse myself in geography revision in order to escape from the thoughts that were tormenting me. I knew I couldn't face Tyler. I had been stung by what I saw as his disloyalty to me in encouraging Amelia and her friends, even flirting with them, but part of me was now ashamed of this reaction. Tyler was free to be friends with who he wanted. It certainly was not my place to dictate who he should speak to and who he should ignore. Perhaps he had wanted to be friends with Amelia for a while and only resisted because of his loyalty to me. Or out of pity. I couldn't bear the possibility that Tyler was my friend out of pity, but what else was there?

Other students began to filter into the room and I braced myself for another English lesson on a poem that I could not make sense of. English felt like a series of puzzles I wasn't quite able to solve. I couldn't comprehend the indefinable grading of achievement at all. In maths and science, there were concrete facts and formulas you either remembered and knew how to apply or you didn't. Answers were either right or wrong, black or white, and the more you got right, the better grade you got. In English, there were just different shades of grey. Some answers to the same question were completely different, but still correct and worthy of the same grade, and some answers said more or less the same thing, but one was much better than the other. It was too vague and imprecise for me, and I have to admit, I didn't put in a huge amount of effort to understand.

I watched for Dan's entrance, as I always did in English (he was the only thing that made it tolerable for me) but he didn't arrive with two of his friends like usual. It was odd; I was sure I had spotted him earlier before the bell went for registration, but I assumed he was in a football meeting, or a cricket meeting, or a meeting for another sort of sport he was good at.

'Ok,' shouted Miss Purcell. 'We're going to work on English language writing skills for one lesson a week for the next couple of months. I want us to think about what the purpose of our writing is, and how we can come up with the best possible plan to make sure that our writing achieves its purpose.' (She always spoke to us in the first person, as if she were going to take the GCSE right alongside us and she was as confused as we were about the purpose of our writing).

'Ok,' said Miss Purcell, 'so we're going to plan our writing in groups.' (No surprise there then) 'Four brains working together should be able to come up with enough ideas to keep us going.' She smiled enthusiastically, as if the class were going to knuckle down and brainstorm ideas for a paper two writing task, and not chat about anything and everything to avoid it. I sighed. I hated group work. There was always a dominant member of the group, who thought they knew everything, a quiet member of the group, who seemed to know nothing, a lazy member of the group, who spent the whole time making faces and throwing things at their friends in different groups, and me.

She separated us into groups of four. Looking around I could see the logic in her choices. There was indeed, in each group, one person that liked the sound of their own voice, one who barely spoke and another one or two (depending on the size of the group) who were kind of in-between. In my group, I guessed I'd be the in-between one. First there was Charlotte Keenan, who I'd describe as a wannabe witch, or a witch in waiting. She was there on the fringes of the clique but couldn't quite make it in. Sometimes it seemed like she was in (I'd see her walking down the corridor chatting with Jilly maybe, or one of the other minions) but she never quite made it to the inner enclave and achieved an audience with Queen Amelia. I suppose she was pretty, in a red-haired, freckly kind of way, but from what I could remember about her she lived in the wrong direction (the wrong side of school) to be witch material. I'd say she was definitely the one who liked the sound of her own voice, although I think she was slightly isolated there. Most of us had been guilty of rolling our eyes when she'd waved her hand about in the air and we'd heard the words, 'Shall I read mine out?'

The third member of our group was Zainab Malik, a studious girl who never volunteered her opinion or asked questions in class, and who would look like a rabbit in the headlights if ever called upon to give the most straightforward answer. She was tiny, under five feet tall and painfully thin, with huge dark eyes and delicate features; she had to weigh about a third of what I did. I assumed she was bright. She always seemed to achieve highly in assessments, but I'd never spoken to her, and she'd never spoken to me, so she was somewhat of an unknown quantity.

'Ok, said Miss Purcell, 'so we're going to write something with a real purpose this time.' (implying all the other 'practice papers' had been pointless? I knew what she meant, but I was just in the most contrary mood.) 'As you know, there has been a question mark hanging over the prom this year. It is felt that spending a huge amount of money on this one night is extravagant and thoughtless, given the fact that our school focus this year is raising money for the Village Endowment Trust, which empowers the ultra-poor in rural Africa to lift themselves out of poverty through small sustainable businesses and savings groups.' (She sounded like she was reading directly from the leaflet.)

No-one spoke. I think the class were split on the issue of the prom. I knew a lot of the girls were horrified at the possibility of no prom, which meant they lost the opportunity to feel like a movie star for a day. No outrageously expensive gown, no chance to have their make-up and hair done by a professional, no chance to exit whatever ridiculously ostentatious form of transport Mummy and Daddy had paid a fortune for just so that their little princess could be belle of the ball. Limousines and Stretched Hummers were passé now. In recent years, students had arrived at the prom in helicopters, on white horses, and even in a World War Two tank painted white. Although I had been impressed when one boy a couple of year before had driven his dad's tractor there. At least that was funny.

The prom, to these people, was a rite of passage. It was something they had dreamed of and looked forward to for years. Even I could see how cancelling the prom, for whatever worthy reason, would be a devastating blow for many.

For the other half of the year, cancelling the prom would probably be somewhat of a relief, for numerous reasons. Our school catchment area straddled two very different boroughs. There were quite a few affluent areas to the north from which, probably, the majority of the students came, but on the south side there were a number of estates where those students with much less prosperous parents lived. Parents who wanted their children to thrive but struggled to keep up with the steady stream of requests for contributions to school trips and chosen charities. The school had, until recently, been a grammar school, and it seemed like the governors and senior leadership team were keen to retain the air of exclusivity it had previously enjoyed.

Whereas other local schools perhaps visited France and Germany and travelled by coach for their school trips, Westfield High organised expeditions to Peru and Tanzania. (Theoretically, students would fund raise frantically to raise the finance needed to be part of these life changing excursions, but the reality was more that rich parents would provide their children with the thousands of pounds required and nothing would be mentioned.) Even the skiing trips did not escape the same elitist touch. No France or Austria for Westfield (that would be far too affordable). Westfield skied in Canada.

As a result, those students whose parents were from 'the wrong side of the school' were excluded from many of the activities 'offered'. They knew this, and accepted it I think. I know I did. Although my parents were comfortably off, and could probably have found the money from somewhere to finance maybe one trip during my time at Westfield, it would have had to be a case of sacrificing our family holiday, or the new car Dad needed, or the kitchen extension that had made Mum so happy a couple of years before. Luckily for them, I never wanted to go anyway. Why would I, when most of the others who would be going made me feel like an outsider, unwanted and unwelcome in their gang?

Similarly, the prom was really designed, I considered, to suit the more desirable students (in the eyes of the powers that were), the ones whose parents' net worth allowed them to attend such an exclusive and sophisticated celebration of their success, whether about to be earned, or inherited. To buy a dress from Topshop, or hire last year's style of tuxedo, and arrive in your Dad's eight-year-old Ford Mondeo would be embarrassing at best.

Money was not the reason I dreaded the prom. My friends and I had parents who could pay for reasonably priced clothes and transport, and none of us were what I'd call materialistic or pretentious. I just knew that I wouldn't enjoy it because I wasn't like them: the others. Then again, I wasn't like my friends either.

Miss Purcell continued. 'Obviously, the issue of the prom and what to do about it is extremely pressing. If we do hold a prom, it will need to be organised and booked as a matter of urgency. However, I think it has been decided that a 'traditional style' prom is unlikely.' She made a quotation marks gesture in the air to emphasise the unlikelihood of a 'traditional style' event.

Some of the girls began to mutter and look around at their friends in dismay. They had, I think, assumed that everything would happen as it always had, and ignored the rumours that had been circulating around school for months. Charlotte looked as if she was going to cry, and I felt strangely sorry for her.

'Ok, I know it's disappointing for some of you, but that's the reason I've chosen to focus on this issue. I think we can come up with some amazing ideas for an alternative prom that will blow the stuffy old sit-down meal out of the water. Who's with me?'

No-one was.

Miss Purcell looked uncomfortable, then recovered. 'Ok, so let's just back pedal a bit shall we? Let's tweak the task a little. I said unlikely, not impossible, so let's tell the governors exactly what we think. If you are completely against the idea of changing the format of the prom, you need to persuade the governors not to change it. If you quite like the idea of a new and innovative arrangement, you need to persuade the governors of this. The main thing is, you need to agree as a group what you're going to argue, and make it as convincing as possible. Ok?'

There was a general, unenthusiastic agreement, which Miss Purcell gratefully accepted (She must have been relieved that a full-scale rebellion had not ensued) and she began to write the task on the board.

'The board of governors at your school have made it clear that in their opinion, to hold a traditional style prom would be extravagant and wasteful, given the focus on charity and selflessness this year. Write the text of a speech in which you argue for or against this view.'

'Ok, let's engage those brains!' she beamed.

I looked at Charlotte and Zainab. Somehow I didn't think it was going to be as easy as Miss thought to agree which way we were going to argue.

Over Charlotte's head I saw the door open. Then Dan Sweeney walked in and gave a student support slip to Miss Purcell. His head was down and he seemed to be trying to avoid eye contact with anyone. After a brief conversation, she scanned the room and turned back to him. There was another short conversation, and then he turned and looked at me, well, at us I suppose, before slowly walking over and sitting in the chair next to Zainab.

As soon as I'd seen him look in our direction I'd known he was going to join us, and my heart was beating out of my chest by the time he reached the table. I could barely breathe, let alone speak. The others obviously felt the same, as an uncomfortable silence descended, until Miss Purcell breezed over and took control. 'Charlotte, bring Dan up to speed with what we're doing won't you? I'm expecting great things from this group,' she smiled, then moved on to the next table, who had started laughing at something that sounded very unlike the task we'd been set.

This was the nearest I'd ever actually been to Dan, and he looked frighteningly big and real up close, like a person, not a fantasy, although his dark skin and eyes were so perfect it was a little like seeing a close up of a film star. I couldn't imagine being able to control my breathing, let alone my voice. A flush of embarrassment was already creeping up my face.

When Charlotte started to speak, I wasn't quite sure what she said as she sounded as if I was hearing her from a distance, but Dan lifted his head and turned towards her to listen. Once I felt it was safe, I looked at him out of the corner of my eye, facing Charlotte though, as if I too was intent on what she had to say.

If I didn't know better, I would have said he'd been crying, or at least upset. His brown eyes were still slightly watery and red, and he took a couple of deep breaths as if to compose himself. Seeing him looking so differently to the way he had before, or maybe the way I'd imagined him before, was weird. He looked so restless and vulnerable that I suddenly felt a wave of empathy toward him.

When Charlotte finished speaking, Dan straightened up and smiled. All traces of the anxiousness I'd perceived a moment earlier disappeared and left me wondering if I'd invented them. Maybe he had hay-fever, or he'd just sneezed, or both, I told myself. What did Dan Sweeney have to worry about, let alone cry about? It was obviously a figment of my over-active imagination.

Still, it had distracted me for a moment from my pathetic hero-worship, and I gradually began to make sense of the conversation he was now having with Charlotte about the prom.

'I can't believe they'd actually let us leave without having a prom,' Charlotte was complaining. 'Some people I know have already bought their dresses. It's so unfair that the governors have all the control. They don't understand the significance of it all. If it was their prom and they had to miss out, maybe they'd feel differently.'

'You have to see it from their point of view though? Dan countered gently. 'The school's supporting The Village Endowment Trust and it's all over the radio and the newspapers how we're all making huge sacrifices to help those less fortunate than us. Can you imagine how hypocritical it would look if we held a prom like last year? You've got to admit it's all getting a bit out of hand?'

'What do you mean out of hand? It's one day.' She sighed heavily. 'It's just one day.'

'Exactly,' Dan continued. 'Have you any idea how much some of those cars cost? And the rest? Say it's thirty pounds a head and two hundred people go, that's six thousand pounds. Add on what people spend on clothes and make-up and things like that and I bet you're talking upwards of fifty thousand. Just think what you could do with that in Africa.'

Charlotte cast her eyes down. There was no way she could argue further with Dan without sounding like a spoilt, selfish brat.

'It's not all or nothing,' I said. I couldn't quite believe that I was speaking, let alone in what sounded like a calm, even confident tone.

'What?' Charlotte's head swiveled towards me, as if she'd just remembered I was there.

'It's not like the prom has to be completely cancelled,' I answered. 'We just have to think of a theme that fits in with the school's view on charity at the moment.'

Dan looked at me and smiled approvingly.

I carried on, buoyed by his support, 'We don't have to sacrifice the prom, just the extravagance that goes with it nowadays. No-one really needs to arrive in a helicopter do they? What do you really get out of that?'

'Apart from everybody knowing that your parents are rich,' Dan laughed.

I looked over at him. 'I think everybody probably knows whose parents are rich anyway, without having it shoved down their throats.'

He laughed and his eyes crinkled up at the corners.

I couldn't seem to tear my eyes away from his face, so I was grateful when Zainab spoke. It was so unexpected I think I might have even jumped a little, but at least it saved me from making the way I felt about him even more obvious.

'What sort of theme?' she asked quietly, looking at me.

I stared back inanely. I could hardly remember my own name, and the conversation we'd been having previously was a complete blank.

'What sort of prom theme do you think would fit in with the charity focus,' she repeated slowly, as if talking to a small child.

Gradually, my composure returned and I started to recall the thoughts I'd been having earlier. 'Maybe a second-hand theme? Everyone has to wear second hand clothes? We could buy them off Ebay or just the shops in town?'

I could tell from Charlotte's body language that for her, this was an alarming suggestion. She started to scrape the thumbnail on one hand and her face contorted into a frown. For a second, I even thought I saw her lip curl in disgust.

'That will be a no then,' I conceded. 'What about fancy dress? It doesn't cost much and it could be funny?'

'What sort of fancy dress?' asked Dan. 'Just anything, or narrow it down to movie stars or pop stars? What about Mardi Gras? Lots of feathers and masks and sparkle?' I could see he was becoming more enthusiastic.

'Mardi Gras would cost a fortune,' Charlotte piped up. At least she was considering ideas though.

'Yeah, I suppose. I was just getting a bit carried away,' grinned Dan.

'An era maybe?' I was clutching at straws. This was a lot harder than I'd anticipated. 'The fifties, or forties? A war theme with uniforms and stuff…'

'The seventies?' Zainab cut in.

I swung my head round to face her and she dipped her head self-consciously. There was a slight pause before she spoke.

'Sorry, I didn't mean to interrupt, but all your ideas are going to end up costing quite a lot of money. The seventies is easier. It's quite fashionable these days so I bet people already have stuff in their wardrobes they could customise. You can buy loads of accessories really cheaply too.'

Charlotte suddenly came to life. 'We could have a festival theme. You can make that as basic or as glamorous as you want. You can just do shorts and wellies, or the whole Kardashian over the top thing.'

'No-one would know what you'd spent,' I admitted. 'We could do it on the school field and just have takeaway vans. We could put together a band to do some of the music. And I know there's a couple of lads who like DJing in our year. Either way, it's something different.'

Miss Purcell's voice rang out, 'Ok year eleven. We only have a couple of minutes left of the lesson so I want you to agree on the way you want to argue and for homework come up with some ideas for your paragraphs. You need different points in each paragraph and between the three or four of you, it should be easy to come up with four good persuasive reasons why the governors should decide your speech is the most convincing. I'll speak to Mr. Harding and I'm sure he'll make sure the governors realise how much you care and take your feelings seriously.'

We looked at each other. 'Festival?' Dan asked, raising his eyebrows and opening his palms.

'Yeah, I think maybe I can cope with that,' Charlotte sighed.

Zainab and I just nodded.

'Ok, we'll spend more time on our plans next Friday before we actually write the speech. I want us to stay in the same groups throughout then we can get to know each other's writing styles, hopefully share our views and help each other improve. It might be a good idea to get together in the interim and discuss what we have so far then we know we're not overlapping.'

My heart started beating faster again. Should I suggest meeting up before next Friday? Would someone else? No-one actually did that though, did they? You'd look like a complete nerd if you took homework *that* seriously. Wouldn't you?

We were putting our chairs under and making our way to the door. If nobody said anything soon we'd just melt away into our normal lives and not see one another for a week, just like the other groups. It was agony. I wanted to say something, indifferently, as if it didn't really matter either way, I was just putting it out there. 'What about meeting up Monday or Tuesday, to make sure we have enough points, that we haven't duplicated each other's ideas?' I could say noncommittally.

I didn't though, and then it was too late. Dan twisted his head round and for a moment I thought he was going to say something, but he didn't. He just smiled at us and followed his two friends down the corridor.

Chapter 8

It felt like a cruel case of déjà vu, sitting there in the hospital, unaware of the seriousness of Dan's condition. Only a few months ago I'd been here, in the same hospital, with its clinical white walls and bright lights, waiting to hear whether he was alive or dead. Now I was waiting to hear the same news again.

A year ago, I'd barely set foot in a hospital. Mum told stories about a couple of incidents when I was small, an isolated and unexplained fit I had as a baby, and a visit to A and E when I put my teeth through my lip and she'd panicked. I myself remembered only one; I'd somehow managed to wedge a crayon so far up my nose that no-one could reach it and I can still see the huge frightening instrument with which they finally extracted it.

Now I felt I was coming to know this place, was beginning to navigate the spacious corridors and decode hitherto indecipherable signs with ease. I recognised the corridor I'd hurried up and down when Dan was brought here all those months ago, and although this time I'd been directed to a waiting room and was sitting in a comfortable chair, the sensation was the same.

A few tattered magazines remained in the rack by the door and I flicked through them to pass the time. They were the sort of magazines delivered free through your door, full of glossy advertisements for local kitchen and bathroom fitters, restaurant reviews and the occasional article about a local semi-celebrity. Mum always commented on how much they must cost to produce when most people just threw them straight in the bin. We'd been receiving them for years, but every month she'd mention it. I wondered why nobody brought in the sort of magazines people actually spent their money on, so obviously wanted to read.

The phone in my pocket vibrated, and I was jolted back to reality. 'On way there,' Tyler had texted. 'Mum is bringing you something to eat.'

I looked at the time: '12.38'. How long had I been here? It had been half-past eight when the bus had passed Dan's house, and so much had happened since then. I couldn't remember noticing the time when I first sat down in this room, but it must have been two hours before. No-one had come to update me about Dan's condition. Why was that? Was it a positive sign? a negative one? Had they just forgotten about me?

Chapter 9

Even though part of me was disappointed, I told myself it was for the best. I hadn't made a fool of myself; imagine how I'd have felt if everyone had mumbled an embarrassed, 'no thanks.' Or made lame excuses. No, it was definitely for the best. I relived the experience all weekend and looked forward to Friday safe in the knowledge that no-one thought any the worse of me than they had before.

Oddly, I recalled, I hadn't sensed any negative vibes, even from Charlotte, the whole lesson. I was mulling it over in my head again on the way to our steps on Monday when Olivia fell into step beside me. 'Where were you on Friday?' she asked. 'I was late but I got here way before the bell. Faye said she thought she saw you when she came into the yard but by the time she made it to the steps you were gone so maybe it wasn't you. I thought you might be ill but then I remembered it was Friday. You'd drag yourself in off your deathbed for maths.' She chuckled at her own wit and I couldn't help joining in. I was feeling much more positive since Friday.

'Then I thought I'd see you at lunch but Faye said you were doing some homework in the library,' she looked at me and frowned, as if this was the strangest thing she'd ever heard. 'I couldn't believe it. You never go to the library!'

It wasn't that I didn't work hard. I liked working hard, but the library was so outdated. There were lots of novels in there, fiction, which I hated, and although they probably did have lots of non-fiction, even text books, text books were obsolete as soon as they were published. How pointless were text books when you had the internet? The thought of reading an actual book would never enter my head. I did all my studying online on my laptop at home as the computers were so slow in the library and they were never free as you had to book them in advance. And studying at home gave me a reason to go to my room, which recently was the only place I wanted to be when I was at home.

'I wanted to get started on my English homework as soon as I could,' I lied. How could I tell her that I hadn't wanted to see her because I was jealous of the fictitious marriage between her and Dan that I'd fabricated in my weird, obsessed mind?

'English? Since when did you care about English? You hate English, or so you say.' Olivia teased. 'Or…maybe you secretly love it like you love maths and science and you've made up this irrational hatred for it just to make yourself seem more normal. It's not normal to be good at everything so you pretend you're rubbish at English to fit in with the rest of us thickies.' She waited for me to respond but I just laughed. They were always kidding me about being clever but it was all good-natured and in fun. They were proud of it really, even kind of competitive on my behalf. They'd ask what grade I'd been given in assessments, then always follow up with, 'What did everyone else get? Were you top? Did you beat Amelia? Did you beat Will?'

'You're doing it wrong though,' she carried on. 'You need to be bad at something to be in our gang. There's no point telling us how useless you are and still being in set one. You'll have to drop at least one set to qualify. I can show you how to be bad at English if you want. I'm in set three and I'm still struggling.'

We were both laughing now. I playfully pushed her away from me and she doubled up clutching her arm. 'Ahh, you've broken my arm,' she screamed between giggles. Then she linked up with me. 'Come on, speed up a bit. I need to sit down.' She caught my eye. 'Heavy weekend,' laughing again, 'You know how it is?'

When we reached the steps, George and Faye were deep in discussion. We flopped down, still linked up and laughing. 'What's happening dudes?' Olivia quipped.

It was clear from their reaction that whatever was happening was not funny, and we quickly sobered up. Faye looked at George, then back at us. 'Tyler's mum and dad have spilt up,' she said gravely.

'You're joking,' Olivia said. 'I mean, I know you're not. No-one would joke about something like that. It's just…I'm just shocked, that's all.'

I was speechless. Tyler's parents were great. His mum was lovely, always smiling and laughing; laid back, my parents called her. I loved sleeping at his house. She was a fantastic cook and would make delicious home-cooked meals every night. There were always home-made brownies and scones in tins piled up in the 'cake cupboard', and her bacon butties were legendary. She never seemed irritated by Tyler or disappointed in him; it always seemed like she just wanted him to be happy, and if he was happy then she was happy. She was always hugging and kissing him, and while he pretended to be embarrassed and told her not to, he loved it really and ended up laughing and hugging her back.

His dad was amazing too, really witty and entertaining. He'd have us all in stitches every time they came round, even Mum. Dad said he should have been a stand-up comedian. I suppose that's where Tyler got his wit from. Nobody could fail to be entertained by Tyler. He was effortlessly funny and would come out with hilarious one liners so naturally that I was sometimes in awe of him.

Oh my God, Tyler. It suddenly hit me how devastated he would be. I couldn't imagine how it would feel to be told that your whole world is about to be turned upside down and everything you took for granted is about to be taken away from you.

By the time the bell went, he still hadn't arrived. 'Where is he?' I asked Faye.

'He's at home. I don't think he can face coming in today. They sat him down and told him yesterday and his dad left straight after. They'd obviously planned it because he's sorted out a flat near his work. I just can't believe it. I'm so gutted for Tyler.'

We sat in silence for a couple of minutes. I was imagining what it would be like if Dad left us and finding the idea too awful to even think about. When I glanced over at Faye, I realised that she was probably reliving the time when her dad did leave, which was even worse.

'You should go round after school,' Faye told me. 'I don't think he'll want a lot of visitors but you should be there for him. He'll need someone to talk to, even if he doesn't know it yet.'

I texted Tyler at break but there was no reply by lunchtime so I tried again, 'Did you get my text?' By the end of school, I'd have no choice if he still hadn't replied.

I spent most of the afternoon planning what I was going to say to Tyler and rehearsing it in my head. I'd let him do most of the talking and decide how much or how little he wanted to tell me. I predicted he'd probably put on a brave face and make a joke out of everything like he usually did if things were tense. Mind you, were things ever tense at his house? I couldn't imagine it. He'd probably encountered most of the tenseness he'd experienced at my house, when Mum was in one of her moods when neither Dad or I could do anything right. She was never rude or unpleasant to him, in fact she seemed to be even more friendly and warm to Tyler when she was annoyed at us, and the incongruity made it even more uncomfortable. Snapping at us with a face like thunder, then switching her smile on like a light bulb when she spoke to him. Yes, he definitely knew what tension was.

I took my time on the way to Tyler's house, walking slowly as if delaying the inevitable would make it easier, but I couldn't put it off absolutely so when I arrived I went quickly to the door and knocked. I decided that further procrastinating would only prolong the agony.

His mum answered pretty much straight away, opened the door to let me through and then gave me a big hug. She always hugged me if she hadn't seen me for a few days, but I could feel the extra emotion in that hug.

She pulled away and smiled at me. 'He's in his room.'

The house was more of a tip than usual, if that was possible. There were piles of washing waiting to be ironed on the stairs and every surface was covered with papers, coins or some other paraphernalia Tyler's mum couldn't find a home for. It couldn't be more of a contrast to my house, where everything had its place, and had to be in its place, or my mum would sulk, or stomp around shouting about having to do everything herself and how nobody else cared.

Normally, I wouldn't have knocked. We'd never knocked on each-other's doors before, just barged in like siblings would. That was how our relationship had always been. Knocking seemed so formal, so awkward, but then this situation was awkward, so I knocked.

'I'm fine Mum,' Tyler responded from the other side of the door.

I pushed the door gently and popped my head around it. 'It's me.'

He looked up through his mop of curly blond hair, surprised for a minute, then sighed. 'Oh...come in then.'

He looked pale. If that was possible. Everyone said that he only had to look at the sun to get a tan, and it was weird how dark his skin was compared to his bright blond hair and light brown eyes.

My mum always said he looked like a lion, with the tan, the blond mane and the yellow cat's eyes.

Everything I'd planned to say mysteriously disappeared out of my head. I fidgeted for a couple of seconds, then asked, 'Are you ok?' Talk about a stupid thing to say. Of course he wasn't ok. I made a mental note to smack myself in the face as soon as I was alone again. What an idiot.

He didn't seem to notice though. He looked at me for a while, as if trying to decide which path to take, the usual one where he'd relieve the atmosphere with humour, or the truth. When his eyes began to fill, I realised the decision had been made for him. He stood up and came towards me, arms outstretched, and I wrapped mine around him. I wondered when I'd grown taller than him. I'd always pictured us as the same height; we definitely used to be the same height, but now his arms naturally fitted under mine and I could almost rest my chin on his head. Tyler had such a huge personality, such an aura of confidence, that he seemed larger than life somehow, and it was a shock to see him look so physically small.

I'd never seen Tyler so vulnerable and helpless before and I suddenly saw our relationship from a distance, as perhaps other people did. Tyler was the strong one, the confident one who didn't need support or encouragement. I was the one who went to him for those things, and I'd always taken it for granted that it would always be that way. Now he needed me, and I knew I had to come through for him in the way he always had for me. It felt good. I hated him being hurt so much it was almost painful, but it felt good to be needed. I steeled myself. I had to be strong for him to help him get through it.

When he stopped sobbing he rubbed his face with the towel he always kept thrown over the back of a chair. There were many words I could have chosen to describe Tyler, but tidy was definitely not one of them. His mum said life was too short to worry about tidying the house, and the sentiment had not been lost on him. I wished my mum would realise how short life was.

'He's already gone you know? They've been planning this for weeks and I didn't even suspect.' He groaned. 'What does that say about me? They were so unhappy they couldn't stand the sight of each other and I didn't notice. I've always known I was stupid, but this is ridiculous. Do I go around with my eyes closed or something?'

'You're not stupid. They obviously didn't want you to know so they acted as if everything was fine. Nothing's your fault and they'd be gutted if they thought you were blaming yourself. Things just happen, that's all. Have they said anything about why?'

'They've just…fallen out of love with each other.' He made quotation mark with his fingers in the way Miss Purcell always did to emphasise the cliché. 'I don't know yet who fell out with who because they're being all united about it to try and make it easier for me. 'We still love each other, we're just not, *in* love anymore,' he mimicked, 'and all that crap.'

'Maybe it's not crap,' I suggested. 'Maybe they do feel that way?'

'You know what's really bothering me now?' he glanced towards me, then cast his eyes down. 'How are me and Mum going to live now? Mum's never really had a job, well, not a career sort of job anyway. She used to childmind and she was a dinner lady at school for a bit but how much does that pay? We'll have to sell the house! Dad won't leave us penniless; I'm not saying that, but he's not going to pay for this place and his own *new life* is he? I'm not being materialistic. I don't care about the money, or moving really, it's just, what's she going to do? She's no qualifications. She was never great at school. Remember, she always used to say I got my brains from her.' He laughed miserably.

'And it's made me think about my future too. What am I going to do? You know how thick I am. I've never thought about it before because I never had to. Maybe deep down I thought I'd still be living with Mum and Dad at forty, with Dad still supporting me. Well, that idea's down the pan now, isn't it?'

'Stop it!' I snapped. 'You're not thick, you just aren't academic. That's not everything, you know?'

'Easy for you to say,' Tyler retorted.

'No, but you're good at so many things. You can do anything. You're brilliant at sport and games. You can just pick them up instantly. Remember when your dad took us playing golf and after one round that lady asked how long you'd been playing and wanted to put you in the team? What about the way you are with bikes? Everyone knows if their bikes need mending or tuning or whatever to come to you.'

I couldn't believe Tyler was saying these things. I'd never thought for a minute that he wasn't exactly the confident, optimistic free spirit we all saw, and I felt guilty. When I had moments of weakness, and there were a lot of them, I'd moan to Tyler for a couple of hours and he'd build me back up again. Now I had to do that for him.

'You know what the main thing is about you? You can do anything you want because you've got it. Ok, maybe not heart surgery, but most things.'

He laughed, but looked at me and listened.

'Everybody likes you. You've got charisma. You're funny and interesting and kind and honest and all those things, but it's not just that. You've got something else…I can't put my finger on it…charisma's the best I can do.'

'The X factor. I have the X factor.' His delivery was dead pan.

'See!' We high fived each other and collapsed laughing. It felt so good to make him laugh.

Later, when Tyler's mum shouted that dinner was ready, he walked downstairs with me. 'Hey,' he said quietly. I turned and he smiled at me, a sad smile that didn't quite reach his eyes. 'Thanks.'

When Tyler's mum had asked if I wanted to stay and have dinner with them I hadn't even considered it. A Tyler's mum style meal would not so much ruin my diet as torpedo it completely out of the water, and I was enjoying it now. I always did like the feeling of complete control that a diet gave me, once I was safely on it.

I never would have told anyone I was 'on a diet'. That would have made me even more a target of ridicule for the wider school population, in particular those who revelled in the misery of others. It would also create a situation with my friends where they felt they had to convince me I wasn't fat all the time. The last time they'd become aware I was trying to lose weight, they tried every tactic in the book to persuade me there was no problem, to the point where it became quite irritating. I knew I wasn't huge, probably ten to twenty pounds overweight at most, but the flab seemed to settle in the most unattractive places and my confidence plummeted as a result. Everyone on social media and all the celebrities I seemed to see had toned and tanned bodies and I felt like a freak when I looked at my bulk in the mirror. I could never go swimming looking like I did, and I spent all summer in a variety of big T shirts, disguising the shape underneath.

Once I was officially 'on a diet' in my mind, I was the best dieter ever. I'd eat very little and ask for chicken and tuna salads for lunch, filling up on fruit and water. I'd be on a kind of 'control high' and the hunger was part of that. When my stomach shrank I didn't even feel so hungry, just a little self-satisfied at being so disciplined and virtuous. As a result, I was able to lose weight pretty quickly, and my confidence grew as my waistline shrunk. There was nothing like the feeling when I looked in the mirror and could see my jawline reappearing, or when I tucked in my shirt and there was enough space for my hand to fit.

I felt guilty about not staying, as I could see that Tyler's mum would have really appreciated the company. I would have made the house feel less empty I think. But I had to think about my diet. However ashamed I was for prioritising my weight above her feelings, I justified it by telling myself that I needed to be strong to support Tyler. He did not need a fat, needy basket case right now, he needed a solid, reliable friend he could depend on. And I was determined to be just that.

Most of the time, he was doing a very good job of concealing his anguish, at least in front of others. On Tuesday, he walked to our steps sporting a black eye and a line of butterfly stitches over a large cut on his cheek. 'Rugby,' he answered our shocked expressions. Then to me, 'I know, modelling career in tatters as well now!'

The week dragged. Even though I spent a lot of time thinking about Tyler and how I could best distract him from the situation at home, I could not forget that on Friday, Dan would be sitting across from me, or next to me, in English, and that he would be talking to me, and listening to me. Our eyes would meet. It felt wrong to be so exhilarated when my best friend was suffering, but also like a delicious secret that only I could enjoy.

On Thursday, I saw Dan briefly. I'd been sent from the all-weather pitch to fetch a stop watch for PE and was passing the student support area when I saw him emerge from one of the counselling rooms. He looked furtively about but I was partially hidden behind a pillar so he mustn't have seen me. Then he hurried away, head down as if he was trying to avoid being recognised. There was no-one about, so he was probably relieved at not being spotted, or at least at the fact he thought he hadn't been spotted.

The counselling room was where students with 'problems' went. Some were open about their troubles, and spent most of their free time in and around the student support and counselling area. There were a number of people in my year with sporadic attendance caused by different issues either at home or at school and we couldn't help but speculate at times. We'd express our concerns and sympathise with whatever condition we decided these people were suffering from, but we didn't enjoy it. At least, I don't think we did.

Other people, like Amelia and the witches, probably relished the thought of anybody else being miserable. I could imagine them laughing at the misfortunes of those weaker than them and less popular. 'How sad,' I could almost hear Amelia crowing, 'to have to spend your lunchtime with all the other misfits and loonies.'

Others visitors to the counselling rooms, I was sure, would hate anyone to know they were suffering. Like Dan; he definitely looked like he would hate anyone to know he was struggling.

I wondered what he was struggling with. It was at least the second time he had been 'counselled' as I remembered the slip he'd given to Miss Purcell the Friday before, so it had to be an ongoing issue. I supposed they all were; it had to be ongoing, because if you had a problem and then you solved it, there would be no need for counselling, would there? I pondered the matter as I dawdled back to PE with the stopwatch.

Dan was gorgeous, not just ordinarily attractive, but stunning, like a young Elvis in the films I used to watch with Mum. He was over six feet tall and his hair was thick, dark and shiny, worn long on top so it flopped over one eye. He had dark eyes with long eyelashes which looked slightly oriental, especially when he smiled and they crinkled up at the sides. Until last week, I hadn't ever been close enough to see that, but a couple of times, when he'd immersed himself in the task and relaxed, I'd seen it, and it had made him even more striking. His mouth was wide and generous, and when he smiled he had quite a large gap between his front teeth, which on anyone else might have seemed like an imperfection, but it just added to his appeal. He also had a slightly lopsided grin, which reminded me of a photo of Elvis on the cover of one of Mum's CDs. If I had to find fault, I suppose his nose was on the large side, and a little hooked when seen from the side. But it just looked manly on him, and kind of right. He certainly could not complain about his looks.

Then there was the athletic ability. Dan was in almost every sports team the school fielded and probably would have been in them all if they hadn't clashed with each other. Apparently he was also an amazing swimmer when he was younger, but had given it up about a year before. I thought he must be reasonably clever too, as he was in my top set for English, and although we didn't have any other lessons together, I assumed he was in higher sets for everything else too. In my mind, if you were clever, you were clever, and it never entered my head that some people excelled in one area but struggled in others. He was popular, and seemed to have a number of good friends he hung around with as a rule. I didn't know much about his family, but I'd heard rumours that they were 'a bit rough', whatever that meant. Whatever it did mean, I think it added to the air of mystique that swirled around him, and made him seem even more exotic and appealing.

How could someone so blessed be worried about anything so much that he had to visit a counsellor at school? I was baffled, but I knew from experience that not everything was always as it seemed.

Chapter 11

Dan was already sitting across the desk from Charlotte with his back to the door and they were chatting merrily away when I got to English the next day. I'd arrived just on the bell as I didn't want to look all keen and geeky, but it seemed they hadn't missed me. Dan was laughing at something Charlotte had just said and she was flicking her red hair irritatingly. It was the kind of hair that would make people stare in the street, glossy and fiery, although I'd never noticed before. I would have sworn she'd had it professionally styled if it wasn't a Friday morning. Surely hairdressers didn't open that early did they? She was also wearing a lot more make-up than I thought I'd ever seen her wear before; not that I'd particularly noticed. She looked like a clone of Amelia Clarke. I felt my lip curling and only just managed to rearrange my face before they both turned and greeted me.

'Hi,' they chorused, like a couple.

I took a deep breath and answered. 'Hi,' exuding an enthusiasm I did not feel. I was relieved when Zainab quietly took the seat beside Charlotte. I sat down next to Dan and Miss Purcell began to speak.

'Ok, the first thing I want us to do is share the ideas we've had during the week and start thinking about a plan for our speech. Think about organising your points in order of persuasiveness, most persuasive point first and so on. When you're presenting your idea to the group, make sure that you explain how you're going to develop the argument too? Let's aim to spend about twenty minutes for starters shall we? Any questions?'

There were no questions, so we discussed roles within the group and decided that Zainab should write, as she was the neatest (I could have seen that stereotype a mile off; the quiet girl does the writing then we don't have to worry about her) Charlotte would be the director (as she was the loudest) and Dan and I would do the 'other' roles, which I think we called the encourager (meaning Dan would prise as much out of Zainab as he could) and the co-ordinator (meaning I would make sure Charlotte didn't talk too much).

We worked well, I thought, stayed on task more than usual and actually came up with some sound ideas for our proposed prom. Zainab gave her opinions reasonably freely, becoming more comfortable as we progressed, and Charlotte proved herself to be a surprisingly good listener (A voice in my head reproached me for prejudging). Dan and I performed as I had known we would, he being his easy-going, charming and delightful self, and me calculating every word in order to give the impression that I was the same.

'Ok year 11,' Miss Purcell clapped to gain attention. 'I'd like us to work in pairs now. Look at the plan we have and evaluate it honestly. Is there anything that doesn't work, or anything we want to add? We'll take ten minutes and then reconvene and draft a final version. If your back is to me just turn around and work with the person next to you.'

My mouth felt suddenly dry and my heart sped up. I was going to have a conversation with Dan, just Dan, without the buffer of the other members of the group, for ten minutes! How would I manage to do that without betraying my feelings? A flush started to creep up my neck.

'I know you saw me,' Dan almost whispered to me, 'outside the counselling room? I know you saw me.'

I stammered, 'I…I wasn't spying. I—'

'I know,' he cut in, sighing. 'I just need to know you won't tell anyone, that you won't…discuss it with anyone.'

I shook my head, 'No, no I won't.'

'I don't know why I went there. It's stupid.' Another sigh. 'You know what it's like here. People gossip. They'll talk about it and make things up. It will be like Chinese Whispers and by the time they've finished I'll be suicidal or something.'

'Are you ok?' I asked. I don't know why. Like he'd tell me anything if he wasn't. 'You don't seem like yourself.' If I could have, I'd have taken that back immediately. How did I know whether he seemed like himself or not? I didn't know him at all. I kicked myself.

He didn't seem to notice though. 'Yeah, I'm good honestly. It's nothing honestly. It's just something that I need to work out for myself.' He glanced over. His expression didn't convince me. 'Honestly,' he repeated. Obviously he felt the same. 'You won't tell anyone?'

'I won't tell anyone.'

Walking down towards the nearest reception area I wondered what to say. I wasn't family, and I was under the impression that hospital staff were unable to disclose information to anyone except close family, although I wasn't sure whether I'd read that, or seen it on the TV, never mind whether it was true or not.

I decided I'd speak to the nurse on reception as if I was a family member of Dan's. I wouldn't lie, I just wouldn't mention it. In the end, it was academic. She had no information and all she could tell me was that as soon as the doctors were able to, they'd come to the waiting room and let me know what was happening. I rushed back there, hoping I hadn't missed them.

Next, I rang the police. It hadn't occurred to me. I had been so desperate to make sure the ambulance came as quickly as possible and so concerned about Dan's condition, I hadn't even contacted the police. I had no idea how the emergency services shared their information, but at the very least I needed to check that they were aware of the situation. A woman, a police officer or an admin worker, took the details down and said they'd be in touch.

Before I could decide what to do next, Tyler and his mum arrived. She immediately pulled me into her arms, squeezing me tightly and not letting go for what must have been a full minute or more. She set down the food she'd brought in a Tupperware container and looked at me sternly. 'Eat,' she ordered. 'You'll be no use at all to him if you don't keep your strength up. I'm going down to the entrance to wait for your mum,' she told me, then stared at Tyler meaningfully before leaving. I listened to her heels clicking away down the corridor.

'She insisted,' he said, palms up apologetically.

I shrugged. What did it matter either way? Sitting down, I opened the container and began to eat. Even Tyler's mum's sausage rolls tasted like cardboard, but I knew she was right. I had to be strong for Dan.

Chapter 13

Although I did worry for Dan (what could be sufficiently embarrassing that he was so desperate to keep it a secret?) I liked the clandestine nature of what was between us. I felt like I had a connection to him that no-one else did, and I savoured it, my own secret.

The next couple of Fridays were fun too. We'd become comfortable in our group, and were genuinely enjoying the task. After we'd finalised our plan, we'd begun writing, swapping books at frequent intervals to proof read, evaluate and give constructive feedback on each-others' work. I was nervous at first. English was a subject I had never felt comfortable with, considering my own strengths lay in factual subjects and not ones which required a good imagination. However, Zainab said she thought I wrote well. She was impressed with my accuracy, my sentence structure and wide vocabulary. And you didn't have to be all that creative when writing non-fiction, she'd added, laughing, which I took on the chin. You can't have everything.

When I assessed their work, I could see what she meant. Grammatically, neither Dan or Charlotte wrote as accurately as I did, and I could see that their sentences could have been more varied in length and linked by more diverse connectives. That was just using a formula for me, and that was my forte. Give me a formula and I was happy. Their speeches however, were powerful in a way mine wasn't; I could actually hear the impassioned tone of voice, and all of a sudden, effect on audience actually meant something to me.

Miss Purcell had arranged that one member of each group would present their speech to Mr. Harding, the head-teacher, in assembly at the end of term. He had, apparently, promised to consider each idea seriously before deciding which of them he was going to support. It was unclear whether 'support' meant put into practice, and I knew that at least a couple of the other groups had gone down a vehemently reactionary line, arguing that the traditional prom was an institution and should be reinstated; I couldn't see how that would work. I admit, I was cynical. Still, there were another five groups, including ours, so we'd just have to wait and see.

We discussed it between us and unanimously voted Zainab should be the one to present her speech. Well, the rest of us were unanimous. It was brilliant. It sounded like she'd had seven spin doctors write it for her and we were in awe. There was no competition.

Unfortunately, she was absolutely adamant that she couldn't do it. No matter how much we cajoled, begged and tried to bribe her into it, she refused to agree.

Eventually, we relented. 'You could read Zainab's speech Charlotte?' I suggested (the original impression I'd had about her liking the sound of her own voice was still lodged in the back of my mind). She didn't look as ecstatic as I thought she would.

Dan spoke then, looking straight at me. 'No, you should do it. You're the most articulate one. I think you'd be able to deliver it in the way that it deserves to be delivered.' He smiled at me. 'What do you think Zainab?'

'Definitely.' Both she and Charlotte were nodding.

'Right then. That's settled. I'll go and let Miss Purcell know what's happening.' And he was gone before I could open my mouth to protest.

I didn't get up to leave when the bell went at lunch time, just said good-bye and watched them leave. Dan noticed before he reached the door and retraced his steps. 'You're not angry with me are you? I didn't mean to force you into it. It's just, I think you'd be the best one to do it.' He sat down.

'I've never done anything like that before though,' I fretted. 'I've never spoken in front of people, or done anything in front of an audience. It's ok for you. You're used to it with all the teams you're in. You probably love having an audience.' I could hear the whining tone that had crept into my voice. 'Everything must be easy for you.'

I stared out of the window at the students beginning to stream out into the sunlight. In the English classroom, it was dark and increasingly silent. Miss had switched off the light, obviously assuming that everyone would automatically follow her down the corridor. The sound of students laughing and shouting was becoming more distant, and I was painfully aware of Dan's closeness and the fact that we were alone.

Eventually, Dan spoke. 'I did love it…once. And you're right, I am used to it. You forget people are watching and you just play.

It's like second nature. But it's not easy. I mean, the sport's easy. I've been doing it all my life. It's the only thing I'm good at.

You're good at English? I suggested.

'I'm ok…but English isn't a priority in my house.' He made a sound, half way between a sigh and a laugh, and shook his head gloomily. 'When I go into the family business, English isn't really going to help me. You don't need much in the way of creative writing to build a wall.'

'Is that what you're going to do then? Go into the family business?' I tried to sound interested in order to lighten the mood.

'Yep,' He took a deep breath in, then blew out forcefully as if he was trying to compose himself, all the time gazing dolefully out of the window.

'You don't sound too happy about it,' I ventured, and when he remained silent, 'why don't you think about something else you'd enjoy more?'

'There's no point thinking about anything. It's not like I have a choice. That's what happens. It's inevitable. There's no escape. My brother left school and went to work for Dad straight away, which was fine, because he wanted to. That's all Ryan ever wanted to do, work with Dad. They're the same, you know? They like the same things; they laugh at the same things; they're like friends. I've just never been like them, that's all.' He sighed again.

'What do you mean?' I asked.

'I don't know,' another long, deep breath in and out, 'everything I do irritates him. He used to be proud of the way I was a fast runner and when I first started playing football, he bragged about how good I was all the time with his friends. Now he says it's just a waste and I need to stop thinking I'm special. He says things like, 'once you're working you'll come back down to Earth with a bump', as if I think I'm better than him and Ryan or something. I never mention winning matches or races or anything to do with school, but the more I try to be invisible the more he hates me.'

He paused for a while and I started to feel guilty for the way I'd automatically assumed his life was perfect. The sun had disappeared behind a cloud and the room seemed to be darkening as he spoke.

There didn't seem to be anything I could say to make him feel better, and I was half relieved when he said, 'Anyway, I've still got a few months left and I'm doing a course in electrical installation at college so I'm going to be out of his way for a while yet.'

'Thank God,' he added, almost inaudibly.

The sound of numerous people running and laughing interrupted his thoughts and he was shaken back to reality. 'Sorry, you don't need to hear all this. We started off talking about you and now I'm just rambling on about my crap life. Do you want me to tell Miss Purcell I'll do the pitch instead?'

'No.' I was embarrassed by his honesty and the pain he was obviously in. 'I'll do it. I was just being pathetic.'

We stood up to leave just as two year-ten boys burst into the room to retrieve a jacket that had been left behind.

'Do you want me to go through it with you?' Dan offered.

'Yeah that would be great, thanks.' Strangely, there was no tone of hero-worship or desperation. We were friends, new friends, but friends. It felt comfortable.

We walked down to the dinner hall together and when I veered off in the direction of our usual table, Dan asked, 'Do you think they'll mind if I sit with you lot today?' He nodded in the direction of Tyler, Olivia and Faye.

My stomach churned instantly and the familiar feelings of dread returned. I wanted to check whether Faye had make-up on or Olivia had her hair down but I had to answer. It would seem weird if I hesitated. What could I say anyway? 'Sorry, no, my friends look too attractive today and you might fancy them.'

'Yeah course you can,' I said, with all the enthusiasm I could muster, and we made our way over.

We were initially met by puzzled expressions, which subtly transformed as my friends realised Dan was actually coming to sit with us. Olivia and Faye started to look slightly uncomfortable, as if they'd have preferred to have the time to fluff their hair and powder their noses. Olivia moved closer to Faye to allow one of us space to sit down and almost sat on Faye's knee. 'Ow,' Faye yelled, 'you trod on my foot.'

I needn't have worried.

As usual, Tyler took centre stage and put everyone at ease. 'Hi Dan, here for some goalkeeping tips from the school's new star striker?' he quipped, and everyone laughed gratefully.

Strangely, it didn't feel as uncomfortable as I had envisaged. What I had pictured, and I had definitely pictured it numerous times, was Dan suddenly seeing either Olivia or Faye (it didn't matter which one) as if for the first time and falling hopelessly in love, staring at them, transfixed, or at least engineering it so he sat next to one of them, before spending the rest of lunchtime huddled up with them, so absorbed in each other that no-one else might have existed.

Obviously none of this happened. Probably because we weren't all living in a particularly bad romantic novel. Dan sat next to Tyler and I slid in next to Olivia, and by the time George arrived, having been kept behind in detention in science, we were all getting on like a house on fire. Having a new addition at the table instantly made all our old, worn anecdotes new again, and I couldn't remember the last time we all laughed so much at lunch.

Surreptitiously, I glanced over at the table Dan would usually sit at with a few of the football team and a couple of other lads. They didn't appear to be overly shocked, but one or two of them looked over a couple of times.

During the next two weeks, the presentation was never far from my thoughts. I veered from complete terror, imagining scenarios where I was unable to speak at all, or everyone was just bored and started talking over me, to something nearing excitement, where I pictured everyone laughing hysterically at my ad libs and applauding enthusiastically at the end.

I practised all the time. In the shower, I'd incessantly perform Zainab's speech to the sink and the toilet. I'd read it in the car, making sure every word was perfect. Poor Tyler was subjected to repeated readings where he'd be the prompter if I forgot my words, and I have to say, he was priceless (the hilarious ad libs were mostly his ideas, predictably).

Dan was as good as his word, and towards the end of the first week, he caught up with me in the corridor to check how I was feeling, and ask whether I wanted to get together and go through the presentation. We arranged to stay after English and practise at lunchtime.

In the end, Zainab and Charlotte stayed too. I think deep down I was relieved, because standing up in an almost empty room and presenting to Dan would have been an altogether more intense and nerve-wracking experience.

'Oh my God. That was amazing!' Zainab responded when I'd finished. 'It was exactly how I pictured the delivery, but better. I love the bits you've added. You're so funny.' She sounded so awe-struck I was quite embarrassed, although exhilarated by the praise at the same time.

'That was Tyler,' I admitted, blushing. 'Most of the ad libs were his idea,' I blurted out. Not all of them had been. In fact, when I actually thought about it, it was probably half and half, but it seemed trivial now to bring it up.

'Yeah, but the way you performed it was so professional,' Dan added. 'You sounded like a politician when you were doing the serious parts and a comedian in the more relaxed places. It was brilliant. You need to go into public speaking as a career.'

We all laughed at his exaggeration, but I was buzzing from their reactions and even allowed myself to start looking forward to the assembly where we'd be presenting our ideas to the head.

Chapter 14

On the morning of the assembly, I was sick with nerves. I couldn't decide whether or not I was actually ill, or it was just a symptom of my anxiety. Mum was her usual sympathetic self, dismissing my feelings as ridiculous, arguing that even people who had been performing for years suffered from stage fright and it would disappear once I was up there.

Up there. Or rather down there, in the case of my school. On the stage. In front of two hundred of my peers. In front of Amelia and the witches. I said I thought I was going to be sick, and that was when she lost patience with me, forced me into the car and screeched off the drive. 'You're doing it!' she barked, and didn't speak for the rest of the journey.

At first, it was like I was in a trance. The seven victims (of course I mean presenters) had been told to convene in the head's office, and the six of us (one was conveniently off sick; presumably with the same illness I'd been suffering from earlier) sat in near silence, all of our faces different shades of grey. I suppose this should have made me feel better, reassured me that we were all similarly terrified, but I was trapped in my own prison of fear.

Before our fellow students filed into the auditorium, we were told to sit on six chairs facing the audience, like death row inmates, waiting to be executed one by one. I couldn't imagine whose idea that had been. At best it was thoughtless, at worst, downright sadistic. Still, there was no escape once we were in place, so maybe that was the logic behind it. I know if I hadn't been in full view of the whole year, I might well have made a bid for freedom.

The audience shuffled in, chatting and relaxed. Most of them looked at us and we could see some of them discussing us, looking back and pointing, as if to say, 'that one, the one next to the end,' before turning back and finishing their story.

From this perspective, the auditorium seemed much bigger than I'd ever seen it look before.

It sloped up steeply, designed so that every single person in every single seat could see (and be seen) clearly. At no point in assembly could you hide behind the person in front of you and nod off, a fact which had always irritated me before. Now I could see it from this side, I realised how well it was built for its purpose and I hated it even more. Lots of natural light spilled in through the skylights, which were positioned directly above the stage and served as spotlights, illuminating the six of us in an excruciatingly bright circle.

I could see Dan, Zainab and Charlotte on the second row, alongside the other members of our class who had avoided the ordeal. A few rows behind, Amelia and her cronies gossiped and giggled. It had been easy to spot them as their uniform big hair stood out from the rest of the normal sized heads and their faces were more colourful, even from a distance. It never ceased to amaze me that certain people seemed immune from having to follow the school's dress code. I suppose it didn't actually stipulate a maximum size of hair, but it certainly said make-up was banned, and I remembered quite recently a girl in my class being banished to the toilets with a wet wipe to wash off what, in comparison, was no more than a subtle enhancement. Amelia's face made the Kardashians look restrained. I couldn't make out from where I was who they were targeting, but given the circumstances, I felt there was a good chance their venom was directed at me.

Amelia had her phone out and it looked as if she was videoing something. Wasn't that invasion of privacy; I was sure it was illegal. Our parents had to sign permission slips if we were pictured in the background on sports day! Why wasn't her phone confiscated? Had it been ninety-nine percent of the school, some eagle-eyed teacher would have swooped down, snatched it and hauled her off to the isolation room.

As I was scanning the sea of faces for Tyler, Olivia, Faye or George, Miss Purcell's voice rang out. 'Ok year eleven. I think most of you are aware that set one have been on a mission for the past few weeks to save our prom!' She emphasised the last three words as if she expected a cheer, but none was forthcoming. My stomach churned. 'So, without further ado I will hand you over to Mr Harding, who will introduce the candidates one by one to present each proposal on behalf of their groups. I hope you will give them all your support as they have worked fantastically hard and are excited to share their ideas with you.'

There was sporadic clapping which soon petered out, and then Mr Harding stood up to speak.

The next few minutes was a blur. I couldn't have told you what he, or the first three 'candidates' said if my life had depended on it. It made us sound like election hopefuls and I think we all cringed a little bit further down in our chairs. I was vaguely aware of polite applause after each presentation and Mr Harding's voice announcing the next pitch, but I felt quite light-headed, like I might faint away at any moment.

I was suddenly aware of an elbow in my ribs and the girl next to me hissing, 'It's you. He's just introduced you. Go on!'

Somehow I reached the podium. I became aware of the microphone first, and gradually the rest of my surroundings started to materialise from the mist that was my brain. Lifting my head, I scanned the front rows and my eyes lighted on Dan. He was smiling, and I could almost feel him willing me on, wanting me to do well. He believed in me and I wasn't going to let him down

After a shaky start (I had to stop and go back to the beginning after muddling up my introduction) I found that I knew the speech perfectly. I injected just enough pathos into the paragraphs where we explained the reasons why it would be self-indulgent to hold a traditionally extravagant and ultimately wasteful prom. Even the ad libs were embedded solidly in my memory. Tyler had gone through the timing so many times that it felt natural when I paused, for what he called 'comic effect'. When people started laughing along, my confidence soared and I genuinely enjoyed the final third of the presentation, even making eye contact with the audience and grinning when I saw Tyler waving inanely.

The crowd really did erupt, at least it felt like it to me, and I was elated. I floated back to my seat on a cloud of euphoria, made up perhaps of two parts adrenaline and one part relief.

The rest of the day was torture. Although my friends assured me there was no competition and we must have won, I myself had no real recollection of listening to (or certainly hearing) the other candidates' presentations. My friends would say that, wouldn't they? They would have said the same if I'd been awful. In my heart of hearts, I did know how well I'd done, but I couldn't let myself celebrate too early. My cynical self knew there were other factors in play that had nothing to do with whose was the best speech, although surely taking that into consideration realistically gave us a better chance. Zainab had certainly put a substantial amount of spin in there.

Fifteen minutes before the end of maths, Miss Purcell appeared at the door. She was accompanied by the other candidates and together we made our way to the head's office. My heart was beating out of my chest. I don't think I realised quite how badly I wanted to win until that moment.

Mr Harding thanked us all for our hard work and spoke for a while about how impressed he was and how difficult the decision had been. I could hardly stand still I was so full of nervous excitement. If the decision went against us I thought I would deflate like a helium balloon until there was nothing left of me.

When Mr Harding announced that he and the rest of his leadership 'panel' had chosen our idea, I was so happy, not just for me, but for the team. I couldn't stop smiling, and I'm not even sure I tried to hide my triumph, or commiserate with the others. I couldn't wait to tell everyone.

It was only that night, at home in bed that it hit me. The 'team' had served its purpose. There was no more English group, and next Friday's lesson would be just another lesson. It was over.

For the next few weeks, I barely saw Dan. We had mocks to revise for and school had made sure that our parents were left in no doubt as to how important they were. Mum insisted I come straight home after school to study; our predicted grades for college courses would be based on our results and Mum never tired of reminding me whenever she glimpsed my phone or heard me talking in my room. She'd stand at the door pointing to the non-existent watch on her wrist, then make gestures that meant 'take off your headphones and turn off the PS4.'

Sometimes Dan would be in the canteen with his friends, laughing and pranking each other. He would occasionally glance over and nod, but we often missed each other. It seemed like I'd dreamt the closeness of our conversation that day after English, and if he was still depressed about his dad and the way his future seemed to have been mapped out, he was hiding it pretty well.

I felt a little bit embarrassed for having thought that he was my friend. We'd been thrown together and he'd made the best of it, but we were from different worlds. He'd obviously gone back to his.

Chapter 15

I awoke to feel myself being gently shaken and hear Tyler speaking, almost whispering my name, as if we were in a church or a library. 'The doctor's here.' Faye was standing behind him, her eyes wide and anxious.

It took me a few seconds to remember where I was, what had happened.

We were told that Dan was in a coma. The doctor explained that his head injury was severe, blunt force trauma she called it, which meant that he had either been hit by a blunt object such as a baseball bat, or had fallen on or collided with a blunt object, maybe a hearth or a window sill. That there was increased pressure on his brain was undeniable, but whether caused by swelling or bleeding in the layers of the brain they were uncertain. He was in intensive care and being monitored closely; they had given him drugs to reduce the swelling but at this point that was all they could do.

'Will he be ok?' Faye asked, her face ashen.

'The honest answer is we don't know,' the doctor told her. He could come out of it tomorrow and return to his previous level of functioning almost straight away.' He paused. 'You have to be aware though, that there is a chance his brain will be permanently damaged, and also a chance that he will never wake up.'

Faye turned to Tyler and collapsed, sobbing, in his arms. Tyler and I looked at each other in shock. I couldn't speak.

'I'm sorry,' the doctor looked at us all in turn, then quietly left the room.

When she'd gone, Tyler's mum came into the room, followed by mine. She didn't hug me now. Maybe she felt it wasn't her place, with Mum being there, but she looked into my eyes with such sorrow and genuine concern that I felt her warmth from across the room.

I didn't look at Mum.

We sat down again with our thoughts, all thinking and dreading the unthinkable. Dan couldn't die. He was full of life.

For me, it felt like he was my life. I could not envision life going on without him. In the future that I saw for myself, there were different scenarios, and they all ended in different ways, but one thing was constant. Dan and I would be in each other's lives forever. I just always imagined forever to be a long time.

Tyler's mum left the room and I heard her heels again, clicking down the corridor, getting fainter and fainter until there was almost silence, apart from Faye's occasional sob or sniff, or the sound of one of us shifting in our chairs.

I was staring at the floor, and I couldn't help seeing Mum's shoes there, next to Faye's, both feet planted on the floor. I started to feel anger building up in me. Why was she here? What right had she to be here? She'd never met Dan and she never wanted to. That was clear. I wanted to scream at her, 'Get out! Get out!' but something deep-rooted stopped me. Maybe it was the hospital environment; You couldn't shout and scream in a hospital; it was disrespectful. But I knew I couldn't remain in the same room as her.

I pushed myself out of my chair and tried to swerve around the table, tripping over the corner in my haste. Regaining my balance, I stumbled out of the door and started to pace down the corridor. I didn't know where I was going. I only knew I had to get away from her.

After I rounded the next corner, I leant against the wall, breathing heavily. I felt sick, and for a minute I thought I was going to faint, but the feeling passed, and I leant over, hands on my knees.

Faye arrived then. She'd quietly followed me and allowed me to compose myself before showing herself. 'He'll be ok,' she soothed. 'I don't know how I know it. I just know. Come on, let's go back. They're worried about you.' She put her hand on my shoulder, and I grasped it.

'I can't sit in there with her. I can't. If it hadn't been for her, this might not have happened. If she was like Tyler's mum, I would have asked if he could stay at our house.'

Faye didn't respond, just let me continue.

'She's poison,' I spat, still staring at the floor. 'She made me feel like dirt. I hate her. I can't go back there.'

Tyler's mum's heels clicked into earshot. She was walking slowly, quite close to me now. She'd probably been there for a while but in my rage, I'd blocked out any sound except the roaring in my head.

'I'll sort it out,' she said, I assumed to Faye, because I never looked up, and she clicked away around the corner in the direction of the waiting room.

Tyler came to collect us when she'd gone. His mum had persuaded her to go back home and wait for me there. They'd left together.

In the waiting room, Tyler showed us leaflets his mum had brought, advising the family and friends of coma victims about what was possible. We could talk to Dan, let him know we were there, hold his hands, play music he liked, sing to him, and a host of other suggestions. Nobody was sure if any of it worked, but previous coma sufferers reported being able to hear and feel things, even if they were unable to respond.

It was something positive, something we could do to help Dan. I clutched the possibility hard. I could help him.

Eventually Tyler and Faye persuaded me to go home. Faye's mum picked us all up and dropped Tyler and me off on the way. I was so preoccupied it wasn't until later when I thought about it that I realised I hadn't thanked her. I couldn't remember responding at all. I hoped I hadn't been rude, or that if I had, she'd understand.

Chapter 16

Over the Christmas holidays, I made a comment to Tyler, which was meant to sound light hearted and in jest, about how Dan had dropped us. He turned and looked at me, screwing up his face. 'Are you actually joking?'

When I didn't answer, he shook his head. 'You were like a bloody recluse for weeks. You hardly had time for anybody. How can you blame Dan for that? Everybody understands that you go off the radar around exams because you're so swotty; we just overlook it, but it's you, not anybody else that's the hermit.'

He was right. After the Christmas holidays, I was pleasantly surprised. Dan increasingly seemed drawn to us; the mocks were over, and he would spend part of quite a few lunchtimes at our table. The more I saw of him, the more I liked him. He was nothing like the person I had imagined, and I was ashamed of my narrow minded initial reaction to him. To assume things about someone just because they were good looking was surely as bad as prejudice based on skin colour or religion, wasn't it?

Tyler's mum and dad were 'dating' and 'seeing how it went' and although he joked about it and pretended to be cynical, he was secretly hopeful.

Miss Purcell had asked me to join the Prom Committee, which sounded far too American and apple pie to me; I said I'd think about it, but that I had my revision and my piano exam coming up and I'd probably be busy. Of course, when I found out that Dan had accepted, I changed my mind and offered my services.

The rest of the term was, if I'm honest, one of the happiest times of my life. Part of the transformation was down to my weight. I'd been so busy over the last few months I'd hardly had time to think about food, and everything had gone so well for me that I hadn't felt the need to take refuge in my bedroom, eating junk and feeling sorry for myself. I'd lost at least fifteen pounds, and although I wasn't as slim or as toned as I'd have like to be, I didn't hate looking at myself in the mirror any more. The witches hardly bothered me now. There was an odd time when I'd hear a snigger or a hoot and turn around to see them watching me, but generally I was able to ignore them in a way I couldn't when I felt fat.

The Prom Committee turned out to be good fun too. Olivia and Faye decided they'd join too (how much of that was down to Dan's membership I couldn't say) and the four of us had a laugh. I wasn't jealous of them any more either. There was no sign of anything other than a friendly interest on Dan's part as far as I could see, and I had searched his face for those kinds of signs. Not that I was an expert, but I remembered Tyler's face when we used to go roller skating in town a couple of years before and he bumped into Ianthe, a girl from Beaconhead High with braces and badly dyed red hair. He would turn his face toward her and gaze at her when she didn't know he was looking, laugh hysterically at her rubbish jokes and always make sure he was behind her in the queue in order to charm her with his magnetic personality. He never did.

At the time I thought that Dan laughed at my jokes the most, and I was sure he paid me more attention than he did them, but then when I thought about it afterwards I knew I must have imagined it. He enjoyed my company as a friend. I couldn't hope for any more than that.

Tyler and George argued that they'd rather have math's homework every night for the rest of their lives than admit they were on the Prom Committee. In reality, it wasn't anything like they thought. Yes, Olivia and Faye were in charge of the year book, but they were putting their own slant on it, and it promised to be both hilarious and touching if they could pull it off. Dan was in charge of the entertainment, and had put together a band who would play on the night. I say put together, the drummer and guitarist were already in a band together, so Dan had just found a bass guitar player (no mean feat apparently; everybody wants to play lead) and a singer. He was busy organising rehearsals, canvassing the students for must play songs and putting together a playlist. Thankfully, so close to the GCSEs, competitive team sport had tailed off considerably or he'd never have had the time to do it.

My job was accounts and finances, which was fine with me. I worked out how many tickets we'd have to sell and at what price to be able to put on a reasonable spread, pay for lighting and sound and still make an impressive profit to donate to The Village Endowment Trust. I knew the only reason Mr Harding had agreed to our idea was the publicity we'd promised it would generate for the school. My scintillating speech had been persuasive, but the promotional opportunities had been the golden goose.

I was on the crest of my own personal wave so didn't notice that Dan was quieter than usual when he joined our table one lunchtime. 'What's up?' said Faye quietly across the table. I couldn't help but hear as I was sitting next to Dan, but I had been so engrossed in the tale I was regaling Tyler and Olivia with that I had been oblivious up till then.

'Nothing,' he replied, straightening up and smiling brightly. 'I'm just tired, that's all.'

I recognised the tone. He was anxious again and I wondered what had happened. Maybe it was something at home again linked to his relationship with his dad. I determined to ask him later if I could, or at least let him know I was there if he wanted to talk. I figured if anyone could understand how your personality could clash with one of your parents', I could.

I'd avoided confrontation for a couple of months with Mum, mainly because she was so thrilled I was looking almost 'normal sized' these days, and never being at home had helped. However, if anything, she seemed more anxious now than I'd seen her for a long time, and that manifested itself in constant criticism and nagging if I was there. She'd blame me for not doing housework she'd never asked me to do, berate me for not doing my own washing and ironing (even though I was forbidden to do it anyway as I'd obviously ruin perfectly good clothes) and generally make me feel guilty for existing. I did try to anticipate situations that might irritate her, keeping my bedroom tidy, emptying and filling the dishwasher and tidying up the kitchen as soon as we'd finished eating, but there was always something I could have done, or could have done better, to frustrate her.

If I wasn't at Tyler's house, I was at school sorting out the prom finances or revising in the new ICT suite. The computers in there weren't perfect, but it was better than facing the constant barrage of disapproval at home.

Dan wasn't in school the next day, or the next, which was a Friday, so by the time I did bump into him it was the Monday of the last week of term. He looked quite dejected, trudging through the school foyer with his head down, but I pressed on and fell into step beside him. 'If you want to talk…' I began.

'I don't. I'm grateful, but I don't,' he said blankly. Then, 'sorry,' and he sped up, away from me.

On the Friday, we still hadn't spoken and I was feeling uncomfortable. In the morning, sitting on the steps, Olivia and Faye both asked if we'd fallen out, or if it was something one of us had done to upset Dan. Tyler just said to leave him alone and stop worrying about it. Maybe he was just back in with the jock's table. Then he laughed, but I don't really think he thought it was funny.

In the canteen Dan sat with the football team again and I told myself to forget it. Maybe Tyler was right and he'd had enough of hanging with our third rate crowd. Still, it hurt to think that. I thought I'd got to know him better than that. I thought we were friends. And although I told myself that I was cured of the crush I'd had on him, I knew I wasn't. I felt sick with longing.

Dan's table was particularly rowdy that day too, singing football songs and generally being annoyingly 'laddy'. I suddenly had a flash-forward to what they'd be like in their twenties, drinking too much, eating too many takeaways and going out with bimbos. No doubt some of them would play semi-professional football and be local celebrities, until their beer bellies got too big and the bimbos moved on to the next, younger and fitter batch. Not that I was bitter, but I was definitely beginning to sulk.

Was Dan singing too? I couldn't see his face as the boy between us was standing and had his back to me, blocking my view. I hoped not.

After a couple of minutes, the singing stopped and Ewan Reid, the huge blond-haired striker, started to howl with laughter. I'd always disliked him. He went to my primary school and in year six he already looked like a man and had a six pack. I imagined he had a list of criteria you had to fulfil before he'd speak to you even then and as I was useless at sport I'd never made the cut. My dad was a big believer in physiognomy, where a person's facial features or expressions reflect their character, and to me, Ewan was a perfect example. He seemed to wear a permanent sneer, and he had a habit of looking sideways and down at people. I imagined him to be a condescending and even potentially cruel boy; he probably tortured insects as a toddler. Maybe I should have learnt a lesson about prejudging after getting it so wrong with Dan. Or maybe not. After all, he did seem to be back in the popular fold.

'That's so gay!' Ewan bellowed, creased up with laughter. 'Hand sanitiser? You're actually using hand sanitiser? Are you really that gay?'

His table joined him in the hilarity, even the boy he was mocking (another nameless football player to me). Even most of the students on other tables looked over, amused for the most part. The victim of the teasing was obviously finding it funny, enjoying being the centre of attention, so no harm was being done.

Ewan was enjoying the wider audience. 'What do you think lads? I'm not sure we want a queer on our table do we? You might have to go and sit with the other queers.' He waved his hand vaguely in the direction of a table by the door. The laughter had abated now, just a few of Ewan's followers continuing to snigger. Around the room, the atmosphere was becoming uncomfortable.

'We don't want to have to be watching our backs all the time, do we?' He kept up with his now completely incongruous guffawing, not sensing the rapidly cooling atmosphere and the way people had started to shake their heads and mutter to each other.

Suddenly, I heard the sound of a chair hitting the ground over his chortling, although I didn't see or know why until Dan marched out of the hall, stone faced.

It was so unexpected that Ewan stopped laughing abruptly and watched as he slammed through the double doors. You could hear the squeaking of their hinges as they swung back and forth for a few seconds over the silence that had descended.

Gradually, the room came back to life, rife with condemnation and speculation. Heads turned to watch Ewan as students discussed his indiscretion and bigotry. Westfield was a middle-class school which used to be a grammar school. Students considered themselves to be educated and tolerant. I think most would have said their attitudes were quite liberal on the whole, certainly in public.

We eyed each other anxiously. 'Do you think you should go and talk to him?' Faye asked me.

I wasn't sure. He'd certainly made it clear that he didn't want to talk to me. I knew he was worried about something and in his troubled state of mind Ewan's behaviour might have upset him more than usual. Also, even though I'd known him for a relatively short time, I was sure that this sort of blatant homophobia would make him feel uncomfortable. He was probably ashamed of his friend and worried that he would be considered guilty of the same bigotry by association. I felt relieved that he'd left the table. How would I have felt if he'd stayed, or even worse, stayed and laughed? That would have been awful. At least now I knew that he hadn't been acting when he'd appeared so thoughtful of others' feelings recently.

'What do you think?' Faye persisted. 'You're the closest one of us to him and nobody else even seems bothered.' She waved a dismissive hand in the direction of Ewan's table and made a disgusted face.

'I don't know,' I stammered pathetically, but their faces were all so wide eyed and expectant, willing me to do the right thing, whatever that was, that I pushed back my chair, hoisted my bag onto my shoulders and started towards the double doors Dan had stormed through. As I walked by Ewan's table, I could see one of the male math's teachers and a lunchtime cover supervisor waiting for him to collect his things; no doubt he would be taken to the head's office for a dressing down and then thrown in isolation for a day. I couldn't envisage anything major happening to him; he was the football team's star striker and came from an affluent and influential family, exactly the type of student Westfield were desperate to attract.

One or two of the other boys watched me as I passed. I wasn't sure, but I thought I could detect something other than the complete indifference I had previously experienced from them.

As the doors closed behind me, shutting in the general hubbub which had resumed, I noticed how quiet and cool it was in the corridor. No-one was around, and I realised that Dan could be anywhere. How was I going to find him when he could be anywhere in the school?

After wandering around aimlessly for a few minutes, I headed to the counselling rooms. Maybe that's where he'd go. That was the obvious place for someone who was upset to go, wasn't it? I hung around for a while, tried a couple of doors which were locked and then the last room, which was open. When I couldn't hear any sound from inside, I peeped cautiously around the door, which confirmed this room was also empty. Sighing, I pondered what to do now.

If I went back, they would think I didn't care and hadn't tried hard enough to locate Dan. If I continued to search, there was no guarantee I'd find him, and if I did, he might not be happy about it. In the back of my mind, I knew that was my main concern. Would Dan rebuff me again? Was I over-estimating our relationship in considering us to be friends?

For no real reason, I headed in the direction of the English department. Maybe thinking about Dan had subconsciously lead me to the place where we'd spent the most time together. I dawdled down the corridor, half-heartedly looking through the glass in each door for any sign of movement or a light on, until I came to Miss Purcell's classroom. Peering in I could see Dan sitting in the corner, in our group's corner of the room. He was staring straight at me as I quietly opened the door. The room was quite dark and silent and I briefly wondered whether to put the light on before deciding against it; I didn't want him to feel I was there to interrogate him.

Sitting down, I said nothing, and for a while he just continued to watch me, as if waiting for me to speak.

'You think I'm like them, don't you?' his voice cracked a little and his head was down now, eyes fixed on his hands, fingers of one hand rubbing the nails of the other.

I hesitated. Of course he was like them. He was good-looking, popular, sporty; everyone wanted to either be his friend, or be his girlfriend. Of course he was like them.

But then, did I think he was like them? Did I think he was arrogant and bigoted and homophobic and insensitive, like Ewan? Of course I didn't. I was desperate to believe that he was nothing like them. But what did I know? I knew so little of him that I couldn't be sure—

'Oh my God, you do, don't you!'

I'd hesitated too long. Dan stood up, throwing his chair backwards. Pain was written on his face, an expression of pure desolation. He blundered into the table before pushing it out of his way and lurching towards the door.

Standing up I grabbed his arm, hoping he wouldn't simply throw me off in anger. 'No!' I shouted frantically. 'No, I don't. I don't. Sit down. Just sit down and talk to me. Come on.'

He stopped, breathing deeply, taking huge gulps of air before blowing them out forcefully. Then he covered his face with his hands, pressing the ends of his fingers into his forehead.

'Come on,' I repeated gently, 'just sit down.'

Eventually, he sat down on the nearest chair, head still in his hands and shoulders hunched over as if protecting himself from attack.

'I don't think you're anything like them Dan. Honestly, I don't. I think you're a kind, thoughtful person who'd never intentionally hurt or offend anyone, no matter who they are. Just because Ewan's your friend doesn't mean you think like him.'

'It's not just Ewan,' Dan was relatively calm now, his face devoid of emotion and his eyes still locked on his hands. He looked defeated, as if he had given up on something, or lost something precious. 'I'm not saying they're all *that* bad, but the ones who aren't just let it happen and laugh along. I don't know whether they find it genuinely funny or they just do it to fit in, but I know one thing, I don't fit in with them any-more, and I don't want to. I hate it. The weird thing is, they have no idea.' He laughed bitterly. 'They've no idea how much I don't fit in with them.' The bitter laugh again. 'They're all I know. They've been my friends since,' he hesitated, 'oh, I don't know, since forever. They're all I know, but now it's like I don't know them. I don't fit in with them, but I don't fit in with anyone else either.'

'You fit in with us.' How could he think he would have a problem making friends? Everyone liked him. No-one could fail to like him. 'No-one will blame you for what Ewan said. When you left, it sent a message to everyone that you don't feel that way. People'll get to know you and you'll show them what you're really like. Even if some people have prejudged you, you can prove them wrong.'

The irony of what I was saying was not lost on me. Most people had probably prejudged him, just like I had before getting to know him, and maybe it was going to be a bit harder than I was making out to convince some of them. Still, at this moment, he didn't need to know that.

The bell rang. Dan was nodding, still rubbing his nails and looking at his hands, but his expression had changed and he looked less grey than he had a few minutes before.

In the distance, the sound of chatting and laughing reached us. The students had been ushered out of the hall and in from the yard and were making their way to lessons. 'Come on,' I said, 'we'll have to go.'

The noise was closer now, maybe on the English corridor. I slipped out. 'See you later,' I looked over my shoulder and smiled.

'Thanks,' Dan said quietly, before we were engulfed by the wave of year sevens careering along the corridor.

Chapter 17

Over the next few days, I was reminded of the reasons why I had chosen the friends I had. Ok, some of it had been luck, but other people had come and gone, while the five of us had stuck together. We could rely on each other, and I knew that each one of us would be there for Dan now, to help him through whatever trauma he was going through. Somehow, I knew that the unravelling of childhood bonds wasn't the only problem he had to deal with. Obviously, he wasn't ready to talk yet, but once he came to trust us more, perhaps he would, although I already had a feeling the issue was at home, and concerned his dad's attitude towards him. I wondered what had happened, or changed, to make him so hostile.

Tyler, Olivia, Faye and George welcomed Dan into the fold whole-heartedly, waving him over to our steps in the morning and making sure he knew there was a space at our table in the canteen.

There was gossip, while other students speculated. Why had Dan decamped to our table in particular? Had he completely severed all ties with Ewan and the football team? There were surreptitious glances directed at us from many different groups of students but generally the interest subsided once it was clear there was going to be no confrontation between the two groups.

Ewan blamed Dan for the fact he'd been sanctioned for his behaviour. They clashed before a PE lesson a couple of days later and Ewan behaved like the arrogant brat I'd always thought he was, blaming Dan for his punishment and not his own loud, insensitive remarks. Apparently, Dan's chair crashing to the floor and his thumping out through the double doors was what alerted the staff to the situation. He'd only been joking and everyone was laughing. He didn't know what Dan's problem was. Dan had changed. He used to be a laugh but he was just weird now. Ewan had no time for him.

The confrontation with Ewan in the changing rooms was, if anything, quite convenient. It meant Dan didn't have to explain his defection; Ewan actually gave him an easy way out. The reactions of the other members of the team, previously Dan's best friends, were diverse. Some sided with Ewan and blanked him completely (Dan said he was aware of the odd sneer and some sniggering behind his back), others, apart from perfunctory nods, avoided contact. There were those who reached out to him and tried to act as if things were normal, but never when Ewan was there.

My heart went out to him. Around school, he was self-conscious, hyper-aware of the shift in his social status, and in the changing rooms, he was almost shunned. We'd always do our best to cheer him up though, and gradually, he started to smile again.

Another concern he had, he told me confidentially, was the band. He didn't want anyone to worry, but there was something missing there. He couldn't quite pinpoint what it was, and

they sounded ok, he said, but not great, not even good. The singer was always missing rehearsals and forgetting her words, the others were frustrated and they just weren't gelling. With only two months to go, I could imagine the anxiety that would create.

I texted Tyler about it that night. The tickets were selling fast, and it looked like we'd probably surpass our targets by a substantial amount. For me, the pressure was minimal. Once I had the money in, I could relax. Dan, however, would not be able to relax until after the night and would also feel responsible afterwards if the band wasn't a success.

'What about Faye?' Tyler suggested the next day. 'She's an amazing singer. Do you remember her in the choir at primary school? Remember when she did that solo at the leavers' assembly?'

I did, and he was right, she had a fantastic voice, deep and resonant when she sung the low notes, but with a range that meant she was also able to hit the high notes perfectly. She'd been having singing lessons since she was about eight, and used to compete in festivals, very successfully Olivia said.

'I don't think she'd do it. She hasn't sung in public for ages,' I replied. Faye had been quiet and unassuming at primary school, but because of the festivals, she was used to performing in front of an audience so had been expected to sing at school. I don't think, back then, she felt she had a choice. Mrs. Masterson, who'd run the choir and organised all the school plays and concerts, would liaise with Faye's mum, who would arrange for Faye to learn and practise anything she was required to sing, and she would sing it. It wasn't an option for her back then.

Now it was, I knew she'd be horrified at the thought of performing in front of the whole school. In year seven, she'd been tall, but no taller than the other tall girls. Then in year eight she grown taller than all of them and the boys in our year. It had made her profoundly self-conscious and she'd begun to stand and walk with a severe stoop. We'd all tried to convince her that her height was an asset but to no avail. Talking about her height just upset her; none of us wanted that, so we hadn't mentioned it for years now, even though, as we'd moved up school other girls had grown as tall as her, and quite a few boys substantially taller. I estimated she was about five feet eleven inches (we could never have asked) which I didn't think was abnormally tall, but her stoop remained. It seemed like part of her now, which was a shame because it made her look permanently submissive, even frightened.

It was in year eight that she'd refused to sing in any more festivals, although I knew she still took lessons, and occasionally I'd hear her singing when she thought no-one else could hear, or she forgot herself.

Tyler was sitting on his bed, surrounded by a mess of clothes. I couldn't tell whether they were dirty or clean, and I'm not sure he knew either. My mum would have had a coronary if she'd washed my clothes only to find them mixed up with worn socks but as far as I knew, Tyler's mum was cool about it. I'd seen him sniffing socks until he found clean ones and still not putting the old ones in the wash.

'I could ask her?' he said. 'I think she might, if I ask her really nicely.' He grinned at me.

I wasn't sure why Tyler thought that Faye would sing 'if he asked her' rather than me, but it was worth a try.

As I predicted, she was indeed 'horrified' and refused to even consider it the next morning when he ventured the question. Undeterred, he told me, 'Never fear. All is not lost.' And he tapped his nose with his forefinger to show he had a cunning plan.

At lunchtime, Olivia and Dan were a few minutes late and came through the doors together, laughing hysterically. Olivia in particular was creased over, holding her stomach and hardly able to breathe. There was something about their shared mirth which I found uncomfortable; they looked far too familiar with each other all of a sudden. The feeling of anxiety I thought I'd all but conquered was back.

When she eventually regained the power of speech she still couldn't stop breaking out into giggles intermittently, which was annoying. Apparently, a wasp had got stuck in Jilly's hair and she had gone absolutely wild, running around screaming. Then Mr Wright had told her to stand still and tried to get it out, and when it did fly out it hit him in the face and he jumped back and got his foot stuck in the bin.

With hindsight, it was a funny story, and the others were soon hooting along with them. I tried to laugh but I was too aware of the closeness of their bodies to focus on what Olivia was saying properly. She kept bumping her arm against his every time she remembered something different before giggling, 'His face though,' or 'What did she sound like?'

I noticed Olivia was wearing make-up, not a huge amount but enough to make her green eyes look feline and exotic. When had that started and why hadn't I seen it before? Did she usually wear her hair down like that? I always pictured her with a pony tail as until recently she'd played so much sport after school. Now though, it was waving over her shoulders, black and glossy and bouncy. Had she styled her hair for school? It was naturally curly but it looked different somehow. When had she started spending so much time on her appearance? Was it when Dan began to sit at our table?

I'd never sensed an attraction between them before, but how could he fail to be captivated by her? She was stunning. I marvelled again at the fact that I'd never noticed how attractive my best friends were.

I became aware that Olivia was talking to me. She waved both hands in front of my face and shouted, 'I said tickets! How are the sales going?' Her face was glowing after all the laughing and she looked so beautiful it hurt my eyes to look at her.

'Yeah good,' I tried to smile and act normally, even though I felt sick and my heart was racing. 'even better than we expected.'

Luckily, Dan interjected at this point. 'Oh no,' he groaned. 'Not the tickets,' he added hastily, 'it's the band. It's going to be a complete disaster if something doesn't go my way soon. Rosie's more or less told the others she's not doing it. She's angry at them for being angry at her for not turning up for rehearsal. Theo can't stand her and he says she's rubbish anyway and keeps going wrong with her timing and putting them off. I don't know anything about that but I do know she's a diva. She says she doesn't need to practise and they're just jealous because she's too good for them.'

'How good is she?' Tyler asked.

'Honestly? She's…she's ok. She's not as good as she thinks she is, but she's ok, and she's all we've got…that's if we've still got her. She's been dangling her resignation over my head for about two weeks now.'

'How good is she Faye?' Tyler raised his eyebrows while he waited for Faye's response. 'Come on, I remember when she used to do all those festivals with you and you always beat her. She told all her friends you cheated and wouldn't speak to you.'

'She's ok,' Faye replied eventually, tucking a strand of her long, straight, blonde hair behind her ear. 'But will you stop it? I said no and I meant it. I don't sing in public anymore because I don't enjoy it. You just never give up do you?'

She wasn't angry, more amused. She was blushing, but more with pleasure than with embarrassment. I wondered what Tyler had said to her.

The next morning was a Wednesday, and the sky was dark as if a storm was brewing. When Dan walked across the yard his face looked like the thunder we were expecting. 'She quit!' he snapped. 'I started to explain why Theo was frustrated and she just screamed at me that she was too good for them, she was too good for a pathetic school prom and why couldn't I see it? I thought she was going to say 'Do you know who I am?''

I'm not sure Tyler and George really understood the implications of her decision. Their initial reaction was to laugh, which I understood, given the ridiculousness of her arrogance, but the rest of us were dismayed. There was a week to go before Easter, which was late, and then we were on the home straight. It was four weeks until the GCSEs started, two weeks after that was half term and three weeks after half term was the prom. It may have sounded like a long time, but in reality, given the time we'd all have to spend revising, it left little for finding a singer, the singer learning the songs, the singer rehearsing the songs with the band. It was a nightmare for Dan.

Distant thunder rolled and the sky became even more gloomy. 'Hey, come on,' Olivia spoke first. 'We'll think of something.' She linked up with Dan, and like an afterthought, with me too. 'Come on Faye,' she called over her shoulder. 'The four musketeers,' she giggled. 'Sorry you two. You can't be in our gang unless you're on the Prom Committee, or unless you can sing.'

Tyler and George launched into a shocking rendition of 'Let Me Entertain You' by Robbie Williams.

That night I received a message from Dan. 'We're going to hold auditions! What do you think?'

'Great idea,' I messaged back with a smiley face to reflect the opposite of my present feelings. I wondered who 'we' were. I ate a second helping of pasta to distract myself.

The next morning Dan confirmed that 'we' were indeed Olivia and himself. Apparently, it was Olivia's idea and they'd gone through it the night before, obviously messaging back and forth, planning when and where the auditions would be. Olivia had already designed posters and put information on her Instagram and Snapchat accounts. Could we all do the same then as many students as possible would be made aware of the opportunity?

I had to admit the posters Olivia brought were impressive, eye catching in a cool way and with all the information required concisely included. She had added a few incentives to persuade potential auditionees that not only would they become local celebrities, but that the experience may also be to their advantage in other ways; they could use it to pad out their CVs, or they may be spotted by talent scouts eager to find a singer for the next international super-group. There was a slightly tongue in cheek tone, but would-be lead singers certainly might be influenced by the possibility of fame.

The auditions were scheduled for the next day. There was no time to waste, as if the band were missing a lead singer by the time we broke up for Easter, it would be almost impossible to find someone who could manage to learn and rehearse the songs in seven weeks or so whilst revising for their GCSEs. George had already mentioned that his mum had told him categorically that he would not be allowed to do it at such a crucial time. The fact that he was tone deaf made me think she may have been joking, but many parents of genuine hopefuls might seriously feel that way.

We all helped stick up the posters around school and all that was left to do was wait. Dan asked if I wanted to take part in the audition process, and while I was tempted to retort petulantly, 'I think you and Olivia could probably manage it between you,' I was so interested to see the response and hear the potential singers that

I bit my tongue, smiled and said I was looking forward to it. Faye was similarly eager to take part in the judging procedure and when Tyler arrived, grinning mischievously, none of us had the heart to disappoint him.

On Friday lunch-time we set up in one of the music rooms. Permission had been granted by the head for the four of us to miss period four if the process overran and we would provide any contestants who themselves were made late for lesson with a slip to explain where they had been.

The music room we'd been allocated was relatively large, with desks in rows and a large area at the front where students would perform. There were various guitars on stands scattered around, a piano, two keyboards propped against the wall gathering dust and a set of drums. Woodwind instruments like flutes and clarinets were stacked on shelves alongside violins and other smaller instruments and a couple of cellos and a lone double base were pushed back into a corner. Although we were a modern school, the original building having been knocked down ten years before, the orchestral instruments themselves were largely old, their cases well used and battered, and there was a musty, airless smell in the room.

For ten minutes we waited, and no-one came. The tension in the room rose perceptibly; if no replacement for Rosie was found, then the whole prom was in jeopardy. You couldn't have a 'festival' prom without live music. Olivia tried to stay positive, assuring us that there would soon be an influx of wannabes. They would be queueing out into the yard according to her. I supposed she had more invested in the process than Faye or I. It was her idea after all, a fact that I became more grateful for as the clock ticked on.

Each time noises could be heard in the distance, we willed them to be potential auditionees on their way to sing, and finally, eleven minutes after the start time, there was a knock on the door.

Dan shouted, 'come in!' and we were in business. Unfortunately, both the first two entrants were disappointing. They had not read the poster correctly, had not provided backing tracks or prepared anything particular to sing. One did an acapella version of an Ariana Grande song (I wasn't sure which one as it was unintelligible) and the other only knew two lines of 'Let It Go' from Frozen, which she repeated until we did, gratefully, let her go.

After they left, we had to laugh, or I think we'd have cried. Five minutes later, a boy I'd seen around school but didn't know arrived. He was painfully thin and pale with wispy growth on his upper lip, and looked like he was terrified. On the plus side, he'd downloaded a backing track to his phone and could sing in tune, although barely audibly. Dan told him we'd be in touch.

We saw three more girls and a boy, all of whom, for various reasons, were completely unsuitable, and were beginning to think wispy moustache (with an industrial sized microphone) may be our man, when Amelia and Jilly walked in.

My first reaction was surprise. For me anyway, this was completely unexpected. As far as I knew, the witches had never taken part in any extra-curricular activities, be they sport, music or subject related. I was also amazed that they would want to put themselves in a position where they were being judged by us. Then I realised, Dan was completely on or even above their level socially (or had been until recently), and Olivia and Faye were popular in their own way too. It was only their association with me that affected their status in my mind.

I wondered who was going to sing and who was there for moral support. Maybe they were both going to sing, or they were going to sing together. At the very least, I was intrigued.

By the time I had picked up my lower jaw from the floor, Dan had taken Amelia's details (Jilly was there for the moral support) and she was ready to sing. She had obviously taken extra special care with her appearance that morning, her highlighted hair cascading down around her shoulders and make-up immaculate, accentuating her large eyes and full lips. Her uniform always looked like something off the catwalk, fitting and flaring in exactly the right places of her tanned and toned body. There was no way her skirts and shirts came from the supermarket. Even so, there was something plastic and fake about her which was unattractive, at least to me.

The song she had chosen, 'Shout Out To My Ex' by Little Mix, seemed like a reasonable choice to me, and I wondered if she really could sing. How would I feel if she was amazing? All I knew was I hoped she wasn't.

When she started to sing, she certainly didn't seem nervous. She was definitely loud enough, but after a while we started to realise that this was not necessarily a good thing. Her voice was generally in tune within a limited range, but outside of it she rarely hit the notes. In particular, on the high notes, she'd simply push her voice as far as it would go towards the note she was aiming for, ending up belting out a completely flat version of the line she was targeting. In addition, her voice had an unpleasantly harsh tone, which was starting to grate by the end of the song, never mind a whole set.

It was a shame really, because she certainly acted the part, closing her eyes when reaching for the high notes, pointing at us (the panel) as if we were the 'ex' and using her hands to reinforce the fact that we'd 'made her who she was'.

Afterwards, she made a gesture with her hands to suggest that she had 'smashed it' and stared straight at Dan, challenging him to disagree. Jilly was clapping and whooping in the corner, and I couldn't help but think she was tone deaf too to allow her friend to embarrass herself like that.

There was an uncomfortable silence before Dan spoke. I wondered if I'd heard Amelia's voice differently and subconsciously distorted it because I disliked her so much. Maybe to the others she sounded like Beyonce? She and Jilly obviously thought so. There were another couple of boys waiting to audition outside and I heard muffled giggling, as if they were struggling not to laugh out loud. Maybe it wasn't just me then.

Dan took a breath. 'Thanks Amelia, you really put everything into that.' He raised his eyebrows knowingly at her. We have a couple of others to see yet, so we'll let you know when we've made a decision.'

'I'll look forward to it,' she pouted playfully, hands on hips and body thrown forward. 'Speak soon.' And she sashayed out, followed by Jilly, whose sashaying needed a little more practice.

We looked at each other, speechless, before Tyler said, 'Well she certainly made that song her own!'

It broke the tension and we laughed. When we'd collected ourselves, Olivia stood up and walked towards the door. 'Come on, let's see whether either of these two are the next Ed Sheeran?'

They weren't, and even Amelia's performance failed to conceal the fact that we'd run out of options. Ten auditions and not one genuine potential lead singer for the band. Dan's head was in his hands. 'I'm so sorry. I know how much work everyone has put into this and I've messed up. I've let everyone down. I'd sing myself but I'm worse than Amelia. I'll have to go to Miss Purcell and explain that the band won't have a singer. Do you think people will be ok with it? We can still dance, can't we?'

Olivia and I made unconvincing noises as we glanced at each other over his head.

Faye stood up, walked to the piano and started to flick through the music strewn across the lid. 'Can you play 'Someone Like You' by Adele?' she asked, staring at me.

'If the sheet music's there, I can.'

'Come on then!' she seemed to have made a decision and was wanting to get it over with as soon as possible.

Suddenly, she didn't look like Faye. As she prepared to sing, she pushed her shoulders back and stood up to her full height, gathering up her heavy blonde hair in both hands and putting it over her shoulders, out of her way. She lifted her chin and took some deep breaths as I started to play.

I remembered Faye being a good singer at primary school, but then the rest of us were useless, and the only other singers we'd seen were on 'X Factor'. This though, was something else. Her voice was unbelievable, strong and rich but never shouted, perfectly pitched whether at the top or the bottom of her range, and with a unique pure tone that genuinely almost brought tears to my eyes. Olivia was wiping her eyes as the song ended.

'Wow.' Dan was looking at Faye as if he'd never really seen her before, and I knew how he felt. How had she kept such a huge talent hidden for so long? Strangely, she hadn't seemed self-conscious at all while she was singing, although as soon as the music ended, she became herself again, her shoulders drooped and she stared at the floor. 'That was amazing Faye. You can't keep that to yourself any more. You need to share it with people. Do you even know how good you are?'

Faye looked up. Her blue eyes were shining and her cheeks flushed. I hoped the adrenaline rush would convince her to agree.

'Ok,' she said, quietly smiling, and we all clapped, laughing, with relief? exhilaration? I don't think we knew.

Olivia jumped up and ran to hug Faye, still laughing. 'It's going to be awesome!' she squealed with excitement. Then she ran and hugged me, still jumping up and down. 'It's going to be so awesome!' she repeated, and ran to hug Dan, who hugged her back. Did they hug for longer? I thought so. She eventually

calmed down and let him go, and Dan caught my eye. He smiled
and nodded at me, and I nodded back.

Chapter 18

During the first few days, I kept expecting Dan to wake up. I'd rush to see every message and answer every phone call I received, thinking it could be someone letting me know that he was ok.

After a week, I realised the situation wasn't that simple. I remembered the doctor's words, 'a chance he'll never wake up.'

We drew up a rota for visiting Dan. At first, I didn't want to leave him at all, but Tyler reasoned with me, using the whole of his repertoire of persuasive techniques, from guilt tripping to threats. 'When he wakes up, what is he going to think if you've thrown away your education because of him? What are you going to talk to him about if all you do is sit by his bed? You'll bore him into a deeper coma. You need to let us share this with you. He needs all sorts of different stimulation. If you won't let us try, we might miss saying or doing something that might have reached him.'

In the end, I allowed myself to be persuaded, and together with the doctors, we decided on a two-hour evening slot each weekday (no more than two people at once) and an afternoon and evening slot at weekends.

We would take in music; we played anything and everything we thought may provoke some response, trigger a memory which may haul him back to life. Faye would sing to him and describe what was happening in various TV programmes they both liked. Tyler performed comedy routines on his nights, adding new material each time, but honing the jokes and anecdotes he'd told before as well; he would ask Dan his opinion, and sometimes it looked like they were actually having a conversation, with Tyler imagining Dan's replies.

I would read books to him. I wasn't funny or talented, but Miss Purcell, for want of another way to praise me, had always gushed about my reading aloud.

I would sometimes stop reading and just watch his face, and my heart would swell with…what? Admiration, affection…love? All I knew was that this man was the kindest, most beautiful soul I thought I'd ever met. I remembered the long, glossy, black wedge of hair which constantly flopped over his right eye and how he'd sweep it back habitually. His hair was growing back now, but unevenly, in some places thicker and seemingly longer, in others, hardly at all. I'd lean over and stroke it back and to the side. I wondered if he could he feel my touch, hear me speaking or sense my presence? I hoped he could.

Chapter 19

The band were as blown away with Faye as we were, and rehearsals seemed to be fun rather than a chore. There was at least one of us at each rehearsal the first week to give her moral support, but as time went on, she didn't seem to need it. I'd heard of actors who were painfully shy in real life, but when in character they felt protected. This was the way Faye appeared on stage. It wasn't just her voice, but her whole aura. Tyler in particular loved to watch her, pretending to be her manager, requesting more and more extravagant additions to her 'rider' and threatening to pull her out of the show if his demands were not met. He set up a group where he would post pictures of Faye, usually with her arm across her face, hiding from the camera, and asked for ridiculous ransom amounts, accompanied by pictures of his gangster face. The band thought he was hilarious.

Over Easter, we'd agreed that we needed to revise. Apart from the band's rehearsals, arrangements were firmly in place. Dan had already sorted out the stage, the lighting and the sound before Rosie left the band. Pretty much all my work was done; tickets sold, outgoings and profits estimated; the remainder of my role would be calculating actual profits and liaising with the charity in order to transfer the money and collect receipts. The year book was complete apart from the prom photos, which would be added later, so Olivia was finished until after the exams too. Apart from Faye, our jobs were done.

I was looking forward to Easter until the last Friday of term. Dan, by his own admission, had wimped out of letting Amelia know that her services were not needed. I had to admit, a week was a long time, and I secretly thought he was being unfair. Obviously she thought that too.

In the morning as we sat chatting on the steps, Amelia approached us with Jilly and another couple of members of the coven. It was like an ambush.

'So you decided to go with the giraffe then?' She sneered at Faye. 'Figures. You could never handle a real woman could you? Or is it her?' she spat, gesturing her head towards Olivia. 'You do know I dumped him, don't you? You didn't, did you?' she was directing the venom at Olivia now, obviously deciding that she was the new love interest. 'I suppose he's trying to keep it quiet. I dumped him because he was pathetic. Fumbling around like some little primary school kid. It was embarrassing. He was too scared to even kiss me.' She turned back to Dan. I was shocked at the way such a pretty face could twist into the grotesque mask of bitterness it was now. A small crowd had gathered, straining their ears to hear while trying to appear indifferent. 'I can't believe you'd get your revenge like this Dan. They must all wonder why you didn't pick me for the band.' She flung her arm out dismissively in our direction. 'Well, now they know. And I hope you're proud of yourself. You know I could have put that band, and the prom on the map. My dad would have made sure of it. Well I hope it bombs. And don't even think about even looking in my direction again. There's no way in the world I'd give you the time of day after this.'

She spun around, swishing her hair, and swept towards her bench, followed by her friends, who imitated her sneer before their spins. The effect was so dramatic that it almost looked like it had been choreographed, which perhaps it had been.

The crowd quickly dispersed, ambling away with their backs to where the action had been, not wanting to be caught watching.

'What an absolute bitch!' Olivia exclaimed, saying out loud what the rest of us were thinking.

George turned and stared at Dan, his eyes wide and mouth open. 'Did you really go out with her?' blurting out what everybody wanted to ask but didn't know how to.

The bell went and we stood up to head inside. Dan hadn't spoken and his head was down; I could see Olivia staring at George, who had his hands out, palms up, like he hadn't a clue what he'd done wrong. There were daggers in her eyes and if they were real he'd have been dead. She was protecting Dan, and to me it was a sign of how much she'd come to care about him and how close they'd become. They'd fallen for each other, just as I'd feared months ago when I first met him, although at the time it seemed so unlikely they'd ever actually meet that I'd dismissed the idea as my own paranoid imaginings. Ironically, it was me who had brought them together, and finally put to rest the ridiculous fantasy I'd entertained where we were living in a parallel universe and there was a chance we could be together.

I swallowed down the ache of despair in my throat and shook my head physically. I had to shake myself free of my feelings for Dan and be happy for them. I'd always known it was an impossible dream and that I was living in a fantasy world, but at times I had seen glimpses of hope. Sometimes I had caught him looking at me, and we would smile at each other, a secret smile filled with possibility, or that was what I'd let myself believe when I'd replayed them in my mind…in my imagination. That's obviously what it was, my overactive and treacherous imagination, which had deceived me into believing there could be something between us. I blushed with humiliation, my only consolation being, at least he was unaware of my stupidity.

When Faye, George and I arrived at our table in the canteen, Olivia and Dan were already there, heads bent towards each other, deep in conversation. They pulled apart as soon as we sat down; did they jump a little, as if startled or caught out? I had to stop thinking this way. If they were 'together' or on the verge of it, if they did have feelings for one another, they'd tell us, wouldn't they? It was irrelevant anyway, I told myself. It wouldn't affect my relationship with Dan one way or the other.

Dan waited until Tyler arrived to put us out of our misery, although it was clear that he had already confided in Olivia. He and Amelia had never been 'boyfriend and girlfriend'. Dan's dad had built an extension at her house and was desperate to make a good impression, hoping it would lead to other jobs in the area (the houses were huge according to Dan and the bigger the house the more his dad made). Dan had been doing some labouring and she'd hung around more and more as the time went on. When Amelia had asked him go to a party with her, his dad had forced him to go. After that, they'd gone to the cinema and bowling a few times but it was always arranged between Amelia, her parents and his dad. He hadn't really felt he had a choice in the matter, and anyway, there wasn't anything in it. Then she'd started messaging him; sending pictures of herself in sexy poses and wording them like they were in a relationship. For a while he'd just sent back noncommittal replies, keeping it firmly 'in the friend zone' and hoping she'd get the message. But then they'd gone to another party. He couldn't remember why he'd agreed to go and he'd have refused if he'd known what was going to happen. She insisted on holding his hand and showing him around, introducing him as her boyfriend, and he was so uncomfortable. And then she'd kissed him on the stairs, and he was horrified. He didn't think of her like that at all and it was just so awkward. She was certainly right about that.

He said he tried to explain, to let her down gently, but she became nasty and abusive, like she'd been that morning, and ended up calling him all the names under the sun and 'finishing with him'.

'I can't believe you did that,' George marvelled. 'I mean, she's a cow, but she's fit. I don't think I'd throw her back if she threw herself at me like that.' He laughed, his spiky head turned to Tyler for confirmation. Tyler recognised the inappropriateness of the comment but just shook his head and smiled.

'God, you're such an idiot,' he chided, good naturedly.

'She's not my type,' Dan continued. 'At all,' he added. 'And even if she was, she's not the kind of person I want to be with at all.' For a split second, he glanced at me, and my heart leapt. 'She's self-obsessed, arrogant and mean. I feel sorry for the person who ends up with her. She'll make their lives a misery.'

To say I over-thought that momentary glance would be an understatement. All afternoon I agonised, convincing myself to let go completely, then allowing a snapshot of that glance to flood my mind. By the time the bell went after period five I was as exhausted as I was confused.

However, my confusion was not to last long. As I walked across the yard I saw Olivia and Dan waiting together by the gate. Reeling, I watched as a large, white BMW pulled up and they both picked up their bags and climbed in. I saw Olivia's mum turn around to laugh at something Dan had said as it pulled away.

Chapter 20

Easter was unbearable. I tried to submerge myself in my studies, avoiding social interaction, in fact, avoiding civilisation completely. My phone was the most difficult. Obviously, as with all addictions, after a couple of days' withdrawal I was going insane, unable to sit still and concentrate on anything other than my phone, not so silently beckoning me from its hiding place under my pillow.

I'd endured hours of constant buzzing before I finally turned my phone off vibrate. I convinced myself it was because I couldn't be bothered to get up, but I think the buzzing kept me company in a strange way, even though I had forbidden myself to read or respond to any messages. Even a buzz from under my pillow was better than absolute silence. At least someone knew I was alive.

A visit to Nando's had been arranged for the Thursday before Good Friday, so I knew that some of the messages would be everyone making arrangements for that. I did consider going, but I simply couldn't face it. Pretty soon, I'd have to pick myself up and give myself a good talking to, but for now, I preferred to wallow.

I did revise. I wasn't stupid and I was not going to jeopardise my future. If nothing else, I told myself, I was clever enough to succeed in my exams, and once I'd forced Dan out of my head, I could use all the left-over space to make sure I beat everyone. Never massively competitive before, I decided that I'd get over Dan by challenging myself to come top in everything, apart from English; I could never write like Zainab. I might not achieve it, but it was a tangible goal I could switch my focus to.

The other focus which seemed to have crept under the radar as I was moping, was food. Mum was out at work for most of the day, so I set about eating everything in the house. Bread was a favourite. There were lots of slices in the bag and I didn't count. There were still quite a few left however many I ate so I could tell myself I'd just had a couple; I didn't count the butter. It was the same with cheese. You couldn't really tell how much had gone as long as the remaining chunk was the same shape; I'd just had a couple of small wedges.

I wore track suit bottoms and sweatshirts every day, and rarely ventured out apart from to the shop for packets of crisps or chocolate bars. Neither did I look in the mirror. What was the point? I wasn't going anywhere.

Half way through the first week, my phone beat me. Justifying my decision by telling myself I needed a short break from studying, I thought I'd just have a quick look. Predictably though, once I'd had that one glimpse, I was well and truly hooked again.

Checking my messages, there were no real surprises. Multiple unopened posts from our group, a couple of private messages each from Tyler, Faye and Olivia, a few from other people, mostly on group chats I rarely contributed to now, and one from Dan. I opened the rest first, the usual pointless messages people send each other to avoid revising: How's the revision going? Not too well or I wouldn't be wasting my time on here!; What's that supply teacher called with the purple hair?; Have you heard about any prom after parties yet? There were lots of posts on our group chat about Nando's on Thursday, and the few private ones were asking me why I hadn't joined the chat and was I coming or not? Tyler's were brief. 'Has your mum got you strapped to a chair in a straightjacket in front of GCSE Pod?' 'Have you died?'

Finally, I opened Dan's message. It couldn't have been more unrevealing if he'd tried to make it as vague as he could; maybe he did: 'Are you going on Thursday? Haven't been to Nando's for ages.'

I didn't reply to any of them.

I opened the pictures one by one; as usual, everyone was having fun with filters, stickers and funny voice change videos. How happy they all seemed, and how perfect they all looked. It amazed me how even Snapchat, with its focus on silly faces and voices, still felt that it had to erase any blemishes from snappers' faces so that they appeared almost cartoon-like in their flawlessness. On a roll now, I checked Instagram. Predictably, it was full of ab shots and pouts. Why did people feel they had to advertise how good looking they were over and over again?

There had been a time, probably when I was first allowed on social media, when I spent most of my time requesting friends on Facebook (before I realised that nobody cool used Facebook) adding friends on Snapchat, and following people on Instagram. The more friends you had, the more popular you felt, so everyone at school added everyone else, whether they'd ever spoken or not, and everyone ended up with thousands of friends. So it didn't really mean anything, but if you didn't have thousands of friends, what did that mean? Did it mean you were unpopular, that no-one wanted to be friends with you?

I was 'friends' with most of the football team, although none of them had ever given me the time of day and I was pretty much invisible as far as they were concerned. I also followed them on Instagram. I think at the time I thought it was a two-way thing, that me following them would be like adding a friend, and they'd automatically be following me too; it took me a while to realise that you only amassed Instagram followers if you were popular, if people were interested in the pictures you posted and the things you had to say. If you were a relative nobody, and I soon realised I was, no-one was interested, and you were left with a measly number of followers who were basically made up of your mum and your best friends.

The football team boys I followed wouldn't know it. I don't know why I even looked at their pictures, theirs and the witches'. It was as if I had a masochistic compulsion to make myself feel worthless. Their lives seemed so exciting and desirable.

When I saw the boys at school, most of them looked fairly normal, if in a more cool and athletic way than some. On Instagram they were like Greek gods, with perfect tans and gym honed bodies. There was never an ordinary or unflattering photo, and I wondered if they really did look like that under their uniforms, or whether they'd photo-shopped themselves. Celebrities photo-shopped themselves, really badly in some cases, so why not them; I looked for wonky walls and uneven arm sizes but never had any joy. I just had to accept that maybe most of them actually were that buff and shiny.

The girls were even worse. Hundreds of different sexy top close ups and bikini shots would pop up as I scrolled down. And the pouting was ridiculous. It never failed to amaze me how different they looked on photos to the way they looked in real life. There would be photos of Jilly, who had always been as skinny as a toothpick since primary school, and whose lips were on the thin side, looking like Jessica Rabbit. When Jilly's photos came up, I had to read the caption, as my first reaction was always, 'Who's that?' I was clueless as to how she managed to create such huge pouty lips, knowing the limitations of her natural ones, although I did have theories regarding how her figure seemed to be filled out in all the right places on camera.

Both the girls and the boys continually posted numerous snaps of the fun things they filled their weekends with, the fashionable places they went to and the popular people who were with them all the time.

When I thought about it, I wasn't sure the filtered, Photoshopped alter ego was such a good idea. Surely your real life couldn't fail to be a disappointment to anyone who believed the publicity. Not only that, how disappointing was your own real life when you compared it to your social media life?

Of course, these were the things I tried to tell myself, and I knew they were true, but they didn't stop me obsessing about the body I didn't have, the places I didn't go to and the life I'd never have. When I compared myself to those people, I would always find myself lacking, and although I considered myself to be intelligent, and I knew how I was being misled, envy was a very powerful emotion, and it had me in its grip.

The worst pictures I saw that fortnight had to be the ones from Nando's though. Silly, smiley pictures of my friends, arms around each other, pulling faces and laughing, with angels' wings at either side of their heads, or rabbits' ears; Voice changing videos where their faces were distorted into weird shapes and they sounded like cartoon mice and one where one of the staff had obviously been asked to take the photo. The four of them were sitting in a booth, Tyler and Faye on one side of the table, and Olivia and Dan on the other. Faye and Olivia were in the foreground, leaning back against Tyler and Dan then the photographer could take more of a close up. Tyler and Dan were leaning over the table, arms on each other's shoulders and other arms around the girls. Someone had obviously said something hilarious, because they were laughing. It was the kind of photo you rarely manage to take, posed, but somehow not posed, natural, but unflawed, like an advertisement for Coca Cola. Completely central, framed by the seats of the booth so no photo-bombers (intentional or unintentional) no double chins or closed eyes or the blurred faces you get when one person moves. Four good-looking people, two picture-perfect couples having a fun double date.

I couldn't have put into words then how desolate I felt. I'd been trying so hard to convince myself that I fit in, I had completely forgotten that I didn't. If I'd been there, where would I have sat? Everything would have been uncomfortable, the sides of the table odd, with me obviously tagging on awkwardly. It had been my decision not to go, but the photo just confirmed how wise a decision it was. I would have felt like a spare part, a non-entity. Wasn't it better to feel isolated when you were in fact on your own? At least you had an excuse then. I'd heard the saying 'feeling lonely in a crowd', and I had understood what it meant for a good while now. I was different to other people. I was different to my friends. And it was going to get harder and harder to endure.

Back at school, I was quiet. My plan had been to blot everything I was feeling out by concentrating on my studies and striving to be the best, and I could almost believe it was working when I was at home, ensconced in my room learning facts and formulas and munching on whatever I could put my hands on. At school though, it wasn't so easy.

The first day back I'd put on my new school trousers and found I couldn't fasten them. However hard I tried, they just would not stretch enough for me to yank the zip up, let alone button them. Relieved I hadn't thrown my old pairs away, I pulled some on, my heart sinking when I realised how well they fit. They weren't as tight as they had been in the past, uncomfortably tight, but in two weeks, I'd certainly managed to fill them out.

There were only four weeks to go before my first exam, and I intended to use this as a reason why I'd be spending less time with the others. It wasn't permanent, I told myself. As soon as I could get my head around Dan's relationship with Olivia, I'd ease my way back in. It was mind over matter. I would convince myself that my feelings for Dan were completely platonic, and that I was happy for them and then I would move on. It was raw. I was struggling, but give it time and I knew I could manage it.

Sometimes, I caught Olivia and Faye in deep conversation, but when I approached, they'd go quiet, pause, then start chatting about something else. It was pathetic really. Didn't they realise that I knew they weren't the least bit interested in 'Hollyoaks' or whatever the first thing that came into their mind to put me off the scent was.

We still messaged. It was easier to lie when you weren't face to face. I would just imagine the message I would have sent had I not felt this way and send that. My social media alter ego was ironically unaltered, while the real me had changed. I think Olivia thought it was down to my weight. Nobody had mentioned anything about me being heavier, but they couldn't have failed to notice. For years they'd watched me yoyo and put up with the different person I was when I was fat, to the one I was when I felt slimmer (not slim, I'd never reached the perfection of the Instagram set) so part of me hoped they would put it down to that.

One Monday, Faye was waiting for me after physics revision class. 'Hi!' she breezed, falling into step with me. I was immediately on my guard. Straight away she started to babble, explaining why she was up here on the science corridor at exactly the time my class was due to finish. I indulged her. If she did have an ulterior motive, then she'd have to reveal it sooner or later.

Her discomfort was palpable as we made our way downstairs and through the door. 'You aren't upset at Olivia and Dan being friends, are you?'

'No,' my response was much too fast and nowhere near as casually delivered as it was meant to be.

She looked at me searchingly from under the hair she'd allowed to hang down, hiding her face, protecting her from my reaction?

'No,' calmer this time, with a hint of 'what a ridiculous thought' and an incredulous expression. 'Where has that come from? Is it because I haven't been on the group text?' I tried to make it sound as if they were being trivial and immature, thinking that any absence from social media was a potential concern. It was condescending, I knew, but I had to make it convincing.

Faye squirmed. 'I just...we just thought maybe---'

'Look,' again that patronising tone, 'I need to spend the next few weeks with my head down. I want to get into UCL and if I mess up now I'll never forgive myself. Messaging and sending silly photos and stuff will just have to take a back seat. I'll be back to myself as soon as that last exam's in the bag.'

'But you have to relax sometime. All those websites you go on tell you that if you take breaks you retain more. You can't work through all your breaks and lunchtimes.'

'I'll come to the canteen this week,' I said. She was right. I couldn't completely cut myself off.

'So,' she paused, then came to the point, 'you're not jealous of all the time Olivia's been spending with Dan?'

I almost choked. Was it so obvious? 'You're joking! Course I'm not,' I laughed as if it was the most outrageous thing I'd ever heard. 'We're all friends. I don't expect anyone to wait around for me, especially when I'm so busy. Everyone can see each other anytime, whether I'm there or not. Who thinks I'm jealous?' I could have won a Bafta for that performance. She couldn't possibly doubt my sincerity.

'No-one,' she lied, 'I just wondered why you'd vanished off the face of the earth lately. Anyway, canteen tomorrow?'

'Yeah, I'll be there,' I conceded.

I was as good as my word, and for the last two weeks of the half term, I joined the others for lunch a few times. I wasn't sure who had been discussing my behaviour, apart from Faye and Olivia, that much was obvious, but nothing specific was mentioned in relation to Dan and Olivia. Tyler and George teased me relentlessly for being a swot, which I didn't mind, I freely admitted it, and apart from that, things were relatively normal. Everyone was becoming more and more excited for the prom and much of our time was spent discussing the band and how amazing they were.

Faye was modest, but Dan said everyone who heard them was blown away. They were rehearsing that night and did I want to come and watch? He and Tyler would be there too.

'Come and watch us,' Faye smiled. 'You haven't seen us for ages. We've compiled a proper set list now – about twenty songs so far. We won't do them all, just the first set tonight. You can give yourself one night off can't you?' she wheedled.

What could I do? I agreed, not because I had to, I found, but because I wanted to. Being back together with my friends had reminded me how much I missed them, and I looked forward to it.

It was English period five, so Dan and I walked to the music room together. On the way, we chatted about English, the prom and various other safe subjects, avoiding anything which might prove awkward, or at least, I did. I had no idea whether Dan was privy to the 'jealousy theory'.

As we turned to walk across the foyer towards the music department, Ewan Reid and another couple of members of the football team were standing at the bottom of the stairs, leaning against the bannisters. On the other side of the bannister was Amelia, who looked like a queen holding court with her suitors. When Amelia saw the two of us she laughed, then bent down to whisper something to the boys. They turned around in unison, spotted us and creased over, theatrically stifling giggles and punching each-others' arms. Ewan said something to Amelia about Dan's new *friend* with a particular emphasis on the word *friend* that I couldn't work out. Dan ignored them, but we walked more quickly to the double doors to avoid their stares.

It was the same room in which the auditions had been held, but looked very different. The band had asked permission to change the layout at the front of the room so that their instruments were ready to play as soon as they arrived. The main difference was that the drums now stood in the centre of the playing area, like they would do on stage, with the lead and bass guitar on stands at either side. Faye's microphone was set up at the front, and a maze of wires covered the floor.

'You want to be careful,' I joked, 'or health and safety will be after you.'

Theo and the bass player arrived soon after and began plugging in and tuning up.

'Faye said you're a keyboard player,' Theo shouted over the noise. 'You don't fancy joining us on a couple of numbers do you? Keyboard players are rarer than bass guitars. James is crap; we only let him join because we were desperate.'

James laughed good-naturedly and went back to reading a message he'd just received. 'They're going to be ten minutes,' he said.

'I'm not joking.' Theo continued. 'We're doing some old stuff. You know, with it being a festival and all that, and some of the songs would sound so much better with a keyboard. We're doing the Beach Boys, some 70s Beatles and Queen, Bohemian Rhapsody; not exactly Woodstock, I know, but we researched it and no-one will have heard of any of the bands that played there. You want to hear Faye's voice on Bohemian Rhapsody; It's awesome. It doesn't sound half as good without the keyboards though. Do you want to have a go? We've got the music. Where's that carrier bag with the sheet music in James?'

He was so keen I didn't have the heart to refuse. They'd forget about it anyway. Dan dusted off the less ancient looking keyboard, plugged it in and wrestled with the stand for a few minutes before it finally gave in and clicked into place.

It was surprisingly easy to keep time with the band, which was my main concern, especially when Woody, the drummer, arrived with Faye. After a couple of run throughs, Faye sang with us, and Theo was right. Her voice was awe-inspiring. In the past, I'd played at family get-togethers accompanying various aunts and cousins; it had been a tradition in my mum's family that on Boxing Day, we would all entertain each other by showing off our 'talents'. No-one was allowed to escape, and if you really couldn't sing, you'd be forced to learn a poem to recite. Luckily, because I was the only one who could play the piano since my Grandma lost her sight, I was immune; I suppose you could say I was showcasing my talents at the piano instead. I didn't mind; all eyes were always on the singer, either because they were genuinely talented, like my cousin Georgia, or they sounded like they'd overdosed on helium, like my cousin Maisie.

None of them compared to Faye's voice though. It was truly beautiful, and made them all look like karaoke singers at best.

We found some sheet music for 'Good Vibrations' by the Beach Boys and I was pleasantly surprised at how well I played it and how much I enjoyed it. As Dan switched off the lights after the rehearsal, Faye came running over to me. 'You will play on some of the songs at the prom won't you? They sound so much better with the keyboard on.' She looked at me with puppy dog eyes and I had to laugh, which she obviously took as a yes as she threw her arms around me and gave me a squeeze. 'I've missed you so much,' she smiled.

For me, half term was already organised. I'd worked out a revision timetable which left me very little time to think about anything else, let alone go anywhere, or see anyone. If I needed time out, I'd factored in a couple of hours every day where I could stick my headphones on and lose myself in the mindless enjoyment of Fortnite, although Tyler always won; I could imagine the ratio of serious revision versus perfecting his Battle Royale strategies that was going on in his house. Alternatively, I'd join in with whatever undemanding game was popular on Checkpoint, the gaming hangout I visited when I needed to unwind.

Faye called around on the Monday with the sheet music for the other three songs which 'would not sound right' without keyboards and her excitement was tangible. Her skin glowed and she looked so alive. Although I still harboured doubts about standing up in front of my peers and performing, I couldn't let her down. Anyway, I reasoned, it would be just like Boxing Day parties; everybody would be focusing on Faye and I would be more or less invisible.

The week passed quickly, and then we were all plunged back into the midst of the exams. Apart from a couple of anomalies, where I couldn't for the life of me understand what one of the questions on the physics exam meant, or where we'd definitely not covered a particular part of a topic in geography, I was comfortable in the fact that I'd absolutely prepared as well I could do for every subject. At times, it was embarrassing when other students spoke about an impossible question, or a formula they had completely forgotten. I was quite relieved to be able to join in when people started mentioning the physics question and the missing knowledge of petroleum geology.

Even the couple of problems I'd had turned out to be someone else's fault; the rogue question we'd struggled to work out was all over Twitter the next day and even made it onto the national news. How could someone whose job it was to write GCSE science papers get it so wrong? Likewise, our geography teacher informed us that she hadn't taught the particular strand of petroleum geology that had appeared on the paper as it was an A level topic, and not supposed to be on the GCSE syllabus, although maybe she was just covering for a mistake she'd made, as there was no nationwide coverage of this error, and it did appear that our class was isolated in its ignorance. Still, I was secretly happy that it wasn't my own oversight.

The prom was scheduled for the Thursday of the third week back at school, when all but one of our exams were over; I was just glad I didn't have Product Design at nine o'clock in the morning the day after. We had thought at first that a Saturday would be the ideal day to hold a festival, but various members of staff had pointed out that an actual festival required entertainment, lighting, sound, refreshments (the list was endless) and staff to provide these for a full day. The health and safety implications would be huge when planning four hours cover, let alone another however many more. We had deferred to their greater knowledge and accepted the Thursday graciously.

I'd seen more of the others since the first rehearsal I'd attended. Faye was always there obviously and Tyler seemed to be everywhere she was recently. It had crossed my mind before that he fancied her, but I'd never seen any outward signs from either of them so I'd always felt it might be in my imagination. Also, Tyler was, in his own words 'compact', which was the perfect way to describe him. He'd always been what I'd call 'wiry' as a child, not an ounce of fat on him and a six pack when he was eight, but as we got older, he'd become less skinny and more muscular. Other people would simply have called him short, or small, but compact was better. It implied solidity and toughness, and that's what Tyler was, like a perfectly put together package of power and energy.

In contrast, Faye was tall, taller than most of the girls and a lot of the boys too, and painfully aware of this. I knew she'd have more of a problem with their size difference than him. Tyler was just Tyler, and his personality made him appear taller than he was. No-one ignored Tyler or bullied him. Personality wise, he was always the biggest person in the room. But Faye, I thought, would struggle, because his lack of height would emphasise how tall she was. It was ridiculous how stereotypical ideas about relationships inhibited some people from being with other people they'd be perfect for.

Dan had also been to most of the rehearsals, but I felt awkward around him, glad that I was playing then it didn't look like I was avoiding him. I still didn't know whether he also had the impression that I was jealous of his and Olivia's closeness, but the thought of it was excruciating. When I thought of how easily we'd chatted in the past and how much I enjoyed his company I would develop a lump in the throat.

I did also feel that he had pulled away from me, which would suggest he was embarrassed too, mortified probably, and was keeping away so as not to lead me on. He would stand in front of the band at the beginning, adjusting the volume of our instruments until the sound was just right and then watch from the back of the room, sometimes stopping us to make suggestions. It was darker there as we only used the lights at the front of the room where we were playing, but I still sometimes caught his eye, and we would both look away self-consciously.

Olivia was the one I felt most awkward around though. Since the conversation with Faye, she had been quiet when I was there, not rudely so, and perhaps no-one else noticed, but as if she felt permanently uncomfortable. It felt as if she would go out of her way to sit at the other end of the table, and if I was talking, she wouldn't respond. Gone were the days when she'd link up with me and boss me around, telling me off about feeling fat and joking about my having body dysmorphia. I missed our friendship hugely.

Chapter 21

On the Tuesday of the week of prom, I arrived at rehearsal an hour early in order to go through a last practice on my own before the others arrived; as we'd finished most of our exams, we'd officially left school, but teachers were unaware of who still had exams to finish and who didn't so it wasn't as if we were being herded off the premises. In our case, they knew we were most likely on official 'prom business' and had permission to use some rooms, so our presence was completely overlooked.

Dan was already in the room, fiddling with one of the amps, and I considered trying to escape before he saw me. He'd heard the door bang shut though and turned to see who'd come in. When he saw it was me his expression changed fleetingly to something between confused and pained, before he smiled, nodded at me and returned his attention to the amp. I was tempted to switch the keyboard on and run through my songs anyway; it would be less embarrassing than trying to pretend nothing had changed and keeping a stilted conversation going for an hour.

Walking across the room I decided to brazen it out. I'd make a little small talk, then start to practise. As I put down my bag I could see out of the side of my eye that Dan's face was turned in my direction, as if he was waiting for me to speak or waiting to speak to me. I felt the atmosphere between us crackling. Why wouldn't he speak? What did he have to say to me that was so difficult?

Eventually I couldn't bear it any longer. 'What?' I sighed. 'What's happened? You just need to get it off your chest, whatever it is.'

He stood up and walked over to the drum stool, putting the drums in-between us like a protective barrier. 'I need to tell you something.' He paused for a long moment and the silence in the room was palpable. 'I'm not what you think I am.' Another pause. Was I supposed to respond, or just listen? I was frightened of what he might tell me. 'I've been using you and your friends and now I'm going back to the in crowd? We think it's hilarious that you believe I could genuinely be interested in you? It's all been a big joke?'

'What do I think you are?' My voice cracked and I cleared my throat.

'You think I'm confident and cool and that my life is perfect. You think that whatever issue I have must be insignificant. You probably think I'm just attention seeking.' He was getting into his stride now and his voice sounded harsh and bitter. 'You think I'm good-looking and great at sport and all the girls fancy me so what could my problem possibly be?'

I looked at the floor. It wasn't too far from the truth.

'I know you think your dad hates you, but you're probably just clashing because you're different.' I ventured, hesitantly. 'He expects you to be just like him and your brother but you're not. I don't think he hates you; he just doesn't get you. My mum's the same. She wants me to be just like her. The problem is, she's already disappointed in me. I've always been a disappointment to her. She was great at sport like you – she was a county level cross country runner at one point – and she wanted me to be sporty too but I'm useless…'

Dan laughed, a fake laugh that said, 'you don't know anything,'

I broke off, aware that it wasn't about me. Maybe I'd said too much but I so wanted him to know that I understood.

'If he was just going to be disappointed in me, I think I could handle that. If I could tell him how I feel and the worst he'd feel is disappointment, I'd tell him. But I can never tell him. If I tell him, he'll hate me. He won't want anything to do with me. He'll throw me out.'

I must admit I was unconvinced. I'd never met Dan's dad, but he couldn't be that bad. What could be so horrific that he thought his dad would never get over it. Whatever it was, he'd surely get over it in time.

He was looking at me, weighing me up, trying to work out what I was thinking. I didn't know what to say that wouldn't make it worse. His eyes were desperate, red ringed and almost pleading.

Suddenly, I knew what I had to do.

'Tell me,' I said.

Noises could be heard in the distance. Laughing and shouting.

'Tell me. I might be able to help you.'

The sounds were closer; on the corridor outside footsteps thudded towards us.

His eyes on mine were frantic as he fought with himself.

I could distinguish Tyler's voice above the hubbub, then the chorus of laughter that followed.

'Whatever you've done, it can be sorted. Just tell me.'

We looked at the silhouettes passing by the frosted glass in the door. Soon they'd be Tyler's and Faye's.

He took a deep breath. 'It's not what I've done,' his eyes locked on mine.

'It's what I am.'

The door swung open and Tyler bounced into the room as Dan wrenched his eyes away and spun to face him.

Dan's voice was emotionless as he spoke. 'I have to go home now. Can you sort the sound Tyler?' he said, getting up from the stool and grabbing his bag from one of the tables. Then he just walked out, leaving me standing there, stomach churning, not knowing what to think or feel or how to explain what just happened.

For a few seconds, I was dazed. What did he mean by 'It's what I am'? What did 'I'm not what you think I am' mean? The obvious answer was almost a cliché, more than a cliché in fact, but too ridiculous to even entertain. My head was spinning with different possibilities, but each one seemed more unbelievable than the last.

Tyler broke the spell. 'What's wrong with Dan? What's happened?'

I couldn't answer. Not just because I had no idea how to; I didn't know what had happened, and my mind was still reeling. What was wrong? I needed to go after him. I couldn't leave it like this.

Picking up my bag I rushed out of the room, looking both ways down the corridor for any sign of Dan. Obviously, he had disappeared; I'd been so slow, such an idiot; I should have gone after him straight away but I'd just stood there like some kind of senseless halfwit.

He'd head home I assumed, probably choosing the route whereby he'd be the least likely to encounter fellow students, as he certainly hadn't seemed like he was in the frame of mind to chat. I turned left, in the direction of the south exit, avoiding the foyer and the canteen where groups of students who'd had exams would usually congregate after school. I started to run; if I missed him now, who knew when we'd have the chance to talk again? The pain was etched on his face, and I couldn't stand the thought of him having to live with whatever his agonising secret was for one more night.

Slamming through the double doors, I scanned the field, and when I couldn't see him I sprinted around the front of the school and searched the paths and car park, scrutinising each tall figure, expecting to recognise Dan's dark, floppy hair. Unable to spot him, I carried on walking towards the front doors, hoping I'd chosen the wrong direction and he'd miraculously appear in front of me, but he'd vanished.

It was warm, but the sky was darkening and there promised to be a storm. I waited for a few minutes as the flow of students became a trickle, before accepting that he'd gone. Dejected, I started up the front steps, wondering what to do. The darkness reached inside the foyer, as if the eyes of those inside had gradually adjusted to the waning brightness and failed to realise they should be switching on the light. Unsure of where to go or what to do, I stood motionless in the gloom, which is why Olivia almost knocked me over on her way out.

She jumped, obviously startled to see anyone lurking in the shadows, and even more so when she realised it was me. We looked at each other for a few seconds, before tentatively saying hello, but then what were we to do? We hadn't spoken to each other alone for weeks, and there was an unspoken feeling, on both sides I thought, that our friendship was somehow damaged. I'm not sure either us could have explained why, other than our respective relationships with Dan, Olivia feeling I was jealous of hers and me feeling embarrassed about mine.

Olivia spoke first. 'How did the rehearsal go?' something she obviously thought was a safe subject; she couldn't possibly have known how wrong she was.

'Fine,' I lied.

She looked up into my face, as if trying to read the truth there, and her eyes glittered in the darkness. She'd been crying, and I suddenly wanted to hug her, but the invisible barrier between us remained.

'Are you walking home?' I asked. We lived in the same direction and often walked home together in the past. I certainly couldn't face returning to the rehearsal and I didn't know where Dan lived (not that I'd have followed him anyway). I needed to get home, retreat to my room and think, or not think and spend a couple of hours on Checkpoint.

We walked out together and fell into step.

There was a rumble of distant thunder which relieved the tension for a while, and we chatted about how hot the weather had been, and how much we hoped that if there was a storm, it would be clear again for Thursday. It would be awful if it rained at the prom, although we could sell those plastic macs you can buy at theme parks for a profit and make even more money.

The silence descended again momentarily before a louder growl of thunder interrupted it.

It seemed to galvanise Olivia and she announced loudly, 'Dan says he's gay,' in a flippant tone of voice.

The emotion I felt was indescribable. Obviously, the first thought that entered my head when Dan had said the words, 'It's what I am,' had been that he was telling me that he was gay. It was something that writers and film makers had made into a stereotypical 'coming out' statement. Maybe that's why I'd questioned it. Was it too obvious? Was I assuming something because of the connotations of the statement?

What did I feel? I was certainly shaken: my heart was beating out of my chest, but I couldn't have put my feelings into words.

I'd been contemplating other implications continually since the words came out of his mouth, but if I was honest, this was the one I had kept coming back to. Everything about Dan screamed straight; he was the archetypal, perfect straight boy, so maybe that was why I couldn't accept what he desperately wanted me to know. Had he wanted me to guess, to save him the need to actually say the words? Did he now think that I had guessed and didn't approve and that's why I didn't immediately follow him? Was he regretting telling me and picturing all sorts of repercussions?

I wanted to run away, to shout and scream? I didn't know. To be on my own, think about how I felt and allow my emotions to calm down? But I was trapped. Olivia knew nothing of my feelings. Anyway, I lectured myself, nothing has changed. He was out of your league; he's still out of your league. End of story.

'I don't think he really knows though,' Olivia continued. 'How can he know when he's only sixteen? His hormones are all over the place and he's probably just confused.'

She stopped to allow me time to answer, but I was speechless, partly because I was still thinking about how Dan would be feeling right now and how he may be suffering, and partly because I couldn't quite believe what I was hearing.

'What do you mean,' I asked.

'I told my mum last night,' Olivia admitted quietly, 'I was in such a state, she came into my room and it just came out. And she said lots of people go through this phase of hormones all over the place and thinking that must mean they're gay. She said a lot of people change their minds when their hormones stabilise, you know?'

'What do you mean, stabilise?'

'Well there's the TV and films and things too. There are so many gay characters on TV nowadays that people are influenced. They think it's normal, you know?'

'What do you mean, normal?' I was struggling to recognise my friend.

'You know I don't mean it that way. I don't mind people being gay. You know I don't. It's just that Dan isn't like that. He's into sports and all his friends are sporty. He isn't the slightest bit camp at all. I think you can tell when boys are gay and I don't think he really is. I just think he's confused. I'm sure we had a connection. I really felt that there was something between us, and…maybe he's just scared, you know, like Amelia said, maybe he's scared of relationships.'

Her tone was almost hopeful, like the fact that she wanted Dan, and the way her mum had spoken had convinced her that there was still a chance for them. She was so deluded, I felt sorry for her. Did she really think that anyone would put themselves through the torture Dan was enduring because they were scared? He was tortured because he wasn't confused, because he knew. While he was confused, and I was sure there was a long period of confusion and denial before he finally admitted the truth to himself, he probably tried to ignore his sexuality. He was scared, she was right there, but he wasn't scared of her, he was scared of him. My heart ached for him.

The sky was suddenly brightened by a sheet of lightning and I realised she was again waiting for my reaction.

'Maybe you're right,' I said. I wanted to argue with her and show her how ridiculous she was being, but the truth was, I didn't trust her. Olivia wasn't a malicious person, but she was hurt, and she was probably embarrassed. If she felt there was a chance for her, she was less likely to tell people what Dan had said before he was ready to do that himself.

She told me how they'd become close over the last couple of months; she was sure it wasn't in her imagination, but she thought he was just too shy to take their friendship to the next level, so she'd tried to kiss him and he'd pulled away, like Amelia said he had with her. She was going to give him space and let him work out what he wanted, but she was sure he couldn't be gay. If he was, she would have known. She would have felt it.

We had come to the fork in the road where we separated. There was a huge clap of thunder, and I turned to her, 'Better get home quickly or we'll be soaked. Don't shelter under any trees, will you?'

'Yeah, I know,' she said, 'Don't tell anyone, will you?'

'Course not.'

I watched her walk away, wondering when and how we'd become so different. Another flash of lightning lit the sky and she turned and waved before starting to run.

Sitting down on the garden wall of the nearest house, I saw isolated damp patches appear on the pavement, although when I put my hand out to check for drops, none seemed to materialise. I watched as one by one they multiplied, seemingly avoiding me until the first one glanced lightly off the side of my nose. Unable to dodge me any further, the rain began to fall more and more heavily, pounding the pavement and bouncing back, until I was soaked to the skin.

Only then did I stand up and head for home.

Chapter 22

Mum would drive me to the hospital and back, which made me uncomfortable. I felt like such a hypocrite accepting lifts when I couldn't bring myself to speak to her. If I could, I would have walked, or taken the bus, but logistically, that would have been impossible. Once I'd caught the bus home from college and eaten, it was usually approaching six o'clock. It would take me over an hour to walk, and the visiting slot we'd agreed was from six until eight. I swallowed my pride and told myself I was doing it for Dan.

She talked to me in the car. I tried not to listen, but she knew it was the only time she had the power to force me to hear. She would apologise over and over again, pleading with me to forgive her, and trying to explain why she'd behaved the way she had. She would sometimes cry and sometimes become angry with me for my lack of understanding.

I was merciless. As far as I was concerned, I'd never forgive her.

Most of all I blamed her for Dan being in a coma. If she'd been the kind of mum I felt she should have been, I would have told her about Dan's situation, and she would have insisted he come and live with us. We would have plucked him out of hell and everything would have been perfect.

She tried and tried, most nights in the car, but she might as well have been talking to a block of ice. She could chip and chip, but the hurt inside me went so deep that if she hacked away forever, she would never find a layer of forgiveness.

I would never forgive her.

Chapter 23

I saw Dan fleetingly on the Wednesday, just the back of his head during the biology exam. He had ignored all my messages since the night of the rehearsal and slipped in and out of the exam hall unseen. I grew more anxious about him by the minute, and Olivia and I looked meaningfully at each other all day, the unspoken reply always being a subtle shrug or eyebrow lift which meant, 'No, I haven't heard from him either.'

When Faye, Tyler and George asked about him in the canteen, oblivious to our collusion, we pretended to be as mystified as them regarding his absence. Tyler shot me a few cynical looks (he was still curious as to why we'd both suddenly abandoned the Tuesday rehearsal) but didn't delve any further.

Faye and Olivia allowed the rest of us a sneaky peek at the almost finished prototype year books. Apart from prom pictures, they were complete, and it had been arranged for the official photographer to send all individual and group photos, with names, to the company producing the book in order that they were ready on results day to collect. For some I supposed, it would be the icing on the cake; for others less satisfied with their performance, a reminder of the time they'd wasted.

There were lots of pictures of Dan. Dan holding a trophy aloft as part of the football team after winning the county schools championship, after hitting a century as star batter of the cricket team, winning the inter schools' cross country and the one hundred metres race at sports day. I could imagine there were plenty more but Faye and Olivia had been forced to choose the best few winning at sports pictures to avoid it becoming the Dan FanBook. There were a couple more of Dan, with a group of friends on a Duke of Edinburgh expedition and laughing after stumbling off a roller coaster with Ewan Reid, arms around each other for support.

How would Dan view his year book? Would he remember the fun he had at school fondly, or the lie he was living in some of these photos?

The next day was Thursday, prom day, and the weather forecast was still uncertain. The prom committee met for the final time that morning to check all plans were in place and discuss the possibility of rain. Miss Purcell said she'd organised a deal with a local supplier to collect two hundred plastic macs if it was still looking like it might rain when school closed.

The stage had been erected and sound and lighting towers were being installed as we spoke. Zainab and two friends, who had volunteered to decorate the area, had brought boxes and boxes of fairy lights and fake flowers to create a festival feel. Miss Purcell had roped in about twenty boys to actually put up the decorations; Zainab had made it clear that she was the designer and she was prepared to supervise but not climb any ladders as she had such an extreme fear of heights that high heels made her feel faint.

One of the art teachers and her year nine class had spent weeks preparing two huge fake flower creations spelling out 'WestFest', one for the stage and one to be hung on the fence next to the front gate as a surprise gift for us, and Miss Purcell was so touched she scrabbled in her bag for a tissue to dab her eyes. 'Hayfever,' she assured us, shaking her head.

The only absentee was Dan. When he still hadn't shown half an hour into the meeting, I texted Tyler to ask if he'd deputise until Dan arrived. I made it sound like this was a certainty. A lie, but for the greater good I thought.

When Miss Purcell asked where Dan was, I made it sound like everything was under control. Dan was running late and Tyler was going to stand in until he arrived. We still had a final rehearsal to run through, checking that the sound and lights were working as well as making sure we were fully prepared and timing our set list. I sounded much more confident than I felt.

Straight after the meeting, I ran outside and messaged Dan. At this point, the immediate issue of the potential collapse of the whole prom was upsetting me to the exclusion of all else. My message was abrupt, and maybe a little harsh in the circumstances, but I was panicking.

'You need to get here now. A lot of people are depending on you and I can't cover for you much longer.'

When there was no reply, I realised how it must have sounded, what Dan was afraid of, and I messaged again.

'No-one knows. Olivia and I spoke. We are both completely supportive and haven't told anyone. We can help you deal with this after the prom.' A lie, but for the greater good.

Ten minutes later, he messaged. 'Ok.'

The relief was immense, not just the fact that he was coming, but that he was there, that he was ok. I hadn't allowed myself to acknowledge my biggest fear, but now he was ok, I almost cried with gratitude.

Tyler helped the sound and lighting crew we'd hired set up until Dan arrived. The stage was adorned with strings of colourful fabric flowers by now and I had to admit when Zainab asked me to come and look at the final product, fairy lights twinkling at the back of the stage in the dark, it was impressive. As it was June, and the last DJ we'd scheduled after the band was finishing at twelve, we'd only have an hour where it would be dark enough to see the lights elsewhere, but she assured me it would look amazing. I believed her; she had worked her labourers like Trojans and the whole festival area looked unbelievably impressive, better than we ever could have hoped when we were planning our pitch all those months ago.

When Faye and Olivia returned for the rehearsal after doing some last-minute shopping I pulled Olivia aside. 'I told Dan we'd agreed not to say anything and that we're both supportive,' I whispered, hoping she'd been genuine about 'giving him space'.

She looked away, but nodded.

Dan arrived just as the first song started. He looked grey and drawn, his hair limp and lifeless, as if it hadn't been washed for days and dark shadows under his red ringed eyes, as if he'd not slept either. Everyone had to have seen, but no one said anything, just waved and smiled as if he wasn't late and didn't look like hell. I wondered if it was too obvious, but he didn't seem to notice, just smiled back wanly.

Olivia smiled and waved, but kept her distance. Maybe it had been genuine after all.

After twenty minutes, I was starting to feel uncomfortable. Maybe I shouldn't have pushed him to come. 'Come into the foyer,' I told him.

I set off, and he followed me. Right then I didn't care what people thought. I just wanted him to know that things weren't as bleak as he thought. There were people who cared about him enough not to care about this.

'Has anything happened?' I asked.

He shook his head.

'Ok, then you need to forget about it, for one night, or for one year, until you're ready to deal with it. It might be tomorrow, and it might not, but this is not everything you are.'

'And you'd know all about that I suppose? You don't know anything,' Dan snapped.

'Oh for God's sake, being gay or straight or bi or trans isn't everything you are. You can enjoy things that have nothing to do with sexuality or gender or anything like that, can't you?' He was looking at the floor, biting his lip. I realised I'd sounded harsh and adopted a more diplomatic tone. 'Can't you just be a person tonight? We'll deal with the rest tomorrow, or whenever you're ready.'

He sighed heavily.

'Come on!' I took a chance. 'Stop sulking and let's get this party started!'

Looking at me for the first time, he laughed, and I smiled back.

Standing up, he came towards me. I wasn't expecting it, or ready for it, but he put his arms around me and hugged me tightly, not letting go. Eventually I put my arms around him and we stood there for maybe half a minute. I could feel the warmth from his body against mine and my breathing quickened.

'Thanks,' he said, as he pulled away from me, 'I'm sorry, I just…'

He turned towards the door and we walked out together and towards the back of the stage where the band were finishing off their first set.

'And wash your hair,' I called as he made in the direction of the steps. 'It smells bad.'

He didn't look back but shook his head, and I knew he was laughing.

After the second set, we got together again and said our goodbyes. In a couple of hours, we'd be back here to find out if all our hard work had paid off. The excitement and enthusiasm seemed to have infected everyone, including Dan, who now looked healthier by far. Before we left, he looked over and smiled, and my heart gave a little leap.

Clouds were still looming in the sky but they seemed less grey to me now, although I knew I could have been imagining it. I dared to hope that the sun would triumph and the promised rain would simply evaporate into nothing.

Chapter 24

One day, as I was eating, I watched Mum as she tidied the kitchen. When did her hair start to go grey? I hadn't noticed before, but there were streaks above her ears and at the front of her hairline. Her hair had always been a mid-brown, the same colour as mine. Maybe she'd dyed it before; I didn't know. The wrinkles around her dark brown eyes were deeper than I remembered too. I cast my mind back a few months. Not that I'd ever really looked for them, but I was sure the wrinkles and the greys weren't there before.

It was as if she'd aged ten years in a couple of months. Most of the time now, my animosity was silent, but at first, I was vocal in my hatred, describing the way she'd made me feel as vividly as possible, telling her about the times I'd thought about a way out. When I mentioned suicide, she'd crumpled, and put her hands over her face, whimpering in distress. Did I enjoy watching her suffer?

I think I did. Maybe she absorbed my cruelty and the outward manifestation of her agony was the grey hairs and the wrinkles.

Something moved inside me, just a tiny flicker, as if a corner of the ice encasing my heart had melted and dripped away.

I shook my head and stood up, taking my plate and cutlery to the dishwasher. She turned and smiled at me with sad eyes, so much longing in that one action.

I didn't smile back.

Chapter 25

As the year eleven students pulled up at the gates, their faces were a testament to the success of our choice of venue at least. We'd known that holding the prom on the school field would be a gamble; no-one associated coming back to school with having fun. But Zainab and her friends had transformed the whole area, creating a magical festival world full of flowers and sparkle. It was rewarding to watch the surprised expressions and hear the admiring comments. Many of the students, we knew, had been cynical at first, even hostile to the idea, but now it would seem most approved.

Most of the girls had made a huge effort with their appearance, some having gone down the traditional route, dressed as seventies hippies in tie dye tops, peasant blouses, frayed jeans and ankle-length cheesecloth maxi dresses; others in a more glamorous version of the festival genre. Hair was generally styled in long loose waves, flowers interwoven, either subtly or as part of complex creations obviously crafted by a professional hairdresser, and make-up typically incorporated glitter of some kind. Although they might not have had the opportunity to wear a sophisticated evening dress or ball gown, they certainly hadn't squandered the opportunity to shine.

The boys' outfits, although much more understated, were usually designed to be more entertaining than sophisticated, and there was definitely a fancy dress flavour to their choices. Again, tie die was popular, but huge flares, suede fringed waist coats, long wigs and leather thonged peace pendants were also abundant.

From the off, the atmosphere was fun, everyone admiring the girls' skills in putting various impressive outfits together and either giggling or hooting with laughter at the boys, depending on the ludicrousness of their attire. That's when they weren't taking selfies, of themselves, with their friends, with any stray teacher available, with people they'd never spoken to in five years at Westfield, and any other random stranger running a hot dog or ice-cream stall.

Olivia arrived with Tyler and George in Tyler's dad's car. We'd requested that any money parents may have spent on impressive transport to the prom was donated to the charity instead, and surprisingly, I thought, all but the most ostentatious students had persuaded their parents to comply. In fact, some of the parents were vying for recognition by driving the oldest and most clapped out bangers they could, which all added to the entertainment.

She looked amazing, in a particularly flattering pair of frayed denim hot pants and multi-coloured crocheted crop top, emphasising her tan. Accessorising reasonably tastefully with strappy flats and a matching floppy hat, she managed to look classy and sexy at the same time. A large daisy on her hat and a couple of smaller ones painted on her left cheek finished off the look perfectly.

I was impressed, but nothing could have prepared us for Tyler and George, who alighted from the car in garishly bright, flowery, flared all-in ones which left nothing to the imagination, wigs and headbands. Their outfits were identical except for the different patterns, and the look was so outrageous that everyone around the gate was creased up in hysterics. Tyler's dad waved at me, shaking his head and smiling.

We made our way in after watching most of the year arrive and proceeded to people watch for a while. Some of our classmates were barely recognisable in their get ups and we marvelled at the authenticity of various ensembles. Dan wasn't there yet, but I had kind of expected him to be late so as to miss being the centre of attention when arriving. For a lot of our peers, that was the best bit; Ewan Reid and three more of the football team had come as The Beatles, blaring out 'Love, Love Me Do' while doing a prepared dance exit from their car and pointing at various girls along the way. I felt like pointing out that they were a little out of their era at Woodstock in their smart suits and mop-tops, but I swallowed down my cynicism for the sake of the greater good (and because I'd have never dared to mention it anyway).

A lot of the girls were queueing up for the face painting stalls, then spending the next few minutes taking pouting selfies, smiling selfies, tongue out selfies and any other selfies they could think of. There must have been thousands upon thousands of selfies flying through the air at any given moment, some to phones only a few metres away, and some up and away into the distance, to friends from different schools, family members and anyone else who might be the slightest bit interested.

Faye and the band were beginning to tune up while one of the boys DJ'd the first 'arrival' slot, so I said my goodbyes, made my way over and climbed the steps up to the stage. I was shocked to see Dan sitting in the darkness behind the drums as I'd certainly not seen him arrive and I'd been at the front gate for the greetings for ten minutes before the first students appeared. He had on a black open neck silk shirt with large seventies collars and a pair of black flares. If he was trying to blend into the background, he was failing. I didn't know whether he realised it, but he looked even more like a young Elvis and would have all the girls literally swooning.

'Got here early,' he explained with his gap-toothed grin, 'couldn't face all that flash photography.'

We were doing my set, well the set I was playing in, first. Standing there in the spotlight, the reality of what I'd signed up for was beginning to hit me. The others didn't look nervous at all to me, and I searched Faye's face for any sign of fear. She caught me looking and laughed. 'I'm shaking,' she said. 'Feel my hands.'

I could tell though that a lot of that adrenaline was excitement and not fear. Faye was more at home behind a microphone than in real life, and being in the band had made her so much more confident as a person. She was wearing an ethereal white dress which looked like it was made from sparkly cobwebs and her blonde hair cascaded in waves down her back. The minimal make-up she'd chosen and lack of accessories (her feet were bare) made her look like a beautiful ghost.

'Can I pull the keyboard back a bit out of the light?' I said quietly to Dan, who was taping up wires behind the stage.

'You'll be fine once you get started,' he smiled reassuringly and nodded. 'Anyway, you need to get started. The first set starts at half past eight. Is everyone in place?' he shouted. 'Let's run through 'Hey Jude' as a sound check.' We'd cut 'Hey Jude', thinking it was too down beat, but we all knew it, so we might as well use it for something. Five minutes later, we began playing, and immediately the crowd started to move in our direction. After a couple of hitches: amps needing to be moved and plugs plugged in properly, we made it to the end of the song, by which time there were maybe a hundred people surrounding the stage.

My heart was still pounding, but I'd played the song perfectly, and was starting to feel more comfortable. Dan was standing in the wings, leaning against one of the roof supports, perfectly still, watching. I could see his eyes glittering as the lights flashed and I smiled across, just in case he was looking in my direction.

I enjoyed myself more and more as the night went on. Faye sounded better than most of the singers I'd seen live at festivals (not that I'd physically been to any, just watched them on TV) and the crowd were loving it. She had them in the palm of her hand, not just with her singing, but with her stage presence. For each song she had a new act, not a dance exactly, more a movement to the music, and she used the whole of the stage, gesturing to either side of the audience as she approached them. I needn't have worried about being self-conscious, as Faye was the focus, and no-one could take their eyes off her. Although we were only half way into our first set, they were dancing and swaying their arms to the music; even those who'd stayed away at first were now at the back of the crowd, and most of the stall holders had walked over to join in too.

During one of the songs where the keyboards weren't needed, I wandered over to the side of the stage and sat down on the steps to cool down; the lights were becoming unbearably hot and I wondered how Faye managed to look so cool. If I'd have been twirling and stamping around like that in front of their blazing heat, I'd have melted by now.

In the lull between songs, I heard a strident voice sneering, 'Oh my God. What does the giraffe look like? Who does she think she is? Ellie Goulding?' followed by a loud sniggering and Jilly's unmistakably nasal reply.

'She thinks she sounds like Adele,' she brayed, the irony completely lost on her. She was the only one laughing at that one.

'And him. Gay boy,' Amelia spat. 'He must be gay if he's frightened of a real woman. Or maybe he can only handle these prom committee geeks. It's pathetic.'

I stepped around the corner, suddenly brave with indignation, wanting to defend my friends.

'She sounds better than Adele,' I said loudly, 'don't you think?' I challenged any of them to argue. Ok, maybe I was taking a risk, I mean, Adele is…Adele, but in terms of the sound of Faye's voice, I did believe it was richer and purer, especially on the high notes.

Jilly snorted, 'are you joking?' but the rest of them didn't laugh, or even speak. I had directed my comment at Amelia, and she was glaring at me with pure malice.

As if on cue. Faye launched into a haunting acapella rendition of 'Somewhere Over the Rainbow'; it had been Tyler's idea, and he had begged her to do the Eva Cassidy version because apparently his mum loved it and he wanted to video it for her birthday. The sound was so pure and clear that a couple of the girls turned around as if spellbound. The whole crowd gazed at Faye, entranced, and apart from her beautiful voice ringing out like a bell, there was silence.

Even Amelia and Jilly were rendered speechless, and it was a few seconds before Amelia regained her composure. Her face was twisted again in the same way as before, when she'd confronted Dan in the canteen, and I was reminded of a film I'd seen where the main character is hypnotised into seeing people only as they are on the inside; kind and caring girls looked beautiful and mean and selfish ones ugly. The thick make-up she was wearing only served to accentuate the malevolent expression on her face and I couldn't help thinking she looked like a pantomime villain. Her outfit, which had probably cost a small fortune, even added to the effect, a long, red off the shoulder gypsy dress with long sleeves that hung down to a point and a red choker slashed across her neck. She hadn't been able to forego the massive hair either, which if possible looked even bigger, and her eyelashes were huge; I couldn't imagine how she could possibly lift them far enough to open her eyes.

'Who asked you?' she spat, 'Who are you anyway? Nobody would even know who you are if you hadn't started hanging around with Dan, following him around like a puppy dog.' The coven smelt blood, and a couple of titters ensued. Empowered, she continued, and the rest of the witches turned around to watch the show, arms folded, enjoying my discomfort. I reddened with humiliation. 'I don't know what he sees in you lot. Maybe he just feels sorry for you and he's letting some of his popularity rub off on you. Mind you,' she cackled, obviously having thought of something cutting and hilarious to say, 'It looks like it's worked the wrong way around. Your geekiness has rubbed off on him. He isn't even popular now. None of the football team even speak to him.'

The spite dripped from her fangs as she sniggered at her witty comment, and the rest of them followed her lead. I glanced around at their sneering faces, all identical to hers, and I felt the rage rise up from my stomach.

'I don't know which one of those tragic friends of yours he's after, but he's certainly lowered his standards.' Another burst of laughter. 'Maybe he fancies you!' she exclaimed, and there were louder hoots of laughter. 'Yeah, maybe that's it. That would explain a few things.' She laughed as if what she'd said was hilarious and her white teeth looked huge, like some kind of evil predator.

I exploded. 'What is your problem?' I suddenly blurted out, and most of them stopped laughing. 'You must be really unhappy. Is your life so sad that the only way you can get off is to snipe and bitch and make other people's lives miserable? And the rest of you,' I was louder now, and a few others from the crowd around us were watching. 'You're pathetic. You're worse than her because you just watch her do it and let her do it because you're so desperate to be popular. You must know what she's doing's wrong but you're too weak to stop her, or leave her, so you join in. You're pathetic.'

I hadn't noticed the lull in the music or the quiet that had descended as I was shouting, but most of the people close enough to hear were staring, some nodding in agreement. Further back, people were straining to see what was happening.

Gradually, the red mist lifted and I began to realise why it was so quiet. The last song of the first set was 'Bohemian Rhapsody' and I was needed on stage. Theo was playing the first couple of bars continually, probably in a bid to gain my attention and remind me I was needed. I glanced around contemptuously at the circle of girls around me, one by one. How could I have let myself be so intimidated and cowed by these people I didn't care about and had no respect for? Then I turned and walked around the corner of the stage and towards the steps.

Dan was waiting. 'Thanks,' he said quietly, 'for standing up for me. I wanted to back you up…but, it seemed like you were doing ok on your own.' He sighed, looking down at the floor. 'That took real guts. I need to grow a pair.'

'What, a pair of guts? Do we have two?'

He laughed, then breathed in sharply as if he'd just remembered something. 'Oh My God, you're on. They're going to kill me. Everyone's waiting and I said I'd come and find you.'

It was a Saturday, and after I'd finished the assignment I needed to hand in on the Monday we set off for the hospital. It had become a habit now, a routine, as much part of our lives as college, or piano lessons, or part time jobs.

Today it was just me. Tyler and Faye were at a family wedding somewhere obscure; I couldn't remember where, although Faye had definitely told me. Did that mean I was a useless friend? I made a mental note to listen to them more carefully and take an interest in their lives. Just because they weren't in a coma shouldn't mean they weren't important to me.

I arrived at three and immediately started to feel guilty about being late. Our afternoon visiting slot was two until five. Although the staff had made it clear that there were no actual visiting hours on Dan's ward, we had talked to doctors and counsellors and they'd agreed that it was pointless us spending too much time at the hospital. One of the doctors, a young Asian woman with huge kind eyes, had sat with us on the first week and discussed what to do. She told us we had to get on with our lives and do all the things we would normally do. If Dan could hear, he needed to be stimulated. If all we did was sit by his bed, it would be boring for him. He needed to be told interesting stories about what was going on in the outside world. He needed to want to come back.

I was pretty sure she was thinking about us rather than Dan, but it made sense all the same, and we stuck to the routine we'd drawn up back then.

'Sorry I'm late,' I told Dan as I sat down, 'I had to finish an assessment.'

A nurse called Cherry was fixing Dan's PICC line. 'Don't worry,' she breezed, 'your mum was in this morning.'

'What do you mean?' I snapped, shaken for a second.

Cherry seemed surprised. 'She comes in most days; I think on her dinner hour? She sits with him and talks to him like you do. Didn't she tell you? She always comes on a Saturday morning. I thought she was part of your rota?'

How did I not know that? Did everybody else know and they were hiding it from me? I was angry. Why would she come to see

Dan? She didn't even know him and the one time she'd seen him with me she'd been cold and cruel. Why would Dan want someone like her talking to him?

I would tell her to stay away. I would tell her today.

Chapter 27

I felt strangely elated after my confrontation with Amelia, as if I'd purged some kind of disease from my soul. 'Bohemian Rhapsody' was a fitting end to the first set, and everyone sang and swayed along.

During the break, another aspiring DJ took to the decks and Dan stayed to sort out his sound and lighting. The genre was a bit heavy for me, mostly rap and hip-hop, but the throng in front of the stage loved it, jumping around and chanting along. The selfie taking was still in full swing, and the crowd continually flashed and glittered.

I sat with the band on the grass, far enough away from the stage to be able to chat, and we talked about how well the first set had gone. Everyone's face was glowing with adrenaline, although maybe the heat from the lights had a little to do with that too. Theo asked me where I'd been before the last song and told me how awkward it had been waiting on stage while the crowd started muttering and fidgeting with impatience. He embellished and exaggerated as he went on and Faye and James fell about laughing. 'Shut up Theo! We're not Coldplay. You've got a future in politics ahead of you!' James chuckled.

Tyler joined us and said we were brilliant. Everyone said so. He said we needed a manager before we were taken advantage of by some unscrupulous music company executive and tied into a contract that would leave us penniless in our old age, so he was offering his services in order to protect us.

He was serious when he turned to Faye and told her how amazing she was though. He spoke to her as if she was the only person in the world and the rest of us felt like eavesdroppers. Woody gestured his head back towards the festival ground and said innocently, 'Are we going to get something to eat?' nodding at James exaggeratedly when he seemed oblivious to our ploy.

As we walked back towards the music, Theo said, 'He's got it bad for her. Do you think she fancies him?' It was directed at me; I was their best friend.

'I don't know,' I answered truthfully. If I was honest with myself, I'd been so self-absorbed over the past few weeks I hadn't really considered it seriously. I'd seen the attraction, and thought fleetingly about it, but not really studied their body language, or discussed anything with them.

The second set was supposed to begin at ten, but due to various slight hitches, Dan hadn't rearranged the equipment between sets until a quarter past. Faye and the band were back up on stage and about to start when Zainab came flying up the stairs. 'Come on,' she grabbed my arm, 'you have to come and see this.' She was pulling me out of the wings of the stage and down the steps.'

'What?' I laughed.

'I can't tell you, it's a surprise,' She was wearing a sparkly blue salwar kameez, very ethnic looking and in keeping with the theme, and her glossy black hair was in huge ringlets.

'What about Dan?' I remembered, and she sprinted back up the steps, vanished into the wings and then reappeared, dragging a bemused looking Dan behind her.

'Quick,' she yelled as she grasped my arm again and pulled us towards the back of the crowd. 'The view will be better here.'

She was jumping up and down with excitement and clapping her hands like a little girl, her huge eyes wide in anticipation. Dan and I exchanged glances and smiled.

It was dusk now, and suddenly the lights turned off, plunging the scene into darkness. Before our eyes could adjust to the lack of light, the stage was suddenly covered in multi-coloured fairy lights. There must have been thousands of them; I'd only really been aware of those inside the stage unit, but they were everywhere, spiraling up the lighting towers, covering the amplifiers over the front of the stage and at the side and all over the metal structure that held up the roof. She'd also threaded lights around the WestFest sign. There was an audible gasp of disbelief and wonder. My jaw literally dropped open, the effect was so unexpected and magical, and Zainab squealed with delight at the success of her creation.

'That is awesome,' marveled Dan, speaking for both of us. 'Where did you get them all from? How did you get them all up?'

'My dad got them as a job lot,' she explained, 'I asked the crew if they could fix them up when they were putting the stage up and they said no problem!'

After a couple of minutes, during which the band came to the front of the stage to get a better view, the music started again. It was a more modern set, comprising of eighties, nineties and noughties classics, and some contemporary songs. Dan had kept it pretty cool and alternative rather than cheesy, as befitting of a festival, and every one sang along, swayed or danced depending on the tempo of the tune for the duration. We stayed at the back, and Tyler and Olivia joined us, George having 'pulled' some nameless girl as soon as the opportunity arose, according to Tyler.

'Honestly, we spend all these weeks coordinating our look and he jumps ship at the first sniff of a snog.' He retorted, in mock irritation.

Standing there, with my friends, some close and some a little further away, I felt elated. The prom had been more than a success. It had been a triumph, and testament to the hard work of everyone involved. This prom would be remembered for ever in the minds of everyone here as a fantastic night, and tomorrow we would find out exactly how much money we had raised for the poor people our chosen charity would help. The stall holders and stage equipment hire company had agreed to split their profits for a share of the publicity, and from what I'd seen, those profits would be substantial. Everything had been professionally videoed by the mother of a student in year ten, who'd volunteered her services for free, and the videos would be on sale as soon as she could arrange it.

At first, we'd jumped on the festival theme and charity angle purely as a persuasive device to use in our speech, never really considering the genuine value of the gesture, but now I felt proud. We'd done it, and we could hold our heads up high and say we didn't spend obscene amounts of money on transport, clothes and a venue for one night, money that then could not have been put to good use. We had sacrificed those material things, would now be helping others less fortunate than ourselves, and had the best time I could have imagined in the process.

We danced and laughed and took selfies and photos of each other until the end of the set, then made our way to the stage to help pack away. The final DJ came on and played dance tracks for a while, before gradually calming the atmosphere down with some chill out music.

By midnight, the stalls were gone, along with half of the crowd, and the remainder were making their way towards the gates, before heading off in groups, maybe to an after party, or home to bed, having been picked up by parents. Woody and Theo had left in Woody's dad's van after we'd all helped load the drums, guitars and amps into it, and James said his goodbyes soon after.

We sat there on the empty stage in the dark, apart from the security lights nearer the school which stayed on all night, and the moonlight. I didn't want it to end. The sky had cleared completely now and the stars looked large and bright as I lay on my back gazing at them. Olivia said George had tagged along with the girl he'd met to an after party down by the river. She could have gone too, she said, but she just wanted to spend time with us. I wondered who she meant by 'us', but then rebuked myself for being uncharitable.

Miss Purcell came over soon after and joked, 'haven't you any homes to go to?'

I was surprised that she didn't start the question with 'ok' as usual, but I figured that was just her teaching voice, and as we weren't her students any more, she didn't feel the need to use it.

'We have to lock up soon so if you're ready we need to be making our way out.' Her tone was apologetic, as if she'd rather let us stay, but she had no choice. I knew she was just thinking about health and safety. 'Health and safety you know,' she joked, and I laughed.

'Thanks for everything you've done,' she continued. 'There were times when I thought we'd taken on too much but you were all so brilliant I needn't have worried. I think I might get a promotion on the back of all your hard work. Ok, I'll give you another ten minutes and then we're out of here.' She started walking towards where the rest of the staff were loading various things into their cars, then stopped and looked at us.

She smiled at us for a long time, and I wondered what she was thinking. 'I'm so proud of you,' she said, eventually, and continued walking.

'This is it then,' Dan sighed, and I thought I heard his voice crack. 'We won't be together like this again.'

It was true that Dan and George had opted for a different college to the other four of us, but I'd never really looked at it that way before. I thought of our table in the canteen, empty now, and soon to belong to another group, like us maybe, year nines, as we had been when we'd adopted it as our own. The college we were going to was huge, with a sprawling layout of different buildings. Would we make new friends and sit with them? Faye and I were both doing A Levels, but Tyler had chosen a BTEC in engineering and Olivia was doing an Art Foundation Diploma.

Suddenly, the enormity of the situation hit me. It really was the end, in a way, of everything we'd known. A lump formed in my throat and I had to swallow it down.

'Don't be stupid,' Olivia's voice was confident and upbeat. 'It's not like we live hundreds of miles away from each other. We have these magic things called phones. We can message each other all the time and meet up whenever we can. Remember that day at Nando's?'

I certainly did. How long ago did that seem now?

'We can do that every couple of weeks, or even every week. Let's make a deal. We'll make sure we meet up at least once a fortnight from now on unless we're out of the country, or in hospital, or dead!' She giggled and said, 'Come on, we have to shake on it or else it's not binding.'

We stood up and started shaking each other's hands, agreeing to do just that, making a date for two weeks away.

'Oh no! I'm visiting my grandma in Scotland that week,' Tyler moaned. 'You'll have to take a cardboard cut out of me for the photos.'

'I can't make it either. I'm working all week over the holidays,' Faye wailed. 'Can we do it on that weekend?'

'Working Saturday and Sunday,' I added.

'I'm labouring for my dad during the week,' Dan said quietly, but I sensed the apprehension in his voice nevertheless.

Was this what it was going to be like? never being able to synchronise calendars, drifting further apart until we only shared the odd message on the group chat and seeing pictures of each other having contrived fun with our new friends.

Faye started to cry. 'I'm sorry,' she sobbed, 'I can't help it.'

Olivia put her arms around Faye and they hugged for a while, then Tyler stepped forward and put his arms around both of them. They leant their heads in so they were touching and just stayed there, unmoving.

I looked at Dan and our eyes met. He stepped towards me until he was close, enough to hug? or kiss? He stopped, and we stood, close to each other, but so far away. I was unable to move, to tear my eyes away from his, but the barrier separating us was too strong to break through. We could have reached a couple of inches and touched hands, or lips, but instead we were frozen in an agonising tableaux of confusion and fear. I could almost hear the screaming torment in his mind, mirroring mine.

Then Tyler shouted, 'Hey, come on, group hug!' and the spell was broken. We moved away from each other, backing first, as if to increase the distance between us and relieve the tension, before walking over to the others and joining the circle they'd created. Two spaces, on either side of Olivia. Was I grateful for that or not? Would it have been agony to have had to put my arms around Dan and feel his warmth beside me? Or was that what I wanted? My head spun, and my legs began to feel weak. I'd never fainted, but I assumed this was what it was like and I took a deep breath and shook my head to clear it.

'I'm proud of us too,' Dan said quietly, and I thought I heard his voice crack slightly.

After a couple of minutes, Olivia broke free of the circle and hugged me. Then Tyler was hugging Olivia and Faye hugging Dan, and we made our way around, saying our goodbyes and promising we'd see each other all the time. We'd stay close and not lose touch. Our friendship was too important to let go.

Dan was the last one I came to, and my heart pounded as I embraced him. There was no way out. Anything else would have seemed strange in the circumstances, so we threw our arms around each other and hugged tightly. I thought I felt his heart thudding against my chest for a moment, and then we let go.

'Thanks for everything,' he whispered, 'Bye Jake.'

Part 2

'It must be faulty,' Dad complained. 'all the other ones fit perfectly so how can this one be so wrong?'

'You must have forced one of the others in Mark. Either you or Jake has got to have forced one or it would fit. They cut it out of one big sheet of cardboard with the picture already on so they have to fit.' I could tell Mum was getting irritated. The jigsaw my dad and I had just finished had covered one half of the dining room table for over a week and it was driving her insane. I could see her glancing at it like it was her arch enemy while we were eating, and now, all she wanted to do was say, 'Well done. Let's take a picture. Great. I'll put it away now and be able to breathe again.'

'Did you force any in Jake?' Dad was oblivious to her discomfort, and I had the feeling he might just take the whole thing apart and start again.

I said I didn't think I had, but I might have done when I was rushing, and offered to check the whole 1000 pieces to make sure.

I often wondered what had attracted my mum and dad to each other. He was so calm and laid back, with a dry sense of humour, whereas she was the most highly-strung person I knew. It was probably because she was my mum, because she tried hard not to show her anxious, irritable side to others (often unsuccessfully) but I was always aware that the slightest deviation from what she expected might set her off. As a result, I felt that I was always looking ahead, locating obstacles in her path and removing them, anticipating the explosion that might ensue if I didn't.

When they'd had a drink or two I thought I could see it. Mum looked younger and prettier; She kept herself slim and never went out without her shiny brown hair blow-dried in a bob that slightly flicked out at the ends and subtle make-up. She wore lots of bright colours too; It was weird the way that lately, her hair and clothes had become the only cheerful things about her. Dad smiled more after a couple of drinks too, and I could see that he could probably be considered attractive for his age. He'd be more sociable and take control a little more and she'd relax and let him. They'd laugh and become more affectionate; I even saw them kiss a couple of times at house parties.

The best times were when Tyler and his mum and dad came round. Tyler's dad would crack everyone up with his impressions and anecdotes, and my dad would always sort out the games. We'd play in teams. Tyler's sister was six years older and even when we were only seven, she was at the point where all she wanted to do was go on Facebook, when Facebook was all the rage. She'd sulk if forced to play so I think in the end they just gave in; it made the teams equal, which was a second benefit. Tyler and I would be on separate teams and the whole game would be about letting us think we were valuable members of the team, but as we grew older, we always wanted to be on the same team. Mum would say, 'We're not going to let you win,' but they did for a while, and then they didn't. Everyone said we were telepathic, and sometimes I used to think we were, it was so uncanny how similar our trains of thought were.

It was ages since we'd had a games night. Obviously, things had been rocky between Tyler's parents for a while, and I'm sure Mum knew, and probably Dad too. Although they were back together now, we still hadn't seen them. Maybe Mum and Dad knew something I didn't.

I leant over the jigsaw and began to search, methodically at first, but that became unbelievably boring very quickly so I stood up and scanned the whole picture. I'm not sure how I thought that was going to work because we'd already been doing that for over half an hour with no success.

The picture was a painting of a shipwreck, so there were large patches of stormy sea which had taken ages to put together as they were so similar. Dad had completed the sinking ship and worked outwards, and I had taken the easy option of a life boat with one survivor in and some rocks on the left hand side, before starting on the multi-coloured sky, which was harder than it looked. I had no idea who'd bought the jigsaw for Dad (I think he'd once said he quite enjoyed them and after that, he'd been inundated) but he hated waste, and although it was clearly something he'd had for years, he had to help it fulfil its destiny at least once.

I leant back, allowing the light to shine on the joins in different areas, hoping that I'd suddenly see that one piece was slightly out of kilter, sticking up infinitesimally more than the others, or that the picture had lifted up a little from being squeezed into a place where it didn't fit.

There was nothing, and I went back to the original plan, examining each piece individually and hoping the offending fragment was towards the top, where I'd started, rather than the bottom.

Half an hour later, I reached the bottom, still none the wiser. I tried the rogue piece again but it was hopeless, not only was the shape completely wrong, even the shade of the sea in the last space was different. I put it back down on the table; it looked so isolated there I had an irrational feeling of empathy. I knew what it was like not to fit in when everybody else did, to try to squash yourself, unsuccessfully, into a different shape. Maybe if I cut a couple of legs off and taped them onto the other side no-one would notice. I would notice though. I would know.

I slumped over the jigsaw, brooding, turning the exiled piece over in my fingers. What solution could I come up with? Dad would hate the jigsaw not to have been finished correctly, and I understood how he felt. As a mathematician, your whole life is about finding the correct solution, and it was frustrating me too. On the other hand, I didn't think Mum would survive another night of not being able to tidy the kitchen properly, plus she hated the painting because it was depressing.

I decided I'd leave it and come back to it. In half an hour the incorrectly placed piece would probably be screaming, 'Get me out of here! My square interlocking pieces have been squeezed into round holes and they're killing me!'

Dad was watching tennis when I sat down and Mum was in the shower. 'How did you do?' he asked.

'I looked everywhere but I can't find it,' I groaned. 'I'll try again later.'

'Give over,' he laughed, 'put it back in the box and your mum can take it to the charity shop. Or is that too evil?' He lifted one eyebrow and looked at me with the evilest expression he could muster.

I laughed too, with relief. I didn't know my dad half as well as I thought I did. Obviously he was more laid back than he was a mathematician, at home anyway.

'Jake,' he called as I headed back to the kitchen. I turned to him and he was smiling meaningfully. 'I'm proud of you. You know that don't you? I'll always be proud of you.'

Our eyes met for a long moment, and then he turned back to the tennis. I wanted to say yes, and to hug him, but the moment had passed. For a short time, I hung there awkwardly before leaving the room.

Maybe I was the one who was desperate to fit the piece in. I looked at the lone piece, 999 pieces that fit perfectly and only one that didn't. Picking it up I put it in my pocket, mocking myself as I did so; how ridiculous to identify with a jigsaw piece.

I pulled the jigsaw apart and put it back in the box, but not before taking the piece with the tiny lone survivor on it and putting it in my pocket next to the other castaway.

I'd put the jigsaw in the recycling when the bags were out. One ill-fitting piece might be funny, but two missing pieces was just mean.

Chapter 29

The summer holidays flew by. I worked during the weekend at a factory within walking distance from our house, packing gifts for a catalogue company; It amazed me that some people had already ordered their Christmas presents in August. It was easy work, I was allowed to wear my headphones and the pay was more than I'd expected. Often, they'd ask me to work during the week too, and I'd jump at the chance. I'd started saving for a moped to ride to college and give me a bit of independence and I'd really been bitten by the saving bug. Logging on to my account each week, I'd enjoy the rapid accumulation of my funds. Having chosen a make and model, the dwindling difference between how much money I had, and how much I needed, was exhilarating.

Mum was against the idea. How was I going to pay for the insurance and the petrol, not to mention repairs if it broke down? She was never one to look on the bright side.

I saw Tyler as much as I could. I say saw, but most of our interaction was via the games we'd play. Mum kept nagging me to go out and actually see my friends; I think it irritated her the way we'd be laughing and chatting with each other and playing the same game, but not in the same room. I tried to explain to her that it was a culture thing; this was the way people communicated these days, but she didn't understand. 'Why doesn't Tyler just come here and you can play together?' she'd complain.

'We are playing together,' I'd reply, but she'd just tut, and sweep out of my room as if I were from another planet.

Dad just teased me about my headphone hair, which I had to admit, sometimes looked more extreme than others. No matter how much water I rubbed into it, there was still a line across the middle of my head.

We spent ten days in Italy, which was my mum and dad's favourite place; they'd honeymooned in Venice and loved the food, the architecture, and the weather obviously. I enjoyed it, especially the food, but it was coming to a point where I missed my friends and missed gaming more than I liked spending time with my parents. It might have been different if I'd had a brother or sister to share it with, but they'd struggled to conceive me, and afterwards had been forced to accept that I was all they were going to get. Maybe that was why I felt so responsible for Mum's moods and general dissatisfaction. I was all they had, and I wasn't good enough.

Tyler's holiday unfortunately didn't coincide with mine, so there was a month in the middle of the summer where I felt very sorry for myself. All of us chatted sporadically, but everyone seemed so busy, and I was anxious about feeling rejected if I suggested getting together. It was crazy really. These were my best friends, but I was acting as though they were strangers.

In a way, some of us were becoming strangers to each other. George had always been Tyler's friend as opposed to mine, and he had started to splinter off from the group way before the prom; my relationship with Olivia, once so close, had never fully recovered from the misunderstanding over Dan, and Dan was working hard all week for his dad. He occasionally commented on the group chat, and I'd even had a couple of private messages from him, but it was all very impersonal, platonic and decreasing as the time progressed.

We had nothing in common: I was useless at sport and he was a superstar and he was a Greek-god whereas I was a mere mortal. Perhaps that's why I didn't message him until he'd messaged me first. I thought about it, but always discounted the idea. He was the one with the power, the superior one, so I waited for him to contact me.

It did occur to me that Dan didn't actually know I was gay. Nobody knew I was gay. But how could he not know? What had passed between us was obvious wasn't it? Then again, I didn't know how he felt about me, because he hadn't told me. And how could he possibly know what I felt about him if he didn't even know I was gay?

And the others. I was lying to them every time I spoke to them or messaged them. The person they thought they knew didn't really exist; he did once, but over the last few years he had disappeared and been replaced by another version of himself. I wanted to think I could just tell them and everything would stay the same, but I knew it was impossible.

I was painfully aware of people's opinions about homosexuality. Obviously, my ears pricked up at the first sign of blatant homophobia, but most of my friends, family and even acquaintances would argue vociferously that they weren't the slightest bit prejudiced against anyone on the grounds of sexuality. They would never make deliberately homophobic comments, but they were products of their environment and would say things in front of me that they never would if they knew I was gay. Olivia was a case in point. She'd used the word 'normal' when arguing that Dan couldn't be gay. She'd said, 'They think it's normal,' implying that it wasn't.

Other people talked about nature, stopping short of using the word 'unnatural' but the implication was there. At barbecues or family parties, when the subject came up after a few drinks, tongues would loosen and I'd hear things: 'I don't mind as long as they keep themselves to themselves and don't force it on everybody else'; 'Why does every soap have to have one now'; and the one which frightened me the most, 'I feel so sorry for his parents.'

I often felt I was a spy from another world, attending the party dressed as a human being to secretly gauge human reactions. 'I like them. I've nothing against them,' the humans would say, 'but I wouldn't want to be one, or for one of my family or friends to be one.'

It was such a mess.

Chapter 30

Her reaction when I told her was not what I expected. She didn't cry or plead. She simply said, 'No Jake, you can't tell me what to do. Yes, I visit Dan because I feel guilty, obviously I feel guilty about the way I treated you, and I feel guilty about the fact I never met him, but there's no point in feeling guilty and doing nothing. I've changed Jake. I know you don't believe me and you say you don't care anyway, but I'm a completely different person now. I'm ashamed of everything I said and everything I did. I've told you that a hundred times but you don't hear it. I can't make amends with you. You've made that clear. But maybe I can with Dan. Maybe he'll forgive me when he wakes up.'

'So it's all about making you feel better?' I growled. 'All you care about is yourself.'

She screwed her eyes up in pain. Was that another wrinkle I'd caused? 'You're so wrong Jake. I love you so much. But I can't reach you. Maybe I can reach Dan.'

She walked away from me slowly, her shoulders hunched. I thought of the million times she'd told me to stand up straight and put my shoulders back. 'When you go for an interview,' she'd say, 'Your posture is the first thing the employer sees. If you look nervous and frightened, you'll never get the job.'

'I'm eight,' I'd think. 'I don't want a job.' But it stuck, and my shoulders were always back. What did I read into her posture now? I thought about it for a while. Despair? Depression?

Finally, I knew what it was. It was defeat. She looked defeated.

She continued to visit Dan. Tyler told me nobody else had known about it either, which at least meant it was only her deceit. She was the only one lying to me. Could I hate her any more?

Chapter 31

Results day was a blur. I was so full of nervous excitement during the days leading up to it that I struggled to eat at times (which was a first for me). Faye, Olivia and I met up at the gates at half past eight as agreed, all of us unable to stand still or talk about anything else. We waited for George, who had said he'd be there, but when he still hadn't arrived twenty-five minutes later, we decided to make our way in. Tyler was still on holiday and Dan was working; I thought it was weird that he couldn't get the time off to collect his GCSE results given he was working for his dad, and the negative side of me thought maybe he was simply avoiding us.

We'd been told the results would be available at nine, and as we went through the doors, George came puffing up, apologising. 'I overslept,' he panted. 'I think my mum turned the alarm off.'

'You slept?' Olivia's mouth gaped. 'I haven't slept properly for days!'

In my heart of hearts, I knew I'd done well. I knew I'd been ultra-prepared and I was good at exams anyway; to a certain extent, I enjoyed them, like when you play a game you know you're better at than everybody else. The only problem with exams is the time you have to wait before you find out whether you've won.

As I'd known they would be, my results were outstanding, and myself and four others were ushered over to have our photograph taken for an article in the local newspaper. 'Westfield High Achievers', the headline read. It was good to have a reason to smile so much, as I don't think I could have physically wiped the smile off my face if I'd tried. My face ached from smiling, I was so elated. Luckily, it seemed like everyone was happy. We'd all succeeded, and the next two years of our futures were mapped out.

At the end of August, Faye sent out a group text suggesting we meet up at Nando's again. She couldn't possibly have known the anguish the last visit there had caused me, and knowing what I knew now, I felt very embarrassed about my reaction. My jealousy of Olivia proved to have been completely unfounded, and even if it hadn't been, I'd behaved childishly.

We arranged to meet on a Friday night, not ideal for me because of work, but I looked forward to it so much. My mum drove Tyler and I into town. Dad usually shared the taxi driving with Tyler's dad, but Mum said he'd had a hard day at work so she'd fill in. She was quiet on the way there, even with Tyler, which was unusual; I put it down to her being irritated at having to drive.

We were the first to arrive and grabbed a table by the window so we could people watch while we ate. 'Did Dan tell you why he's not coming?' Tyler asked as he sat down.

'I only know what you know from the chat,' I replied. I think I might have been a bit snappy, because in truth, I was hurt by the lack of communication from Dan, especially when his thanks had seemed so heartfelt on prom night.

Tyler was oblivious. 'Don't turn round now,' he whispered covertly behind his hand. I turned around immediately.

'I said don't! You idiot! Don't turn round!' he was shaking his head and laughing. He pretended to talk about something else for thirty seconds then tried again. 'Don't turn round yet, but I think that girl over there,' he gestured his head obviously (if she had been looking the game would have been up!) to your (he calculated) right, I think she's got it bad for you. Obviously hasn't brought her specs!' he grinned.

I blushed furiously. Would I have been embarrassed if I'd been straight? Maybe a little. But this was not about a girl fancying me, it was about lying to my best friend. If he knew I was gay he would never have said it, and if I told him now, he would be embarrassed. Not that I was planning on telling him anyway. I was ignoring it, like I had done for the two years I'd known the truth deep in my heart.

'The one in the black top with the big…eyes!' he gestured clumsily again. He'd never make a spy, or a diplomat.

I forced myself to look in the direction his eyebrows were lifting towards just as the table of girls looked over. It was obviously me, because as soon as they realised, they spun around and fell about giggling and the one in the black top put her hands over her face in embarrassment and desperately tried to shush them.

'She's fit,' said Tyler, eyebrows leaping up and down in a 'what do you think. Are you up for a bit of that?' fashion.

I could see she was a pretty girl, alternative looking, with shiny brown hair in a cool, angled, chin length bob and a nose stud, but that's all she was to me. I could see why a girl would be attractive to other boys, but I'd never felt that attraction.

When I was younger, I just thought it was 'normal'. None of my friends had girlfriends and we just hung around and played on our consoles and never really mentioned girls. When Faye and Olivia started hanging around with us they were just friends that were girls; it didn't seem strange. Faye went to the same primary school as Tyler and me and she met Olivia and introduced her to us when we first moved to Westfield. Tyler brought George in the same way. Lewis, another good friend from primary school, moved abroad in year eight so that just left the five of us. I never looked at Faye and Olivia in that way, and I never looked at any girl in that way. It was only when other friends did that I started to realise.

I think my friends just thought I was shy, or a late starter 'in that way'. Olivia once told me that a girl in her form fancied me, and I must have visibly squirmed, because she laughed and said, 'You're good looking you know? Now the rest of your face has caught up with your teeth. You'll have to get used to girls fancying you.'

I'd gone home that night and looked in the full length mirror in Mum and Dad's room. I had certainly grown; I was as tall as Dad now, maybe five feet eleven, and since I'd had my braces off, my teeth did look completely different. The front two used to be much longer than the rest, making me look like a rabbit I thought, but they were almost in line with the rest now, and I could see what Olivia meant. Without realising, I'd turned into a man. My head was actually bigger and now my teeth looked pretty good. I supposed I *was* actually quite good looking, in an ordinary way. Brown hair, grey eyes, still a few pounds overweight, but if I was honest, not that you'd notice now if you saw me dressed, and nice teeth.

'She's ok,' I managed to force out, squirming in my seat. What if Tyler said something? What if he asked them to join us, or one of them came over and asked us to join them? I remembered Dan's story about Amelia and I began to panic.

Tyler was, very noticeably, observing them in what he considered was a discreet manner, when I saw Faye through the window and breathed a huge sigh of relief. Olivia followed her inside and they made their way to our table smiling. After lots of hugging, Faye sat next to Tyler and Olivia took the seat next to me.

No doubt black top girl would think she was my girlfriend and direct her attention elsewhere.

I felt safe for a moment, but Tyler nudged Faye in the ribs. 'Ten o'clock,' he muttered, and started doing the whole furtive act again.

'What?' whispered Olivia loudly. 'What are you talking about?'

'That girl over there in the black top.' Both of them turned around and I cringed. 'She's got the hots for Jake big style, been staring over since we got here. And now you've come and cramped his style,' he laughed.

'Can we just order? I'm not interested and you're just making it embarrassing. Will you stop looking over? I'm not interested, ok!' I was raising my voice and getting upset and it was obvious.

Faye looked at me meaningfully. 'Shut up Tyler,' she chided. 'We haven't seen each other for ages. I want to know all the gossip.' She picked up two menus, passed Olivia one and said, 'I'm starving.'

She held her menu for Tyler to share and he took hold of his side and began studying it closely. Our eyes met over the table and she smiled sympathetically, and held my gaze for a few seconds.

I tried to regain my composure and enjoy the night, but it was ruined for me from then on. I had to tell them. The pretence was agonising, and it was only going to get worse. There was an anxious knot in my stomach all night, a knot which was growing and growing. Before, I could control it, focus on something else and forget it for a while, but now it was taking over.

I couldn't remember the last time I'd felt content and relaxed and I knew I couldn't live like this.

Chapter 32

If Tyler was surprised by my behaviour that night, he didn't mention it. We gamed together as usual for an hour or two most nights as the weather didn't seem to realise it was summer (it had rained every day for the whole holiday) and sometimes we'd go round to each other's houses to appease our mums; apparently, Tyler's mum was as clueless as mine when it came to modern style socialising.

Faye private messaged me more than usual I thought. I inferred a concerned, sympathetic tone under her breezy comments and wondered why. Did she suspect? Had I done anything to cause her to suspect? I replayed the last few months in my mind. Unless she had guessed my feelings for Dan?

Dan's messages had all but stopped. I missed them, but not seeing or hearing from him at least meant I wasn't permanently hanging on to an impossible dream.

The first day at Beaumont College was exciting and nerve-wracking at the same time. I arrived at the main entrance with Tyler, but our courses were at opposite ends of the campus so we agreed to message when we were ready to leave and meet back there.

There were about twenty students in my first class, more boys than girls which was strange. I was used to girl heavy classes at Westfield as all the set ones were generally three quarters full of girls. In this math's class, there were thirteen boys and seven girls. I quickly recognised Will, who'd been in my classes pretty much since year seven; we'd never been friends, but would always acknowledge each other on the corridor and say hello if we saw each other in town. Luckily he spotted me almost at the same time and I was relieved when he shouted my name and waved me over.

Will had grown massively over the holidays. He used to be very small and skinny with round glasses, and we always said it was ironic that he looked like Will from The Inbetweeners, but he seemed to have shed his geekiness with his glasses. He looked relieved not to be sitting on his own any more, and when we saw Matty, another Westfield graduate, we motioned him over too.

We walked to the canteen together after the lesson, and chatted about the teacher (less monotone than Mr Fearns, the math's teacher at Westfield, and with less eccentric fashion sense) and what we'd been up to over the holidays.

After about ten minutes, Faye came bouncing in, saw me and rushed over. Maybe she didn't bounce in, but she was completely transformed from the Faye I'd known up until recently. Her stoop was all but gone, and she walked confidently and with her head held high.

Behind her was a good-looking boy who could have been Tyler's brother. The resemblance was so uncanny I think my jaw may have dropped a little. 'This is Olly,' she announced, before introducing Will and me. Matty introduced himself, as he and Faye had never really known each other at school.

'A pleasure,' Olly beamed theatrically, leaning over to shake our hands one by one. He had the most perfectly proportioned white teeth I'd ever seen, apart from the very front two, one of which ever so slightly overlapped the other. Like Dan's, this tiny flaw actually made him look more attractive. His hair was exactly like Tyler's, longish, curly and unruly, although Olly's was chestnut brown in contrast to Tyler's blonde, and whereas Tyler tanned to a nut colour if he even saw the sun, Olly was paler and heavily freckled. He was dressed in yellow jeans and a faded blue hoody which matched his eyes. On anyone else the jeans would have looked quite ridiculous, I thought, but on Olly, they just looked right somehow.

They would also be roughly the same height, which emphasised both their similarities and their differences. They looked like the same avatar in different colours. I wondered whether that was what had drawn Faye to him, but she didn't mention it, and neither did I.

Olly was what my dad would have called 'a character', another thing he had in common with Tyler. He had the rest of us in stitches for forty-five minutes before the bell rang and we went back to class.

Will and I made our way to further math's and Matty went off to his computer programming class, planning to meet in the canteen the next day at the same table, or as near as we could manage. I was having a great day.

'He's definitely gay!' Will leaned in and said discreetly as we arrived at our further math's classroom.

My stomach twisted into more vicious knots. 'Does it matter?' I said, in a more cheerful tone than I felt.

'Nahh! He's hilarious. He reminds me of Graham Norton. You know, that Irish one. My mum loves him. His accent might be what does it, or the way he laughs like him?'

I relaxed a little. Olly was funny. My stomach was still hurting from laughing at his anecdotes. He was also unashamedly camp.

What must it be like to just be yourself and everyone love you anyway? I felt a prick of envy but quickly admonished myself. Who said I couldn't be myself? A tiny chink of hope opened up in the distance.

When I arrived home, I was impatient to talk about my day. I felt it was the beginning of something new, not just college, but in my life. I needed to tell someone how positive I suddenly felt. Not why, it was far too soon for that, I just needed to share my happiness.

I threw my bag down on the stairs and went into the kitchen to find Mum. When she wasn't there, I shouted up the stairs, 'Mum!' but she flew out of the living room door, finger to her lips, shushing me frantically.

'Your dad's asleep,' she hissed, then dragged me into the kitchen. 'He was sick at work today and one of the partners brought him home. He's probably eaten something that didn't agree with him. Let him sleep and take your bag upstairs. You need to tidy your bedroom too. I asked you to tidy it yesterday.'

She didn't ask about college, and the bubble of excitement inside me all but deflated. I tiptoed past the living-room door, then opened it a crack and looked at Dad. He was asleep, but he looked grey, and thin and old. His breathing was raspy and uneven. When had that happened? He was only fifty-one, but he looked seventy.

Chapter 33

The next few weeks passed quickly. There was so much to learn and what I'd heard about A Levels being more challenging than GCSEs was definitely true. I found I really had to work hard to keep completely on top of the work, especially in further math's, but I was still determined to achieve the best results I possibly could. I still secretly wanted to beat everyone else too, but these were the best mathematicians from a number of schools, who had chosen the subject because they were good at it, and I could see it was going to be more of a challenge than I'd anticipated.

Tyler and I caught the bus to college together, and met after lessons to travel home together most nights. The main change was separate canteens. It took about fifteen minutes to cross the campus, and we both agreed it would leave us too little time to eat after getting there and back so we'd eat in our own canteens. If I did buy a moped, I wouldn't see Tyler at all during a regular day, and that, coupled with Mum's antagonism towards the idea, pushed the notion to the back of my mind.

Faye and Olly had settled into a pattern of splitting breaks and lunchtimes. Sometimes they'd sit with the drama crowd, who were a colourful bunch, lots of multi-coloured hair and piercings, and sometimes they'd sit with Will, Matty and myself. I expected Faye to start wearing more ethnic style clothes and dying her hair pink. Or maybe going over to the dark side; some of them tended to wear mostly black, but those people would also sport gothic make-up and piercings, which, to me, made them metaphorically colourful. She didn't though, just continued to be herself, apparently uninfluenced by the trends around her. Olly's eclectic style didn't really fit into any genre; it was definitely unique. Nothing he wore ever really matched; he'd wear shorts with a jumper and coat, or track suit bottoms and a smart blazer. The colours and patterns always clashed, but somehow he made it look right.

"Can you imagine one of us in that outfit!' Will said one day. 'We'd look complete idiots.' He shook his head. 'It does look kind of cool on Olly though? Why is that?'

The more I saw of Olly, the more I was drawn to him. It wasn't just the humour. He was one of the nicest people I thought I'd ever met. Miss Purcell would kill me for using a word so vague as 'nice', but it was the most accurate way I could describe him. He was entertaining, but that was only one side of him. Whereas a lot of funny people seem to find it hard to listen to others (I think they spend the time when they're not talking thinking up their next quip, rather than concentrating on what other people are saying), Olly was a great listener, and he made everyone feel that they were interesting and funny too. I even felt I became more interesting and funny in his presence, as if some of his humour was seeping through into me via a process of personality osmosis.

Will and Matty appeared to like him too, and on the days when it was just the three of us, I think we all felt something was missing. Even when other students sat with us, it seemed kind of grey without Olly and Faye.

Half way through the term, Faye asked if we'd like to watch a show the drama class were putting on which would serve as their first assessment. They'd been asked if they wanted to invite family and friends, so hopefully the audience would be sympathetic and not too critical of what would be their first public performance. It was a very exclusive ticket, Olly added. Imagine being able to say, 'I was there when Olly Dillon performed his first soliloquy.' He held up his hand and spoke dramatically as if he was Hamlet talking to Yorick's skull.

'He's not doing a soliloquy!' Faye shook her head and tutted in mock exasperation. 'Don't put them off! We do want an audience,' she tutted. 'We're working in pairs so he has to let me have a look in,' she explained. 'We have five minutes to capture exactly who we are using music, acting, mime, costume, staging…anything really.'

'We have two and a half minutes each to show everybody exactly who we are, what our hopes and dreams are and how we'll achieve them. Should be a doddle. How do I mime 'gentleman of leisure?' he grinned. 'No, seriously, we're scared to death, aren't we Faye? We were hysterical before. This calm demeanour is a testament to our superior acting ability.'

The show was scheduled for the last week of the half term, and I was excited to see what Faye and Olly could produce. I hoped Faye would sing, although I knew it was about more than just having a good voice.

A couple of nights after telling us about the show, Faye messaged. 'What am I like?' she put, with a wide eyed emoji.

'What do you mean?' I replied, with a confused emoji.

'What sort of person am I? Olly's got loads of ideas but I can't think of anything for me.'

I thought for a few minutes. Faye was just Faye, solid and reliable and loyal and kind, but I didn't think she meant that. She wanted to shine too, and beside Olly, it might be difficult. 'You're you!' I messaged back, 'You don't change for anyone, you don't follow the crowd and you don't have to market yourself or pretend to be something you're not.'

It was true. Faye never posted filtered, Photo-shopped pictures; in fact, she rarely posted any pictures, not for any reason, I thought, but because she didn't feel the need to. She wore minimal make-up and her blonde hair either in a pony-tail or just straight and natural. She always looked good, but in a casual, effortless way. Most days she'd wear jeans and trainers with either a T shirt or a sweater, depending on the weather. She didn't have her hair coloured or her nails or eyelashes extended. She was Faye, and you could take her as you found her or not at all.

'Thanks Jake,' she replied, followed by a smiley emoji. 'I have an idea!'

Olivia sent a group text the same night. She said we all had to meet up. It was a month since we'd seen each other and she was missing us.

'Do you think they'd mind if I brought Olly?' Faye asked the next day.

I said no, but it did occur to me that Olivia had wanted it to be 'just us', the old gang back together again.

On the way home, I asked Tyler what he thought and his reaction was particularly defensive. He tried not to show it, but he was obviously irritated. Maybe I should have advised Faye not to bring Olly this time, but selfishly, I wanted him to be there. Increasingly, I enjoyed his company more than anybody's. He made me feel comfortable with myself. Seeing the way he was accepted by everybody, not just accepted, loved by everybody, made me feel that there was hope for me, and I was a happier person in his presence.

In the end, only four of us met up, in Nando's again at Olivia's request. Dan had sent his apologies; he was playing in a football tournament for his college team, George simply messaged that the date clashed with a prior engagement and told us to have fun, and ironically, Olivia also pulled out at the last moment, having been struck down with a mystery illness that morning. Uncharitably, I wondered if the mystery illness would have materialised if Dan were coming.

Like the last time, Tyler and I were first to arrive, and he was definitely not in the best of moods. After five minutes I asked him if he was ok, had anything happened? Maybe there was trouble at home again, but he replied that he was fine. Even that was snapped, so I rambled on about my course, which must have been beyond boring, as we waited.

Faye arrived next and hugged Tyler warmly, while he was a little stand-offish, which was very odd. The atmosphere was beginning to make me feel uncomfortable, and I couldn't wait for Olly to get there. He would have us in stitches in minutes, I thought, and everything would be ok.

Eventually, he came through the door and swivelled his head around looking for us. I stood up and waved vigorously, but as I sat down I saw the sour look on Tyler's face.

Faye and Olly hugged dramatically, and I smiled. We'd been teasing them both for weeks about turning all theatrical, and they were now playing up to the stereotype and acting out the most exaggerated gestures they could. I guessed it was an in joke, because Tyler clearly didn't find it funny.

Faye introduced the two of them and we made pleasant chit chat for a few minutes (I say pleasant, it really wasn't, and I was mystified as to what was going wrong). Tyler was monosyllabic to the point of being rude, and Olly had reigned in his flamboyance to the point where he barely even seemed camp any more. Faye and I tried to lighten the atmosphere, retelling old anecdotes which Olly politely laughed at and new ones which Tyler struggled to raise a smile at. It was painful, and after a strained meal, we excused ourselves and left.

'What the hell was all that about?' I barked at Tyler on the way home; We'd decided to walk as it was only half past nine. 'It was embarrassing. I know you'd rather Olly hadn't been there but you could've made an effort and pretended you didn't have a problem with him being gay. I thought you'd be relieved when you found out he wasn't a threat to you but obviously that's not the issue.' I couldn't believe my best friend would treat someone like that and I strode off ahead of him. I didn't want to talk to him or walk with him.

I didn't look around, and at that point I was so angry I intended to walk home without even speaking to him. It was dark now and I was pacing from street light to street light, only looking up to cross roads and check I was going the right way. My head was spinning.

'Jake!' Tyler shouted, after a few minutes, and after I didn't answer, 'Jake, stop! Will you stop, for God's sake stop!' I heard his steps; he was running now and then he grabbed my arm and spun me round. I couldn't quite read his expression. It could have been anger or frustration but soon turned to uncertainty, like he was wrestling with an important decision. He took a deep breath and exhaled, blowing out the air like it was an effort.

'I don't give a shit that Olly's gay! I couldn't care less. Faye told me weeks ago anyway.'

'So why treat him like a leper back there? You made it painfully clear you didn't like him and wanted to get out of there as fast as you could. Why else would you do that? I thought your attitude was because you thought Faye fancied him. I was looking forward to the look of relief on your face when you realised.'

We were passing the park and Tyler sat down on a bench. The night was quiet and still, and sitting under the street light, he looked like a prisoner about to be interrogated.

'You remember when you told me I had something no-one else had? That I'd always succeed because I had that…that thing that you couldn't put your finger on?'

'The X factor,' I remembered.

'Well I don't, do I?' He challenged me to answer. 'I don't have what no-one else has do I? Not anymore, because Olly has loads of it doesn't he? More than me. He's got tons of it, hasn't he? Faye hasn't stopped talking about how funny he is and how much everyone likes him since the first day at college. You and her spend all your time messaging about some hilarious thing he's done or said. The group chat's like the Olly appreciation society now.'

I couldn't tell him how relieved I was. My best friend wasn't homophobic, he was just jealous and grumpy. I didn't quite know how to deal with it though. What could I say? How could I reassure him that just because Olly had charisma, didn't mean that he hadn't? Just because we liked Olly, didn't mean he'd replaced Tyler in our hearts.

'I can't believe you thought I didn't like Olly because he was gay,' Tyler's tone was incredulous now. 'What the hell made you jump to that conclusion? Have you ever heard me say anything that would make you think I was homophobic?'

Not intentionally, I thought.

'I even thought you might be gay at one point,' he laughed mirthlessly. 'You know, you're crap at football and you hate sport, I always beat you on Call of Duty (It wasn't true; he was just making a joke), and you never join in when we talk about '*birds*'.' He emphasised the word birds because I'd once pulled him up on it (I think it was something mum had been lecturing me about) and the other boys had fallen about laughing.

The adrenaline that had been pumping through my body for the last few minutes probably had something to do with what happened next.

I could have reacted in the way he expected me to, and allowed the lie to remain between us, but then it would have meant the lie grew bigger. It was one thing not to have told Tyler the truth, but responding to this in the way he expected me to, laughing as if it was ridiculous, was tantamount to saying to him, 'I'm not gay!' and that would be patently saying, 'I don't trust you…I don't know you at all.'

My hesitation was all he needed. I wondered whether he had seriously considered the possibility before and had purposely brought up the issue to gauge my reaction, giving me an opportunity to reveal my secret. He stood up and took a couple of steps towards me.

'Jake…Jake?'

I had to tell the truth at some point. Why not now? There was never going to be an ideal time to do it, was there? But I couldn't force the words out. What would I say? And how? 'Actually, I am gay. So now you know, let's just carry on like nothing's changed; everything's just the same.' Instead, I just stood there, staring at the floor, as still as a statue, while the silence grew more and more oppressive.

'Jake,' Tyler repeated softly, 'Are you? Are you gay?'

The silence was roaring; my stomach was churning and I felt light-headed. I waited for him to say something else, to make the decision for me and take control.

In the end, I couldn't stand it, 'Yeah.'

He didn't say anything. He just walked back to the bench and sat down, leaving me standing there in the darkness. A car drove past, but as it disappeared in the distance, the silence became even more apparent. I could hear the pulsing of blood around my brain.

After perhaps five minutes, he spoke. 'How long have you,' he searched for the right word, 'known.'

'Since about year nine.'

'Are you sure?'

I laughed bitterly and he was quick to apologise. Like I'd put myself through this for a joke.

'Why didn't you tell me? Why didn't you tell us?'

'Because I didn't know how to,' I admitted, eventually, 'I blocked it out of my mind a lot of the time and pretended it wasn't happening. I just concentrated on something else and it went away.'

I imagined the cogs turning in his mind. I imagined what he'd be thinking. 'What do I feel? What should I feel? What should I say?'

'It doesn't matter,' he said, like I'd spilled something on the carpet and he was trying to make me feel better. 'It's fine. You're still the same person. It doesn't make any difference.'

All the right things he was saying should have made me feel better. I should be relieved and hugging him with gratitude, but it didn't feel right somehow. The words felt emotionless and blank, like he was reading from a script: How to react when your best friend tells you he's gay.

'Ok,' I said. I felt like I should say thank you, but I couldn't do it. He'd said all the right things but I felt so desolate and alone, as if someone had died. I knew it was unfair of me but I couldn't help it. The knot in my stomach threatened to take over my whole body. 'Come on,' I said, and started walking again.

We came to Tyler's house first and he turned in. 'See you tomorrow?' he asked.

'Yeah, see you tomorrow,' I replied.

I started to run. I wanted to tell them. I wanted to tell my dad. He'd said he'd always be proud of me, didn't he? I just wanted someone to hug me and tell me they'd always be there, and say it didn't make any difference because they loved me, and not just because that's what they *thought* they should say. I felt like I'd explode if I didn't let it out, like it was growing like a cancer inside me and if I didn't let it out it would kill me.

I burst through the door and into the living room. 'Where's Dad?' I panted, frantically. I had to tell him. There were tears in my eyes and I couldn't see straight.

'What's wrong?' Mum stood up. She was wearing her dressing gown, the way she always did when she and Dad watched TV together at night. He would always put one of the same two pairs of threadbare old shorts on and an old T shirt. I looked at his chair but he wasn't there.

'Where's Dad?' I repeated, wiping my eyes. I had to do it now.

She turned down the TV, a sign that she didn't think this would take long and she'd turn it back up and resume her watching when we'd finished. 'He's in bed Jake. What's happened? Keep your voice down or you'll wake him up.'

'Can we wake him up?' I sat down on the sofa and grabbed my hair, tugging it as if I could pull out the poison that way. I realised I was rocking like a madman. 'I need to tell you something.'

'No Jake, he's still not feeling well. He's not been sleeping. What's happened? Tell me love.' Her voice was softer, as if she'd realised it was something serious. She walked over to the TV and turned it off, then sat beside me on the sofa and put her arm around me. 'Have you fallen out with someone?'

It felt good to sit there with her. Her voice was soothing and I put my head on the top of hers; I hadn't realised before how much smaller than me she was.

'Come on, it can't be that bad,' she cajoled.

I took a deep breath, and the first tears started to fall down my cheeks. 'I'm gay,' I told her, heart in my mouth.

I heard her swallow audibly, and her body stiffened.

'Don't say that,' she answered firmly. Her voice took on the tone she used when she was angry, but trying to remain calm.

I squeezed my head between my hands and my eyes together desperately. 'Please let her try to understand. Please make her listen,' I was screaming wordlessly inside my head. 'Mum, I am. I need you to understand,' I was trying to stay calm now. I couldn't cry. I had to make her understand.

'You're only just sixteen. You don't know anything about that yet,' the same slow, measured tone.

'I know. I've known for two years Mum. I tried to pretend it would go away. I was desperate for it to go away, but it hasn't. I'm gay. I'm sorry, but…'

Her tone changed and she became suddenly authoritative. 'You are not gay Jake. I would know if you were. I know you and you are not gay. Maybe you're confused, but believe me, you are not gay.'

She took her arm from around my shoulders and stood up. Then taking a deep breath, but not turning around, she asked, 'Has something happened? Something to make you think you might be? Has someone done something? You can tell me, Jake. I won't blame you.'

It felt like the walls were physically closing in, like she was backing me further and further into a dark corner.

'Nothing's happened. For God's sake, there's nothing like that! I just am, that's all. It's in me. I think I'm in love with a boy. I've never fancied girls…never!'

'Stop shouting,' she hissed. 'You'll wake your dad up. How can you do this? You know your dad's ill. He might be very ill. We didn't want to tell you until we were sure, but now this has happened.' She turned on me now. 'Do you feel left out? Haven't we been giving you enough attention?'

'It's not attention. Nothing's made me do this. I didn't know Dad was ill.' All of a sudden it hit me. Dad was ill. The weight loss and the tiredness; had I been too self-obsessed to even ask? Maybe Mum was right. 'What's wrong? What's wrong with Dad?'

'He may have cancer. We haven't got all the results yet but it's not looking good. So you need to forget all this for now. By the time we know for sure you might feel differently. And if you don't, we'll just have to sort it out then. You can't mention this to your dad. He would be devastated. It would kill him.'

She was crying now. Tears rolling down her cheeks and dropping onto her dressing gown. I could see how distraught she was about Dad, and how desperate to shield him from my awful secret. 'Promise me,' she sobbed, 'promise me you won't tell him. We have to think about your dad now, not ourselves. I don't want him upset. We have to make things as normal as possible. He's not strong enough for that.'

I promised, and she hugged me, not the hug I wanted, the hug that made everything alright, but a hug of gratitude. She was grateful to me for promising to lie to my dad; she was grateful that for now, and maybe for ever, he could live in blissful ignorance. In the worst case scenario, he could die thinking that his son was normal, and would meet a girl, get married and have babies, and that would allow him to die happily.

In the best case scenario, he would get better, and I could tell him when he was stronger. But could I? Mum had left me in no doubt as to what she thought his feelings would be. *'He would be devastated. It would kill him.'*

There was going to be no hug, and no one was going to tell me that they loved me, and it made no difference.

As I climbed the stairs to my room I felt so tired, like I could sleep forever, but I knew I wouldn't sleep. The knot in my stomach was tightening, and growing, threatening to burst out, but I had to keep it down; I had to keep it inside and hide it.

I put my phone on charge on top of my bedside table. The two jigsaw pieces were there, and the tiny man on one of them seemed to challenge me. If I cut one of the tabs off the ill-fitting piece and stuck it on the other side, I could probably squash it into the other piece. It wouldn't exactly fit, and it would need the square tab cutting into a rounded tab shape as well, but it could be done, and maybe no-one would notice.

It was ironic, I thought, as I considered the potential disfigurement, that jigsaw pieces are called male and female, because they fit together like males and females should do. Males do not fit males, and females do not fit females. The only way it works is the right way, and there is no other way.

Gradually the shock of what Mum had said began to wear off and was replaced by an increasing fear. I'd been so angry with her I'd irrationally thought that perhaps she was making it up, or at least exaggerating Dad's condition to force me to keep quiet, but now a cold dread began to creep under my skin as I thought about losing him.

I went to bed racked with guilt, feeling more hopeless and alone than I could ever remember, and cried myself to sleep.

Chapter 34

'How're things at home' Tyler asked quietly, one night as we sat by Dan's bed listening to music. I shrugged. We never really talked about anything but Dan now; what might stimulate him to wake up; whether he could hear us but not respond; how impotent we all felt.

After a couple of minutes, Tyler said, 'I've told Mum everything. About you, and Dan... everything.'

'What did she say?'

'She said it made no difference at all. She didn't care at all. She said she wouldn't care if it was me or my sister either.'

'Brilliant,' I thought. Tyler could have come out and everything would have been just lovely. He would have had all the support he needed from his mum and not have had to pretend to be anything other than what he was. I wasn't sure if that didn't make me feel worse.

'Sorry,' he said, as if he'd read my mind. He told me then that she also said it wouldn't be as easy with his dad. It would take time for him to come to terms with it but she knew he would. His love for them was stronger than his narrow-mindedness, and she knew it would win in the end.

'She said your mum will accept it too and not to give up on her.' He glanced over at me. So that was where the conversation was going.

I spoke with a vehemence that shocked even me. 'I've given up on her already,' I snarled. 'She made me think that I was shocking...disgusting.

'She was just...'

'I don't care Tyler,' I was stone now. 'It's too late.'

'Can I see Dad?' I asked, before I set off for college the next morning? I saw the momentary panic on Mum's face and reassured her. 'I won't say anything.'

He had obviously been asleep, but the slight click of the door as I opened it must have woken him, as his eyes opened and he turned his face towards me. He started to lift himself up on his arms but I rushed to stop him. 'Don't get up, I just wanted to see how you were before I set off,' I tried to keep my tone light. 'How are you feeling? Did you get some sleep?'

'Yeah, I think I slept all night. I feel much better now just for that.' He smiled at me in what he probably thought was a reassuring way. 'I'll get up soon and potter about a bit. I've got the week off so I might as well get things done I've been saying I'll do for years. Might not get the chance again if I'm back at work next week.'

He looked better than the last time I'd seen him, maybe with a little more colour, and I thought maybe the doctors would see his results and it would be an infection or a virus, something curable. Or even if it was cancer, people survived loads of cancers now; Faye's uncle had had throat cancer for a year, or maybe two, ago and he was fine now. He'd done the chemotherapy and the radiotherapy and had an operation and they'd cut the cancer out. He had to keep having check-ups, but he was back to normal, even riding his bike competitively like he did before. Cancer wasn't the certain death sentence it had been years ago. We had to stay positive.

'You need to get some rest though Dad, or you might make it worse and be off work for longer. Don't do too much, will you?'

'No, no I won't. What subjects do you have today?' he was trying to be interested and keep the conversation going but I could see it was a challenge to simply keep his eyes open.

'Maths and Physics,' I replied, standing up. 'I'd better go now or I'll be late.' I leant over and kissed his cheek. I don't know why. I'd never done it before but it felt like the right thing to do. He didn't seem to notice. 'See you tonight,' I called, as I pulled the door shut, but I think he was asleep.

The next few days were difficult. Tyler was restless on the way to college the first day, as if he was wrestling with a dilemma. He'd start talking about some random topic: Brexit, the state of the toilets at college, the tool he was making on his course, and then fall silent again. Did I want him to ask me about it? I don't know that I did. After what had happened with Mum, and the situation with Dad, I couldn't 'come out' so what was I going to do? Having told him at all seemed pointless now; it had just made things awkward between us for no reason.

I wasn't going to bring it up. What would I say? 'Shall we talk about me being gay?' I knew what his reaction to that would be. The same as his reaction when we were bored and watching 'Brokeback Mountain' on Netflix at Faye's one day and he realised it was about a gay love affair; it had been as much of a shock to all of us I think, the creeping awareness of what was happening. He'd just jumped up and said, 'Right, I'm off. I can't sit here and watch two men kissing!' and off he'd gone to play football, or indulge whatever macho activity he thought it would take to get the image out of his mind.

We gradually settled into a similar routine as normal: small talk on the way to the bus; messaging or gaming on our phones on the bus; and some more small talk on the way from the bus stop to college.

But the elephant was in the room.

At times, when I was with Faye and Olly, I all but forgot what I was feeling. If I focused on them, and what had become a kind of double act (with Faye as the straight man) I could enjoy myself. It was like I was part of the audience, concentrating on the show to the exclusion of all else.

They were excited, but wouldn't tell us anything about their act, no matter how hard we tried to wheedle it out of them. Even bribery was futile. After Olly complained that he was dying of thirst one day, Will changed his approach, 'I'll give you the rest of this can of Coke,' he offered, raising one eyebrow as if he was being cunningly underhand, 'if you give us one clue.' But Olly simply smiled and raised his eyebrows.

The other acts from their drama class were fair game though, and both of them spoke freely, voicing their opinions, whether positive or negative, on their rivals' concepts.

'Evan and Adeel worry me,' Faye admitted one day. 'They're both really natural actors. You forget who they are and you start believing they're the characters. We haven't seen anything. They don't do any practising in college at all. I mean, the rest of us all kind of know what everyone's doing, whether it's singing and dancing or comedy or whatever, but those two are beyond serious. I bet they're rehearsing every night.'

'Yeah, but you have to know your audience,' Olly argued. 'It's not as if we're performing at The National Theatre. Our audience won't know their Henry V from their Twelfth Night…No offence,' he grinned at Will and Matty and me, 'They aren't going to appreciate 'The Tragedy of Evan and Adeel in dramatic verse' are they?' He continued, throwing out his arms melodramatically and making exaggerated faces. 'Be not afraid of greatness Adeel. Some (like us) are born great, and others (like everyone else) doth have greatness thrust upon them. We are such stuff as dreams are made on, but others wilt crasheth and burneth.'

I had no clue what he was talking about, but his over-acting was so intense it was hilarious. Faye tried to admonish him but she was laughing so hard that she could barely speak. 'Don't be so mean!' she giggled.

'I don't mean it. It's just the green-eyed monster,' Olly grinned. 'I've always wanted to play a great Shakespearean hero, or villain, I'm not fussy, but no-one ever takes me seriously.' He put the back of his hand against his forehead and affected a theatrical sigh.

It was difficult to tell whether they were genuinely worried about the competition. It wasn't a competition, but I could tell that both Faye and Olly were out to win, and as the night of the show approached, they spent most of their breaks rehearsing.

'Who else is coming?' I texted Faye a couple of nights before the show. I'd already talked to Tyler about it and we'd left it at 'he'd probably be there', which I thought was out of order. It implied that if a better offer came along, he might not come, and I thought that was really disloyal, given the length of our friendship with Faye. Still, he might come, and Faye would never know he'd considered not going; I certainly wasn't going to tell her.

Tyler and I hadn't seen or spoken to each other properly (other than on the journey to school) for ages, and I didn't really know whether it was on his part or mine. He was rarely online anymore; at least not at the same time as me. We needed to talk, and I told myself that I would arrange it, and we'd talk, and say all the things that needed to be said, and move on, but procrastination was easier.

'I've invited Tyler, Olivia, George and Dan,' there were a couple of other friends from school and the rest were Faye's family. Apparently, space in the auditorium was rationed, and each student could have twenty tickets each. As Faye had a large family, Olly had kindly donated ten of his tickets to her, arguing that his family was smaller and they'd go to waste otherwise.

I hadn't seen Dan since the festival, and my heart started pounding at the prospect of being in the same room as him again. I couldn't decide whether I'd missed the feeling, or whether it was just adding to my already mounting anxiety.

Chapter 36

Dad didn't go back to work. It was decided to extend his leave until something more certain was known about his condition. He seemed to be having tests continually for weeks, but then it seemed weeks would go by before the results of the tests were analysed and ready to feed back to him. Mum was a nervous wreck, although she took care to hide it from him, and I'd often find her weeping in the living room after he'd gone to bed.

In a way, the not knowing was torture, but on the other hand, it allowed me to live in hope that the doctors would find it was something they could treat and cure. There was nothing else to do but wait.

On the night of the concert, I sat with him for half an hour before I set off for the bus. I had hoped Tyler would text and say his dad would take us, as his parents knew about Dad and I knew they'd rally round as much as they could to help; his mum had already brought casseroles and pasta dishes a few times, saying it made her feel useful.

When he didn't, the realisation hit me that he wasn't coming, and I began to feel guilty. Was it my fault that he wasn't coming? Had the distance between us made it too awkward? I tried to tell myself that it was his irrational dislike of Olly, rather than connected to me, but I couldn't shake the feeling that it was. Not only had I lost my friend, I had driven a wedge between Tyler and Faye too.

Olivia and George were there when I arrived. I was surprised to see George as I'd assumed he'd send his apologies as before. He'd moved on, but I didn't resent it. People did move on, for various reasons. They went to different colleges, made different friends, met girlfriends and boyfriends, and there were only so many hours in the week. I understood that, and I was glad to see George. Maybe his presence would fill some of the void left by Tyler's absence. I didn't think so, but maybe.

Matty arrived, then Will, and last of all Dan. I was shocked by his appearance. He'd cut off the thick, glossy mass of hair that used to flop over his right eye and now it was completely shaved at the back and sides. It was still longer at the top with one of those fashionable lines between the long and short sections, but he'd lost weight, and if anything, his new haircut emphasised the fact. His cheek bones and jaw line looked too prominent and he looked like one of those catwalk models periodically featured in tabloid newspapers in articles about them being too thin and influencing others to follow suit. He had on black jeans and a black hoodie, which, while typical of other groups of students, were quite a deviation from his own previous look.

It was his eyes that worried me the most though. He nodded to me from his seat, but they were glassy and expressionless. He'd taken on the kind of look some of the second-year students at college had. They'd hang around outside smoking, and most people agreed that their cigarettes smelt strange. There were also rumours of more serious drug taking, although we didn't know them and had no idea whether this was true.

After we'd said our hellos and made a little small talk, Olivia caught my eye. There was genuine concern in her eyes and I made a mental note to talk to her alone later.

The auditorium filled up rapidly and I spotted Faye's mum and sister and waved across. I wondered where Olly's family were and looked around to see if I could spot anyone with similar features. Tyler's curly blond hair was just like his mum's, so I looked to see any curly brown heads in the audience; there were a couple of possibilities, but neither were freckled like Olly, or looked the slightest bit like him.

People were still arriving when the lights went down signalling the start of the show. I twisted around to see if perhaps Tyler was one of the latecomers, although I realised it was wishful thinking. Dan caught my eye, and seemingly read my mind. 'Tyler not here?' he mouthed, a puzzled expression on his face.

I shook my head and lifted my shoulders slightly to indicate that I didn't know why, thinking that Dan would find it strange. Not only was Tyler absent on what was a hugely important night for Faye, the girl he obviously felt strongly about, but I didn't know why. It would definitely have him speculating as to what may have happened over the months during which he hadn't seen us. He would probably be guessing at some kind of fall out, and in truth I would rather it had been a fall out; at least then we'd all know what the issue was. As it was, as far as I knew, Faye had no idea about Tyler's dislike of Olly, and she would be devastated when she found out he hadn't come to support her. She was also completely unaware of the situation between Tyler and me, and the possibility this had influenced his decision. Should I have told her? Would that have created a host of different problems?

It was too late now either way, and I was determined to put the whole thing out of my mind until after the show. I owed it to Faye to give her performance my complete attention, and that's what I was going to do.

In the end, I needn't have worried on that score. Some of the groups were so impressive it was like watching professional actors and comedians. A couple were also so cringe-worthy that I had to bite my lip to stop myself from laughing. It was all I could do to avoid catching anybody's eye because I knew we wouldn't be able to control ourselves.

Evan and Adeel's performance was brilliant. They had, as Olly predicted, channelled Shakespeare heavily, and I presumed most of their dialogue was Shakespearean, but their concept was clever. They had created a situation where two actors audition for the main part in a Shakespeare play, and along the way each one tries to undermine and manipulate the other in order to make sure they aren't given the part. In the end, Evan's character became more and more Machiavellian to the point where they used costume to emphasis his wickedness, and the twist was that the casting director asked him to play the villain instead of the hero, so both characters were happy. I was torn over the ending. I found myself wanting the character to fail, to be exposed and condemned, which I imagined was the intention, but I could see that the ending was a clever twist, so I decided to discuss it with Faye and Olly later and see what their opinions were.

Two girls presented what, half way into the performance, I realised was a comedy routine. It was a sketch set in a pet shop (I assumed) and one of the girls was supposed to be a dog (or a cat, it wasn't clear). Like me, the rest of the audience had also misunderstood the humour, and spent the first few minutes desperately trying to work out what was happening. When we eventually recognised that their purpose was to make us laugh, a few people tried to summon up some half-hearted titters, but it really was dire, and the last couple of minutes were uncomfortable to watch. What it must have been like for them, when they realised that their script was completely unfunny, I couldn't even imagine. I admired them for managing to make it to the end. It showed they were troupers at least.

Eventually it was Faye and Olly's turn to shine, and I found that I was both excited and nervous for them both. When they walked on to the stage, Faye was wearing a sparkly gold dress with feathers at the neck and sleeves, a big gold pendant and matching earrings, a long, wavy, brunette wig and one of those huge feather headdresses the dancers wear at the Moulin Rouge or Las Vegas. She also had some red sparkly platform shoes on to match the headdress. I was mystified. I'd never seen Faye look so little like herself and she seemed massively uncomfortable.

Olly, on the other hand was wearing jeans, a plain white long-sleeved T shirt and trainers that looked suspiciously like Faye's. She towered above him, and I wondered if that was making her feel even more awkward. When I looked closer, it was clear that something was slightly amiss; both outfits made them look at least twenty pounds bulkier than they were, and I guessed that at some point in the proceedings, we'd get to see what they had on underneath.

I looked at Olivia quizzically, but she just raised her eyebrows to indicate that she was as clueless as me.

Waiting until the audience was completely silent, Olly stepped forward into the spot light. He looked at the floor for a few seconds and then began to sing, slowly and unaccompanied, 'I am what I am, I don't want praise, I don't want pity.' His voice was clear and tuneful, but not strong, and his posture was stooped, as if he was nervous and out of his comfort zone. It was understandable in the circumstances. I hoped Faye wouldn't belt her lines out too loudly to emphasis the contrast.

She didn't, singing the next four lines in a disappointingly ordinary voice, almost not like her own. 'I bang my own drum. Some think it's noise; I think it's pretty. And so what if I love each sparkle and each bangle. Why not try to see things from a different angle?' I hoped she hadn't curtailed her voice to this extent in order not to outshine Olly. It would be just like her to do that, but if so, the audience wouldn't be able to hear her immense talent. Olivia and I looked at each other with matching frowns.

Then they sang the final three lines of the verse together, Faye harmonising perfectly and the true beauty of her voice escaping, unintentionally I thought, as there was no real power there. 'Your life is a sham, Till you can shout out, I am what I am.'

I wanted to stand up and shout, 'Sing it properly! Show everyone how amazing you are! Don't hold back!' but I just sat there in despair.

Suddenly, the music started, and the introduction to the song rang out. This time Faye began, quietly at first but building in volume, 'I am what I am. I don't want praise; I don't want pity.' She reached up and pulled of the gold earrings, throwing them to the floor.

Olly picked them up and put them on. As he sang the next four lines, Faye took off the pendant from around her neck and placed it over his head. His voice was louder now, and he stared defiantly at the audience.

While they duetted on the next three lines, Olly walked around to the back of Faye and undid the zip of her dress. She then started to sing the first four lines of the next verse while pulling her arms out of the dress and revealing the plain white T shirt and jeans she had on underneath.

Her voice was more powerful now and soared effortlessly above the music.

Stepping out of the dress, she flung it to one side, while Olly sang his lines, pulling the white T shirt over his head, hurling it to one side and revealing a sparkly red basque style costume underneath.

The audience loved it. Some laughed and some just gasped in surprise, but when I looked around at people's faces there was a smile on every one.

He and Faye duetted on the last three lines of the second verse, and he pulled off the trainers and jeans to uncover the rest of the costume. It comprised the leotard, elaborately embroidered and boned and completely covered in red crystals, a feather tail which covered the bottom half at the back, and red fishnet tights. The audience clapped and whooped. Faye circled behind Olly and fluffed up the feathers which had obviously been squashed under his jeans and T shirt.

Their voices were forceful, challenging the audience to disagree, their postures had straightened and their heads were held high and proud. Olly's voice was impressive, and they both looked so comfortable and in control there on stage I felt a pang of envy.

While they sang the third verse, Faye put on her own trainers and gave the red platforms to Olly, who now looked slightly taller than her. She took off the wig and headdress and passed it over, and while he adjusted it on his head she peeled off the false eyelashes she was obviously wearing, and swept liquid eyeliner over his lids, flicking it out dramatically at the corners.

Before they sang the last section of the song, Faye took out a wet wipe from one of the back pockets of her jeans and a lipstick from the other, passing it theatrically to Olly. At the same time as she wiped off the scarlet lipstick, Olly applied his own. Then they stood together and sang, hand in hand, their voices crescendoing stirringly.

I am I am I am good
I am I am I am strong
I am I am I am worthy
I am I am I belong
I am I am I am useful
I am I am I am true
I am I am somebody
I am as good as you

It was a song I'd heard many times before at family parties, but I'd never listened to the lyrics before. I felt like they might have been singing it to me and me alone, inspiring me to accept what I was and be proud of who I was. I glanced at Dan, wondering if he too could feel the healing power of the words.

When the music came to an end, Faye and Olly stood there, basking in the applause that thundered around the auditorium, him resplendent in full cabaret costume, and her relaxed and comfortable in her simple clothes of choice, both smiling and glowing with pride. They had completely fulfilled the remit, illustrating their personalities perfectly. We stood up and led the clapping, whooping and whistling to show our appreciation.

Not being a thespian, I couldn't evaluate the different performances for acting ability or comedic or dramatic effect. In fact, I wasn't sure how the teachers could assess so many different genres against each other. However, Faye and Olly had certainly provided the best entertainment in my opinion.

For me, it was more than entertainment. I felt moved, as if their performance had stimulated something inside me that couldn't be extinguished.

For me, it wasn't just entertainment. It was hope.

Chapter 37

After the show, there were refreshments served in the room adjoining the auditorium and we shuffled in, struggling to see how so many people were going to fit into such a small space. 'What does everyone want?' shouted Olivia, 'I'll go to the counter and you can all give me what you owe when I get back. We might as well stay in the auditorium and wait for them? Jake, will you help me carry?'

We took orders from the others and settled in for the long queue ahead. 'Who thought this was a good idea,' Olivia complained, 'they must have had an idea of numbers.' Then she changed her tone and lowered her voice, 'Dan looks like he's on drugs. Do you think he is? He hasn't asked for anything to eat or drink.'

'I don't know,' I replied truthfully. He definitely looked strange, but I had little experience of drugs, and as far as I knew, neither did Olivia. Maybe she was just being dramatic. I hoped she was just being dramatic. 'He brought some Pepsi with him,' I added.

'I thought he was dealing with it. He seemed to be dealing with it. After he told me and you? She left the question hanging in the air. I couldn't answer. I didn't know how he was dealing with it. I'd hardly spoken to him since the festival.

'I'm not stupid you know? I've grown up Jake, and I do realise how pathetic I must have sounded to you that night. I thought I was in love with him.' She paused. 'It wasn't love, it was just hero worship, but I wasn't ready to let go. I'm so embarrassed when I look back.'

'You don't have to be embarrassed,' I said, 'It was only me.'

'I know Jake. That's why I'm so ashamed.' She looked down at the ground, then back up into my face. I was confused, and about to ask her what she meant when she put her arms around me and drew me into a hug. 'Are you going to talk to him?' she continued. 'I think you should talk to him. Tell him we're here for him whatever, that it doesn't matter to us?' She looked up at me and raised her eyebrows. 'Will you let me know what he says?'

We reached the counter and she ordered our drinks and paid, passing three to me and carrying the other two herself. 'Where's

Tyler?' she asked as we wove our way back through the crowd. 'I wouldn't have thought he'd miss this for the world.'

'He couldn't come,' I suddenly felt the need to lie, to cover for him. 'He was sick!' I blurted out, immediately regretting it. 'He probably ate something. He'll be ok.' Why had I said that? I was a terrible liar and my face was already reddening.

When I saw Will coming out of the toilets, I thrust the cans into his hands and mumbled something about bursting for a pee. Luckily a cubicle was free and I darted in without checking whether anyone was waiting and pulled my phone out. 'I said you were sick,' I messaged. 'Back me up. Speak later.'

Faye and Olly ran out together, both unable to stop smiling. We all stood up and Faye hugged us one by one, before she suddenly realised she hadn't introduced Olly to Olivia, George and Dan. 'Oh God, sorry,' she lifted her hands to her cheeks in mock horror, 'Where are my manners?'

When she'd finished, it seemed to dawn on her suddenly that Tyler wasn't there, and she looked at me inquiringly.

'He was sick this afternoon.' I explained, 'He thinks it was something he ate…or maybe a bug.' I couldn't believe I'd just embellished what was a lie in the first place. Was I going to run to the toilet again and tell him why he was supposed to be sick?

For a moment she looked crushed, but then recovered quickly. 'Oh well, he can watch the video,' she smiled ruefully. Obviously deflated, she headed to the refreshments room to speak to her family, leaving Olly to entertain us. He'd changed into a pair of red shorts and a yellow sweater, but still had the false eyelashes on and glitter all over his face. 'I'm going to wear these for ever.' He stroked the eyelashes lovingly.

'You don't want to do that,' Olivia teased. 'You'll wake up with your pillow glued to your face! So tell us where you found your inspiration for that number?'

'Mum! Dad!' Olly shouted to a couple further along our row. He made exaggerated arm gestures beckoning them to come and join us.

I was surprised at how old they looked, and how ordinary. I'd expected Olly's parents to be young and vibrant, older versions of him I supposed, but these people were nothing like the way I'd pictured them.

When they reached him though, the warmth of their relationship was obvious. He put his arms around them both and they stood there for a few seconds hugging, while they told him how wonderful he was and how much they'd enjoyed the show.

Eventually, they turned to us and Olly introduced Will, Matty and I as 'the math's geeks', which must have been how he referred to us at home. 'Olly!' his mum chided him, and they both rolled their eyes and shook their heads in mock horror. 'We have tried to bring him up better than that, but he just gets worse,' she smacked him playfully on the arm.

After the other introductions were made, I watched as they charmed everyone, asking questions and seeming genuinely interested in our lives. It was clear where Olly had learned his social skills.

When Olivia repeated her question, Olly started to explain how his dad had originally come up with the idea for their performance, and we turned to him as he told us how Olly had asked for a tutu for Christmas when he was four. 'He loved that tutu. Do you remember Ann? He used to wear it while Strictly was on and twirl around knocking all the furniture over.'

They all laughed at the story, and Olly added a few more amusing anecdotes from his childhood. He had us in stitches, and I thought, not for the first time, that he'd make a great stand up comedian.

As I watched them together, I wondered what it must be like to know that no matter what you are, or do, or choose, your parents will always support and love you in exactly the same way. I felt an unpleasant twinge of jealously.

Will and Matty excused themselves at nine as Matty's dad was picking them up, and George cheekily begged a lift half way home with them.

After another couple of minutes Oliva poked me in the ribs surreptitiously before dragging Olly and his parents off to meet Faye's mum. 'Talk to him!' the poke was supposed to mean, subtly, but Dan wasn't naïve; he knew exactly why we'd been left on our own.

'She seems back to her old self,' he smirked. I didn't recognise his voice.

'Yeah,' I agreed, unsettled, then remembering, 'To be honest, I've only seen her in passing since we left school till now. 'She seems good though.'

'Go on then,' Dan sat down and sprawled one of his legs over the seat in front. 'You've obviously been left with a job to do, so you might as well do it.'

When I didn't speak, he asked, 'What do you want to know? Have I lost weight? Yes. How much? About twenty pounds. Did I lose weight on purpose? No, it just fell off. Have I cut my hair? Yes. Why? Because it looks less *gay* this way!' He spat the word gay with venom and I was shocked at the way he looked at me. His face was twisted into an ugly sneer that I'd never seen him wear before.

'You haven't told your dad then.' A statement, not a question.

'Obviously not.' The same disdainful tone.

'You don't have to do it on your own.' I remembered what Olivia had said. I thought back to what Tyler had said when I'd told him. What was wrong with the way he'd responded? What had I wanted him to say?

'We like you for the person you are,' I started. 'If you're gay, that's part of you…' I was sounding like a therapist in some American drama. I hadn't thought about being on this side of the equation.

'It's not part of me because I won't let it be. It's mind over matter and if I'm strong enough I can beat it.' He was staring at the same spot in front of him, eyes boring into the seat as if he wanted to rip it out and crush it. 'All that liberal crap. We like you for the person you are.' He adopted a girly, squeaky voice, mocking my attempt at being empathetic. It's not like I'm Olly is it?' he looked up, narrowing his eyes, and I could see they were watery and red, not like he'd been crying though, something else.

'If I was like Olly, everyone would already know, wouldn't they? I mean, it's obvious.' He swept his arm towards the stage clumsily, and suddenly I knew why his eyes looked odd. He'd been drinking. Perhaps that's why he looked so awful, because he was drunk. 'Everybody loves a camp comedian don't they? Like Alan Carr? Yeah, Alan Carr, everybody loves him don't they? I bet everyone loves Olly, don't they?' He paused for a few seconds.

'What if you're not funny though?' He shouted, and I almost shushed him. The last thing he needed was to be thrown out of the building. And the last thing Faye needed was to have one of her guests thrown out of the building. 'Eh? What if you're not funny or camp and no-one wants to be your friend because you're not what they thought you were? What then Jake?' His eyes were huge and round and empty.

I started to speak but he cut me off again. 'You said you were my friend but you weren't really, were you? Hardly heard from you since school.' He seemed to have become drunker.

'Well you probably won't see me again because I've got new friends now, and they think I'm so cool. I'm a babe magnet,' he sneered, viciously. 'I can do it if I'm drunk enough. Anyway, I'm going. Tell Olivia I said thanks for trying, but it isn't that easy.' His tone was so out of character and vicious it chilled me.

'Dan,' I called after him as he swaggered down the stairs, long thin arms swinging; he didn't look back.

I ran down the stairs and into the corridor after him, calling again, 'Dan!' A couple of people turned and pointed to the double doors leading out on to the car park. Rushing through them I scanned the area but I was too late again. I was angry with myself. Why did I always wait too long before making a decision?

I was also ashamed. I had let Dan pour out all his bitterness and self-hatred and not once genuinely thought of doing the one thing that may have helped. He thought he was alone and that no-one understood how he felt, but there was one person who understood exactly how he felt, and that person had failed him.

Was he really going to live like that? Pretend to be straight and block out his real feelings? It didn't seem like it was working for him so far. He looked bitter and hostile, although I guessed he'd saved that up just for me. As far as I knew, Olivia and I were the only ones aware of Dan's real feelings so the only ones he could open up to. When I thought back, he'd been quiet when he arrived, but perfectly friendly to everyone; it was only when left alone with me that he'd changed.

I compared Dan's life with Olly's. He was obviously torturing himself, trying to keep his secret and be what he thought everyone wanted him to be. I didn't think I'd ever seen anyone look so unhappy. In contrast, Olly was full of life, secure in the knowledge that he was living exactly the way he wanted to live. It was clear from his performance that he wasn't prepared to compromise. He'd shouted out to the whole audience, 'This is me, and if you don't like it, tough!' But they did like it, maybe not all of them but most of them. And there's always someone who doesn't like you for whatever reason, so most people, especially those I cared about, was enough for me.

I decided then and there I was going to come out, not to everybody (I couldn't risk my mum and dad hearing about it from someone else) but to the people I trusted and genuinely believed would say 'so what?'

After that, I was going to tell Dan.

Chapter 38

After a couple of months, Dan's outward injuries had faded to nothing. The bruises were gone and the cuts had healed. His hair had grown, and he was recognisable as the Dan I loved. He was still painfully thin, but there was some colour in his face now and his long black eyelashes were no longer hidden underneath the bruising and swelling that had originally covered his face like a mask.

The doctors told us that there were other injuries to Dan's body, suggesting a pattern of physical abuse over years, rather than months; broken ribs had shown up on the scan, with the possibility of other breaks elsewhere, and multiple scars, which were unlikely to have been acquired accidentally, covered Dan's body.

I cried when I imagined the kind of life Dan must have been living, while I was complacently envying his easy life.

'How could his mum have let it happen to him?' I thundered at Tyler. I couldn't believe a mother could let her child suffer like that. Why didn't she stop him, leave him? She could have gone to a refuge or something. Mums were supposed to protect their children and make sure they were safe and happy. They were supposed to prioritise their children above all else. I was consumed with an overwhelming hatred for her. I was so absorbed in my vitriol that I failed to notice his reaction.

Suddenly Tyler shouted. 'For God's' sake Jake. You're not perfect you know!'

He had never been angry at me before, and I was stunned. 'Have you never read about victims of domestic abuse? She was probably terrified of him. You've talked about the culture Dan described. Women don't leave their husbands. It would mean leaving everything they know.'

I caught his eye and he must have seen the shock on my face because he stopped, took a deep breath and carried on in a much more controlled and measured tone.

'Nobody knows how someone in that situation feels. It's easy for you to say, 'I would have done this, or I would have said this,' because you've been brought up in an environment where there's no violence, there's no threat. Your parents brought you up to be

strong. You wouldn't accept it because they told you you don't have to. She obviously wasn't brought up like that.'

He sighed. 'God Jake. You're so angry. It's like the thing with your mum. She's trying so hard now. She's going to the support group with my mum. She knows what she did…how she acted was wrong and she's trying to make up for it. Unless you've never done anything wrong in your life you can't refuse to forgive her?'

If I could have put my fingers in my ears like a child, I would have done. I didn't want to hear it. I refused to hear it.

In the end, I walked away.

Chapter 39

I made my way back to the refreshments room to find Faye and Olly. If I had the chance, I'd tell them now, before I backed out again.

Faye's mum almost walked past me. It was only the recognition on my face that made her stop and take a better look. Her mouth opened in shock. 'Jake? It can't be. How much have you grown? Faye, how much has Jake grown?' she shouted to Faye, who was at the other side of the room. 'Bella, come here. How much has Jake grown? You've lost all that baby fat you used to have, haven't you?'

I smiled, blushing. I had grown taller, but also I didn't seem to have had the time lately to obsess about food and my weight. I'd only noticed the difference when my joggers started to slip down over my hips and I had to keep pulling them up, and even then it didn't seem important. How things had changed.

It was embarrassing, but most of the crowd had dispersed now and only a few stragglers remained. Faye's large family were treating it as an impromptu get together, standing and sitting in clusters chatting. Olly's mum and dad had been welcomed into the fold and looked as if they'd known the group they were talking to for years and Olly was holding court in one corner, a couple of Faye's aunties and three cousins hanging on his every word. Every so often, they'd erupt with raucous laughter and Faye would turn around from her circulating and shake her head, smiling.

When she eventually circulated her way round to us we were in deep conversation; or rather, Faye's mum was in deep conversation, extolling the success of the prom.

'Mum, come on, they're wanting to go home,' she scolded, gesturing her head towards the tables where the refreshments had been. The three ladies had packed all their wares away and were standing, boxes in arms, waiting for the last of the loiterers to leave. 'Olly! Auntie Julie! We need to go!' she shouted over, and they started to make their way over to us.

Finally, one of the ladies switched off the lights and we spilled out through the double doors onto the car park.

'Sorry Jake, she can't help herself,' Faye laughed. 'Thanks for staying and saying hello to everybody. I feel guilty that I left you all but once I got in here I couldn't escape. Did you like it then?' She asked, her eyes shining.

'I loved it,' I said, honesty. 'You were absolutely brilliant. I was so proud of you. Both of you.'

'Why thank you sir,' Olly approached, having overheard, bowing dramatically and removing his imaginary hat. 'She is unbelievable isn't she?' He was staring at Faye now in pure admiration. 'She taught me to sing. In five weeks she taught me how to sing.'

'Don't be ridiculous,' she rolled her eyes. 'He could sing already,' she told me, 'he just needed a few pointers on breathing and projection and he was good to go.'

Faye's mum called her over, starting the car and beeping the horn. 'Sorry, I've got to go. Thanks for coming. See you tomorrow,' she called over her shoulder as she ran across.

Olly and I stood watching as they drove past, Faye's mum driving, her auntie in the passenger seat and Faye, her sister Bella and one of her cousins in the back, all five of them waving madly. As they passed us, Bella wound down the window and started blowing kisses at us as if she'd been the star of the show, 'Love you all, love you all!' she shouted as they pulled away.

In the next car, another of Faye's aunties was giving Olly's mum and dad a lift, all of them beaming away. 'You can squash in between your mum and dad Olly?' she shouted, but Olly waved them on.

'I'll walk with Jake to the bus stop,' he told her. 'We're only round the corner.'

'You two *were* great tonight,' I said, as we started to walk towards the road. I wondered whether I could tell him now. We were alone and it was the perfect opportunity. Although I felt I should tell Faye first. Would she resent me telling Olly, who I'd only known for a couple of months, before her? I could feel myself increasingly overthinking it and I knew I was in danger of missing my chance again.

'Thanks Jake,' he replied, smiling, and after a pause, 'It's true about Faye. She was just being modest. I was so useless at first. I've never sung in public before and I was like 'I can not do this!' but she just built me up and built me up until I believed I could.

It's like she hypnotised me.' He swung an imaginary watch in front of his face and chanted, 'you are Gloria Gaynor, you are Gloria Gaynor. And hey presto,' he adopted a diva stance, one hand on a thrust out hip and the other behind his head, 'I am what I am!'

'What time's your bus?' he asked. 'I'll wait with you.'

'They're every ten minutes,' I told him. I had to do it now. The bus stop was only 200 metres away and the bus might come as soon as we got there. Unless I said it now I wouldn't have time.

'I've never listened to the words of that song before,' I ventured. If there was ever going to be an ideal way in, this had to be it.

'I suppose you wouldn't,' he sounded thoughtful. 'The first time I heard it I knew it was about me. I think I was about ten and it was on one of those top hundred eighties anthems or something. I printed the lyrics off at school and kept it in my drawer until it disintegrated. Seems like a long time ago now.'

'Did it inspire you then? You know,' it was harder than I thought, actually saying the words, 'to come out?'

'I was never really in,' he grinned. 'My mum and dad have been awesome. They said they knew when I was a toddler and it just never mattered to them. I never felt like I was different at all because they just let me be whatever I wanted to be. It was a bit of a shock when people started noticing at school, you know? That I was different.' He paused for a while and looked wistful, as if remembering something difficult.

'Anyway, my mum and dad, they just said 'Be yourself. Don't listen to anyone who doesn't like it.' It was hard at first. Some people were so aggressive. You know, blatantly homophobic? And others were…they just stopped talking to me, kind of moved away from me. I didn't understand it, so Dad had to sit down and explain it all to me. He had to tell his gay son that outside our house, there would be people who hated me because I was gay, but I had to ignore them because they were just quite stupid, and we really should feel sorry for them.'

'You're lucky to have them,' I said, 'I know a lot of parents wouldn't find it so easy.'

'It wasn't easy,' Olly jerked his head round. 'They felt guilty that they hadn't prepared me well enough, that they hadn't been honest. They have a thing about honestly. I'm adopted, and I've always known it, ever since I can remember. When things got worse at school, they blamed themselves. Can you believe they blamed themselves for making my childhood too happy? Like they should have told me, 'Olly, you're not like other people. You're going to be ridiculed and bullied by some of them just because you're different.' Nope! I prefer their way. I did what they said. All my friends are real friends and if anyone has a problem with me, then I just ignore them and they go away.'

'Like I said, you're lucky to have them,' I repeated. 'Ok, it's never easy, but they made it as easy as it was ever going to be?'

'Oh I know that, and I'll always be grateful for it. Sorry I snapped at you, but I know it's been harder for them than they let on. Mum was a wreck when I was being bullied at school. They think I don't know, but I heard things and saw things they tried to hide.'

We walked on in silence for a while, but then he seemed to shake off the past and be himself again.

Tonight was the best night,' he smiled. 'I'll never forget it. I loved being on stage. I wonder if I could actually do it for a living? Wouldn't it be great to get paid for something you enjoy?' He turned to me. 'Do you think I'm being naïve? Dreaming of becoming a star? Am I delusional?' he laughed.

I shook my head. 'If anyone can do it, you can,' I replied, and I really believed it. Olly would have so many more nights like this in the future. I could see he was going to be a star, maybe on stage in the West End or maybe even with his own show on the TV. He was so charismatic (as Tyler would say, he had the X Factor) I couldn't imagine there was anything he couldn't achieve.

Olly suddenly veered to the right and bent over what looked like a pile of clothes lying in the gutter of one of the sidestreets. Probably a homeless person who hadn't made it back to their doorway or a drunk. I waited for him to come back, watching as he knelt down, shook the person's shoulder lightly and started to speak.

'Jake! Jake, help me with him!' Olly shouted urgently, and he started to pick the man up and turn him over. 'Help me!' he began to heave the body out of the road and I bent down to grab his feet.

As we dragged him to the pavement, under a street light, the hood fell away from Dan's face and I dropped his feet.

'Oh my God Dan. No... Dan!' I fell to my knees and held his face with my hands. It was cold. 'Oh my God, is he dead?...Dan!'

I started to shake him and slap his face. Was he breathing? 'Olly, what do we do?'

Olly was already speaking on his phone, calmly giving the street name and nearest house number to the operator followed by details of what was happening. He gave the phone to me and turned Dan over onto his side, into the recovery position. Why hadn't I done that? An empty Pepsi bottle rolled out from underneath him and Olly reached over to grab it. After sniffing the bottle, he put his face close to Dan's and said 'Tell them he's breathing, but not conscious. I think he's drunk. Tell them alcohol, maybe drugs, we don't know. Tell them he's cold, to hurry up.'

It seemed like an hour before we heard the sirens in the distance. Olly took off his sweater and put it under Dan's head, and we covered as much of him as we could with my jacket. I waited at the end of the street for the ambulance; it felt like something I could do to be useful, which I certainly hadn't been so far.

Eventually, the paramedics lifted the stretcher carrying Dan's unresponsive form into the ambulance and the one who'd been driving, a man in his twenties, asked, 'Is one of you coming with him?'

'I'll come,' I told him immediately. Olly had only just met Dan, and knew nothing about him, but I'd been a pitiful excuse for a friend to him, letting him suffer alone when I could have helped him. I was determined to make it up to him. If I had the chance. The thought struck me that I didn't know what he'd taken or how much he'd drunk. Newspaper articles my mum read out about teenagers dying from alcohol poisoning or taking lethal cocktails of drugs flashed through my mind. Mum was always cutting out stories about teenagers dying accidentally because of their own stupidity. She'd warn me about swimming in reservoirs, walking on the streets wearing headphones and getting into cars with drivers who'd been drinking or taking drugs.

She also talked about suicide a lot, telling stories about how the people left behind had their lives ruined and suicide was selfish. 'They might be escaping their personal hell, but they're condemning their families to a lifetime of torture.' Then she'd try to be more sensitive, 'There's nothing that's bad enough to justify doing that Jake. There's always another way. You must talk to us if there's anything you ever feel worried about and we'll help you.'

It seemed ironic now.

Had Dan tried to commit suicide? I tried to remember the last expression I'd seen on his face. Was it desperation? Hopelessness? I didn't think so; I thought it was contempt. He'd made it clear I'd let him down and his attitude had been, 'You abandoned me when I needed you and now I don't need you. You weren't there for me so I'll deal with it by myself.'

On the way to the hospital, I sat and stared at Dan as he lay there, his mouth and nose covered by an oxygen mask. His beautiful face was grazed on one side, when he'd fallen maybe? and there was an unhealthy sheen to his skin. He'd obviously started shaving, but there was an uneven stubble around his chin, as if he hadn't bothered for a while. It was his colour that shocked me the most though. Now he looked pale as a ghost except for the dark circles around his eyes; he could have been made-up as a zombie and not looked so lifeless.

Olly had told the woman paramedic, who was now sitting in the back of the ambulance monitoring Dan's condition, exactly what had happened while the other had made sure there were no bones broken and that Dan could be moved (I'd assumed that was what he was doing) so I didn't have to explain again, but she obviously felt that she needed to talk to me, so she asked, 'Is he your friend?'

'Yeah.' I swallowed the lump in my throat and sniffed. She handed me a tissue and I blew my nose and took a deep breath. I wouldn't cry. I had to be some use to Dan. All those weeks he'd been away, I'd expected him to keep in touch with us, with me, but why? He was the one who needed reassurance and support. I should have known that, and I should have made sure he knew I was there and I was supportive. But I hadn't, and it was too late now.

'Can you contact his parents? They need to know what's happened and where he's going then they can be there for him. His phone is locked, unless you know the passcode?'

I had no idea how to contact his dad, or his brother. We hadn't known each other long, and given what he'd told me about them, I'd never really wanted to. Maybe Olivia would though. At least once I'd seen him getting into Olivia's mum's car. Maybe Dan's dad might have returned the favour. They had definitely been close once; it had to be worth a try.

'Do you know Dan's home number? Or his address?' I messaged.

'No. Why?' she replied, instantly.

'It's important. Do you think you can find out?' I texted back, ignoring the question. I'd justify my rudeness later. I knew I could ring, but then she'd want an explanation and I hadn't worked out what to say.

As we pulled into the hospital grounds, my phone buzzed. '01471 182171. Don't know address. Is something wrong?' I ignored the question again and the messages that followed. There would be plenty of time to explain later.

The ambulance pulled to a halt and the driver came around to help lift Dan's stretcher down so I jumped down and stood to the side, not wanting to be in the way. Other people in uniform appeared and as they started to wheel him in through the doors and I turned to ask the female paramedic whether she would ring Dan's dad or I would, but she had disappeared.

I remembered how calm Olly had been when speaking to the operator before and how impressed I'd been. Panicking helped no-one. I pressed call, running after Dan's stretcher with the phone to my ear. I needed to be able to tell his dad where to go so I couldn't lose sight of him.

'Hello,' a gruff voice answered. It sounded like I might have woken someone up.

'Hello, I'm ringing about Dan,' I started.

'Dan? What about Dan?' I heard another voice in the background and there was a muffled conversation as the phone changed hands.

'Dan!' An angry voice now. Dan's dad, I assumed. 'Where are you? What do you think you're playing at?'

'I'm not Dan,' I shouted. I had to make myself heard now. 'I'm not Dan. I'm a friend. He's been... he's been taken to hospital. He needs you here. It's Belle Vue in Torton.'

'Who is it? Where is he?'

'He's in Belle Vue Hospital. We've just come through Accident and Emergency and we...' The stretcher and its entourage turned left into a room and the doors closed behind it. 'I'll just ask where we are,' I said into the phone, and looked around for anyone I could ask. The corridor was lined with people, but none of them looked like staff.

'What happened? What's he done? Where is he?'

'I don't know. We found him...in the street.'

'In the street. What do you mean? What's happened?' I couldn't tell whether he was still angry, or just panicking? I decided to simply tell the truth.

'He seemed drunk, but it may be something else too. I don't know. He was lying in the street so we rang an ambulance and he's in with the doctors now.' I assumed he was with doctors, but no-one had told me what was going on. I needed to find out. 'I'll ring you back when I know where we are and what's happening. Can you come though? He needs you to be here.' I pressed to end the call and looked around me. All the corridors looked the same, all white and shiny with the same bright lights illuminating them. I could hardly remember which one we'd come down, let alone how to get back. I waited for what seemed like hours, but couldn't have been more than ten minutes, thinking that at some point, a doctor or a nurse, or even a porter had to come past and I'd ask them.

As I paced up and down, trying to decide what to do, but not wanting to leave Dan, two gowned men came rushing down the corridor and into the room into which he had been taken. I panicked then. What did that mean? Should I go in and ask or would that disturb the people helping him? After a couple of minutes, a woman emerged and started to walk away. 'Excuse me!' I gasped frantically, 'what's happening? Is he ok?'

'Are you family?' she asked, and I lied, more easily than I'd ever lied before. 'He's in the right place.' She put her hand on my arm. 'Fingers crossed,' she added, and started to walk away again.

'Where shall I tell his dad to come,' I called. 'What room?'

'Emergency room 16,' she answered, smiling sympathetically over her shoulder.

I slid down the wall and sat on the floor outside Dan's room. 'Please let him be ok,' I repeated under my breath, 'please don't let anything happen to him.'

My phone buzzed in my pocket. Ripping it out, I blurted, 'Hello,' expecting Dan's dad, or his brother? It was Olly. 'What's happening?' he asked, voice full of concern.

'I don't know!' I almost sobbed. 'Nobody's telling me anything. I told Dan's dad. I think he's coming. Nobody will tell me anything. I don't know if he's even alive.'

'Ok,' Olly's voice was calm and soothing. 'Listen,' he said, 'take a few deep breaths. You have to keep it together for Dan. Do you want me to come down?'

I told him I'd be fine. The deep breaths had worked and I felt more in control. He was right. I had to function properly for Dan. His dad was coming and I couldn't let him down. I wasn't sure what I'd say, but I had to be sensible.

He needed to know where to come first, so I tried Dan's home number again, but it rang out continuously. Of course, it would. They were probably both on their way here. How stupid could I be? I put my head in my hands and rested my arms on my knees, screwing up my eyes in frustration. I had to go back to Accident and Emergency and wait for them, then I could bring them here.

Taking one last long look at the closed door, I started to make my way back. If they'd set off straight away, it couldn't take them more than fifteen minutes at this time of night. I'd probably reach the doors at the same time as them, and then we could come back and wait.

Scrutinising every person who entered, I sat by the doors of A and E, looking for any resemblance to Dan. I knew not everyone looked like their parents or siblings, but it was all I could think of. Never having met his dad, I had no idea what to expect. He might be adopted for all I knew.

Most people were obviously prospective patients, or with injured family members, but I knew I was looking for a man, probably aged about forty, and maybe with a younger man (I realised I had no idea how old Dan's brother was). Every time the door opened, I looked up expectantly, but it was never them. Why didn't they come! If they didn't come soon, I'd go back to Dan's room. Maybe he'd woken up to find he was alone. I couldn't let him think he was still alone. I had to go back.

I stood up, walked to the door and scanned the car park, but there was no sign of them. I'd go back now.

As I turned, I heard the screech of tyres and a large white van swung into view and parked in the first space it came to. A man, who I assumed was Dan's dad, got out, followed by a younger man who was obviously his brother, and they started to walk towards the door. As they approached, I could see that the man was tall and imposing with a thick head of dark hair and stubble. He was a little heavy around the middle and his shirt buttons strained slightly, but I could see in him exactly what Dan would look in his forties. Following him was Dan's brother, who was also dark, but shorter and less well built than his dad and Dan.

Waving my hands, I stopped them. 'Dan's dad?' I said, urgently. Not waiting for an answer, I started back through the doors. 'He's in Emergency room 16,' I called over my shoulder, while walking quickly in the direction of Dan's room.

Half way across the waiting room, my arm was grabbed and Dan's dad spun me round to face him. 'What do you think you're doing?' he spat. 'Haven't you done enough?'

I was stunned. What had I done?

'Dad!' Dan's brother put his hand on his dad's arm and his body between us. Then to me, he said firmly, 'We're here now. You can go.'

Momentarily speechless, I was rooted to the spot as they approached the counter for directions, but then I found my voice. 'But I need to see him! I need to know he's ok. I…'

Dan's dad whipped his body around to face me and I saw the raw hatred in his face. He bared his teeth as he spoke and I could see he had the same gap as Dan between the front two. Bringing his face close to mine, he growled, 'My son said. You can go.'

I stood in the doorway of A and E, staring out at the car park. It had started to rain now, the fine drizzle you can hardly see but wets you through to the bone. I was aware of people rushing in and limping out, but I didn't see them, and they probably didn't see me.

I thought about Dan's dad's hostility towards me, and what might have caused it. Had they guessed Dan's secret, and they'd assumed I was with him…in that way? Had they confused me with someone else? Should I find them and try to explain? Remembering the venomous look on Dan's dad's face, that wasn't an option just yet. I considered staying in the waiting room and asking someone to find out what was happening with Dan, but I wasn't family, so they probably wouldn't be able to tell me anyway.

When I looked at my phone, I realised it was half past one and Mum hadn't texted, or called, and that started me panicking for a different reason. Mum always texted if I was late, and if I didn't answer, she'd phone and shout at me for being thoughtless and selfish. Why hadn't she done that tonight?

What should I do? The buses weren't running, and it would take me at least an hour to walk home. Should I ring Mum? What if she'd gone to bed exhausted and I woke both her and Dad?

In the end, I decided to walk. If Mum was worried, she'd call, so she must be asleep and unaware I wasn't home.

It was a still night with no wind, just the endless, silent drizzle. Before I left the hospital car park my face was dripping and my jacket covered with millions of tiny sparkles of rain, reflecting the light from the street lamps on the end of every line of spaces. Soon, they'd soak in and my clothes would no longer keep me dry. I started to run.

The sound of my feet pounding on the pavement was almost therapeutic. I counted my steps up to a hundred and then started again, focusing on the regular sound of rubber hitting pavement and the jarring splash which interrupted it at random intervals. If there was any traffic on the road, I was unaware of it.

By the time I reached home my feet were soaking and my hair sticking to my face. I took out my phone and keys and opened the door as quietly as I could, checking for missed calls again and noticing the time was five-past two and I'd made it in thirty-five minutes. I'd never have believed I could run so far without stopping; maybe I was fitter than I thought.

The living room light was on, but as I reached in and switched it off I saw that the fire was still flickering, sending shadows dancing around the room. I pushed the door open and bent my head around it, eyes gradually becoming accustomed to the gloom. Mum was lying on the sofa, sleeping. She had on her dressing gown but wasn't covered, so I bent down, picked up the throw from Dad's chair and put it gently over her.

She suddenly stirred, and as if realising she was sleeping in an unfamiliar place and position, she jumped a little and opened her eyes. As soon as she saw me, her eyes filled with tears and she struggled upright and put her arms out to me. I went to her and sat down, putting my own arms around her while she sobbed uncontrollably.

Eventually, she pulled away and stared at me, her eyes red and puffy even in the dim light from the fire. 'I was waiting for you,' she whispered. 'What time is it?'

'It's late,' I replied. There was no point explaining how late, or why, until I knew what had happened.

'We went to the hospital today,' she said, and another sob broke free. I had been dreading this day. Dad had grown weaker and weaker over the last few weeks, but the doctors had been ambiguous, unsure and maybe 'afraid to make a mistake and have us sue them' my dad had said. Cancer was the obvious cause of the deterioration, but until they had done more tests, they couldn't be absolutely sure, and if it was cancer, they didn't know where it was exactly. While they were unable to confirm or deny anything, it allowed me to exist in ignorance (not exactly blissful, but hopeful). If they hadn't found it, then perhaps it wasn't there, and they'd discover it was an infection, or a virus they could treat. I'd just refused to think about the possibility of my dad dying. He couldn't die. He was fit and healthy; he could still walk on his hands. That sort of thing happened to other people, not us.

'It *is* cancer, but we knew that, didn't we?' Her eyes searched mine in the firelight. Without waiting for me to reply, she continued. 'It's something called Mesothelioma. It's in the lining of his lung (that's why he's been getting short of breath) and it's caused by asbestos. He doesn't know where he could have been in contact with asbestos, but he must have been, the doctors say. There's no other way of getting it.

I stared back into her eyes. There was so much grief there, but I felt numb. There was no way I could block it out any more as this was the confirmation that made it definite. 'What can we do...what can they do for him? Can he have an operation? Can they take it out?'

The next few minutes were torture. We sat facing each other and Mum took my hand while she told me that the cancer was inoperable because of where it was, and there was no cure. No money was being spent on finding a cure, because asbestos wasn't used any more, and the number of people developing the disease would decline rapidly over the next few years until it died out completely. Some people lived a year after discovering they had the disease, some six months, and some less. All we could do was wait, and make him as comfortable as possible.

My dad was dying.

Mum and I walked upstairs together, arms around each other, and when she pushed open the door we stood looking at Dad lying there. His face almost looked like a skull in the half-light from the landing, and his breathing was hoarse and grating. How could I have believed he'd get better? It was obvious now he had been dying for months. Even last year, when I was preparing for the prom, he was always tired, and kept complaining of a sore throat. He kept blaming a cold, a throat infection or some other virus. Why had I spent so little time with him? I wished I taken out all the jigsaws from under the stairs and completed them all with him one by one.

Mum closed the door silently and we clung together and cried for a long time.

Chapter 41

It happened on a Tuesday, at one twenty-five, but I didn't know about it until later.

My phone vibrated at one thirty-two, just as I sat down for a further math's lecture. Taking it out of my pocket, I checked the screen. It was Mum. I put it back. She tried again, then sent a text. I ignored them.

Ten minutes later, my phone buzzed again. I ignored it again. No-one else would ring me at this time. They were all in lectures themselves, or at least knew I was. It wasn't the first time she'd done it. Usually she'd want me to pick something up from the shop on the way home. She could wait.

Just after two o'clock, the door burst open and Faye stood there, panting, searching the class for me. When she saw me, she seemed momentarily unable to speak, her eyes wild.

'He's woken up!' she blurted.

It took me a few seconds to understand, and I remained in my seat.

'He's woken up!' she screamed. 'Dan's woken up!'

One of the counsellors drove us to the hospital and Faye filled me in on the way. Mum had been sitting with him, chatting, and he'd squeezed her hand. When she looked down at him, he'd opened his eyes. Then he'd spoken to her.

She didn't know anything else. Mum had been frantic. She couldn't get hold of me and Dan was asking for me. Faye had tried my phone but also got no reply, so she'd just run out of class and come searching for me.

We ran all the way to Dan's room, and when we got there we were out of breath and unable to speak. He lay there, still so thin and grey, head against the pillow as if he didn't have the strength to lift it. It was almost surreal, looking at him, in the same bed, the same position, but with his eyes open. And smiling. He was actually smiling.

Chapter 42

When I finally closed the door to my room and sat down on the bed, I realised I hadn't thought about Dan since I'd woken Mum up. Pulling my phone out of my pocket, I wondered whether to message. If he'd woken up, he might have his phone with him. Then again, it was half-past three so if he'd woken up, he'd probably have been put back to sleep again. If he hadn't woken up. I couldn't bear the thought of it. If we'd been too late and he'd taken too many pills to block out the pain, the pain I could have eased, I would never forgive myself.

I lay there on my back, fully clothed, in the dark for a while, thinking about my dad, and what life would be like without him. Tears spilled down onto my pillow and I didn't try to stop them, or wipe my face. I wanted to cry for him, and for Dan.

When I woke, it was too light, and I realised Mum had let me lie in. I leant across to grab my phone; it must have fallen out of my hand when I fell asleep and was out of battery. Plugging it in, I waited for the messages to come.

Olly had texted twice. 'What's happened? How's Dan? Are you ok?' Then again, 'What's happening? Is Dan ok?'

There was a message from Tyler. 'Enjoy the skive. Message me if you fancy a thrashing. You choose what at!'

Nothing from Dan. I messaged his phone. 'Are you ok? I need to talk to you.'

I took off last night's clothes and went to have a shower. The house sounded silent, so maybe they were still asleep. The warm water usually made me feel human again, and I'd stand under it for ten minutes while the life returned to my limbs, but today I was immune to its healing powers. I washed myself robotically and dressed in the same way before tiptoeing downstairs. Mum sat at the kitchen table in her dressing gown. Her hair hadn't been washed and there were traces of mascara down her cheeks from the night before. She was clutching a cold cup of tea, and I took it from her and told her to go upstairs and have a shower while I made another.

'I told Tyler you were ill,' she said, as she shuffled towards the stairs.

Clicking the kettle on, I checked my phone for a reply from Dan, but there was nothing. The message had been delivered, but I tried again anyway. 'Did you get my message? Are you ok?' Surely, if he didn't have his phone, his dad would. He wouldn't just leave me to worry? He couldn't be so cruel?

What if he hadn't made it though? They wouldn't be thinking about his phone, or his friends or anything. They would be grieving.

I made a decision and rang the number but it just rang until the messaging service came on. I slammed my phone down on the table and clutched my head, taking deep breaths and exhaling slowly in an effort to calm myself down.

Were they ignoring Dan's phone, or was it in a drawer somewhere at the hospital? I had to know. Nothing mattered if Dan was dead, I told myself, and I rang his home number. If they didn't answer, I'd go to the hospital and demand to be told. I'd walk down to the room he was in and barge straight in.

'Hello,' the same voice as last night. Dan's brother.

'Is Dan ok?' I asked, as calmly as I could.

There was a pause, then he spoke, 'He's still in hospital, but we think he can come home today. He had his stomach pumped and he's on a drip that's topping up his blood sugar levels. The doctors think…they think they caught it in time to prevent…other damage.' He didn't say anything else, just waited.

'Thank you,' I was flooded with the most immense relief, 'Thank you.'

'Don't phone this number again,' the voice was menacing. I heard the click as he put the phone down.

At that point, I knew what I had to do. I had to tell Faye and Olly, and maybe Will and Matty, and Olivia and George, about me. I had to make my peace with Tyler, and I had to tell Dan.

Mum and Dad, I could leave till later, or at least I could leave Mum till later. For now, I simply had to be strong for them both. I thanked God for saving Dan, for letting him live, and I silently promised I wouldn't let anyone down like that again.

When Mum came downstairs she'd done her hair and make-up. She smiled at me 'I'm sorry Jake, I weakened for a second there. It won't happen again. We'll stick together won't we? We'll make sure he has the best care and nothing to worry about? Certainly not why his wife looks like an actress in a horror film.' She laughed, but it was a brittle laugh. 'We'll make sure he has nothing to worry about.' It was a warning, and I remembered her previous words. *'You can't tell your dad. It would kill him.'*

She went upstairs again to see if Dad was still asleep or ready to get dressed and come downstairs and I took the opportunity to message Olly. 'Dan is ok and probably going home today.'

It didn't seem enough. Olly might have, no, probably had, saved Dan's life. 'Thanks for everything you did last night,' I added.

After, I put my phone down and went to see if Mum wanted help, but Dad was already halfway downstairs. He'd obviously had a shower, as his hair was wet, and was dressed in his tracksuit bottoms and a T shirt. He looked better than he had done in a few days, and I let myself hope that he might have longer with us than the doctors thought. There were always those miracle recoveries you heard about, and those people who lived years longer than the prognosis they'd been given. Take Stephen Hawking. He was told he had two years to live and he lived for fifty-five!

I took out one of the jigsaws we'd never done, and he laughed. It was a countryside scene, entitled 'Life in the Slow Lane' and I thought it would be much more relaxing than our last effort. Even Mum admitted it was 'not quite as ugly as the last one'.

'Where do you want to start?' I asked, giving him first choice.

'I'll do the blue barge,' he said, with enthusiasm.

'Right,' I said, matching him, 'I'll do the cottage on the left.'

We toiled for two hours, laughing at the way we'd both become frustrated when one piece seemed to elude us, only for it to appear, on the floor, or under another piece. It was only when Mum came in to ask what we wanted to eat that I realised it was half past twelve.

He was more tired in the afternoon so we watched a film, the three of us. 'Let's watch 'Hot Fuzz' again,' he suggested, and I put on the DVD. I couldn't remember the last time we'd spent so much time together, and it was fun. Dad seemed his old self, quiet, but cracking the odd joke, and Mum laughed at both his jokes and the film.

"I didn't think I'd like it,' she admitted afterwards, 'It's not my kind of film at all. But it was really funny.'

Half term had come at just the right time. It gave me time to spend with Dad and also plan what I was going to say to my friends and when. I decided Tyler had to be first. I could go round to his house and sort it out once and for all. If he wasn't comfortable with it, at least I'd know. After half term, I'd tackle Faye and Olly. The rest could be decided whenever.

Apart from Dan. I had to tell Dan soon.

Chapter 43

On the Wednesday morning, I messaged Tyler. 'Are you in?'

'Yeah, why?' Sometimes I hated messages. Immediately, the tone I inferred was cool. *'Why do you want to know? What's it to you?'*

I set off straight away. It was a warm day for October, and the sun was even threatening to come out. I'd take it as a good omen, I decided.

Walking to Tyler's house, I ran through in my mind the events of the night at Nando's. I'd been upset. I'd misunderstood his reasons for disliking Olly, and I'd been unprepared to reveal my secret just then. It was only because I'd, in effect, been backed into a corner that it had happened. Now I was prepared, and I wanted to tell him everything.

'Hi Jake,' Tyler's mum opened her arms to me as soon as she opened the door, not because she thought it was the right thing to do, but because it was the natural thing for her. She'd always hugged me, and if she hadn't at this point, it would have been odd. 'I'm so sorry love. Your dad is the loveliest man. We were hoping it would be something treatable and we'd be back at yours playing charades soon, but obviously it wasn't meant to be. How's your mum holding up? Do you think she'd be ok if I came round to see him?'

'I think she'd be glad to see you. They both would,' I replied, truthfully. Tyler's mum, and her cooking, were always welcome at my house. She kind of lit up the room when she entered, made it warmer somehow.

Tyler was lying on his bed playing Fortnite when I pushed open the door. I moved a pile of clothes and sat down with my back against the cool radiator.

'You can sit with me,' he said, shaking his head. 'I'm not scared of you or anything.'

He was the same Tyler, wearing a crumpled pair of sweat shorts and a T shirt which couldn't have matched less if he'd planned it, curly blond hair sticking up more on one side than the other (obviously he hadn't showered or brushed his hair yet) but not the same. There seemed to be miles between us, as if he was sitting at the other side of the world.

I didn't move. 'I never thought you were scared of me, just disappointed, like you think I'm not the same person now.'

He took off his headphones. 'Are you? I don't know because you don't talk to me any-more. We just talk about the weather and our courses and stuff like that. You didn't even tell me about your dad. How do you think that feels? When my mum told me, I was so shocked. If you were the same person, you'd have told me about that, wouldn't you? I bet you told Olly and Faye, didn't you?'

'No, nobody knows. I don't know why. I think I just thought if I didn't talk about it, it would go away, you know?'

'Like being gay? Did you think that would go away?' His tone had become warmer now. Perhaps he was relieved I hadn't replaced him in my confidence. 'I was really shocked…surprised…no, I was shocked. I didn't see it coming. It's not like there were any clues, or signs. It was just a bolt from the blue. I didn't know what to say. I've never been in that situation before. I tried to say the right things, but obviously they weren't the right things. I still don't know what I did wrong.'

How could I explain? It wasn't just the things he'd said that night, but all the things he'd said before, when he didn't know I was one of 'them', all the subtle, or not too subtle, comments that created a barrier between us (normal people) and them (gays).

'I didn't tell you because I knew you were glad I wasn't gay. That you'd rather I wasn't gay. I know you're not *homophobic,* but I spent two years listening to people saying, 'I'm not homophobic but…' It was just easier to block it out.'

He looked thoughtful for a while and I let him ponder. 'I'm sorry,' he sighed. 'I didn't know. Obviously, I didn't know, and if I had, I'd never have said those kinds of things…'

I interrupted. 'But you'd still have thought them.'

'That's not fair Jake. I don't know what I'd have thought two years ago because you didn't give me a chance. You didn't trust me enough to tell me. I don't know anyone who's gay that well, so I suppose I'm pretty ignorant. If you'd told me, I would've had the chance to change. I've never thought about it like this before. Do you think I'd ever say anything like that again? Now I know about you, I think differently. I'll never assume anything again.'

It suddenly occurred to me how unfair I was being. Nobody had lessons in how to behave around gay people, or how to react when someone came out, so why had I expected Tyler to perform perfectly? And what was perfectly? What had I expected? I didn't even know that.

'I'm sorry too,' I conceded, and it was a relief.

'Hey,' Tyler snapped. 'Get up here and let me annihilate you again.' He threw me the controller, and I propped myself up on *my* side of the bed, just like normal.

The weather held, and on the Monday morning I walked to the bus stop in the sun feeling that life was changing for the better. I told Tyler I was going to speak to Faye and Olly, and he agreed I had to 'emerge from my chrysalis' as he jokingly put it, sooner, rather than later. 'Are you going to start wearing tutus like Olly?' he added, laughing, and I was relieved at the banter. Tyler had always poked fun at me, and I enjoyed it. Just because I was gay, I hadn't lost my sense of humour, and the fact that he could still do that proved that our friendship was back on track.

Will was sitting at our table in the canteen when I arrived and I considered telling him first, and then just telling everyone as they arrived. I was so optimistic and determined, I almost did, but the more rational part of me said no, look what happened when you blurted it out unprepared to Tyler. I told myself to stick to the plan. I'd waited this long, I could wait another couple of days if need be.

Besides that, I still had to ensure that nothing leaked back home, so I had to confide in only those people I trusted. Mum and I were pulling together as a team, making sure we spent as much quality time as possible with Dad, and that he was protected from any unpleasantness; not that there was much to protect him from; she was a completely different person at the moment, endlessly patient with Dad, and it also seemed to be affecting the way she behaved with me too. Of course, I was desperately trying not to irritate her in any way, constantly searching for chores I could do and things I could tidy away, so maybe that had something to do with it too.

As soon as I spotted Faye at the counter buying toast, I took the opportunity to sort out a time and place we could meet. I'd already chosen the drama studio as the ideal location because if no shows or concerts were in the pipeline it would almost certainly be empty. Grabbing a Coke and scrabbling in my pocket for change, I asked her to meet me in there after college with Olly, and not to mention it to anyone else. I knew it sounded intriguingly secretive and it would drive her mad, but I had to make sure we'd be alone, and have enough time to chat. She looked at me quizzically, but I put my finger to my lips and walked back to the table. If Will noticed, he hid it well.

The day seemed to pass excruciatingly slowly and my excitement increased as the meeting approached. Having spoken to Tyler, I felt I was more prepared for any reaction that might be forthcoming. I was determined not expect a specific response and to give them time to let the information sink in before I elaborated. With hindsight, I realised that the process of 'coming out', was as much about how I dealt with imparting the information, as how they received it. Communication was the key, and I wasn't going to mess it up again.

The drama theatre was deserted, as I'd predicted, and most of the curtains were closed as usual. I supposed that if lighting was used at all they had to be closed. It would be difficult to create different effects and atmosphere with natural light flooding in. Everything was black and grey, unlike the rest of the college, where they appeared to be trying out different colours in each area. I knew that colours were supposed to affect your mood: yellow made you happy, orange made you energetic, and so on. Green must be considered to make you work hard in math's, as the feature walls in our block were green.

Today, the dull colours wouldn't deter me. I was going to emulate Olly, and be myself, be who I really was, rather than try to do what Dan had done and pretended to be someone else. Olly had always been comfortable with his sexuality and his life was happy and fun. Dan's life recently had been anything but.

I pulled three chairs into a circle and sat facing the door.

A couple of minutes passed before I heard Faye's voice outside the door. She was singing a song I hadn't heard before, and she continued as Olly pushed open the door and they walked over and sat down. He was wearing a pair of bright green track pants and a paisley hoodie, and his hair was tied up in a ponytail on the top of his head.

'So, what's with the clandestine meeting?' asked Olly, his eyes wide open and eyebrows raised. His face was so expressive sometimes I thought it must be made of rubber. 'Another attempt to blow up the Houses of Parliament?'

Faye shushed him. Knowing me so well, and knowing how out of character this was for me, she must have realised there was something serious on my mind. I assumed Olly had told her about Dan. Maybe she'd linked the two.

There was no point in putting it off. Recently, my second name had been procrastination, and I had made a resolution to change.

'I'm gay.' I said, decisively.

Faye looked over at Olly immediately and they smiled at each other. I wasn't sure what I expected their reaction to be, but it wasn't this. She must have sensed my confusion.

She turned back to me. 'I've suspected since the festival,' she explained. The way you and Dan…the way you looked at each other; the way he was always more interested in the things you had to say than anything the rest of us might come up with. I tried to warn Olivia but she was oblivious. With you it was more, I don't know, there was a chemistry between you. I wasn't sure though, and when you lost touch over the holidays I just thought maybe I imagined it.'

'I talked to Faye about the night we found Dan in the street,' Olly continued. 'When I thought about the way you'd been so…upset, the way you'd looked as if your life would end if he didn't wake up. It was so…transparent. You had no guard up and you were panicking. It was written all over your face. When I mentioned it, she told me about before, but we thought it was up to you to tell us when you were ready.'

Faye had known, or at least suspected, for months, and yet I'd never been aware of it. She hadn't changed towards me or avoided me. Everything was the same. I felt a warmness flood my body. Maybe it was relief. Although I had been confident that Faye and Olly would be supportive all along, I had still been anxious.

We discussed telling other friends like Olivia, Will and Matty, and George the truth. At first, I was eager to tell the world, but Olly was the voice of caution. He knew about the promise I'd made to Mum, and warned me that once the news travelled further than the small group of people I really trusted, it would become college gossip and would spread like wild fire. In the circumstances, I couldn't risk people I'd gone to school with telling their parents, their parents telling others, and eventually some innocent, or not so innocent, remark reaching Mum. Or even Dad. A couple of his friends were still popping around regularly to show solidarity. They might assume he knew, or feel he ought to know. The scenarios were endless.

It didn't really matter to me now that it might take a while before the truth was really out there for everybody. When I was with Tyler, Faye and Olly, it was like being in a warm cocoon of acceptance. I didn't behave differently, they didn't behave differently and it genuinely didn't feel any different than before, which was all I'd ever wanted. I did regret not having told Dan yet, but that was a bigger issue. Faye had convinced me that my feelings may be reciprocated, and while I was ready to embrace my sexuality, I was nowhere near ready to even think about the possibility of a relationship. That terrified me.

Chapter 44

At first, I didn't know how to react, I just stared at him. Then I looked at Faye and we laughed. I don't know why we laughed, but we did. Then Faye started to cry, and she went to the side of the bed and put her face to his hand and sobbed.

Mum was standing at the other side of the bed, but she moved away towards the door. I walked forward and stood beside the bed, still staring, as if I was afraid to take my eyes away in case he disappeared. I didn't want to touch him either. He seemed to me like a delicate piece of porcelain which might break if handled.

'Jake, will you do something for me please?' he croaked gravely. I jumped at the sound of his voice and nodded enthusiastically. I'd do anything for him.

He put his hands to his head, feeling the hair that had grown there and was now arranged in a tangled lump on the side of his head. 'Get me a comb?' he grinned.

I laughed. It was Dan, my Dan. He was back.

Chapter 45

The next few weeks were a mixture of sadness and happiness.

Dad's condition deteriorated; he was unable to eat much and his breathing became more difficult. On Thursdays, my mum went to Pilates and for coffee with two friends afterwards. Dad and I insisted she keep it up. She had to leave the house sometime, and I was there, so she didn't need to worry.

Increasingly, he'd started to have what he called 'rigors'; he'd start to feel cold and then his body would start to shake uncontrollably. I think he was more afraid of the rigors than anything. They weren't painful, just unpleasant, from what he said, and unlike pain, there were no pills he could take to prevent them.

When he felt a tremor coming on, he'd reach for my hand, and I'd sit with him, holding his hand, until it subsided. Sometimes it would be minutes, but at other times I felt like it would never stop. I felt powerless, and it was torture knowing that he was afraid and suffering, yet there was nothing I could do to help him. I'd speak about college and my friends and what I'd seen on the news, desperate to distract him in any way possible, and he'd nod, and laugh in the right places, but the fear never left his face.

At times he was more comfortable, and he'd respond to me, attempt to have a conversation, but he was always struggling to breathe and speaking exhausted him. Tyler came around a couple of times, and Dad laughed at his stories and enjoyed his company, but again, it was tiring, and he didn't stay long.

At college, there was respite, although I felt guilty about being able to escape. My dad would never have respite again; he had to live with this evil illness tormenting his every waking moment. Mum was also trapped in the house, at its mercy for most of the time.

Olly's grandma had died a couple of years earlier, which had been hard for his mum and she'd needed him to be strong. He was adamant there was no point letting it take over my life when I was out of the house as it would only make me ill and then I'd be no support to either of them. It made sense, and I tried to block it out when I wasn't there. When I was with my friends, I sometimes found that I could forget about it for minutes on end, and then it would come surging back with a vengeance, a black cloud shutting out the sun. My dad was dying.

Faye and Tyler did their best to understand and be as supportive as they could, but I felt myself drawn to Olly. We talked all the time. Not just about dad, but about being gay, and about Dan. It was a relief to talk to someone who understood. Dad was dying, but that wasn't the only pain in my life. He never got tired of listening, and never turned the conversation round to him.

After a few weeks, he broached the subject of contacting Dan. 'Jake, you have to make the first move, or you'll never forgive yourself,' he told me. 'Remember how guilty you felt about letting him down before? He's probably too ashamed to do it himself. He'll be worried about what you think.'

He was right. I knew that. I knew Dan was physically recovered as he was back at college now; I'd texted George and asked him outright and he'd simply replied that yes, Dan was at college. Why?

'I don't know if it's a good idea just now,' I said. 'He has enough worries in his own life. He doesn't need me adding to it all. It wouldn't be fair to burden him with all my problems.'

'They're not problems Jake. Your dad is dying. Don't you think Dan would want to be here for you? You two could have something really special. I think you need him.'

'Maybe it's getting a bit much for you,' I said quietly. 'Me pouring out my feelings non-stop. Are you saying I need to find someone else to listen?'

'Oh for God's sake,' he snapped. 'You're just looking for excuses. You don't want to expose yourself but if you don't, you might lose him forever. Honestly Jake, you need to grow some balls. Ring him, and do it soon.'

He stood up and walked away, leaving me with my thoughts. Olly was right. I was a coward. I had to act now or I'd put it off forever.

That night I sat looking at my phone for hours. I picked it up, searched my contacts for Dan's name, hovered over it, then cancelled. I thought about writing down what to say, then I decided to message. It was easier. It left the ball in Dan's court. I knew what Olly would say though. 'You bottled out. You should have rung him. You're a coward.'

I scrolled down Instagram for a while, then tried again. Looking at his name, Dan, I saw his face in my mind, and knew that if I didn't try, Olly might be right. I may never see him again. My heart beat wildly and my stomach lurched as I touched his number.

For a while there was silence. Dan, calling mobile, but no call tone. Should I break the connection? Maybe it was fate. Maybe I shouldn't be doing this.

After a few seconds though, it began to ring, and then I heard his voice. 'Hi Jake.' It was quiet and I couldn't work out the tone.

'Hi,' I replied.

Silence fell between us, but strangely, it wasn't an awkward silence. It felt like he was in the room with me and he was smiling.

'Will you meet me?' I had to do it before the passion cooled, before the spineless side of me had the chance to talk me out of it.

'Now? Where?' he replied.

In my haste, I hadn't made any specific plan, hadn't thought about details. I started to deliberate. Somewhere quiet, or would that look strange? The park? That would look odd too. Costa or Starbucks in town? We might be seen.

'Nando's at 7?' Dan suggested. I thought about it. It gave me time to get the bus, and it was a familiar place, warm and comfortable. Someone might see us, but did it matter? They'd just think we were friends. I'd go with Tyler without even thinking. Anyway, we were just friends. It was just... I shook my head to shake out the doubts; it wouldn't be me without a bit of over thinking.

Dan was there when I arrived and when he waved I nodded, pointed at the counter and bought myself a Coke. He looked happy to see me, whereas I was looking furtively around for people we knew. I sat down and he smiled, 'Alright?' he asked. It was a question, not just a greeting. Obviously, he was aware something had happened, and the word 'alright?' meant, 'what's not alright?'

We sat, staring at our drinks for a while before Dan said quietly, 'I'm sorry I didn't even say thanks, for that night I mean. I was ashamed. I felt stupid, and all those things I said...it was just stupid.'

'I'm sorry too,' I said. If I'd told him then that I understood how he felt because I felt exactly the same way, it might not have happened. He wouldn't have had to feel isolated anymore, like he was completely alone. 'I should have...' I began, but he cut me off.

'You couldn't have done anything to stop me at the time. I was a mess.' He took a deep breath, put his head in his hands and blew out the air loudly.

Just say it, I told myself. If you start with the small talk the moment will pass and it will be hanging in the air until you're walking home and you realise you've chickened out again.

I took a deep breath. There was enough adrenaline left to force it out. 'I'm gay.'

Dan smiled and laughed a little. He looked at me and said, 'I know…well I was pretty sure. I didn't actually know, but… you must have felt it?'

Now he'd said it out loud, it did sound a bit ridiculous. All the meaningful looks, the hugs that were more emotionally charged than ordinary hugs, it had been relatively obvious for a while. At school, things had been so much more ambiguous. We were so much younger and so frightened that everything was distorted and unclear, but with hindsight…

'Sorry,' I said. 'I should have told you back then, in the music room, or at least the next time I saw you. It might have helped. You might not have gone through what you did.'

'You couldn't though, could you? If it's not the time, if you're not ready, you can't do it. I don't blame you.'

Dan went to refill our cups, and I was surprised at how relaxed I felt. It didn't feel nervous and it didn't feel wrong, sitting there, chatting. It felt normal.

I told him about what Mum had said and he was shocked at first, but then he thought for a while.

'We have more in common than we thought,' he sighed, looking into my eyes. 'Your mum hates what you are, and my dad hates what I am. We're the same. We're together now though? So we can get through this.'

The way he said, 'we' and not 'you' felt good. It was also terrifying.

We fell silent, and I wondered if he was thinking the same thing as me. Where do 'we' go from here, if there is a 'we'?

He said he'd had the same misgivings as me about meeting in a public place, but he'd forced himself. The world was full of different types of people and most of them accepted each other for who they were.

I agreed. 'Olly says, 'If you're unlucky enough to encounter someone so unhappy with their own life that they've nothing better to do than resent and condemn other people's life choices, you just have to realise it's their problem. Obviously, he's quoting his mum and dad there, which must be nice, but it's true. There are loads of people like Olly's mum and dad.'

The silence was between us again, unspoken doubts and fears hanging in the air. One of us had to voice them.

'What do we do now?' I began. I was sick of not knowing, being suspended in a sort of limbo, where everything was uncertain and based on guesswork. I wanted to know. 'Where do we go from here?'

'I like you, and I think you like me? I missed being friends with you…being near you, and I don't want to do that again.'

'Me too.' I agreed. There was still no real answer, no plan.

There was another charged silence, before I spoke again. Honesty had worked so far, so I decided to tell him exactly how I felt. 'I don't know about you, but it makes me nervous…the future, relationships and all that. Can we just take it slowly and see how it goes? We can do this again? It's enough just that we know how we feel, for now?'

Once that conversation was out of the way, my anxiety seemed to evaporate, and we chatted until the staff started to clear away for the night. Dan told me about how his mum had died two years ago, something he'd never told me before; there were so many things we didn't know about each other. I knew it was an invitation to talk about Dad, but I couldn't face it yet.

'Let me know if you need to talk about it,' he offered, as we made our way out of the restaurant.

'I will,' I agreed, and we turned to walk in opposite directions. I still didn't even know where he lived.

'See you,' we chorused, and laughed.

I decided to walk home. It was only a couple of miles, and I needed the air. I felt like I was floating, and as I replayed the night in my mind, I would break out into smiles. Were we in a relationship? Maybe not quite that, I contemplated, but we had a connection, an understanding.

When I opened the door, the house was silent. I tiptoed upstairs and went to bed.

I couldn't wait to tell Faye and Olly about my meeting with Dan. Although he was now as active on the group text as the rest of us, I didn't think there was anything particularly suggestive about the messages on there. They were the same as they'd always been and I genuinely didn't think anyone would have guessed at a shift in our relationship.

I could have private messaged Faye, but it seemed so, 'girly', for want of a better word. I might be gay, but I wasn't the slightest bit interested in being more feminine, and looking back, I think that had confused me even further when I was younger. The stereotypical gay man I'd been exposed to at my house was camp. When my parents and their friends talked about *gays,* in their 'I'm not homophobic' way, that was always the assumption. For years I think I'd believed I couldn't be gay because I wasn't camp, or into girl's things, as if the two were mutually exclusive.

I didn't tell Tyler on the way to college. He'd been with Faye for ages now; I wasn't sure about the exact nature of their relationship, or how serious it was, but they were definitely together in some way; neither of them had said, 'We're boyfriend and girlfriend'. It was just obvious. Then again, their relationship was allowed to be obvious; I'd never seen two boys walking down the corridor at college holding hands.

Faye was sitting at our table on her phone when I arrived but there was no sign of Olly, Will or Matty. Although I contemplated telling her, I decided to wait for Olly and tell them together, even if that meant another *clandestine* meeting in the drama studio. It wasn't that I was afraid to tell Will and Matty I was gay; I was pretty sure they'd be fine with it, but for the same reason as I'd not told Tyler about Dan and me, it felt unnecessary.

Seeing as we were alone, I took the opportunity to find out about her and Tyler. They certainly weren't keeping it a secret, so I guessed it wasn't confidential information.

She told me she'd always known he fancied her, as everyone had; subtlety wasn't Tyler's forte at all, but that she'd always discounted the possibility of anything happening between them, mainly because of her height. She was afraid people would laugh at them because girls were supposed to be shorter than their boyfriends, and she was so self-conscious about her height anyway, the thought of being laughed at for another reason horrified her.

I asked her what changed her mind and she laughed.

'You know the times when Tyler and George would show off in the yard at school doing keepy uppies and that thing where they kicked the ball up and caught it on their backs?'

I smiled at the memory and she carried on. 'Amelia and her friends used to watch them and flirt. Do you remember? I started to think Amelia had her eye on him, so I watched the way she behaved when he was around, and she definitely did. He was flattered too; I could see that. He definitely flirted back. Anyway, I started to panic. I supposed it made me realise I did want him. The thought of them together turned my stomach, so I started being more…receptive to his advances I suppose. I wouldn't call it flirting, I'm so useless at that, but I tried my best to show him he wasn't wasting his time.'

'The audition!' I cried out. It made sense now. At the time I would have bet my life on Faye refusing to sing, but now it became clear.

She smiled and giggled at the memory. When Amelia had sung, and she wasn't bad at first, Faye said her stomach was churning. She'd looked at Tyler and to her he looked impressed. He was certainly gazing adoringly at Amelia; that's how it looked to her anyway. She'd made a snap decision. Tyler kept going on about her singing and how he thought she had the most amazing voice at primary school, so she'd just done it, and it had worked. Since then she felt they had an understanding. He knew she did it for him, and it showed him how much she felt about him. It was a while before anything really happened, but they'd gradually become more tactile and he'd kissed her on the night of the festival.

She talked about the night when Tyler had met Olly, and been so rude and unpleasant. I wasn't the only one to have confronted him about that, and they'd hardly spoken for weeks. The low point was her show. When he didn't turn up she was heartbroken, and forced herself to accept the fact it was over, 'but he came round one night and threw himself at my feet,' she laughed, 'literally, you know what he's like? He begged me for forgiveness and said he loved me and couldn't live without me. It was all very ridiculous, but I was so happy I didn't care.'

It was only when the bell rang that I realised I hadn't told her about my meeting with Dan. Still, there was plenty of time for that.

Chapter 46

After college one night, Tyler and I were waiting at the bus stop, chatting with Olly, when my mum pulled up and offered us a lift. She was 'just passing' she said, which rang alarm bells; Mum rarely left Dad on his own at all, and would do the shopping and any other errands after I returned from college. She didn't seem upset though, and when I asked if she could drop Olly off on the way, she agreed cheerfully enough. 'Your auntie Jen popped over, so I thought I'd get the shopping done,' she explained, as if she'd read my mind.

'So where do you live Olly?' she asked pleasantly; she was always polite and welcoming to my friends, even when she was irritated with me or Dad, she would turn on the charm. Olly told her his house was on the main road so there was no need for a detour and he'd let her know where to pull over.

'Are you on the same course as Jake?' she probed, and I realised that I'd not really told her much about college at all. We had too much on our minds, and rarely spoke about anything but Dad nowadays. When I was sitting with Dad, I'd tell him all about my day, which lessons I'd had, who I'd seen and what we'd talked about. If I was speaking, it meant Dad didn't have to, and he didn't get as tired as quickly. He seemed to enjoy listening to me talk and I would ramble on while he nodded and smiled in the right places. I felt closer to him than I had for a long time.

Olly explained that we'd met through Faye, who was in his drama class, and Mum pressed him for details, telling him she'd loved drama at school, but it wasn't a serious option then for people to pursue, at least, that's what her parents had told her.

When he spoke about acting and performing, Olly came alive. He loved the way you could become another person completely, and lose yourself in the story. He told her he admired the great method actors, who would identify with the part they were playing to the extent that they almost became the character.

Strangely, she didn't respond, and didn't speak again before dropping him off. An uncomfortable silence descended. I'd expected her to agree, and perhaps come up with an example or talk about her favourite actor, but she just drove on, her mouth set in a line. She'd started a conversation, then neglected to fulfil her side of the bargain. I wanted to fill in for her, to ask, 'so who is your favourite method actor?' or something like that, but that would have emphasised her withdrawal from the dialogue.

'It's the one on the left here with the big tree in the front garden,' Olly said eventually. He must have noticed Mum's rudeness, and I was ashamed of her and the way she was treating him.

'Thanks for the lift,' he called to Mum as he opened the door, but she remained impassive, staring forward, and didn't even tell him 'You're welcome.'

As soon as the door shut, she pulled away quickly, as if in a hurry to increase the distance between herself and Olly. I was mortified and wished Tyler wasn't there so I could confront her. He was obviously as bewildered as me, because usually he would take the opportunity to charm her with his wit and charisma. I used to think it was embarrassing how he flirted with her, but then he flirted with everyone, so now I just found it funny.

We passed school and Tyler commented on how small it seemed now compared to college. We'd thought it was huge compared to primary school. Wasn't it weird the way some of the teachers at college insisted on being called by their first names? he rambled on, trying to alleviate the awkwardness. He didn't mind it with the ones who taught him on the practical side of his engineering course, because it felt like being at work, but in a classroom, it just didn't feel right calling the teacher Derek.

When he thanked Mum for the lift, she managed to reply. 'No problem,' she said blankly, but she didn't turn around or smile.

I thought it would be me who spoke first. I was furious. Why the hell had she been so rude and unfriendly? But as soon as Tyler shut the door she snarled, 'You promised me.'

For a minute, I was mystified, then she continued. 'You promised that you would forget all that. We agreed that your dad was the most important thing and you wouldn't do anything to upset him but you obviously didn't mean it.'

What was she saying? Olly was gay, and she'd obviously realised that half way through the conversation and it had shocked her. Did she think there was something between us? Maybe she did think that and she was worried that it would get back to Dad. If that were the case, could her anger be justified? I had promised.

I tried to rationalise her behaviour. She was just worried about Dad and she'd got the wrong impression. 'Olly's just a friend. There's nothing going on. He's Tyler's friend too,' I started.

'It doesn't matter whether there's anything *going on* or not,' she spat as we turned on to the drive. 'People will think things and say things anyway, about what sort of friends you've made…they'll put two and two together and get five. You promised you'd leave it alone for now.' She started to cry. 'If you start going around with people like that, it makes you think…'

'It's not catching Mum. And Olly's not trying to lure me into his gay circle, if that's what you mean. We're friends, just like I'm friends with Tyler.' I was becoming more and more frustrated. 'I don't fancy every boy I meet. I promised you I wouldn't tell Dad and I haven't. No-one else is going to tell him anything. What are they going to say? I just thought I'd warn you that Jake is friends with a *gay.*' I mimicked a sharp intake of breath, trying to emphasise the ridiculous nature of the idea.

'Stop it!' she screamed, 'stop making it out to be some kind of joke. It's not a joke. It's not funny!'

'And you think I find it funny?' I was shouting too. 'This is my life! I've promised to keep it a secret for now for Dad's sake, but this is my life. Yes, I see how Olly lives his life and I'm jealous because he doesn't have to pretend or hide what he is from everyone. I haven't just looked at him and thought, 'being gay looks fun. I think I'll have a go at that.' I've known for years.'

She was sobbing now, but I didn't want to comfort her. I'd done what she'd asked, but I couldn't let her manipulate my life any further. I couldn't let her turn me into what Dan had become. I opened the car door and got out. 'And just to make it clear, when *people* put two and two together, it will make four. I am gay, and there's nothing anybody can do to change it.'

I opened the boot of the car, took out two shopping bags and went into the house, leaving her sitting there in the car.

Chapter 47

If it wasn't cruelly ironic enough that Dan should wake up when she was there, not me, or any of the rest of his friends, his first word was her name. I was jealous, and I hated her for making me jealous. I should be ecstatic. I should be focusing on Dan being awake, on the fact he seemed to be well. He was alive and he didn't have brain damage. I should be overjoyed, but instead the bitterness twisted my insides back into the knot I'd almost forgotten.

When we reached home I jumped out of the car, unlocked the door and went upstairs. So many emotions were spinning around in my head, it felt like they were fighting. I couldn't seem to focus on any one feeling at once, there was just a huge chaotic battle going on.

I sat on my bed struggling to regain control for a while, before deciding to go out. Maybe the fresh air would clear my head? I'd decide on a destination, then walk there and back. At least I'd know where I was going.

But the knot tightened as I came down the stairs, to the point where I put my hand protectively on my stomach. As I opened the door, I felt the tension rise into my chest where it quickly became a pain. Panicking, I pressed my hands to the pain and cried out. By the time Mum reached me I was kneeling on the floor gasping for breath.

Chapter 48

The following weeks might have been awkward, if Dad's condition hadn't worsened as it did. We tended to speak in whispers, as he was frequently asleep, which at least meant he wasn't in pain. The hospital had brought oxygen bottles, which were supposed to make it easier for him to breathe, but it didn't seem to me that it made much difference. Whether he was breathing through the mask attached to the bottle or not, he was fighting for air, and it was torture watching him struggle.

Two weeks before Christmas, he was taken into hospital with heart failure. Mum had woken me up in a panic, screaming, 'ring an ambulance! He's not breathing!'

The rest of the night was a blur. We panicked and cried and hugged each other. We didn't speak. There was nothing to say. Nothing mattered except Dad. We thought we'd lost him then, but the doctors managed to bring him back and stabilise him. There were no visiting hours here. We just stayed. There were only hours left and it would be unforgiveable to ration them.

When he finally opened his eyes, we knew it was the end. He was shrunken and grey and he looked a hundred years old. We knew he'd never leave the hospital and I think he knew it too.

We sat at either side of him and held one hand each. Mum leant over him and told stories about when they were younger. 'Do you remember when…' she'd begin. It was rhetorical. He didn't respond and she didn't need him to. His eyes would close, but she'd carry on talking, quietly and soothingly, and he'd squeeze our hands periodically to show he was still awake, and could still hear.

Mum went for a cup of tea and to stretch her legs after a couple of hours and Dad looked into my eyes. 'I'm not afraid,' he wheezed. 'I'm ready.' He nodded and smiled.

'I love you Dad,' I tried not to cry, but my eyes filled with tears. What could I say? Goodbye? He was leaving, and I was never going to see him again, but goodbye sounded so final, and he might have days left to live. I couldn't say goodbye yet. 'I love you,' I repeated.

'I love you too. I'll always love you, no matter what. Will you remember that? And I'm proud of you. Remember that.' He suddenly coughed, and the cough took his breath away. He tried to recover, but then another cough shook his body. He couldn't breathe in and his eyes started to look desperate.

I ran to bring a nurse or a doctor, but there was no-one around. Mum came through the double doors at the end of the corridor and our eyes met. She started to run, and still panicking, I rushed back; I'd press the buzzer and someone would come.

I reached the bed just before Mum, but it was too late. His eyes were closed but he wasn't asleep. I'm not sure how we knew, but we knew he was gone. I pressed the buzzer anyway and we sat, each holding one hand. Mum quietly crying, until the nurses came to tend to him. They were kind, and simply waited, saying nothing, until we were ready. I rose first, and went round to help mum. She kissed his hand and replaced it gently on the bed cover, before bending and kissing his forehead. She touched his face, and stood there for a long moment. Then she turned towards me, her eyes full of pain, and we made our way out, arms around each other, following the nurse to a warmly decorated room with comfortable chairs. The room where they take people when their relatives have died.

My dad was dead.

Chapter 49

Dad died on a Wednesday, and the funeral was arranged for the following Friday. It turned out that Dad had spent a lot of his time over the last few weeks planning his funeral, and 'putting things in order'. He didn't want to leave us with lots of decisions to make and things to sort out, Mum told me, so he'd written an order of service, picked the hymns he wanted us to sing in church and the music he wanted at the crematorium. He'd also written a 'guest list' of the people he would like to come, although he also said he'd like it to be an open invitation and everyone was welcome.

There were also instructions for the wake. It was to be a 'celebration of his life', not one of those boring affairs where everyone wears black and cries. He wanted to buy everyone a drink, and have them tell funny stories about him and have a good time. The food had to be pie and peas too, because buffets were funeral food and he wanted it to be a party. It had to be from the same company as Tyler's Dad had used for his fortieth birthday party. Dad had never stopped going on about how delicious the pie was, and he was only disappointed that he wasn't going to be there to eat it.

Mum insisted I go into college, which was probably the best idea. Dad's sister, Auntie Jen, was there some of the time to support Mum and help with any unforeseen issues, and like Mum said, everything was done. I had to keep busy to keep my mind off it.

Everyone was sympathetic, and those who'd known my dad talked about what a lovely man he was. He was quietly eccentric, Tyler said, and proceeded to roll out anecdote after anecdote about times when he'd made them laugh. 'Remember when my dad knocked that big teapot off the table and he was mortified. Your dad was like, 'Don't worry, I'll mend it,' and we were looking at him like he was mad. It was in about two hundred pieces. But the next time we came round it was on the table mended. It looked like a jigsaw there was so much glue, but it was mended.' he laughed at the memory. 'Do you remember? My mum and dad thought it was hilarious.'

It helped talking about him, and I ran a couple of stories I thought I might use in my eulogy by Dan one night on the phone. He laughed and said I had to put them in, and then he fell silent.

'My mum was a bit like that,' he explained. I didn't speak, hoping he'd open up to me. 'She hated waste. We used to find tins in the back of the cupboard with sell by dates five years before,' he chuckled. She'd just go, 'It's in a tin. It'll never go off!' Dad went mad. 'He'd have a clear out once in a while and you could tell it was killing her. I know she took them out of the bin and used them though. Once he threw out some tinned peaches that were about four years out of date and the next week we had peach crumble, or something like that. He didn't even suspect, but me and my brother knew. We were really nervous about eating it in case we died of food poisoning, but Dad just wolfed it down and said how delicious it was.' He laughed briefly, 'She kept on doing it and we'd find them but never tell dad in case it made him angry. Nobody ever died from eating her cooking, so we figured she knew better than him.'

It was the first time I'd heard him talk about his family. He'd spoken about the things he'd felt when his mum died, but when I thought about it, they were only things he thought would help me through my own grief, as if he didn't want to burden me with his pain. He'd explain how he'd made a scrap book of photos of her laughing and surrounded by family for the funeral, so people could remember her as she was, and not dwell on the way she looked and felt just before she died. On his bedside table, he had his favourite photo of the two of them framed, and every night he'd remember how she'd still kissed him goodnight, every night until he was almost fifteen and she was too ill to walk, and told him she loved him. He said he preferred to think that he was blessed to have had her in his life for fifteen years, rather than dwell on the fact that she was gone too soon.

I'd already started looking through photo albums, and it was therapeutic. Holidays, barbecues and Christmas parties I'd forgotten came back to me, and I threw myself into the task of creating a display, 'celebrating Dad's life' as he'd wanted. The teapot took pride of place.

'Do you have any family on your mum's side?' I'd asked.

'Not that we see,' he replied.

'Do they live in Ireland?' I ventured. I didn't want to pry, but increasingly I was aware that my relationship with Dan was one-sided. He knew all about me and my family, but rarely spoke about his. Had I asked? I wasn't sure. If so, he'd certainly been economical with the information he'd volunteered.

'Some of them.' More detail was obviously not forthcoming, so I inferred that he didn't want to expand for some reason. Maybe I'd push him further in the future, but this wasn't the time.

In bed one night I pondered my relationship with Dan. Over the past few weeks we'd become close, yet I knew little about him. He'd talked a lot about his mum, mostly I think to help me through Dad's death, to make me feel less alone, but he was reluctant to speak about the rest of his family. I knew he lived with his dad, who was a self-employed builder, and older brother Ryan, who worked with his dad. They were from Ireland, and I knew there were a few uncles and cousins living fairly close by, as he'd fleetingly alluded to boxing matches he'd been to, supporting his brother and various cousins, but that was all.

Dan at a boxing match seemed wrong somehow. He was such a gentle and caring person; I couldn't imagine him enjoying anything which involved violence. Not that he'd complained. As with anything else about his life, there had been no elaboration, simply fact. I'd inferred what I could from throwaway remarks. At school one time he hadn't completed his homework because he thought he'd do it the night before, but he'd forgotten he had to support his brother at a boxing match. More recently he couldn't come bowling because he was attending his cousin's wedding. That sort of thing.

It did strike me as a little odd that we'd never met, or even seen his dad. Most of us were fairly familiar with each other's parents. They'd give us lifts and even if we were only being dropped off, they'd smile and wave at the rest of the gang. I supposed I hadn't known Dan for as long as the others, but it was strange that he always arrived alone, having walked or caught the bus. And he never accepted a lift home either. I remembered the rumours at school about his background. 'Apparently, they're a bit rough…My mum says she heard they used to be gypsies…So and so says his dad's been in prison.'

I don't think I ever really considered them as any more than that, rumours. Dan appeared to be as far from 'rough' as anyone I could think of. Tyler once said that if he'd had an ounce of the talent Dan had, he'd be a professional sportsman, but that Dan just wasn't competitive enough. He won everything at our school because he was so much stronger and faster than everyone else, but out there in the sporting world, where they're all fast and strong, you have to be aggressive, and Dan just wasn't.

Chapter 50

When the day of the funeral finally came, I wore the most comfortable jeans I had and a long-sleeved T shirt I liked. Normally, Mum would have insisted on dressing me smartly; I'd only ever been to my grandad's funeral before and I'd worn my school trousers and shoes and a new shirt specially bought for the occasion. However, she was adhering to Dad's wishes almost obsessively. He'd said he wanted it to be a party, and for people to enjoy it, so she wanted everyone to be as comfortable as possible. She'd posted on Facebook, telling everyone not to wear black and to come prepared to celebrate his life as per his wishes. It worried me a little, the fact that she was clinging to the list of instructions he'd given her as if her own life depended on it. What happened when the instructions ran out, and she was on her own?

I think it was because I felt a little surplus to requirements that I wanted to give the eulogy. Mum was visibly relieved. Auntie Jen would probably have done it, or one of my dad's close friends, but I knew she felt more comfortable with one of us doing it. We were the ones who knew him best, and we were the ones who knew how he'd want to be remembered. I asked her to read it a couple of times, but she said she wanted to hear it for the first time on the day, and she trusted me to speak for both of us.

I was nervous, but I think the adrenaline helped me to get through the day. The church service was moving, even though Dad had tried to pick the most popular and upbeat hymns he could. He told mum he hated those funerals where only a handful of people knew the hymns and everyone else just mouthed the words and wailed quietly and tunelessly up and down where they thought it was going to go, so he'd picked ones that everyone knew and would belt out as loud as possible. She'd posted on Facebook that the hymns would be, 'Abide With Me', 'The Lord is My Shepherd' and 'All Things Bright and Beautiful', if anyone didn't know them could they please try to learn them, and could everyone sing as loud as possible because Dad had said he wanted to hear us.

We weren't religious, and as far as I knew, neither were any of his friends, but that day, we sang our hearts out, and it was beautiful. At grandad's funeral, the church was half empty; half of his friends were waiting for him, grandma said, and he had quite a small family. At Dad's, the church was packed out, and people were standing at the back and in the aisles. When I looked at all those family members, friends, work colleagues and neighbours, singing as loud as they could, just in case he could hear them, I almost broke down, not with grief, but with gratitude. The thought that so many people loved Dad enough to be here for him, for us, was overwhelming.

I didn't break down though. I had to give my eulogy and do him proud, so I swallowed down the lump in my throat, wiped my eyes and took deep breaths until I was in control again.

As I walked to the front of the church and climbed the few steps to the pulpit, I felt a little lightheaded, like I was floating. I gripped my speech tightly to steady my nerves. Although I had learnt the words off by heart, actually standing up there in front of everybody was terrifying, and I needed to know that if my mind went blank, I had back up. Looking out over the sea of heads, I could see Tyler and Faye, his arm around her. On her other side was Olly (I'd told Mum I had to have him there as he'd kept me going through the last few days). Olivia, George and Dan were behind them.

I didn't have to worry about Mum's reaction to Dan. She'd never guess he was gay like she had with Olly, and neither would anyone else. It felt wrong, pretending he was straight, just like it felt wrong pretending I was straight, but he was here, standing there, staring at me, smiling encouragement, just like he had when I'd presented our ideas for the prom, and that's what mattered. He was there for me, to support me and show me how much he cared.

Luckily, my heart didn't start to pound now like it used to do around him, and I didn't feel tongue tied and awkward. Instead, a strange sense of calm came over me.

My eulogy went exactly as I'd hoped. There were lots of funny stories about Dad, and periodically, pockets of the audience would erupt with laughter as they remembered specific incidents. There were also points where I spoke about what a loving husband, dad and friend he was. At sixteen, I'd been at the age where a distance starts to emerge between teenagers and their parents, and I'd felt guilty about that when I first found out about his illness. I could hardly remember a time when we'd been close. Since then, I'd searched through hundreds of photos and videos, each one a precious memory, and I'd realised how very lucky I'd been. Like Dan said, I was blessed to have had Dad in my life for sixteen years. I had to focus on that.

I was relieved at how well I'd dealt with the day so far. Only a few months ago, if anyone had told me I'd be strong and capable, supporting Mum and playing an integral part on the day of my dad's funeral, I would never have believed them. I'd always been the dependent one, rather than the tower of strength. Looking back, I could see I'd drawn most of that strength from Dan. He'd listened endlessly to me as I cried and raged at God for taking Dad. I'd blamed Mum, and Dad himself at times, for the cruel blow fate had dealt me. He'd shared his experiences, and when asked, given advice; most of the time though, he'd listened. He was the reason I was coping now.

At the crematorium, Dad had planned everything again, right down to the cut price coffin. She'd protested at that, Mum said, but he was adamant, and they'd spent an afternoon trawling the internet for cheap coffins, giggling at some of the weird ideas. In the end, he'd insisted on a cardboard one completely covered in peas. On the top it said, 'Rest in Peas'. Mum said that at first she'd thought it was tasteless and worried about what everyone would think, but he was so amused at the thought of their reactions, she had to let him have his way. We were a little nervous when it first emerged from the hearse, but we both agreed he'd have loved the response. After a slow start, and a lot of confused faces, everybody seemed to take it in the way that he'd intended, and it certainly lightened the atmosphere. We laughed, and then I allowed myself to cry, while Mum and I clung together and said our final goodbyes.

All my friends came to the wake, which was held at the rugby club Dad used to play for as a teenager and into his twenties. They set up camp on a table in the corner, and waited patiently. It was over an hour, after I'd finished greeting everyone and my mum was safely surrounded by family and friends, before I made my way over to thank them for coming.

'You've made it such an amazing day,' Faye smiled. Your dad would have loved it. He'd have been so proud of you.'

'I can't believe you actually brought the teapot,' laughed Tyler. 'Seriously, Faye's right, we really are celebrating his life. It's the best funeral I've ever been to! It's exactly what he wanted. I just wish he could have been here.' He turned around, scanning the room, and I instinctively did the same.

As I turned back to my friends, I caught Dan's eye. He smiled warmly. Not having known my dad, he would perhaps feel a little out of place, but it meant the world that he had come, for me.

Not everyone had stuck to the dress code; some had worn black (Like Tyler said, they probably felt *more* comfortable in black, especially if they'd been to a lot of funerals), but most had worn some colour, or dressed casually like me. For the most part, I could see they had congregated in definite groups: work colleagues at one table; friends from the rugby club mostly standing around the bar; mum's family at another table and so forth. There were certain individuals who straddled groups; some of mum and dad's family members knew each other pretty well, and there were neighbours and people from work who had become closer friends and knew others from barbecues and parties.

Along the back wall was my tribute to Dad, and quite a few groups were still working their way along it, pointing and laughing, chatting together and beckoning others over. The free bar was still open, and it was clear that a lot of the them would be booking taxis to take them home. It was exactly what Dad would have enjoyed.

I hunted for Mum among the crowd and when I found her she was staring over at me, smiling. I smiled back, before we both turned back to our guests.

Tyler and I told a few stories about Dad and how eccentric he could be and the others laughed and seemed keen for more. I'd always thought of him as the quiet one, but the way Tyler described him, it seemed like he remembered it differently, almost as if our dads were a double act, whereas I'd always thought of Tyler's dad as the one who was hilarious. I supposed they were both showing off a bit in the social situations we remembered, and Tyler's dad probably wasn't the life and soul when it was just the four of them.

The others chipped in, mostly with funny stories about their own families, and another couple with memories of my dad. Faye remembered when he'd volunteered to supervise a group when we'd gone orienteering at primary school and they'd got lost. Dad said it was fine and they'd just take a short cut back, but they'd ended up climbing over fences and walls and finally a tree, pulling themselves across one of its branches to cross a river. She said a lot of them were terrified they'd fall in and drown, but after they all made it in one piece they were so thrilled. It really felt like an adventure.

'What did the teachers say?' exclaimed Olly in shock. 'It must have been a health and safety nightmare writing that up!'

'It was weird actually,' Faye remembered, 'I think we all knew we'd done something illegal, or at least forbidden, and we never said anything. He didn't ask us not to at all,' she looked at me, quick to dispel any implications that he'd done anything suspicious, 'I think we all just felt that telling anyone would spoil it, make it less exciting. It's weird. This is the first time I've told anyone.'

I smiled to myself. It was just like Dad. Never one to follow a map or ask for directions. We'd had plenty of escapades like that in the past.

As the time went on, the room started to empty. Olivia's mum picked her up and George managed to scrounge a lift again. Olly set off to walk home; it was a couple of miles but he said he enjoyed the exercise.

Once the four of us had said our goodbyes to the others, the atmosphere became a little awkward. Obviously Olly had told Faye about the night we'd found Dan in the street, and I'd told Tyler, but they hadn't seen him or spoken to him until today. Although a lot had happened, I still hadn't confided in the others about the relationship between us having changed, although they were aware we were back in contact. I think Tyler already guessed that there were feelings between Dan and I (or maybe Faye had told him) and wanted to give us time to talk.

After we'd made small talk for a few minutes, discussing our courses and any news about friends we had in common, Tyler stood up. 'We're just going to have a word with my mum and dad,' he said, pulling Faye up with him. 'See you in a bit though. I can see my dad's here for the duration,' he smiled, gesturing his head in the direction of his dad, who was leaning against the bar, surrounded by a laughing audience.

I looked around for Mum, suddenly aware that I hadn't seen her for a while, and saw her deep in conversation with Auntie Jen, Tyler's mum and a couple of other friends. Not that I wanted to escape, but my heart had started racing again.

'Are you ok?' Dan asked, looking straight into my eyes.

'Yeah, actually I am,' I nodded, 'I'm not sure it's hit me properly yet.'

I glanced over again at Mum and he must have seen the anxiety in my face. 'Don't worry,' he smiled sadly. 'I'm just your mate from school. She'd never guess.'

He started to talk about what happened in the weeks leading up to the night of the show. We hadn't really spoken about it at all since that night, and it was obvious he wanted to explain.

He'd always known he could never mention anything to his dad or Ryan about how he felt, but it was as if his dad had guessed. 'I don't know how,' he insisted. 'No-one else has ever guessed. At least I don't think so. Maybe it would be easier if they had, like Olly? There's no keeping that a secret is there? But with me, it doesn't show. I'm like you. It's there, just as much, but no-one knows. It's like this dark secret growing and growing…'

He shook his head, 'I shouldn't be saying this now…here.'

'No, go on,' I said quietly. I wanted to hear.

'He kept implying I was soft. Kept ridiculing things I said and did in a girly voice. The more I tried to be as manly as possible, the more he seemed to see me as a fraud, and it made him even more angry. It was like he could see right through me and knew it was all a lie.'

He laughed bitterly and looked at me. 'Which is ironic really. He's never even tried to understand me, and now he's telepathic! Honestly Jake, he just knew, and he couldn't stand it.'

He took up the story again. When he started college, he'd convinced himself that the best course of action would be to pretend. He said at certain points he almost felt like he could do it. He was still the same Dan as he had been years ago, before he'd realised he was 'flawed'. All he had to do was act the same way as everyone else, and for a while it had worked. He simply blocked any sort of sexual thoughts or feelings completely. He said he'd remove himself from the room if that kind of conversation began, and if the situation arose where it would appear strange that he wasn't 'joining in', such as a house party, he'd make excuses and avoid it.

However, a few weeks after starting college, he'd gone round to a friend's house to watch football with some other lads, unaware that his parents were away and the plan was to invite a few girls around too and have a little party. Comments had been made about his non-attendance at any social get together, and people were starting to become suspicious he thought, so he felt he had to stay. There was alcohol there, and lots of it, and he'd found it was easier to bear when he'd drunk a few glasses of vodka and coke. He even found he was quite enjoying the banter, until it turned around to him.

One of the girls made it perfectly clear that she was interested, and had managed to engineer the seating arrangement so she was next to him on the sofa. There wasn't really room and she was all but sitting on his knee so he'd gone to pour himself another drink, but when he got back, everyone had moved around and the only space was next to her. He absolutely couldn't have sat anywhere else, and it would have looked very strange if he'd left the party then.

Instead, he drank more and more and later on she kissed him. He could vaguely remember this but it was very indistinct, just disjointed flashes of memory. He supposed he must have been kissing her too, although he couldn't remember any sort of control on his part, just a distorted image of her face on his.

In the morning, he woke up in a bed with her, but with no recollection of how he'd got there or what he'd done. She'd jumped on him and started trying to kiss him again (he thought that might have been what woke him up) and he'd been horrified, run out of the house as fast as he could and walked home.

Apparently, she'd spread rumours around college that they'd had sex, and although he was pretty sure that was a lie (he'd woken up with his track suit bottoms on) he couldn't be sure. He could have used the rumours as a cover for years, he supposed, but he just felt sick and knew he couldn't live that way anymore.

That was perhaps three weeks before he'd come to Faye's show, and in the interim, he'd turned to the one thing he now knew would block out the truth and the feelings that went with it. His dad was a big drinker and he and Ryan drank so much themselves they never noticed if he looked or sounded different, or if there was anything missing. There were always plenty of bottles of beer and spirits in the cellar. He thought they might be selling some of it too because it seemed to arrive in bulk and leave the same way.

The night of Faye's show, he'd started early, as he needed some Dutch courage to face us. His dad had come home early and sober, seen his face and known exactly what was going on. He'd screamed and shouted, accusing Dan of being a thief and a liar.

'I just exploded,' he remembered. 'I told him it was his fault I needed to drink, to block it all out, because he was such a crap dad. I said he drove mum to drink too and that's why she died. Everything just poured out of me and he stood there watching me. If looks could kill I would have been dead…then he just said really quietly, like a whisper, 'it's a good job your mum's dead. At least she doesn't have to know you're a queer.'

'Oh my God. He actually said that? No wonder you lost it!' I couldn't believe anyone could be so cruel.

'To be honest, it was a wake-up call. There's no point pretending any more if he already knows is there?

The night at the hospital, his dad and Ryan assumed that I was the person influencing him to behave the way he was. They'd never seen me before and didn't know who I was. They suspected he might be on drugs too, and that I might be supplying them to him. What they hadn't realised was that actually they were his suppliers, and the drug that was openly available in their house was to blame for the change in him.

I had been watching his face as he spoke. It seemed like he couldn't look at me, as if he was ashamed of his behaviour and his family and was trying to avoid seeing my response. His hair had grown, he'd shaved and he looked healthier, more like the Dan I remembered. After a slight pause, he looked up into my eyes and smiled, the familiar lopsided young Elvis grin.

'Pathetic isn't it,' he sighed. 'I don't know what I was thinking. As if I could pretend for the rest of my life.'

'You look happier now though?'

'I am.' He paused and looked at me again, 'You probably don't want to hear this now. I'm sorry, I can wait till a better time. Do you want to go and talk to everyone before they go?'

I looked around. There were still forty or fifty people left, chatting and laughing, showing no signs of wanting to leave. 'No, I want to hear it. I want to know what happened. Was it just alcohol?' I ventured.

'Yeah, I wouldn't know how to get hold of anything else. But I know I was in that state where I'd have tried anything. Everything seemed pointless. There was no-one who'd understand.' Then directly to me again, 'I don't mean you. I know you tried to understand, but I couldn't come and live with you when my dad threw me out, could I? I really believed he would you know…Yeah, I think I'd have taken anything anybody offered me. It didn't matter about the danger, did it? I felt so useless I hated myself. It would have been like a game of Russian roulette and I don't think I cared whether I woke up or not.'

'So what changed?' I asked.

He paused, then sighed. 'I called Olivia,' he said. 'I didn't know what else to do. I couldn't tell you because of your dad. I didn't want to add even more pressure. Olivia was the only other person who already knew. Anyway, we started off just chatting and I just broke down. I couldn't help it. She was being so kind and gentle and I just needed to let it out. I told her everything, about pretending to be normal, and that girl at the party, and about you…'

My heart skipped a beat then. What had he told her about me? He didn't look up at me, just paused. I wanted to ask him, what did you say about me? but I don't think I could have spoken if I'd tried.

'She just told me everything would get better. No, she promised. She said, 'I promise everything will get better. This is as bad as it will ever be.' She asked me if I believed her, and you know, I did. She asked me if I trusted her, and I was so tired, I just agreed. It felt so good to have someone else share the burden, I think I just passed it on to her completely, and then I went to sleep.'

He looked at me and laughed. 'I know. It's weird isn't it. I don't think I've slept without worrying about this for two years, but that night, I went straight to sleep, and I slept for hours.' He looked over my head and gestured, 'Everyone's going. I better get off too.'

'You don't have to,' I blurted. There was nothing I wanted more than to spend time with him, and for a second, I contemplated introducing him to Mum, as a friend of course.

'No, I need to get home anyway. I'll let you get back to your family.' He stood up and started to move towards the door. 'I'll call you. I've missed you…all of you,' he added.

Walking him to the door, I thanked him for coming, and was suddenly overwhelmed with a need to put my arms around him. As he turned around, he must have sensed it, and he pulled me into an embrace. It was one of those one arm under and one arm over man hugs, completely acceptable for a funeral, but I held on to him for perhaps a moment too long before letting him go and turning back to the room.

Mum's face was like thunder as she approached me. Only a few stragglers remained now and she made sure she was near enough to me and far enough away from them not to be heard before hissing, 'You promised. I can't believe you'd do this here, in front of our friends…in front of his friends.'

'He's not here though Mum. I kept my promise and he never knew. He died thinking I was straight, thinking I was *normal*, like you wanted.' My voice was low, but there was a bitterness creeping in.

'So you're doing it to punish me then? Now he's gone you're going to rub it in my face? How can you do this now?' Her voice was wobbling and she grabbed a napkin from one of the tables nearby and started to dab her eyes.

'I'm going to say bye to Tyler and his mum and dad,' I said, and walked away. Had any of it actually had anything to do with Dad, or was it just her own intolerance all along? What would Dad have thought? He told me he was proud of me and that he'd always love me. Perhaps he meant 'no matter what'. Perhaps I could have told him and he'd have said, 'It doesn't make a difference. I love you.'

Now I'd never know. And it was her fault.

Chapter 51

The doctor said he was very lucky. It was rare to wake up from a coma and immediately remember everything. We had to prepare ourselves for the possibility that the trauma Dan had suffered would show itself later, but for the present, it appeared that he hadn't suffered any significant brain damage. The next few weeks would be about gaining strength, she told us. He'd be tired easily and needed to get enough sleep, and he needed to start eating well and putting on weight.

Dan said hadn't he slept long enough? It had been over two months since he'd last been awake. But he didn't argue about the eating. 'I can't wait for a Nando's,' he winked, but he looked exhausted and the doctor ushered us out.

I was worried that if he went to sleep again, he wouldn't wake up. 'What if he falls back into the coma?' I asked weakly, but the doctor said the human body knows what it's doing. If it thinks it's time to wake up, it must know that the danger has passed. She was probably saying it to comfort me, as it didn't sound very scientific, but I allowed myself to be reassured.

Mum told me what had happened on the way home in the car. I hated listening to her, but I wanted to know. She'd been describing holidays we used to go on when I was little, telling Dan how I could swim when I was four but I'd always be under water; people would think I was drowning, but she'd just say, 'He's fine. That's how he swims.'

Anyway, she was holding his hand and she felt a definite squeeze. It had shocked her and she thought she'd actually gasped. Then she looked up and he was staring at her.

'Did you tell him my name?' she asked.

'No, why would I?' I responded tersely.

'He said, 'Louise.' That was his first word. He couldn't remember all the things I'd talked to him about, but he knew who I was. I introduced myself to him right at the beginning, when I started visiting him. I said I was so sorry, and I told him how things were between us, and I hoped he wouldn't mind me coming.'

She looked at me, wide eyed. 'I told him my name, and he remembered.'

I talked to Olly about it at college, but he said not to torment myself worrying about it and thinking about what could have been. From what he'd said, he said he'd infer that Dad wanted me to know he would love me whatever I did or was, and to take comfort in that.

Tyler kind of said the same thing, but less effectively.

Over the next few weeks, I did try to follow Olly's advice and focus on what I'd had with Dad, rather than what I'd lost, but Christmas was hard, and New Year even worse; the thought of a whole year without Dad, and after that another. I missed him all the time and every day reminded me of what he would have been saying and doing if he was still there. There was a gaping hole in every social occasion, and although both Mum and Dad's family tried hard to fill each day with activities to take our minds off it, Mum and I came home early from our annual get togethers; enduring his permanent absence and trying to enjoy ourselves was exhausting.

At Auntie Jen's New Year party, we couldn't face twelve o'clock and Auld Lang Syne without him, and we went home and straight to bed. I think we both cried ourselves to sleep. I certainly thought I heard her sobbing, but I couldn't go in to her. After the funeral, we'd barely spoken, and I found I didn't care. If she didn't want to accept me for who I was, I couldn't force her, but I wasn't going to pretend for her any longer.

The only thing that got me through the holidays was Dan. It was only messages and the odd phone call, but knowing he was there was enough. He listened to me and cared and understood, and that was enough.

After the Christmas holidays, I found I could enjoy college and feel almost normal most of the time. There would be worse days, but on the whole my life went on as it had before. I hadn't actually come out to anybody else, but I felt it was just a matter of the right time. If it seemed like someone needed to know, I'd tell them. On the whole though, if it wouldn't affect our relationship either way, I thought, 'why do they need to know?' What was the point in blurting out, 'by the way, I'm gay,' if it didn't have anything to do with your relationship?

I discussed it with Olly and Faye one night while we were sitting at the bus stop waiting for Tyler. It had become a habit, and he was always late, waylaid by this person or that project he hadn't finished. 'I'll be there in 10,' he'd message, and half an hour later, he'd appear.

Usually Olly would sit with me and wait, but today Faye was having tea at Tyler's so the three of us sat on the wall chatting.

'I could never have coped without you two,' I suddenly needed them to know how crucial their support had been to me over the past few months, allowing me to come to terms with who I was, as well as helping me deal with my dad's death.

'You'd have coped somehow,' Faye smiled, 'but thanks. It's nice to know we're appreciated.'

'Anytime,' Olly added.

A bus came and the shelter emptied. We cursed Tyler, as we always did when this happened, but we never actually minded.

'If I'd been a better friend to Dan, he'd never have had to go through what he did.' I carried on. I told them I was glad I hadn't had to go through half of what Dan had. Yes, I'd agonised over the decision, but when I'd finally made it and told them, it was immediately like a huge weight had been lifted off my shoulders. With Dan, he'd told me and I'd just dithered; he must have thought I was horrified, or disapproved at the very least.

I continued, explaining how Olly had been an inspiration to me, and now Dan. He seemed so comfortable in his skin, as if he didn't care about other people's opinions. I loved his 'take me as I am or not at all' attitude; I rambled on about how Dan and I were going to live like that in the future.

I was so engrossed in my admiration, I failed to notice Olly's reaction, how he'd fallen silent.

It was perhaps easier to accept when it was more obvious, I went on, laughing because Olly was always using his campness as material for his comedy. I said I supposed when everybody already had a pretty good idea when you were four, you didn't have the actual problem of 'coming out' as such. I mentioned the story he'd told me about making evening dresses for his action men out of tin foil and his mum and dad judging them like it was Miss World.

'Olly?' I began, suddenly noticing how quiet he'd become. 'I'm sorry. Did I say something?'

'Be careful Jake won't you? Not everyone deals with things in the same way. Sometimes you have to care about other people's opinions, like your mum? And Dan's…Dan's dad. You might have to take it slowly.'

I was confused. Why was he backtracking now, when everything was going well for Dan and I?

He seemed to realise how negative he'd sounded and smiled, 'It's fine. I'm sorry. Your role-model speech just hit a nerve there. I'm just a bit touched.'

'Touched in the head,' Tyler laughed, rubbing Olly's head and messing up his hair, 'thinking you can copy my hairstyle and automatically be as cool as me.' He'd sneaked up on us unawares and jumped out at the least opportune moment possible. It was typical Tyler, and exactly why we loved him, but he was completely oblivious to the atmosphere he'd interrupted. Faye caught my eye; Olly had taken full advantage of Tyler's arrival, and they were now good-naturedly trading insults.

Chapter 53

At home, the situation with Mum was uncomfortable, to say the least. We should have been pulling together and supporting each other, but neither of us were prepared to back down. The way I saw it, how could I back down? I didn't know exactly what she expected me to do, but I assumed any potential scenarios involved lying and hiding who I was from certain people; that would never be acceptable to me now.

I'd go upstairs as soon as I returned from college, finish my homework and spend an hour playing games on my PS4 if there was time. She'd call me when dinner was ready and we'd make polite conversation over the meal, I'd fill the dishwasher and tidy the kitchen, then she'd watch the TV on her own and I'd go and play some more. Sometimes I'd walk over to Tyler's, or he'd come to mine, but if he did, we'd be holed up in my room rather than spending time with Mum. It was just the same as before, except it wasn't. Mum would usually be watching TV with Dad, but now he was gone, and she was alone.

Maybe I should have felt sorry for her, but I was still too angry at her for that.

I'd look around the house, at the chair that Dad used to sit in, Dad's chair. No-one sat there now. When visitors came, they'd instinctively know, even if they'd never been in the house before, that Dad's chair was sacred. It was brown leather, and had a lever on the side which, if you pulled it, sent out a footrest and reclined the chair. It never reclined now though, just sat there empty in the corner in front of the TV, a slight dip evident from the hundreds of times Dad had watched TV, reclining, with a cup of tea on the nest of tables beside it. It was the same in the kitchen, the chair Dad used to sit in when we ate tea remained empty. We were creatures of habit. Mum would always sit on the end, with me to her right, and Dad to her left. Now the chair to her left was painfully empty, and it felt uneven and wrong.

I increasingly felt I should have confided in him and regretted not doing so when I had the chance. Of course, I blamed Mum for that. She'd made me believe that he would have been horrified, that he wouldn't have been able to cope, but I didn't believe that now. In my imagination, I'd play out the scene I'd convinced myself would have transpired if I had told him, and he'd always end up saying, 'None of it makes any difference to me. I love you just as you are Jake.'

I stopped unburdening myself so much to Olly. I felt a little betrayed by what he'd said at the bus stop. I said as much to Dan when I called him one night. 'It's like he can be who he is, but he doesn't want us to do the same. I don't understand why he'd say that.'

Dan's reaction wasn't what I wanted to hear either. 'He's just saying be cautious Jake. It's nothing personal. He just knows that it was easier for him than it will be for me…for us.'

'Why?' I retorted. 'We're older. We're almost adults now. Why should it bother us what other people think?'

'Jake,' he snapped. 'Olly wants us to be free and happy just as much as you do. It's just not that simple. Look, I've got to go. I'll see you Friday.'

I was hurt when he put the phone down, but I understood. I was so excited about the future, I wanted it to start now. I wanted everyone to know who I was and I didn't care who liked it or not. If Dan just wasn't quite there yet, I had to respect that.

When Dan didn't arrive at Nando's by nine on Friday, I started to feel sick. Maybe I'd pushed him too far. Maybe I was moving too fast. Nothing had really happened between us yet but maybe whatever was between us was making him uncomfortable.

I checked my phone again. Nothing. Olivia caught my eye and checked hers. Nothing. 'I'll try his landline,' she gestured, and walked towards the door, keying in the number.

'I spoke to Ryan. His phone's out of charge and he's got some sort of bug,' she told me as she sat back down. I was relieved, but the churning in my stomach would not go away.

I must have been quiet, because Olivia caught my arm on the way out and said, 'Hey. It's fine. You and him are fine. I promise.'

He didn't join in the group chat like usual. I put it down to being ill. Maybe he was catching up on sleep. Still, it was just a bug? I hoped it wasn't something more serious, then I chided myself for being dramatic. He'd avoided social media for a couple of days, hardly grounds for panic.

Half-term was hell. I couldn't pretend that everything was ok because having a bug for a couple of days was one thing, but staying out of touch for nearly a week was serious. I messaged a couple of times over the weekend, funny, light-hearted messages, but there was no reply. Finally, I sent one more, 'Call me please.' I thought the least he could do if it was over was tell me.

On the Thursday the situation between Mum and me came to a head.

It was silly things at first. I'd been so careful not to leave any dish unwashed, coat on the floor or lawn unmowed since Dad's death, but occasionally I slipped up. This time it was my bedroom. I'd had homework the day before and Tyler had been round playing Fortnite later. In the morning, I meant to tidy up, but I'd overslept and had to rush out, leaving clothes, text books and various papers scattered around the floor.

'Do you expect me to tidy up your bedroom as well as do everything else?' Mum barked as soon as I opened the door.

'I'll do it now,' I said sullenly, and set off up the stairs.

As I started to pick up the dirty clothes, she swung open the door and yelled. 'I can't believe what a disgusting tip it is in here. It stinks. You have one room to keep clean and you can't even do that. I'm sick of picking up after you…'

I whipped around to face her. 'It's one day Mum. I always keep my room tidy. And I load the dishwasher and clean the kitchen. You should see Tyler's room if you want to see disgusting.'

'Tyler's room has nothing to do with me. He doesn't live in my house. He doesn't have to follow my rules.' She was calming down slightly now, but her voice was taking on the sort of ominous tone she used to use when I was younger and she was going to threaten me with a punishment. 'The next time you *forget* to unload the dishwasher, I'll take away the PS4 for a night' it might have been. Now I was older, surely she wasn't going down that route again.

'I'm not sure you and Tyler should be up here in your bedroom all the time.' She said, meaningfully.

It took me a while to understand why she would say that, and even when I realised, I hesitated. She couldn't possibly be saying what I thought she was saying.

'After what you've told me. If what you've said is still…'

'Are you joking?' I cut her off, snarling, looking straight into her eyes. I couldn't quite read the expression there, defiance maybe? The expression she used when she wanted to emphasise the fact that she had the power. I'd seen it before when we'd argued and she felt she was losing. 'If you're living under *my* roof…'

I erupted then with a fury I never knew I had in me. 'Are you joking?' I screamed. 'Tyler is my friend, he always has been! We're just the same as we always have been! I don't fancy him! I don't fancy every male person I come into contact with! I can't believe this. Do you really think…Oh my God, I can't believe you said that.'

Her chin was still lifted, a sign that she wasn't going to back down, but I saw something different in her eyes, a flash of uncertainty maybe?

'Tyler's the straightest person in the world. So if you're worried I'll turn him gay you don't have to!' I laughed bitterly. 'Just for the record, I don't fancy Olly either. He's my friend, like any other friend…so he was never a threat to your bigoted little fantasy view of life either.'

'Don't speak to me like that. I don't know anything about…that. Don't talk like that.' She snapped.

'Like what?' I yelled into her face. 'You mean using the word *gay?* It's not a dirty word you know? It's what I am. How dare you make me feel like this? How can you?'

I suddenly had a huge urge to speak to Dan, to tell him how strongly I felt. If it didn't go the way I wanted, if he didn't feel the same way, I'd deal with it. Whatever happened afterwards, I knew I had to do it.

'You know what though. I do fancy someone. I think I might love him.' I was scornful now, wanting to shock her, wanting to hurt her, to punish her for what she'd said and done to me.

'At the funeral, the boy I hugged? It's him. His name's Dan and weirdly he looks like Elvis. You know the cover of that CD you love so much? I'll find it for you, shall I?'

I ran downstairs and rummaged through the CD drawer until I found it. It was dusty, so I polished it off as I headed back upstairs. Nobody used CDs anymore, not even my mum and dad, but ten years ago, she never had that CD off the player. We'd watch Elvis films together too when I was young, and she'd go on about what a good-looking man he was.

I slammed through the door and threw the CD on the bed. She seemed more upset than angry now but I was in no mood to indulge her. 'There, he looks like that. Do you remember. He might even be better looking. Just think, you might get Elvis as a son-in-law.'

I stood there looking at her for a minute as she sat down on my bed, head bowed. 'I'm going out,' I spat, contemptuously, and I grabbed my coat and ran down the stairs. Slamming the door behind me, I took out my phone.

Chapter 54

If it wasn't cruelly ironic enough that Dan should wake up when she was there, not me, or any of the rest of his friends, his first word was her name. I was jealous, and I hated her for making me jealous. I should be ecstatic. I should be focusing on Dan being awake, on the fact he seemed to be well. He was alive and he didn't have brain damage. I should be overjoyed, but instead the bitterness twisted my insides back into the knot I'd almost forgotten.

When we reached home I jumped out of the car, unlocked the door and went upstairs. So many emotions were spinning around in my head, it felt like they were fighting. I couldn't seem to focus on any one feeling at once, there was just a huge chaotic battle going on.

I sat on my bed struggling to regain control for a while, before deciding to go out. Maybe the fresh air would clear my head? I'd decide on a destination, then walk there and back. At least I'd know where I was going.

But the knot tightened as I came down the stairs, to the point where I put my hand protectively on my stomach. As I opened the door, I felt the tension rise into my chest where it quickly became a pain. Panicking, I pressed my hands to the pain and cried out. By the time Mum reached me I was kneeling on the floor gasping for breath.

Chapter 55

On the Monday, I could barely bring myself to get out of bed. Dan hadn't answered any of my messages and that was a message in itself. I missed the bus and was late to college, avoiding any uncomfortable conversations with Tyler or Faye and Olly.

Will and Matty were already in maths. Matty looked like death and my face must have revealed my concern. 'Self-inflicted,' Will explained. 'I had to bring him straight here because he couldn't stand the thought of smelling food.'

'Family party,' Matty croaked. 'I'm not sure I'm going to make it.' And he laid his head on the desk. Normally I'd have laughed, but I couldn't even raise a smile.

It was difficult to concentrate on the lesson as I was so anxious about Dan. There had been no messages on the group chat, and neither Olivia or I had had replies to our messages. I'd never known his phone be unreachable for any length of time before. Where was he? Why was he avoiding us? Ryan had said it was a bug, but a bug doesn't last over a week. According to George, who had made subtle enquiries, he'd already had two days off college before half term, and nobody had seen or heard from him since.

I received a message halfway through the lesson from Olivia. George said that Dan was in college. She'd set up a group with the six of us in, but not Dan. He was obviously upset and she was worried about him. 'Something's wrong. We need to find out what,' she added.

Olly and Faye cornered me at break time. 'I have a plan,' Olly said. 'You finish at lunchtime today, don't you? And we're working on a script. We can say we're going to Faye's to do it and get the bus to Shuttleworth. We'll arrange to meet George and then we'll just hang around until we 'bump into' Dan on his way out.'

'Maybe it's just me he's trying to escape.' I wasn't comfortable with the plan at all. It could end up making me look like a crazy stalker ex-boyfriend, before I'd even been an ex-boyfriend, before I'd even been a boyfriend!

'Jake,' Olly said, putting his hand on my shoulder, 'there's something wrong. I know there is. It's obvious how he feels about you, and he told Olivia everything. He would not do this to you if he had a choice.'

It was weird walking through the main doors of Shuttleworth College. We didn't belong there and it felt like intruding on Dan's territory. When George met us, I felt slightly less nervous, and as we walked through the corridors no-one looked at us as if to say 'imposters!'

George gave us a short guided tour of the places where Dan might be if he was free, but he wasn't in any of them so we sat in the canteen and waited.

'We'll hang around construction just before they come out and we're bound to see him,' George told us. 'There's only one way out and I never see him in here anymore so he must go straight home or to the gym. We'll see which direction he's heading in and follow him. You know, I think I'd make a good Bond. I'm the international spy type. What do you think?'

Nobody laughed and George sighed. 'Sorry. Don't worry, we'll find him.'

When I saw the back of Dan's head, slightly above most of the other students as always, a wave of relief flooded over me. He was there, so he must be ok, physically at least. I'd been worrying that Olly was right, and there really was something seriously wrong, but it seemed like perhaps we might have had a wasted journey after all. We watched him weave his way through the crowd of departing students and head towards the main road.

'Dan!' Faye shouted, and he spun around, shocked by the sound of her voice. When he spotted us, he turned away and it looked as if he was going to ignore us and keep walking, but then he seemed to hesitate and his shoulders slumped as if in defeat. He stood watching as we approached and half smiled.

'What are you doing here?' he asked, looking down at the pavement. It almost wasn't Dan. Although he tried to look comfortable it was obviously an effort. He looked the same way he had at Faye and Olly's show, kind of grey and rumpled. He hadn't washed his hair, and whereas it usually flopped to the side healthily, it was lank and dull, drooping greasily over his right eye. I wondered whether he was drinking again.

I glanced at Faye, and her expression was even more worrying. She was looking at his face and nervously clicking the nails on one hand with those on the other.

'Shall we go and get a drink in the canteen?' Olly suggested. 'Seeing as we're here?'

'Sorry, I can't,' he replied, still staring at the floor. 'I have to get home. I'll see you soon. Sorry.' He turned and walked away, shoulders still hunched, and didn't look back.

I felt sick. He hadn't even acknowledged me. But then, he'd hardly acknowledged any of us.

'Bruise.' Faye mouthed, as he left, pointing to her right eye.

One word, but it set off alarm bells in my head. I hadn't seen a bruise, but I'd been on the other side of Dan, and his hair must have hidden it.

We caught the next bus home. There didn't seem to be much point in staying.

'What are we going to do?' Faye asked.

Nobody answered.

'I'm just going to ask him,' she retorted, and took out her phone. A couple of minutes later, her phone vibrated. None of us expected it to be him, but it was.

'I was wrestling with my brother and he accidentally elbowed me in the face. You should have seen the other guy,' Faye read. 'He's even put a laughing emoji on it,' she said, shaking her head in disbelief.

Olly turned to me, 'Even if that did happen, it doesn't explain him ignoring you over a week does it, or behaving like that with us earlier?'

'Do you think he was just embarrassed?' George suggested, 'because he hasn't been in touch?' He directed the question to me, and I thought for a minute. If his feelings for me had changed and he was just trying to avoid me, it could explain his behaviour, but the bruise? And the dishevelled appearance?

It just didn't ring true. I knew Dan's brother was a boxer. Why would Dan be wrestling with his brother? From the very little I knew of his family, they certainly didn't seem close enough that I'd believe they were play fighting.

'You need to ring him,' Olly said. 'Don't message him. If you phone you might catch him off guard and he might talk to you.'

I knew he was right and I knew I had to do it that night. For a while now I'd been forcing myself to address issues as soon as they arose. I was determined to stop putting things off and being a coward. I wanted to become someone who was capable and strong, not just for myself, but for others too.

I was so nervous as I typed in his number my heart was thumping and I could feel the pulse in my neck throbbing.

'Hiya,' he answered, cheerfully.

Instinctively, I knew there was something badly wrong. 'What's happened?' I demanded. I couldn't let him manipulate me. I had to catch him off guard, like Olly said. 'I know something's wrong. Why won't you tell me?'

'Yeah, I've done mine. It has to be in on Friday. Yeah, it's about weight and support.'

I was firm. 'You obviously can't speak, but you have to tell me tomorrow. I've told you everything about me. You have to tell me.'

'Yeah, ok. I'll see you tomorrow,' he said, as if it was just a routine enquiry.

Immediately I started to panic. If there was an issue at home and either his dad or brother was violent, had I caused even more problems? If I was his dad, I'd wonder why someone would phone, rather than message. Nobody phoned, not about something that could be answered so easily. I didn't think I'd ever phoned before.

I rang Olly; messaging seemed too trivial. 'There's nothing you can do now,' he reasoned. 'Tomorrow we'll talk about it. Olivia might have some ideas, if he's been confiding in her? We'll come up with a plan.'

I didn't answer. 'Like your last plan?' I almost blurted out. But I knew that was unfair. If we hadn't gone to him, we wouldn't have seen how awful Dan looked, and I'd still have been painting myself as the victim of the piece and him as the villain.

'Jake? Go to bed and get some sleep. We'll talk tomorrow. Ok?'

I knew he was right, there was nothing I could do that night, but I lay awake until the early hours worrying, turning over different scenarios in my mind, each one more frightening than the last.

Chapter 56

I messaged the group early in the morning, and we arranged to meet in the drama studio before college to discuss tactics. It was raining, the sky full of dark clouds which promised a miserable day, and the room was gloomy and colder than I remembered.

'Maybe he'll talk to George, seeing as George is already there?' Olivia suggested, but we all agreed that perhaps he wasn't the best candidate for the job.

'I love George,' Faye said, rolling her eyes, 'but he'd give Trump a run for his money as a diplomat.'

I favoured a frontal assault. Give him no way out, no means of retreat. Physically, I argued, we could ambush him and prevent him from leaving until he'd told us the truth. Faye was dubious. It didn't seem right to bully him like that. If he was already suffering, he needed to be treated kindly and encouraged to talk, rather than forced. I felt myself becoming frustrated. We'd tried that, and he'd just walked away. I also argued there was no point messaging or phoning. He'd just ignore us or lie. It had to be face to face if we were to find out what was going on.

Eventually, we came to a compromise. He had messaged back yesterday, so he was at least back in contact. We'd try to draw him out, separately and via the group. If he was suffering, he'd need to talk to someone, and if he knew we were all there for him, it would probably be one of us. George had told us that Dan seemed to have withdrawn from the group he'd first seemed friendly with at Shuttleworth and he'd not seen him with anyone lately. 'He's a bit of a loner,' were his exact words. 'He'll nod when he sees me, but make sure he veers away before we're close enough to speak. I didn't think anything of it before, but looking back, it does seem weird.' He'd sniffed his armpits. 'Maybe I just smell?'

When all our messages over the next couple of days were ignored, I began to think maybe he'd resented my forcefulness the last time we spoke. If he didn't want to talk to us, maybe it was none of our business. Perhaps he was angry at me and this whole thing was because of that. He could hardly be friends with everyone except me.

Faye was adamant though. 'There's something wrong and you know it. I can't concentrate for worrying about him. Olivia's the same.' She was on the verge of tears all day, and in the end, I had to explain to Will and Matty what had happened. 'Maybe you could go and see a counsellor? You know, the area behind the English rooms? Is it student support?' Will suggested.

'What would we say though?' she sobbed. 'He hasn't spoken to us for nearly two weeks and he had the remains of a bruise on his face on Monday that he said he got play-fighting with his brother? 'It's not a lot to go on, is it? They'll just think he's fallen out with us.'

If we've not heard from him by tomorrow, I'm going to see them,' I decided. It felt good to have a plan.

That night, Olivia forwarded a message that Dan had sent her. 'I'm leaving college. It's not for me so I'm going to work with my dad. Don't worry. It's what I want to do.'

The phone rang as soon as I'd read it. Olivia was hysterical. 'Why would he do that Jake? You know he wouldn't do that. I don't think he even sent the message, do you? What if something's happened to him?'

'We don't even know where he lives,' Faye posted on the chat a couple of minutes later. 'It's like he's just disappeared. How can we contact him now?'

George added to the group five minutes later, '34 Station Road. I told you I'd make a good spy.'

When Olly and Faye both messaged to ask how he knew, he replied, 'What century are you living in? I googled the electoral roll and put his last name in. There were never going to be many Sweeneys around here were there?'

'Calm down,' I told Olivia, with a calmness I didn't feel. 'See, we know where he lives now so there's no panic. I'll go round to his house tomorrow. I'll get up early and see what's going on.' I wasn't sure what I expected to achieve, but I had to do something. I set my alarm clock an hour early and messaged Tyler to tell him I wouldn't be meeting him in the morning.

It felt ridiculous to be hanging around across the road from Dan's house at half past seven in the morning, but I didn't see what else I could do. I had to know what was going on and why Dan had withdrawn so completely from me, from all of us.

I wasn't sure where I'd expected Dan to live, but it certainly wasn't here. The house was a large Victorian Terrace on the main road through town. Most of the other properties were shops, and it seemed like the others had probably been converted into flats, judging by the intercom panels by the doors. Number 34 looked quite dark and dingy, squatting between an off licence on the corner of the next side-street and a chemist's shop. I'd travelled through the area to get to the town centre before, but it wasn't somewhere you'd visit without a reason.

It was a couple of minutes after eight before the door of Dan's house opened and his dad and brother came out. His dad was tall and broad, like Dan, but I assumed Ryan must have inherited his mum's slight figure. He wasn't tiny, but compared to his dad and Dan, he would look like a child. Dan had said Ryan was like his dad, but he certainly hadn't taken after him physically. I could imagine him resenting that. They walked around the corner, Dan's dad finishing off the remains of his breakfast, and after a minute, a white van pulled into sight. Ryan was driving. I watched him check both ways and turn right. Pressing myself against the wall, I studied the van as it drove away. 'Sweeney's Building Services' it said in blue lettering, Roofing, Driveways, Extensions. There was more, but the van was gone before I could read it.

Well, Dan wasn't working with his dad today. It didn't take a lot of detective skill to work that out. I sat down on the pavement and considered my options. I could simply observe the house and see if I could spot him, wait to see if he left at any point and follow him, or the most daunting alternative in terms of discovery and potential disaster: I could knock on the door and confront him. If I did that, he might be angry at me for interfering and slam the door in my face. Even worse, his dad might come back and see me, making the situation even worse. I didn't know what the situation was, but I was pretty sure my intervention wouldn't be welcome.

Whichever route I chose, I wasn't going to make it into college today so I rang the absence line and told them I was ill. Next, I messaged the group and said I wouldn't be in, but that I'd let them know what was happening as soon as I could. After that, I walked across the road and knocked on the door. I didn't feel all that strong or capable, but I figured if I pretended, no-one would know the difference.

For a while there was no answer and I knocked again. I was here now so I might as well do what I'd come to do. After a couple of minutes, I heard movement and someone approaching the other side of the door. The latch was pulled back and the door opened slowly. Dan stuck his head around and saw me too late to disguise the fact that his lip and cheek were bruised and swollen.

The traffic had built up, and people were hurrying to and fro to catch buses or make it to work in time. 'You might as well come in,' he said, blankly.

There was no point in lying now. Whatever had happened, it wasn't right.

'Your dad?' I asked, looking at his lip. It could have been his brother of course, but that seemed the less likely option.

'Yeah, he was talking to someone in the club and they mentioned some rumours going around school last year. Probably Ewan, or Amelia. Actually probably both. Do you remember that day they were on the stairs laughing at us? I didn't even know you were gay then, but they called you 'my new friend' or something like that and I knew what they were implying. Anyway, apparently some of the guys were taunting him, making him look stupid in front of everyone, laughing at him. That's the way he saw it anyway. He was mortified. What did it say about him that his son wasn't a real man? He called me all the names under the sun. I've heard them all before so that didn't bother me. But then he started screaming at me for being disloyal and lying to him. Like I had a choice. Like if I'd said, 'To be honest Dad, I'm gay, I hate boxing and I don't want to be an electrician,' he'd have gone, 'ok son, you carry on.'

'So he hit you for lying?'

'No, he hit me for arguing back, like before the holiday. It's not like he does it all the time; normally he barely notices I'm there, much less actually looks at me or speaks to me. It's just at the moment I can't keep my mouth shut. I hate him. The night of the show I was out of the door before he could catch me, and he couldn't touch me for a bit because I had to keep seeing the counsellor, but before the holidays I snapped at him because he shouted at me for burning the tea. That's why he did it then. But this one...' he swallowed and looked at the floor. This is it for me.'

He stared at the same spot on the floor for a long time, lost in thought.

'What do you mean?' I prompted.

He took a deep breath. 'For my future. The future Mum told me about, where I could escape to the city and it would be paved with gold and there would be lots of lovely, friendly people everywhere.' A lone tear ran down his cheek and dropped onto the floor.

'You can still do it,' I said. 'You have to do it. He'll accept it eventually, surely.' It was coming out of my mouth, but I wasn't sure I was being convincing. My own mum hadn't accepted it, so how was I expecting this big Irish builder, whose son's homosexuality was an insult to his own masculine ego, to accept it.

'My dad will never accept it.' He swallowed again, took another deep breath and wiped his eyes.

The room was small and dark, the curtains still closed and the only light coming in from the open kitchen door. It was decorated in a fairly old-fashioned way, but you could see that in the past, someone had tried to make it homely, with scatter cushions across the sofa. It was a little bit cheerless, but not unclean, a fact that I attributed to Dan. All these things I'd seen gradually though. When I first entered, there was only one focal point.

In the middle of the room, above the fireplace, was what looked like an altar: A statue of the Virgin Mary was elevated on a small stand and in front of this was a large gold crucifix surrounded by candles and other religious ornaments. Behind the display, various framed pictures of religious scenes covered the chimney breast.

Aware that I was looking at it, Dan sneered, 'He never even looks at it, let alone prays. But he certainly uses it against me. Do you know what my name means?' He looked at me and I could see the anguish in his eyes. 'God is my judge. Do you believe that? God is judging me all the time and in the Bible it says that homosexuality is wrong, so God hates me too.'

'Religion's just about interpretation though. It says what people want it to say.' I was out of my comfort zone now. I knew nothing about religion and I certainly couldn't start quoting bits of the Bible to make Dan feel more hopeful. 'Live and let live' I thought I remembered hearing, or something similar.

'Yeah.' Dan sat down with his elbows on his knees and his head in his hands.

'He didn't know what was wrong with me when I was four. I was bigger and stronger and faster than anybody else's kids and he loved it. But when I started boxing I just couldn't do it. I didn't want to do it. He saw something in me then, like I told you before? He just saw it, before I even knew it myself. He hated it, and I think he thought he could knock it out of me then, but when he realised that he couldn't, he just hated me.'

He stopped, and I waited. The traffic noise was heavy and constant but somehow it seemed far away.

'My mum tried to shield me from it, but it was there on his face whenever he looked at me, the contempt, the hatred. Obviously, I didn't understand it until later. I didn't know why he loved my brother, and he'd take him places and do things with him, but he hated me. He was embarrassed... no... ashamed of me. All his friends would laugh at him if they knew what sort of son he'd spawned. Where my dad comes from, men are real men and women do what they're told. She tried to discuss it, to reason with him, I heard them arguing, but he wouldn't listen. He blamed her for making me like that. Said she'd been too soft and too close to me, made me like her.'

He described how much he'd loved the times spent with his mum, where she'd talked about the future like it was a great big adventure. He'd go to college and then university and then he'd be free. He'd meet people who would love him and he'd leave all this behind. She never actually said it out loud, he knew she was afraid to, but she meant people who judged you on what kind of person you were, not on the basis of your sexuality or the colour of your skin.

That's why he'd tried so hard at school. He wasn't naturally brilliant, but he had a goal and he'd done everything in his power to reach it. Like his mum had said, it was the only way to escape.

'When she died, the future she talked about?' he looked at me and paused, 'it died with her.'

'Why? Why can't you still do it?' I asked

'You have no idea, do you?' he sighed. 'Yes, your mum is homophobic and your life is difficult, but she still wants the best for you. Ironically, the reason she doesn't accept you're gay is because probably she wants your life to be easy and normal. She scared of you being gay, she has a phobia. But she still wants to you go to university and become...I don't know, whatever you want to be. She's still going to fund that, isn't she? She's not going to throw you out, is she? You think it's all about her, but I think it's mostly about you.'

I felt stupid then. Stupid and naïve. I suddenly realised why Olly had urged me to be cautious, rather than pushing Dan into doing something reckless.

'I have to act like I'm going to follow the rules. The person I am at home is the Dan that's as close to what dad wants as I can manage. He doesn't have much to do with me. As long as I keep the house clean and cook the meals, we mostly keep out of each other's way, and that suits me. Same with my brother I suppose. He's like a clone of my dad: loves cars and can mend them instinctively, a good fighter; he's been boxing since he was about four, works with my dad as a builder; he'll probably take over the family business, and loves the ladies. Not that my dad is a ladies' man, nothing like that, he just likes *ladies*, like *normal* men.'

'You're not really lying though, are you?' I reasoned, 'If he knows, and from what you're saying, he does, you're not lying?'

'It's not as simple as that. I wish it was.' Another sigh.

'Why? What are you lying about?' I prompted.

'I hate my course. I'm useless at it and it's a pointless waste of time. I wanted to do English and history A Levels but he completely refused. There was no point in arguing. He just said he wasn't paying for me for another five years then I could mix with loads of people who made me think it was normal to act like me. He said I had to train to be an electrician because that's what he needs and it was that or fend for myself. That was practically what he said.'

'But you didn't tell him you hated it? Is that what you lied about?'

'I did for a while. It was easier for me to go along with it and let him think I'd accepted it. I actually tried at first. Like I told you. I made some friends and tried to be like them and brought some of them to the pub to meet him, and he thought I was cured. But I couldn't keep it up. I hated the course and I didn't fit in with the banter. In the end, I just got up and went in and sat there. The tutors tried to encourage me at first but then they just gave up, and the rest of the crowd stopped bothering me.'

'So you lied about enjoying the course? Being committed to it?'

'Well I didn't say I wasn't. I let him believe I was, which I suppose is like lying…until a couple of nights ago, after you came to the college. I told him I was never going to pass the course and I didn't want to anyway. I didn't want to be an electrician and I didn't want to work for him. I was just in one of the moods I get in when I don't care. What's the worst he can do? Hit me? Throw me out? Sometimes I think it would be easier if he did.'

'What did he say?'

'At first, it felt good. He looked like I'd punched him. I felt powerful, being able to cause him so much pain.' Dan's eyes narrowed, and he stared into space, obviously remembering the malice that had inspired his actions that night. 'It didn't last long though. He looked at me as if I was a monster, and asked me to say it again. I calculated what the lowest blow would be, and I aimed. I told him I was sick of lying and I wasn't going to do it anymore. I said I was gay and everybody would know soon anyway and he would just have to get used to it. I don't know what I was thinking, but once I'd started, it was like I couldn't stop.'

'Is that when he hit you?'

'Yeah, and you know, I was almost glad. The fact that he lashed out showed me how much I'd got to him, again. He hadn't hit me for ages until just before the holiday, which showed he was…happy…content I suppose, like he'd forgotten about me. I'd acted too well. I resented that so much, because I wasn't happy at all. You know the night when you were going on about being adults and not bothering what other people think?'

'I'm sorry, I…' I began, but he cut me off.

I watched his face as he spoke, his expression changing from pain to anger.

'When you have to act all the time, it's hard work. It's like you're in a pressure cooker and it's getting hotter and hotter. The steam's building up in your head and when it gets too much it just blows the lid off. That's what happened on Monday. I just couldn't take it anymore.'

'So what happened then?'

Dan told me how his dad had stormed upstairs and not come back down for half an hour. He'd waited, straining to hear sounds of movement, but there was nothing. He said the silence was more frightening than if his dad had been raging around and breaking things.

'Eventually, he came down, and he was calm. His face was like stone but he didn't shout, just said that he'd decided I'd leave college and work with him from now on. There was plenty of labouring to be done. He'd done the same thing for Ryan when he started his apprenticeship so he knew how it worked. He'd sort out the day release and at the same time he'd make sure he changed all the details at college. He said if I couldn't manage the electrician's course, I could do bricklaying. 'You need to learn a trade then you can earn your own money,' he said. 'There's no way I'm wasting another penny of my money on you.'

Dan seemed completely defeated. I would have expected him to be at least planning his escape, but there didn't appear to be any fight in him. 'Can't you leave?' I said quietly.

'And go where?' his voice was monotone, devoid of any emotion.

'What about your mum's family? Your grandparents or uncles and aunties? There must be someone?'

'There's no-one. In our family, everyone thinks the same way as my dad. They'd just feel sorry for him having me as a son. My brother told me some of them have mentioned it. He's ashamed of me too. When he was younger, he was jealous of me because I was bigger and better than him at most things. Now he loves that Dad just ignores me and he's the golden boy. My mum's family are mostly in Ireland, but mum said they were worse than his, you know, homophobic, racist, the lot.'

'You could go somewhere and talk to someone maybe. Maybe student support at college? They could help you move out? Find you somewhere to live.'

He'd been down that road, he said. At first, when he realised he wouldn't pass the electrician's course, not that he'd wanted to anyway, he'd gone to The Citizen's Advice to find out what he could do, what options there were. There was nothing. He wasn't entitled to any money as he lived at home and was at college. He had nowhere to go if he left so he'd just starve to death with no money.

I asked about foster parents or children's homes or anything like that and he told me he'd asked about accommodation but they'd been honest with him and said that unless there was the possibility of homelessness or a real crisis at home it was never going to happen. They'd advised him to talk to his dad and explain his feelings. They were sure he would come around. They'd given him leaflets to show his dad with telephone numbers of groups which helped parents in his situation. He'd thrown them away.

I said I'd try to find out if there was anything else, especially now there was violence in the equation. That was a crisis, surely?

'Don't waste your time. I'm just going to get on with it. I'll just keep my head down for a couple of years and then I'll move out and get away from them. Dad says I'll start next Monday. He said my lip looks a mess and it will put the customers off. You never know, I might be good at bricklaying.' He laughed bitterly.

'You have to go,' he said suddenly. 'They come home for lunch and I have to get it ready and make sure everything's tidy. I've loads I need to do. He said he's not going to keep me for nothing. Now I'm unemployed and not at college I need to earn my keep. Today I need to clean all the windows inside and out and he's getting some paint so I can paint the window frames. I need to make a start before they come back. Go out the back and turn right then you don't bump into them if they come back early.'

'You've got your phone, haven't you? You'll be allowed out? He can't keep you locked up forever?' I needed to know how to contact him. He'd need us more than ever now.

He told me he did, but he was going to lie low for a while. Not to worry about him. He'd be in touch when everything calmed down and they weren't watching him so closely. He asked me not to message and let the others know because he'd have to explain who we were and that would just be something else to annoy his dad. The plan was for him to cut ties with all that, but in time they'd let their guard down and he'd be able to contact us. I think he was trying to sound positive but there was a lack of emotion in his voice that scared me.

'Please don't tell your mum or college or anything like that. It would make things so much worse. He won't do it again. He only does it if I answer back or argue with him. I'm not going to do that anymore, so he won't do it again.' Seeing the doubt in my eyes, he repeated himself. 'Honestly, he won't. Promise you won't tell them.'

I promised. There was no real alternative.

'Stay here a minute,' he said as he opened the back door. I watched as he stuck his head out of the back gate and checked both directions before gesturing that it was safe for me to leave.

'You'll be ok?' I asked, as I slipped by him.

'I'll be fine. Don't worry. I'll text you soon,' He smiled, but his eyes were empty.

Chapter 57

'I can't breathe,' I wheezed. I was having to fight for each gulp of air. My heart felt as if it was being squeezed tighter and tighter. Was I having a heart attack?

'Jake!' she cried, kneeling down beside me and looking into my face, 'Jake, what's wrong?' She looked terrified, and suddenly jumped up and ran to the kitchen.

I could hear her speaking on the phone, and the fear in her voice as she gave the address. Then she knelt down beside me and put one arm around my shoulders and the other round my chest. 'Don't worry,' she soothed, but she was shaking too and I could feel her heart beating against my arm. 'Calm down. Don't say anything, just breathe. The ambulance will be here soon. I'm here. Don't worry,' she continued.

By the time the ambulance arrived, my breathing had returned almost to normal, but I was sweaty and still shaking, frightened that it would come back. We were still kneeling by the open door, her arms around me and head against mine. I hadn't moved, and I hadn't asked her to move because I felt safer with her there. It felt like she was protecting me from harm.

The two male paramedics helped us both up and into the living room, where they sat me down in my dad's chair. The younger man explained that the symptoms I described were consistent with my having had a panic attack, and that these were brought on by stress. Was I worried about anything in particular or had anything happened to upset me?

Mum explained about Dan, and he agreed that the stress I'd been under as a result of Dan's coma could well have triggered the attack. He wasn't sure why it would have happened at the point where Dan was out of danger, but you never could tell with the human body. It was a law unto itself.

Chapter 58

Faye wanted to call the police. 'It's against the law to physically abuse your children,' she stormed. I'd agonised over telling her, but Dan had mentioned not telling adults. When I'd promised, it was the authorities I was promising not to tell, college, the police, my mum. He hadn't specifically mentioned friends, and I justified it to myself this way. In reality, I simply couldn't shoulder the burden alone.

I argued that we couldn't tell anyone because I'd promised we wouldn't. It wasn't like he was a young child. He was seventeen. Would the police even do anything? Dan had said it wouldn't happen again, and we'd never seen bruises on him before had we? I was as worried as she was, but I'd promised, and I was terrified of making it worse. What if the police went round and his dad punished him for it?

'How can you force your son into a job he'll hate though,' she raged. 'It's not even just a job, it's his whole life.'

'It's not against the law though, is it?' Tyler reasoned. 'Lots of people are forced into jobs they don't want to do. We're just lucky our parents don't want to do that. Anyway, maybe he'll make enough money doing the building to pay for college in a few years. That's what he's probably thinking. That's what he said Jake, isn't it?'

'He said he was going to do it for a couple of years then move out,' I remembered. 'If he passes his apprenticeship he can apply for other jobs and then he can rent a house I suppose.'

We sat there behind the bus stop for another few minutes, each lost in our own thoughts. Was there nothing we could do to help Dan? Was he really going to spend two years living in that house and spending all day with two people who hated him? I began to see that my life was easy in comparison. Mum hadn't come to terms with my sexuality, but it was like Dan said, I still knew she wanted the best for me. She wanted my life to run as smoothly as possible, and homosexuality was a definite bump in the road. If only she'd help me smooth out the bump rather than pretending it wasn't there.

The bus came and we sat in silence, playing on our phones, until we reached Tyler's stop and the two of them got off and waved half-heartedly. I continued to watch mindless YouTube videos until the bus pulled up to my stop.

There was a huge Dan shaped hole in my life for the next few days. I missed him so much, and I couldn't seem to shake it off. Speaking at all felt pointless. I was so preoccupied I just sat on my phone or played the most undemanding game I could. After a while, everyone stopped suggesting hopeless escape routes Dan had already found were impossible. It was easier not to bother.

Faye had arrived at college the morning after I'd told her about Dan's situation, having been trawling the internet most of the night torturing herself. 'You do know apprenticeships can last up to four years? His dad's not going to fast track him, is he? Can you imagine him being in this situation for four years?'

I repeated to her what I'd told myself the night before. There was nothing we could do right now. It was still raw and Dan's dad was humiliated. He would be determined to punish Dan for publicly shaming him and alert to any sign of deviation from his instructions. We had to do what Dan said, let the dust settle and wait for the point where he started to relax. Then he could contact us and we could hopefully meet up and support him through whatever was happening.

It all sounded completely insincere, even to me, and I felt like I was abandoning him, but the truth was, we were completely unable to help him. Faye had asked her mum if Dan could come and live with them, and although her mum had been sympathetic, she was also practical. Faye's mum and dad had split up years before, and although her dad contributed, she was still a single mum with three mouths to feed. She'd chosen to keep the house, which was a drain on her income, but which she loved, and she just couldn't see how she was going to stretch that far. She'd also pointed out that she'd only met Dan once and never met his dad. You couldn't just take a teenager away from his family because you wanted to. It probably wasn't as simple as it sounded either, she'd suggested. You had to listen to both sides of a dispute.

Coming from a loving, secure home had always been something I took for granted. Even now, I knew mum would never throw me out. Even if she did, I had numerous family members who would take me in I was sure. When I put myself in Dan's position, I could feel how trapped he was. There genuinely was nowhere to go and nothing to be done about it. He'd just have to endure it until he was in a position to escape.

After a couple of weeks, having received no message from Dan, I was desperate. I ran it by Faye and Olly and we decided that one message couldn't hurt. We decided that she'd send it, and we'd make sure it couldn't be used against him if his dad did see it for any reason. We needed him to know he wasn't alone, and that we were still there; we hadn't forgotten him.

'Hope you're ok,' Faye typed, then deleted it. 'It sounds like we're worried about him, and that implies he's told us what's going on. If his dad sees it, he might take it the wrong way.'

'Or the right way,' I mused.

'How's it going?' she typed in. 'We're missing you!' She deleted the second sentence and changed it to 'Hopefully see you soon' then she deleted that too. She lifted up her shoulders and raised her eyebrows at me. I mirrored her body language, then nodded. She sent the message.

A couple of hours later, there was still no reply. I was starting to panic; the message had been delivered and read. She calmed me down, arguing that at work, it's not like college, where you pretty much have access to your phone at all times. He might have to leave his phone in the van, and he was probably eating with his dad and brother. He was probably thinking it would be easier to leave it till later to message back in case they asked and he had to explain.

It seemed she was right. Faye forwarded Dan's reply that night.

'I'm fine. Thanks for your message. Need to just get on with it for a bit. Will see you when everything has calmed down. Might be a few weeks. x'

What did he mean by 'a few weeks'? Had he even sent the message? How many weeks? It was five weeks until the Easter holidays, although would he even have Easter holidays?

I hardly slept, and the next day the others could tell the situation was taking its toll. Olly reasoned with me. 'Look, you know his position. He has to keep his head down. He's asking us to help him. Anything we do could make his life more difficult. It won't be long.' He looked into my eyes. 'I'm sorry Jake. It won't be long.'

We decided that we'd give him until the holidays and then contact him again. Surely by then it would be safe.

Making the decision was a relief. It gave him breathing space, but I had a definite time and date for our next contact. Dan had asked for time and I was giving him time. Hopefully, the next time I spoke to him it would be face to face. His dad would have to let him out sometime, and he could meet me in secret if it would be difficult to manage otherwise.

Life went on. Mum and I remained civil; sometimes I saw her looking at me wistfully but I quickly turned away. She had made her feelings quite clear.

Most of us had exams to revise for so evenings were busy, but we managed to meet up a couple of times, at the weekend, mainly. Tyler, Faye, Olly and I saw each other most days for varying amounts of time. We'd discuss the situation with Dan, but usually in a relatively positive way. He was seventeen. It wasn't for ever. Soon he'd be out of there and living his life the way he wanted to. I think we almost convinced ourselves.

Chapter 59

Will came into the canteen on the Thursday before we broke up for Easter looking agitated. 'I think I've seen your friend Dan,' he told us, frowning. He couldn't be sure because he wasn't near enough and he didn't know Dan that well. He could be wrong, but he had a really strong feeling it was.

'What's wrong?' I asked. Will's body language was making me nervous.

'If it was him,' he started. 'It might not be…but if it was, he looked awful.'

'What do you mean? What did he look like?' Faye's voice rose in alarm.

'He was thin. I mean, he had no weight on him to start with, did he? But if it was him, he was really thin, and his head was shaved, like a skinhead, you know? That's why I didn't notice him at first. It just looked nothing like him. But this morning, I really looked, for ages, and I think I caught his eye. It was only for a split second, but I thought he recognised me. He turned round straight away and put his back to me but I think he saw me.'

Will explained that some neighbours were having an extension, and different vans had been there for about a week, with various builders, electricians and gas engineers in and out of the gate all the time. He hadn't taken much notice; people on his avenue were always having work done, but one morning he'd just happened to see this one builder, the one he thought was Dan, drop some sort of concrete pipe while he was getting it out of the van, and he heard the loud smash as it broke. He'd tried not to be nosy but he was walking right past just as the man in charge had come through the gate and gone mad, screaming at the lad that he was useless and stupid. He kept on walking but he could see their body language out of the corner of his eyes and it seemed like the lad was cowering away, like he was frightened of being hit. There was something familiar about him then. But it hadn't registered what it was.

'This morning…' Will sighed, and then looked up at me. 'I think it was him Jake.'

'We have to do something Jake,' Faye cried. 'We should have done something before. We need to get him out of there.'

I knew she was right. He wasn't safe at home. That much was clear. But what could we do?

'Do you think you could get a message to him?' I asked Will. 'I'm scared they're monitoring his phone. Could you watch until he's on his own and slip him a note or something? We have to speak to him. We can't just kidnap him.'

Will said he'd try, but what could we do then? We were still in exactly the same situation as before. I turned to Faye. 'We need to speak to someone. I'm going to Student Support now. Someone will know what to do. We've given him time and it looks like it hasn't worked. Are you coming?'

We set off in the direction of the student support area. On the way, we discussed what to say and it suddenly struck me. We didn't know it was even Dan. Will had said he *thought* it was Dan, but he hadn't remembered the names on any of the vans. They were all white, he thought, but he couldn't even swear to the colour of the lettering. We couldn't take this any further until we knew. Faye started to cry again as soon as I explained, but I told her we had to do this properly. We had to be sure and plan what to do now.

Will was still in the canteen with Matty and when we returned, a puzzled look crossed his face. I told him what my plans were and he immediately agreed. We couldn't waste any more time. I wanted to see Dan for myself, make sure it was definitely him, perhaps manage to speak to him or at least pass a note, and proceed from there. We set off straight away, leaving Matty to pass on our excuses to Mr. Cotton, the further math's lecturer.

I hoped Will didn't live too far away and luckily, it was only a short bus ride, even a walk if we weren't in such a rush. The bus arrived within ten minutes, and we discussed what to do on the journey. We couldn't risk being seen, so Will suggested going through the field at the back of his house and climbing over the fence. Then we could watch the house from his bedroom window; we'd be able to confirm the van was Dan's dad's or not at least. If it was, we could try and move somewhere closer?

Will's house was in the middle of a prestigious, relatively new, estate, one that was growing all the time, spreading out and becoming a village of impressive avenues and closes, each one consisting of different designs. On one avenue, the properties would have Elizabethan features with mock timber frames, on the next it would seem the designer had been influenced by Georgian architecture. The houses on Will's road looked to have been inspired by Victorian fashions, with pointed gables and turrets.

As soon as I saw the van from the window, I knew it was the one. I couldn't quite make out the rest of the lettering, but 'Sweeney's Building Services' was clear enough to see from Will's house. We had to get nearer. It was obviously Dan, but I wanted to see him for myself. Perhaps Will had overstated his description, or maybe Dan looked thinner because of his hair. He might come out of the house laughing and joking; It could all have been blown out of proportion. I wasn't sure exactly what I wanted to see. I didn't want to see that Dan was being abused, but then again, if he was, I needed to see confirmation then we could act on it.

We decided it would be easier for one person to sneak up and hide in order to get a better view than two. Will would remain at the window and ring me if he saw anyone leaving the house or if there was any danger of my being discovered. It sounded ridiculously cloak and dagger, and if the circumstances hadn't been so serious it would have been funny. But there was nothing funny about it.

It was half past two before I was safely settled in between two bushes in the front garden of the house next door to the one Dan was working at. I messaged Will to say my view of the drive and the van was good but I was completely hidden by leaves. Unless someone knew I was there, no one would ever spot me from that side. I was also hidden from the back, so didn't have to worry about the neighbours coming home and exposing my position.

For the next forty-five minutes, I sat watching the house but there was no sign of Dan. His brother Ryan came out to the van to collect a bag of something and sat on the floor of the open van having a smoke. As he shut the doors, another van pulled up. The driver wound down the window and they chatted briefly before the van reversed and then parked nose to nose with Dan's dad's van before the getting out and slamming the door. Similarly built to Dan, he was dark and balding, with more hair on his chest, arms and back than on his head, and from what I could see, indecipherable tattoos lurking like huge parasites underneath. The two of them walked through the gate and around the back of the house, Ryan having hoisted the heavy bag onto his narrow shoulders and the other man with a large toolbox in his hand.

Another fifteen minutes went by before I heard the gate slam again. As Dan came into sight, I almost gasped audibly at his appearance. Will had not exaggerated. He looked like a skeleton, skin pulled tight over his skull and sunken eye sockets; the shaven head almost made him look like a grotesque caricature. It was a warm spring day, and he was wearing a pair of dusty jeans which looked two sizes too big and were only anchored by a piece of blue string around his waist. Over them he had on a vest T shirt which emphasised the thinness of his arms and emaciated torso. As he passed me I could see his shoulder blades jutting out sharply.

I had to speak to him. This might be my only chance.

'Dan,' I whispered loudly, taking out the sheet of paper we'd prepared for him. When he didn't react and carried on towards the van, I hissed louder, 'Dan!'

He whipped around in shock, and I could see the fear on his face. Had he recognised my voice and was afraid of the consequences, or was he afraid of someone else he thought had called his name?

'It's me, Jake,' I whispered, and he took a step towards the bush, scanning the leaves. Pulling a branch to one side, I held out the note, folded into a small parcel. If we were interrupted, at least he'd have the details. He darted forward and snatched it, skipping backwards afterwards and slipping it into his pocket. His eyes were huge in his head, the look on his face like a terrified baby animal on one of the nature documentaries I used to watch with my dad.

'We're going to help you. Read the note and meet us.' I mouthed as quietly as I could. He didn't speak, just stared at me, and back at the gate continuously, as if completely stunned and unable to move. As he stood there, I saw a deep purple bruise down the side of his body where his T shirt gaped; I thought he must have seen me notice, as he put his arm down and around his body protectively. When I heard a laugh from the direction of the house, and the sounds of men saying their goodbyes, I was afraid he was going to give me away, he looked so rooted to the spot, but he jumped again and scuttled to the van, never having said a word.

The other man strode through the gate laughing to himself. As Dan turned from the van, carrying what looked like a trowel, he bellowed, 'Alright Danny Boy!' and hunched into a boxing stance, throwing pretend punches, before slapping Dan playfully on the back of the head, climbing into his van and reversing into next door's drive. As he pulled away I noticed the lettering on the van: 'M. Sweeney Plumbing and Gas'.

Chapter 60

They were talking about me as if I wasn't there, and to a point, I wasn't. I stared at the ceiling as I reflected on what had happened. The attack had started with my jealousy of Mum, the fact that I resented her being the person Dan had chosen to wake up to after the way she'd treated him. Really it was more about me though, wasn't it? The fact I couldn't forgive her for the way she'd treated me. In the back of my mind I'd known it wasn't about Dan, it was about me, and I felt guilty about it.

I remembered what Tyler had said about forgiveness. 'Unless you've never done anything wrong in your life.'

Let he who is without sin cast the first stone.

My own resentment and bitterness had welled up inside me like an infection. In the end, my own lack of empathy and forgiveness had attacked me. I was suddenly exhausted, and I closed my eyes.

Chapter 61

We met that night at Faye's house. All of us. Faye had told her mum some of what had happened and when I relayed my story to everybody she agreed that we should go to Student Services. She also said she'd go to the Citizen's Advice Bureau herself the next day and between us we'd sort it out. If Dan had to stay at her house for a while, she was prepared for that too.

'It's fine Mrs Reed,' Olly interjected, 'Mum and Dad would like Dan to stay at ours if he needs to and that's possible. We have more than enough room, and to tell the truth, they're mad enough at me already for not telling them before it came to this.'

I felt guilty that I couldn't tell my mum. We had two spare bedrooms at home and I knew that money was nowhere near as tight for her as for Faye's mum. There had been no thawing of relations though. We were like strangers living in the same house, both still grieving for dad, but separately. I think she blamed me for making a devastating time in her life even worse, and I blamed her for blaming me, and not supporting me through the worst time of my life. We were civil to each other, but it was a cold civility.

On the Friday, Faye and I met outside Student Support half an hour before it opened. 'You always need an appointment,' she explained. 'Not that I've been before, it's just that you always need an appointment anywhere nowadays, don't you?' It was another thing that would have been funny, her speaking as if she were someone's grandma, if I hadn't been so anxious, but I was finding nothing amusing at that point.

When the counsellor arrived, she unlocked the door and ushered us inside with a smile straight away. The room was comfortable, the focal point being two bright blue sofas at the end under the window. They faced each other, with a low-level coffee table in-between; it reminded me of films I'd seen where the main character goes to see a psychiatrist. There was a big leafy plant on the windowsill and a view over the playing fields.

'Take a seat,' she said pleasantly. 'Do you want a cup of tea or coffee?' When we declined, she picked up her coat and bag and opened the door, 'I'll just be one minute,' she called over her shoulder, bustling out.

We sat in silence and I took in the rest of the room. There were filing cabinets, a desk and lots of leaflets in displays on the wall. I started to scan the brightly coloured literature. Bullying, alcohol, drugs…

The door opened again and the same lady came back in. 'Sorry about that,' she apologised, and sat down across from us, smiling again. A plump and friendly looking woman with glasses and frizzy red hair, she put me at my ease immediately. I wasn't sure what it was about her but she looked trustworthy and dependable somehow, like a benevolent aunt. She told us her name was Helen, and asked ours. Then she looked at us both kindly. 'So, what can I do for you?'

I began; Helen looked so motherly and concerned that my fears for Dan poured out of me; maybe it was something to do with not really having an actual mother-figure for the past few months. There was no hesitation. I felt completely impotent, and we were doing what had been drummed into us since primary school. We were telling an appropriate adult. At one point, I became choked up and she turned to Faye, who continued with the story until she came to the visit to Dan's house, and said, 'you tell the rest Jake.' You were the one that saw him…you saw what he was…' a sob escaped her, and Helen passed her a conveniently placed box of tissues.

I continued the story, determined not to leave anything out, and above all, determined not to leave without making it absolutely clear that Dan was in danger. Some might argue that he may have sustained the latest bruise in the course of his work, but I knew that was not the case. I had seen the some of the previous injuries his dad had inflicted, and who knew how many more had remained covered. He had assured me that his dad was not habitually violent, but that's what victims did, wasn't it? When I remembered the conversation we'd had about his visit to The Citizen's Advice Bureau, it was obvious now that he hadn't told the whole truth. If he had described his home life honestly, they couldn't possibly have simply sent him home with a fist full of leaflets and a flippant, 'I'm sure he'll come around.'?

I had to convince her that we needed to act. When I described his appearance outside Will's house, she frowned and rose, walking over to the desk at the other side of the room and taking out some papers and a pen.

Putting them on the table in front of her, she looked across at us gravely. 'If everything you've told me is true,' she began, her eyes on the forms in front of her, 'and I believe it is,' she hastened to add, looking up at me, 'I believe that your friend may be living in an abusive home, and we do need to address the issue as soon as possible. We'll have to involve the police if that is the case?'

She was obviously giving us a last chance to back out, warning us that once certain procedures had been set in motion, the situation became serious. What we were alleging was criminal behaviour and not to be taken lightly. She was checking whether we were willing to stand by our convictions, maybe in court.

I looked at Faye, seeing her search my face for any sign of doubt. I was the one who'd spoken to him. I was the one who'd seen him. It was my word she was agreeing to stand by.

We turned to Helen and nodded together. 'Yeah,' I said. 'I'm sure.'

It was another couple of hours before we left the room. Helen brought in a couple of her colleagues and we repeated our statements while she wrote them down. The three of them then explained that the case would be referred to a specialist child abuse investigation team and social workers would probably be involved. There were various things that the team may do, including arranging an interview with Dan and his dad.

I stopped Helen there. What if his dad denied it? What if Dan backed him up? Would they just drop it then? That would put him in even more danger. For the first time, doubts about what we were doing began to creep in. What if we made the situation worse and Dan was punished for it?

One of Helen's colleagues, a bald man of about forty wearing a creased grey suit and brown shoes, said gently, 'The police know what they're doing, but there are procedures to be followed. Hopefully your friend will confirm what you've told us and they'll be able to take him into police protection, at least until they can provide a more permanent solution. But the procedures have to be followed.'

I knew he was right. The police weren't going to swoop down immediately and snatch Dan away for his own safety until they had investigated our allegations. How long would that take? My heart was knocking against my rib cage. What had we done? Had we just put Dan in an impossible situation?

When we eventually left the room, after Helen had reassured us that they'd keep in touch with us closely and let us know what was going on, I turned to Faye. 'We have to see him. He has to tell the truth then they can take him away. What if he lies to protect his dad? We have to tell him, then he's prepared.'

'You gave him the note, didn't you?' she asked, her tone reflecting her anxiety.

I nodded.

The note had asked Dan to meet us in Nando's at eight on Sunday night. I remembered him telling me how Sunday night was the big night in the club his dad went to. Ryan would go too for the first part of the night, then he'd be off into town, drinking more and chasing women (like all red-blooded men should be). Sunday nights were the times he'd spend with his mum, watching films or just talking, the nights he obviously missed terribly.

If we could persuade him to tell the truth, perhaps he'd never have to go back and he'd be safe.

Chapter 62

All day Sunday I was jumpy. I couldn't even concentrate on the games I was playing online with Tyler, and in the end, he said there was no point. It wasn't fun if there was no competition. We arranged for his dad to pick me up at half past seven, then we'd be there well before Dan just in case he was early.

I went downstairs and sat on the sofa in the front room looking at Dad's chair. Would it have made a difference if Dad was here? Could I have spoken to him about it and could we have come up with a solution together?

The front door opened and Mum came in. Realising everything was quiet, she called my name.

'In here,' I said, and she popped her head around the door.

'Are you hungry?' she asked.

'No, I'm fine,' I answered, and went back upstairs.

Nando's was busy when we arrived, and I worried that we wouldn't be able to get a table. Luckily, Faye and Olly had beaten us to it. 'Jake!' she called, and they waved us over to one of the farthest booths from the door.

They already had drinks in front of them, so Tyler went to order some from the counter. We had decided to eat there, as on a Sunday, it was frowned upon if you simply nursed your drinks and ordered and couple of snacks to share. They didn't usually mind on weekdays, but weekends were the money spinners, so if we didn't eat, it wouldn't be long before our table was commandeered and we were politely asked to leave. We figured the best way of keeping the table was to spend loads of time wondering what to eat, then stagger our orders and eat as slowly as possible. That way at least one of us was eating at any one time. Tyler reckoned we could spin it out for two hours, maybe longer if we ordered puddings.

By half-past eight, Dan hadn't arrived, and my stomach was doing somersaults. Realistically, I knew nothing could have happened this soon. It was still only Sunday, and the counsellors at college had told us that guidelines were in place concerning investigations of this type and contact would be made when information had been shared with the health services, local authority and schools to establish if Dan was already on the at risk register or determine if any previous concerns had been raised. At the weekend, these organisations were either unmanned or employed a skeleton staff, so it was highly unlikely that any action would be taken well into the following week.

Still, my nerves were in tatters, and I could barely listen to the conversation at the table. There was no going back now but I was worried that Dan wouldn't thank us for what we'd done. He asked me not to tell anyone, and I promised. I lied to him, and my conscience was tormenting me.

'Earth to Jake!' It was Olly, and as my eyes gradually focused I could see his were full of concern. 'You've done the right thing,' he said firmly. 'What else could you have done?'

Tyler added his reassurance, arguing that there were loads of explanations as to why Dan hadn't showed up; it didn't have to mean he was physically locked in the house. He might have a legitimate reason; Maybe they had visitors, or there was a family party, or his dad just decided not to go out, and he couldn't get away.

No matter how much they tried to convince me, there were nagging doubts at the back of my mind. By the time the food arrived, Dan still hadn't, and I couldn't face eating. Pushing the wings I'd ordered around my plate, I replayed scenarios in my head where our actions had negative consequences.

At a quarter to ten, I made my excuses and left, declining both Olly's plea that I stayed a bit longer and Tyler's offer to come with me. Dan's house was in the opposite direction to mine, but only half a mile from Nando's and on the main bus route. If I walked up there, I could catch the bus from just past Dan's house. What that would achieve I wasn't quite sure, but I set off anyway.

The lights were on downstairs when I arrived, but the curtains were drawn, as they had been during the day when I'd gone round to talk to Dan. Why would someone always keep their curtains closed? To hide the outside world from those inside, or to hide what was going on inside from the outside world. I felt like charging over there and confronting them, but what could I do against two men, both boxers, and at least one of whom was obviously violent outside the ring?

After half an hour of watching the house, there had been no movement, no figures silhouetted by the light against the curtains, like you see in films. I walked to the bus stop and waited for the bus. I was being ridiculous. I had to let the authorities do their jobs.

But I couldn't shake the increasingly ominous feeling that Dan was in danger *now*.

Chapter 63

I didn't wake until hours later. Mum was sitting on the sofa watching me and she asked if I was hungry. I said I wasn't. I was still tired and thought I'd go straight to bed. I rose, but I was still wobbly and she helped me to the door.

Passing the front door, a feeling of dread washed over me, almost as if I was reliving the attack, but it subsided as I climbed the stairs.

The next day, I planned to set off for college earlier than usual and had already texted Tyler to let him know.

After eating breakfast (I was starving after not having eaten since breakfast the day before) I slung my bag over my shoulder and started towards the door, but before I reached it, I began to feel nauseous and weak. I went back into the kitchen and sat down until the feeling had abated.

Picking up my bag again, I began to walk towards the door again, but this time I felt the same anxiety as the day before. I started to gasp, but the more I tried to breathe in enough air, the more difficult it became. The fear came then and I called out for Mum in-between shallow breaths. If it was possible, this time it felt even worse, and I was convinced I was going to die. I just couldn't seem to take any air into my lungs at all. The more I tried to breathe, the more I couldn't. I tried to call out again but I couldn't make a sound. I couldn't shout or scream. In desperation, I dropped to my knees, putting my hands out in front of me to steady myself.

She ran down the stairs put her arms around me like she had done the day before, soothing and calming me as I struggled for air.

When I started to relax, she steered me into the living room, sitting me down and fussing around me, dabbing my sweaty face gently with a towel, asking if I needed anything, whether I was too cold, too hot, did I need a blanket? Again, I was exhausted and lay there prostrate, answering her questions monosyllabically. But I held her hand tightly. I felt safer that way.

Chapter 64

I slept badly, tossing and turning, unable to shake the worries. On Monday, I was short-tempered with Tyler on the way to college. I knew we had to wait and there was nothing we could do now, but I snapped at him on the bus, 'stop saying that. Just don't say anything!'

He took the hint and we rode for a couple of miles in silence. We passed Dan's house, and I thought about how many times I'd been metres away from him and not known. I strained to see if there was anything different, but the curtains were still closed and the light was still on.

A couple of blocks further on I turned to Tyler. 'Why would the lights still be on?'

Tyler looked at me in confusion.

'Why would the lights still be on?' I repeated. 'It's half past eight on Monday morning. They leave at eight. I've seen them. Why would they leave the light on?'

'Maybe they just forgot?' he suggested.

I suddenly had such a huge surge of foreboding that I leapt up and ran to the front of the bus. 'Stop!' I screamed at the driver. 'Let me off, now!'

Slamming his foot on the brake in shock, he opened the door and I jumped off, sprinting down the road in the direction of Dan's house. I don't know what it was, but I *knew* Dan was in trouble. As I checked the road before crossing, I could see Tyler gaining on me with both our bags bouncing off his shoulder.

The road was busy, and even if there had been any sound from inside, the traffic would have drowned it out. I stared through the window, nose against the glass, hands cupped around my face, in case there was any chink in the curtains, but they were pulled tight and there was no way of seeing anything from the front.

Rushing around the side of the block and down the back street, I checked for any sign of the van. If it was there, it wasn't parked in the same place as it had been the last time I'd been here. I came to the second gate and tried it, but it wouldn't open and when I stuck my arm over I couldn't find the bolt. 'Shit!' I shouted, punching it in frustration.

'Here,' Tyler said, holding out his laced together fingers as a step. He seemed to sense the urgency and almost threw me up onto the top of the wall. I jumped down and slid back the bolt, opening the gate for Tyler.

After all the running, it seemed bizarre that we were now tiptoeing toward the back door, but I was afraid of what we'd find. There was nothing in the kitchen to suggest anything was amiss, but when I peered through the window, the light from the living room was shining through the open door weirdly. Was it weird, or just an oversight, as Tyler had predicted?

'It's open,' Tyler whispered, his hand on the back door handle. Why would the light still be on and the back door open if everyone was at work? The fear was back with a vengeance. A rush of adrenaline filled my body and I walked through the door and across the kitchen, careful not to make a noise. As I walked around the kitchen table, I heard a crunch and felt something under my foot. Glancing down I saw that a glass had been smashed, and the remnants lay glinting in the half light from the living room.

Chapter 65

If anything, over the next couple of days, it got worse. I seemed to panic as soon as I even saw the front door. Mum suggested we try the back door, but the result was the same. I'd become short of breath, nauseous and weak every time any door was opened to the outside world.

The first day, Tyler messaged. 'Mum can pick you up tonight on the way in.' I texted back and told him I was ill.

The next day I had messages from Olly and Faye. I said Mum thought it was flu, and that I shouldn't really come into contact with anybody, especially anybody who may visit Dan. Could they pass the message on? As soon as I was better, I'd be straight in. Mum said why didn't I just tell them the truth? They were my friends and they wouldn't judge me. But I was too ashamed.

When Tyler's mum rang, once I realised it was her, I begged Mum, eyes pleading and hands clasped together as if in prayer, not to tell the truth. Reluctantly, she agreed, unconvincingly paraphrasing my messages.

'I need to see Dan,' I cried. What would he think? It seemed so unlikely that I'd suddenly be struck down with flu at this specific point in time. He would think I didn't care, that I'd abandoned him. I was so angry at myself for being so weak. Who was so weak they couldn't even step out of their house?

Mum was strong though. My weakness seemed to have infused her with a vigour that I hadn't seen since Dad had died. 'Dan knows you're desperate to see him Jake. That is genuine. He knows it must be something serious for it to prevent you from seeing him,' she said, 'It's temporary. It just may take a little time. You will learn to control it. We'll do it together.'

I was desperate for the panic attacks to disappear, and frustrated that I was completely dependent on Mum, but every time I even thought of walking through the door I felt sick. It seemed to be getting worse, not better. Mum took control. 'I'm going to tell them,' She stated. It wasn't a request, more like an order, but I was relieved that she'd taken the initiative. She'd been on the internet and printed a couple of articles off on dealing with panic attacks; we'd tried some of the methods they advocated, but so far, it didn't seem to be working.

She went into college and collected a pack of work from my tutors, explaining that it may be some time before I was able to come in. Tyler and Olly both came round, separately. Then Faye and Olivia dropped by as if they'd just been 'in the area'. It was ridiculous. I wasn't sick, I was just weak. They had probably drawn up a rota like we had for Dan. Mum said why didn't I write to Dan and she could take the letter in? We could be like pen pals. She meant well, but made me feel even more stupid and worthless.

After a week, I felt so pathetic that I pretty much withdrew into my room, coming downstairs only for meals. I told Mum to ask everyone not to come again. It made me feel worse if anything. I was ashamed, and I couldn't cope with their pity. Mum tried to reason with me, but I became angry and refused to listen.

She'd been so kind and supportive, and I'd needed her so much that I'd allowed myself to let her back in. I'd even hugged her and wept on her shoulder. Now though, I was confused again. If I stayed in my bedroom, I was fine. As long as I didn't think about going out or approach the door with a view to going out, I could breathe easily and there were no symptoms apparent, but when she tried to talk to me about trying again and controlling the attacks, the anxiety returned.

Chapter 66

I gasped as I moved forward into the room. The door to the stairs was wide open, and the glass coffee table had been smashed, but the most shocking thing was the fireplace. The makeshift altar seemed to have been purposely destroyed. If there had been a fight in here, things may have been knocked over, or even broken, but it looked like someone had deliberately swept everything off the mantelpiece. On the left hand side of the hearth, candlesticks and candles were strewn about on the carpet and the large gold crucifix lay on its side in the middle of the room, perhaps having bounced off the wall. A couple of the framed religious pictures which had covered the wall behind the altar remained hanging askew; the rest were on the floor on the right side of the fireplace.

The statue of the Virgin Mary was missing. I remembered her specifically because she had stood in the middle of the display, pale and almost luminous, and it was when I saw her that I realised the significance of the Catholic religion in this house. Scanning the room, I expected to see her lying on the floor somewhere or maybe on one of the chairs.   She seemed to have disappeared, but why demolish the rest of the shrine and save her?

There was no sign of Dan, but as I crossed the room, preparing to check the upstairs, I saw what looked like a heap of clothes piled up next to the sofa, blocking the door.

Sticking out of the clothes was a bare foot.

'Dan!' I shouted, kneeling down to touch his shoulder. He was huddled up in a ball, on his knees, but slumped forward with his arms around his head, as if he was protecting himself.

'Dan,' I ventured, more quietly this time as I shook him gently. There was no response. I touched the skin at the back of his neck, feeling for warmth or a pulse. I couldn't feel either, but he wasn't cold.

As I took my hand away from his neck I saw the blood. On the far side of his head, half hidden by the sofa, there was blood, blood that was now covering my hand, soaking the neck of his T shirt and dripping down onto the carpet where a large stain was growing.

'Ring an ambulance!' I screamed at Tyler, who was standing in the middle of the room like a statue, staring, his eyes and mouth open and frozen. I remembered my feelings of shock when we'd found Dan in the street, and how they had rendered me helpless.

Pulling out my phone I rang 999, spoke with a strange calmness I didn't feel, and gave the necessary information. Taking off my jacket, I lay it over Dan and talked to him, stroking his back softly and telling him we were there and that the ambulance was on its way.

'Can you open the front door and wait for them?' I asked Tyler, my voice once again sounding relaxed and controlled, like someone else's voice completely, belying the terror I was feeling. How long had Dan been like this? hunched up here?

The light was still on. The light was on at ten o'clock last night, but why now, when sunlight was streaming through the gaps in the curtains? Had Dan been here like this all night?

Chapter 67

I knew I was being irrational, but I couldn't seem to help myself. One day, she came into my room and said quietly, 'Jake, there's someone here who wants to talk to you.'

I didn't answer. Maybe it was another therapist.

A couple of days before, she'd skyped one online counsellor who claimed to specialise in panic attacks, but he'd sounded just like he was reading from a script. Half way through the session we looked at each other and frowned. Everything he was saying, we'd already read a dozen times in leaflets or on the internet. She stopped him abruptly and said, 'thank you but I don't think you'll be able to help us.' Then she turned the IPad off before he had the time to argue.

We sat there for a few seconds in silence, until she turned to me, an expression of mock guilt on her face. 'How rude am I?' she made a shocked face, before scowling contemptuously, 'charlatan!'

'Charlatan?' I started to giggle. 'Where are we? The nineteenth century?'

It seemed so absurd when I thought about it, so old fashioned and inappropriate to have called someone you'd just skyped a charlatan, that I couldn't stop myself, and Mum must have realised, as she began to laugh too. It felt so good, both of us in a fit of giggles. At one point, I felt a little more composed, but mum was still holding her stomach, with her eyes closed. 'Charlatan,' she repeated, between cackles, 'Why would I use that word?' and I was off again.

When we eventually pulled ourselves together, Mum smiled at me for a long time.

'What?' I asked, still smiling, and when she didn't answer, 'What?' I was beginning to laugh again.

She reached out and stroked my hair to one side, something she'd always done, as long as I could remember, when we'd gone into a restaurant, or before we visited family. It was more an affectionate habit than a serious attempt to tidy up my appearance.

'I'm proud of you,' she said quietly. 'I'm really proud of you.'

I'd wondered then if she'd known how much that meant to me.

I watched the door from where I was sitting on my bed finishing some equations. Mum came in first, and opened the door wide, a welcoming smile on her face. As Dan walked through, she looked at me to gauge my reaction, which I thought was probably sheer surprise. Obviously satisfied that it wasn't horror, she withdrew, asking us if we wanted anything to eat or drink. I shook my head and Dan declined politely, smiling at her nervously as she closed the door.

'She rang me at Olly's and asked if I'd come to see you,' he explained, gesturing at the door.

'You're staying at Olly's then?' It was the only thing I could think of to say.

'Yeah,' he smiled and walked over to look through the window. 'The police said I could go home once I'd been discharged; Dad and Ryan have vanished off the face of the earth it seems. They certainly couldn't get back into the country without being arrested. Anyway, Olly's mum and dad wouldn't let me. Olly said they spent a week doing my room up and his mum would kill him if I didn't come. Now she's trying to feed me up...'

After a pause, he turned and looked at me. 'I wanted to come anyway, but I didn't know how things were between you. You know, with...everything.'

It struck me then, that since Dan had been attacked, I'd never really given Mum the chance to talk about how she felt about me, about what I was and about my relationship with him. I didn't know how things were between us either with regard to her feelings about my sexuality. She'd admitted what she'd done and apologised endlessly for the way she'd made me feel, but I'd never really listened, and I'd certainly never asked her how she felt now. I'd held on to the ignorance and the bigotry as a reason to blame her.

But she'd invited Dan here now, into my bedroom nonetheless. She must have done that to show me. To show me she'd accepted what I was, and she loved me. It was a sign.

'I'm good,' I began, then realised how it sounded. 'I mean, not good, but I think I might be getting better. You know?'

Dan nodded, sitting down on the edge of the bed. He should have shaken his head, I thought. Of course, he didn't know, because I hadn't told him. He was aware of the way I felt about Mum and how much I resented her attitude when Dad died, but I'd never told anyone the truth about why I hated her so much. I wasn't sure I even knew myself until just now.

So I told him, about how I felt to blame for his situation. At first, I'd seen what I wanted to see, I'd never dug any deeper or asked Dan about himself, never thought about what it meant that he didn't talk about his family and we didn't ever see his dad or know where he lived. I should have done more to help after the night he'd collapsed. Then when it became clear he was in danger, I was too quick to let him manipulate me into doing nothing, perhaps because that too was easier for me?

He stopped me. He put his hand on my knee sympathetically and reasoned with me, 'Jake, don't torture yourself. You didn't know the situation back then. No-one did. You believed what I said...What could you have done anyway?'

That was it. That was why I blamed Mum. I wanted to help him escape, to tell him I'd keep him safe. I wanted to bring him to my house, where it was safe and loving and warm. But I couldn't, because of Mum. Then again, I hadn't told her, had I? I hadn't given her the chance. If I had, who knew? Maybe we were both to blame for that.

'I could have been there for you, like you were for me,' I sighed. I could have told the counsellors at college or the police. I could have saved you all those weeks of suffering. I remember what you looked like when we first found you in that house.' A sob escaped from my throat as I remembered how he looked when I'd seen him across from Will's house, terrified, eyes as huge as a baby animal.

'Don't Jake. As soon as you knew, you did what you could. You probably saved my life. I'm alive! I'm free. No matter what happens, I'll never have to go back to that place, ever.' He looked straight into my eyes and spoke firmly. 'You have to do something for me now though.'

I looked at the floor. I knew what was coming.

'You have to get well. We'll all help you. I know it seems impossible. Your Mum told me all about it, but we just have to persevere...keep going.'

I didn't move. I knew he was right, and the way he'd said 'we' rather than 'you' reminded me that I wasn't alone. 'I will,' my voice wavered, and I took a deep breath. 'I will,' I repeated clearly. I looked at him and nodded, and he smiled.

'I'll come back tomorrow,' he promised. He seemed to falter as he rose to leave, then leaned towards me and gently pressed his lips to mine before walking across the room and out of the door.

On my bedside table, the two jigsaw pieces sat beside the Virgin Mary's face. All three, so different, but together, watching, judging. 'It's up to you now,' they seemed to say. 'You can't blame anyone else for this. Dan is alive, he loves you, your friends are waiting. What are you waiting for?'

I woke to the sound of music from downstairs. 'Maybe I didn't treat you, quite as good as I should have. Maybe I didn't love you, quite as often as I could have…'

Memories of listening to Elvis with Mum, watching Elvis films as a young boy and dancing with Mum flooded my mind. 'Tell me, tell me that your sweet love hasn't died…'

Was she sending me a message, saying sorry again? Or was she just listening and reminiscing about a simpler time. A happier time?

As I listened to the words, I thought about the way I'd treated her over the last few months and I knew what I had to do. I ran down the stairs and past the front door without a thought.

She was standing at the sink with her back to me as I entered.

'Mum,' I called, and she turned and smiled. I went towards her with my arms out, eyes brimming, and she opened hers to me. We hugged each other tight, and my tears dripped down onto her shoulder.

'I love you,' I whispered.

'I love you too,' she said, leaning her head against my chest. Then she pulled away and looked into my eyes, her hands on my arms. 'And I meant it before. I'm so proud of you.'

Printed in Great Britain
by Amazon